Carla Cassidy is an award-winning, *New York Times* bestselling author who has written over 150 novels for Mills & Boon. In 1995, she won Best Silhouette Romance from *RT Book Reviews* for *Anything for Danny*. In 1998, she won a Career Achievement Award for Best Innovative Series from *RT Book Reviews*. Carla believes the only thing better than curling up with a good book to read is sitting down at the computer with a good story to write.

Linda O. Johnston loves to write. While honing her writing skills, she worked in advertising and public relations, then became a lawyer…and enjoyed writing contracts. Linda's first published fiction appeared in *Ellery Queen's Mystery Magazine* and won a Robert L. Fish Memorial Award for Best First Mystery Short Story of the Year. Linda now spends most of her time creating memorable tales of romance, romantic suspense and mystery. Visit her on the web at www.lindaojohnston.com

Also by Carla Cassidy

Also by Linda O. Johnston

Discover more at millsandboon.co.uk

DEADLY DAYS
OF CHRISTMAS

CARLA CASSIDY

UNCOVERING
COLTON'S
FAMILY SECRET

LINDA O. JOHNSTON

MILLS & BOON

First Published in Great Britain 2021
by Mills & Boon, an imprint of HarperCollins*Publishers* Ltd
1 London Bridge Street, London, SE1 9GF

www.harpercollins.co.uk

HarperCollins*Publishers*
1st Floor, Watermarque Building,
Ringsend Road, Dublin 4, Ireland

Deadly Days of Christmas © 2021 Carla Bracale
Uncovering Colton's Family Secret © 2021 Harlequin Books S.A.

Special thanks and acknowledgement are given to Linda O. Johnston for her contribution to *The Coltons of Grave Gulch* series.

ISBN: 978-0-263-28359-4

1021

MIX
Paper from
responsible sources
FSC™ C007454

This book is produced from independently certified FSC™ paper to ensure responsible forest management.

For more information visit: www.harpercollins.co.uk/green

Printed and Bound in Spain using 100% Renewable Electricity at CPI Blackprint (Barcelona)

DEADLY DAYS OF CHRISTMAS

CARLA CASSIDY

Chapter One

Callie Stevens walked briskly down the sidewalk toward the sheriff's department in the distance. December 1 began her most favorite time of the year—the coming of the holidays.

Overnight the street crews of Rock Ridge, Kansas, had worked to hang red-and-white lights in the shapes of candy canes on each streetlamp, along with greenery that added to the festive aura.

She loved Christmas and this year she was determined to bring a little bit of the holiday into her work space, something that had been an unspoken taboo for the past two years she'd worked as a receptionist-dispatcher for Sheriff Mac McKnight.

Her cheeks warmed a little against the unusually cold, blustery air as she thought of Sheriff Hottie, her secret nickname for him. If this year went as the last year had, Sheriff Hottie's cranky mood would begin today and last through the holidays.

"We need a little Christmas," she murmured beneath her breath and then opened the back door of the sheriff's office. Her shift was four in the afternoon to midnight, when Glenda Rivers came in to relieve her. She went into the break room, where Johnny Matthews greeted her with a wide smile. "Cold out there, right?"

"Too cold for so early in the season," she agreed as she hung up her white winter coat on one of the hooks protruding from the wall on one side of the room. "Anything popping this evening?" she asked.

"Absolutely nothing," Johnny replied. He took a swig of his soda and then set the can back on the table. "I think it's going to be a long, boring night. It's too cold for even the crazies to be out."

She laughed. "Don't sound so depressed, Johnny. That's the way we're supposed to want things…boring. Who else is on tonight?"

"Cameron and Adam. They're out on patrol right now." Johnny downed the last of his soda, crushed the can and then stood. He was a good-looking guy with dark hair and brown bedroom eyes.

He'd made it clear on more than one occasion that he wouldn't mind going out with her, but Callie had no interest in dating him. She thought of him more like a big brother. She just felt no chemistry with him.

"Guess I'll hit the road," he said and grabbed his coat off one of the hooks. "You still haven't bought a car?"

"No." Callie released a deep sigh. Her old car had finally died two months ago with the repair estimate being more than the car's worth. "Every time I think about the whole process of getting a new one, I get a headache. I can walk to work and to pretty much all the stores on Main Street. I keep asking myself why I really need a car."

"On days like this when the cold wind blows, it's nice to have a car to take you where you need to go,"

Johnny replied and then laughed. "I think I almost made a rhyme. Now I'd better get back to work."

"Stay safe out there," Callie said.

"Always," Johnny replied. As he went out the back door, Callie left the break room and headed up the hallway toward the reception area.

She passed Sheriff McKnight's office door. It was closed but she knew he was probably in there. He was almost always here or out on the streets. It wasn't unheard-of for him to still be here in the office at midnight and be back at seven in the morning. The man was definitely a workaholic.

"Hey, Callie," Maggie Jones greeted her and rose from the desk. "I have a feeling it's going to be a long, boring shift for you. The phone hasn't rung all day."

Maggie was the grandmother of ten, but she refused to be one of those grannies who sat home and baked cookies. With her brassy red hair and raucous laughter, she had been a fixture in the sheriff's office for years.

"I always bring a book with me in case things are really slow," Callie replied. "And today I also brought this…" She reached into her purse and withdrew the large red-and-white candle and set it on the desk. "This will make the whole place smell like peppermint."

"Oh girl, you know that's not a good idea," Maggie replied and cast a quick glance down the hallway.

"Surely he can't complain about one simple little candle," Callie protested.

"A candle that smells like Christmas," Maggie said, raising one of her red eyebrows. "I love Mac to death, but you know he's like Scrooge around this time of the year."

"I'm sure it will be fine," Callie said with a touch of false bravado.

Maggie got up from the desk and laughed. "I just hope you're alive for your shift tomorrow." Maggie gathered up her things and with a goodbye she headed out the front door.

Callie placed the candle on the desk, her purse on the floor, and then sank down in the desk chair. In a small town like Rock Ridge there was nothing technical or complicated about being a dispatcher. Her job was to answer the phone, facilitate help for anyone who came through the doors and use her radio to stay in touch with the officers on duty.

Most of the calls that came in were nonemergency issues, so her job was relatively undemanding. What she really wanted was to become a deputy and work side-by-side with the sheriff.

After high school she had moved to Kansas City and had gotten her degree in criminal justice. She'd landed a job as a deputy on a small-town force just outside the city and life had looked bright. Then tragedy had struck.

She shook her head, unwilling to allow any sad thoughts to intrude into her head at the moment. She got out a lighter from her purse and lit the candle and then settled in for work.

Everything remained quiet for the next hour or so and then she heard the ominous creak of Mac's office door opening. She glanced at the flickering candlelight as his footsteps came closer and then she drew in a deep breath for courage.

As always, her heart fluttered a bit in anticipation of

seeing him. There was just something about Mac that made her feel like a breathless teenage girl with a crush.

He stepped into the reception area. He was a tall, broad-shouldered man. His dark hair was cut short and his features were well-defined. Lordy, the man was hot. His gray eyes now shot to the candle and then back to her.

"Afternoon, Callie," he said, his low, deep voice shooting warmth right to the center of her belly.

"Afternoon, Sheriff," she replied.

Once again his gaze shot to the candle throwing out the sweet scent of peppermint. She heard him draw in a deep breath. "I'm heading to the café for an early dinner," he said. "If you need anything in the next hour or so, that's where I'll be."

"Enjoy," she replied, happy that he said nothing about the candle.

As he headed out the front door, she couldn't help but admire how his khaki pants fit over his sexy butt and down his long legs. She released a deep sigh as he disappeared from her sight.

She'd been working here for almost two years and on most days, she wasn't even sure Mac noticed her at all. He obviously had no idea that she was crazy mad in love with him.

All she wanted was for him to really *see* her, to allow her to bring a little joy into his life. Because she had a feeling from everything she'd seen of the man, he appeared to have little or no joy in his life. To Callie, there was just something a little bit sad about him.

Of course, if he knew she thought that about him, he'd probably be highly offended. He was a strong and proud man who loved his town and had committed his entire career to keeping the citizens safe. The deputies who worked with him all adored him and considered him a fair and supportive employer.

She was twenty-seven years old and wanted to be with the man of her dreams. She wanted to be loved and cared about and begin planning a family. It was unfortunate that the man of her dreams didn't know she was anything other than a capable dispatcher.

The ring of the phone pulled her from her thoughts of Mac. She took the call and then an hour later Mac walked back into the office. As always, her heart quickened in pace just a little bit.

"How was your dinner?" she asked.

"It's always good at the café," he replied. "I had the Tuesday-night special."

"Meatloaf with mashed potatoes and corn," she said with a grin.

"You must eat there often to know the daily specials."

"On my nights off I usually grab dinner at the café," she replied.

"Anything happen while I was gone?"

"Daisy Miller called."

A slow, lazy grin curved his mouth, half-melting Callie's heart. "Let me guess. Bubba got out again and she wanted all the deputies to come over and get him back into the house."

"You got it." Bubba was Daisy's miniature pet pig and about once a week the pig somehow got out of the house and into Daisy's yard. "I told her somebody would get back to her and fifteen minutes later she called again to say she'd coaxed Bubba back into the house with a pan full of roast beef and vegetables."

"I wouldn't believe it was a normal week if Daisy didn't call about Bubba," he replied. "And now I'm going to head out on patrol for a couple of hours."

With a murmured goodbye, he headed down the hallway and exited out the back door and Callie settled back in for another long, boring night.

Mac was back at eight and returned to his office. The deputies came and went, talking and teasing with her and breaking up the monotony of her job.

At ten until midnight Glenda Rivers showed up to relieve Callie. Glenda had just greeted Callie when the phone rang. Callie picked up. "Rock Ridge Sheriff's Department," she said.

"I just murdered a woman. Her body is on Main Street," a deep voice said.

Callie frowned. Was this some kind of a joke? "May I ask who is calling?" The caller identification showed an anonymous number.

"That doesn't matter. She's on a bench in front of the post office." Whoever it was then hung up.

Callie immediately jumped up from the desk, so disturbed by what she'd just heard that she didn't think about calling Mac on the radio. Instead, she raced down the hallway and burst into his office.

"Mac... Sheriff, I just got a call that there's a body of a murdered woman on Main Street on the bench in front of the post office," she explained.

Mac rose from his desk. "Who called it in?"

"It was an anonymous call," she replied. "It was a male, but I didn't recognize the voice." She watched as he pulled on his winter coat. "Mac, could I ride along with you? Glenda is here to take over the desk. Please, you know I've been asking forever to shadow you for more experience."

He hesitated a moment and frowned. "Okay, grab your coat and meet me at my car."

Callie didn't waste any time. She went up front and grabbed her purse, then raced down the hallway and into the break room to grab her coat. This was what she'd been waiting for. She'd wanted an opportunity to work with him. At least now maybe he would be able to see that she'd make a good deputy…or better yet that she'd make a great girlfriend.

"COLDEST NIGHT OF the year and somebody has put a body on a bench? It's got to be a hoax," Mac said as he started his patrol car. "There hasn't been a murder around here in the past four years and that one was a domestic that went bad."

"That was obviously before my time here," Callie replied.

"Yeah, it was," he agreed. He tore out of the parking lot behind the office and turned onto Main Street. He cast a quick glance at her.

With her curly blond hair, sparkling blue eyes and ready smile, she looked more like a cheerleader than a wanna-be deputy. She smelled like crisp fresh flowers with a hint of cinnamon and vanilla. She also smelled of danger…the kind of danger that could get a man into trouble.

He wasn't even sure why he'd allowed her to come with him other than the fact that she asked frequently to ride with him and in the chaos of the strange phone call he'd had a weak moment.

He found her attractive and sexy as hell, so he tried to keep his distance from her. He had no desire to have a relationship of any kind with any woman. He preferred being alone.

He emptied his head as he drew closer to the post office. At least it was cold enough and late enough that the streets and sidewalks were empty of people.

And then he saw her. Despite what had been done to her he immediately recognized her. The dead woman on the bench was Melinda Tyson, a waitress at the café.

"Oh my God," Callie said with a gasp.

Mac pulled his car to a stop. "Stay here," he said to Callie and then he jumped out and hurried to Melinda. She was a horrifying sight, posed with a little red Santa hat on her blond hair and with a dead bird in her mouth. What the hell?

If she still had a pulse, if she had any sign that she still clung to life, he'd do what he could to sustain that life until an ambulance from the hospital could come.

As he got closer to her, he knew she was dead, but he still checked her wrist for a pulse. Nothing. Her eyes were wide open and already had the pale cast of death in them. There was nothing he could do to help her at this point.

He returned to the car and got on his radio, calling all available deputies to the site. He then called under-taker–medical examiner Richard Albertson.

"I've got some protective gear in the trunk," he said to Callie. "We should at least put on some booties and gloves until the scene has been thoroughly processed."

He gazed at her for a long moment. "It's a fairly grue-some scene. Are you okay?"

"If you're expecting me to throw up or dissolve into hysterics, you'll be disappointed because I'm just fine," she replied. "I'm horrified, but I'm good." She raised her chin as if to prove to him she was okay.

"Then let's get moving."

Minutes later they both wore plastic booties and gloves and by that time Deputies Johnny Matthews and Cameron Royal and two more deputies had joined them.

Cameron began photographing the scene, Johnny and the other two deputies collected any and all poten-tial evidence around the bench and Mac wrote down his impressions about the body while Callie stayed back to observe.

Melinda had been stabbed at least five times that he could see, although there was no blood around the bench, letting Mac know she had been killed elsewhere.

She was clad in black slacks and a light blue sweat-shirt. There was no coat or purse anywhere around her to be found.

The Santa hat might just be a nod to the upcoming holiday. However, it was the bird in her mouth that was horrifying and made no sense. It was a bobtail quail, fairly common in their county. Mac knew making sense of it would be imperative in solving the murder. Was the fact that it was specifically a quail important or would any bird have done?

Richard Albertson arrived on scene with his assis-tant, Dean Cooper. Mac stepped back next to Callie as the medical examiner did his preliminary exam.

Mac had only worked with the tall, thin man on a

murder case once in Mac's seven years as sheriff. That had been an open-and-shut case where the guilty party was on scene and confessed to hitting his wife with a baseball bat and killing her in a fit of rage.

Melinda, with a dead bird shoved in her mouth and a Santa hat on her head, was a whole different animal. This was the kind of case that would give law enforcement officials dark and horrible nightmares until the killer was caught.

It took almost an hour for Albertson to finish his exam. "There are ligature marks around her wrists and ankles," he began. "My initial guess would be some kind of a rope, but I'll know more about that after getting her on my table."

"Time of death?" Mac asked.

Richard frowned. "Time of death is a bit of an issue with the temperature and not knowing exactly how long she's been out here in the elements," he said to Mac. "But, due to the fact that rigor mortis hasn't set in yet, my guess is she's been dead no longer than about two hours."

"Cause of death?" Mac asked, although it didn't take a rocket scientist to know she'd been stabbed to death.

"My initial finding is death by stabbing, but again I won't know for sure until I get her on the autopsy table. Right now my ruling is death by homicide." His round brown eyes appeared owlish in the headlights from Mac's vehicle. "If you're finished gathering evidence, then Dean and I are ready to transport the body to my office. If you want to stop by my office within the next couple of hours, I'll try to have a better workup for you."

"Sounds good," Mac replied.

It was just after two when the body was finally carried away and all the potential evidence had been collected. Mac and Callie got back into his car.

"Now I have to do one of the most difficult things my job entails," he said with a deep sigh. Mac had kept his emotions turned off from the moment he'd seen the body until now. But now, along with the sadness of the loss of a life, a rage built up inside him. He was determined to find the person who had done this to a young woman in the town he loved.

"What's that?" Callie asked.

"Make notification to Melinda's parents. I don't want to wait and risk the chance they'll hear it from anyone before they hear it from me."

"We were lucky there was nobody else to see her except law enforcement officials," she said.

He nodded. "I'll go ahead and take you home before I go to their place."

"That isn't necessary. Maybe I can help… You know, a woman's touch and all that."

A woman's touch. God, it had been a long time since he'd felt a woman's touch. And now he found himself wondering what it would feel like to have Callie running her slender hands across his body.

Dammit. He shook his head to empty it of any inappropriate thoughts. Apparently, it was easier to think of the woman seated next to him than the murder he needed to solve.

When he pulled up in front of the Tysons' home a hard knot of tension formed in his gut. He knew Connie and Eddie Tyson. They were good people who had always supported him and he knew how much they loved their daughter.

He cut his engine and stared at the darkened house. He was about to wake up the couple, tear their lives apart and rip a hole in their hearts that would always be there.

"Let's get this over with," he finally said and together he and Callie got out of the car and headed to the front door. An hour later they returned to the car.

Mac had left out the gory details of Melinda's death, but telling parents their beautiful daughter had been stabbed to death had been difficult enough.

He'd actually been grateful Callie had been with him. As Connie fell to the sofa and began to sob, it had been Callie who had held her while Eddie had expressed his grief by yelling and swearing that once the perpetrator was found he was going to kill him.

By the time Mac and Callie left their home, Connie and Eddie were on the sofa together, sitting in the kind of silence that positively screamed with pain and grief too enormous to express.

Callie was silent on the ride home and Mac appreciated the quiet. It was almost three in the morning, far too late tonight to speak to people about Melinda. He'd asked her parents a few questions and had learned that Melinda wasn't dating anyone at the moment, and that lately she'd mostly hung out with people from the café where she worked.

Melinda usually walked to and from work, unless she caught a ride with one of her friends. When she'd left the house that morning she'd been wearing a red-and-blue winter coat. She had worked an early shift at the café and when she hadn't come home from that shift, her parents had just assumed she'd gone out with friends. As an adult living at home with her parents, she had no curfew and her parents often didn't know what her plans were for any particular day.

This heinous murder was the kind that would haunt those who had seen Melinda with that bird stuffed in her mouth. It was definitely the stuff of nightmares.

Tomorrow he'd have a full plate interviewing co-workers and friends of Melinda. At the moment, a tension headache stretched and tightened painfully across his neck. He rubbed it in an effort to ease the pain.

Once again, he could smell Callie's evocative perfume, but this time he welcomed the fragrance after the scents of death and grief that filled his head.

He knew she usually walked to work, but there was no way in hell he was going to allow her to walk home from the sheriff's office at this time of night with the wind chill hovering around freezing and a murderer on the loose.

"Mac." Callie finally broke the silence as he pulled in front of the attractive two-story house where Callie lived on Main Street. He cut the engine and then turned to look at her.

She looked so pretty in the illumination from the dashboard. Had her eyelashes always been that long? Had her hair always looked so shiny and touchable?

"I want to help you with this investigation," she said. "Couldn't you deputize me just for this case and let me be an active participant in catching this creep? You know you can call in Dana Jeffries to take over my shift as dispatcher. She's always eager to work."

The words tumbled out of her mouth fast and furiously. "You only have a small force of deputies and you could use one more working on this case. I have all the qualifications to be a deputy and I really think I could be a big help. Please, Mac. Let me be a part of this."

She looked so intense…so earnest and there was no question he had a feeling he could definitely use another deputy working on this case. Still, he hesitated. Would she be a help or a distraction to him?

"I'll think about it," he finally said.

"You can't give me an answer now?" she asked.

"I said I'll think about it," he repeated in a tone that didn't invite further conversation on the matter.

"Okay, then I'll see you tomorrow." She opened the car door. "Good night, Mac."

"Good night, Callie." He watched as she walked to the front door and then disappeared into the house.

He pulled away from the curb and headed toward the Albertson's Funeral Home. Despite the lateness of the hour, he hoped the medical examiner would have worked up a preliminary report by now.

This was the first time Mac would be challenged as a sheriff, as a man who wanted to keep the people in his town safe. He'd been found inadequate before in his life and that inadequacy had not only destroyed his love of Christmas, but also his ability to ever open his heart again.

He didn't care about the holiday or ever loving again. What he cared about right now was finding the person who had killed Melinda. He definitely hoped this was a one-and-done kind of murder.

However, as he pulled up in the back of the funeral home, he had a very bad feeling about this.

Chapter Two

Mac sank down at his desk a few minutes after seven. He hadn't gone to bed the night before until just before four. He now had before him the initial autopsy report that Richard Albertson had provided to him this morning. Unfortunately, he hadn't had it ready the night before when Mac had stopped by.

Thankfully, he didn't believe anyone in town other than his team had seen Melinda's body. He intended to keep the bird in her mouth and the Santa hat on her head from the public.

He continued to read the report, and was nearly through it when there was a knock on his door. "Come in," he called.

He raised an eyebrow in surprise as Callie walked in. "Good morning," she said with a bright smile. She was clad in a pair of jeans that hugged her long, slender legs and a royal blue blouse that did amazing things to her eyes. The scent of her eddied in the air, a scent he'd noticed the day before and found incredibly attractive.

She carried with her a handful of papers and a foam cup of coffee from his favorite coffee shop. "This is for you," she said and placed the cup on his desk in front of him. "It's made just the way you like it with a teaspoon of sugar and a dollop of cream."

He stared at the cup and then looked back at her. "Is this meant to be some sort of a bribe to get the deputy job?"

Her eyes widened and a charming pink danced into her cheeks. "Oh… I didn't think about it that way." She appeared truly shocked by the very idea. "I… I just figured you were probably up really late last night and I've seen you carry in a cup of coffee from the Beanery before and I just thought…" Her voice trailed off.

"It's fine, Callie," he said with a smile. "I appreciate your thoughtfulness. And for future purposes, if you are going to try to bribe me, I'd expect a muffin or a cinnamon roll to go with the coffee."

She smiled. "Duly noted." She slid into the chair facing him. "I did a little research when I got home last night into the bobtail quail."

He looked at her in surprise. He knew what time she had gotten home the night before. The fact that she had done anything but go straight to sleep was definitely admirable.

"What did you find out?" he asked, certainly interested in any information she might have about the bird that had been stuffed in Melinda's mouth.

He was aware of time ticking away. He had two of his deputies already out talking to people around town to see if anyone had been on the streets the night before around the time that Melinda's body had been left. Mac wanted to get to the café and start talking to people there sooner rather than later. But the bird might be the key to finding the murderer.

She looked down at her papers. "I could give you all the yada yada about species and subspecies, but I don't think any of that is really important in this case. What I do think might be important is that the whistle they make sounds like 'bob-WHITE,' so maybe it's possible our murderer's name is a derivative of that. The species was once considered to be monogamous, but their behavior is now described as ambisexual polygamy."

She glanced up at him. "Am I boring you or do you want me to go on?"

"Absolutely go on," he replied. He'd never noticed before what a pleasant voice she had; it was low and more than a little bit sexy. More importantly, she was telling him things about the bird that might be vital to this case.

She returned her gaze to her papers. "Really, the only other thing is that the birds are shy and elusive and rely on camouflage to stay undetected." When she looked back up at him a tiny wrinkle danced across her forehead. "So, it's possible our perp somehow identifies with the bobwhite. Maybe his name is White or some derivative and it might be possible he's shy and reclusive."

"Maybe. Thanks for your research into this. You've definitely saved me some time." He knew her shift on the dispatcher desk officially began at four, but here she was at seven in the morning giving him information that might be important to the murder.

He studied her for several long moments. She'd shown initiative and he liked that. Her eyes also shone with a fierce determination, an eagerness to be a part of the investigation.

He opened his desk drawer and pulled out a deputy

badge, a police-issued revolver and a holster. He set the items on the desk and pushed them toward her. Her eyes widened once again and then joy filled her features. God, he couldn't remember the last time he'd felt anything remotely close to joy.

"Really?" she said, her voice half-breathless.

"Go on, take them," he said. "Get a uniform from the supply closet and get into it. You are a deputy until four o'clock today and then we'll see how things are going. You haven't officially been sworn in, so you'll ride with me and only do what I tell you to. Now, meet me at my car in about fifteen minutes. We've got a full day ahead of us."

She picked up the badge and clasped it to her heart, then grabbed the holster and revolver and jumped out of the chair. "I swear you won't be sorry about this," she said and then practically raced out the door.

He picked up the phone, made a quick call and then grabbed his coat and headed down the hallway. As he passed the break room he glanced inside. Nobody was there, but there was a stuffed Santa sitting on top of the soda machine.

He knew it was Callie's doing. Nobody else would have the nerve to bring in anything remotely to do with Christmas. All his staff knew how he felt about the holiday.

Still, he had more important things to think about besides a stuffed doll. He headed out the door and to his car, where Callie stood by the passenger door, her coat in her hand. He'd never thought of their uniforms as being sexy, but on Callie the khaki outfit appeared to be made just for her.

The shirt fit her frame perfectly, showcasing her slender waist and the thrust of her breasts. The slacks hugged her long legs and a rivulet of warmth swept through him despite the cold temperature.

He frowned as he unlocked the car. She threw her coat into the back seat and then the two of them got inside. Maybe it was a bad idea for him to have her with him. However, there was no way he intended to let her loose to do her own thing. She was far too green to be out on her own and he hadn't really sworn her in properly.

"I just finished reading the autopsy report," he said once they were both in the car. He'd rather stay focused on the murder than anything he might feel toward his sexy new deputy.

"And?"

He could feel her curious gaze on him as he backed out of his parking space. "We will have to wait on some lab results, but she was stabbed twenty-three times."

"Wow, definitely overkill indicating rage," she replied.

A pleasant surprise filled him at her response. It was exactly what he believed. He just hadn't expected her to pick up on it.

"So, knowing that, what would be the next thing you'd believe?" he asked.

"That the murder was personal, probably committed by somebody close to her."

"That's what I'm thinking, so we're headed to the café to talk to the people she worked with to see what we can discover," he said.

"Sounds like a plan," she agreed.

He doubted that anyone at the café, except the murderer, knew about the murder. Other than the notification to Melinda's parents in the middle of the night, nobody else in town should know.

"What about her missing coat and purse? Do you think the murderer kept them as trophies?" she asked.

"Hard to tell at this point, but I had several of my men check Dumpsters last night looking for the items and they didn't find them," he replied.

"And the ligature marks?" she asked.

"Albertson was ninety percent certain they were made by ropes. Whatever happened to her, it appears she was tied with her wrists and ankles to something."

"It's so tragic," she said softly.

"I definitely agree," he said.

He had to park down the block from the café, as all the parking spaces in front were taken. Seven days a week half the town folks could be found having their first meal of the day in the café. It was the place where gossip ran rampant, the food was great and the coffee was always fresh and hot.

The first person he wanted to talk to was Jimmy Jo Jacobs, aka JJ, the owner and head cook in the café. He and Callie walked in together. The scents of frying bacon and onions and fresh baked goods filled the air, along with the sounds of clinking silverware and the chatter of all the diners.

Linda Richards, one of the waitresses and acting hostess, greeted them. "You two need a table or a booth?" she asked.

"Neither. We aren't here to eat. We need to speak with Jimmy," Mac said.

She waved toward the doorway that led into the kitchen. "He's back there."

With a nod, Mac and Callie headed to the kitchen area. Jimmy Jo was a big man, a walking advertisement for his excellent home-cooked food. When they entered the back, he was working the grill and barking orders to two other cooks.

"Jimmy," Mac yelled to be heard above the din.

The bald man turned to look at Mac in surprise. "Sheriff, what can I do for you? Eggs too runny? Toast burned?"

"No, nothing like that, but we need to talk to you… privately," Mac replied.

Jimmy laid down the wide metal pancake turner he'd been using to flip frying bacon. He wiped his hands on the white apron that stretched across his big belly. "Chris, take over here," he said to one of the men. "Let's go on back to my office," he said to Mac and Callie.

They followed Jimmy through the kitchen and to a small room in the back. Besides holding a variety of supplies, there was also a small desk with a couple of folding chairs in front of it.

"What's up?" Jimmy asked once they were all seated.

"Melinda Tyson was murdered last night," Mac said.

"Oh my God." Jimmy sat back in his chair, obviously shocked. "I wondered why she didn't show up for work this morning."

"Did she work yesterday?" Mac asked.

"She did. She worked the early-morning shift and got off work at eleven." Jimmy shook his head. "She's really dead? I can't believe it. She was a good kid and a hard worker."

"Did she mention where she might be going after she got off work yesterday?" Callie asked.

Jimmy shook his head. "Not to me, but she might have mentioned something to Shelly Steward. She and Melinda were pretty tight as friends. You want me to call Shelly in to talk to you?"

"That would be great," Mac replied.

"Hopefully Shelly will be able to fill in some blanks as to what Melinda did after work yesterday," Callie said once Jimmy had left the office.

Mac nodded. It was definitely important to trace a victim's movements in the hours prior to their death. Somebody somewhere might have seen something that could blow the lid right off the case.

The word would be out now. He figured within hours everyone would know about the murder and all the people in town would be looking to him for answers.

As a member of the law enforcement team, Callie would also now be under scrutiny. Was she really up to the pressure…the stress that was about to take over her life? More importantly…was he?

CALLIE SAT QUIETLY and watched as Mac questioned Shelly. Initially when the auburn-haired Shelly had learned why they were speaking with her, she had burst into tears at the news her friend had been murdered.

Callie admired Mac's gentleness with the grieving young woman. He allowed her the time to cry and once she managed to pull herself together, he began to question her. He was patient and soft-spoken and it was definitely a side of Mac Callie had never seen before, a side she found very appealing.

"What about men?" Mac now asked. "Do you know if she was seeing anyone?"

"She wasn't seeing anyone at the moment. She was dating Roger Lathrop for a bit, but he got a little too controlling so she broke up with him. It was a pretty bad breakup and since then she's been single," Shelly said tearfully.

"When was the breakup with Roger?" Mac leaned forward in his chair.

"About three weeks ago or so." Her eyes widened. "Do you think he…he killed her?"

"We don't know anything right now. We're just in the beginning stages of the investigation. Do you know anyone Melinda was having a problem with, male or female?" Mac asked.

Shelly shook her head. "No, nobody. Melinda is… was…super easy to get along with. Everybody liked her." Tears filled her eyes once again. "I just can't believe she's gone. I can't believe somebody actually killed her."

"Shelly, we're so sorry about your friend," Callie said. "She was wearing a light blue sweatshirt. Do you know if she changed out of her work T-shirt before she left here yesterday?"

"She always changed into regular street clothes before she left here."

"Did she take her work T-shirt with her?" Callie asked.

Shelly nodded. "She always rolled it up and shoved it into her purse."

"We just want to thank you for speaking to us," Mac said. He stood and pulled a card from his shirt pocket.

"If you think of anything that might help us identify the perpetrator, please call me no matter what the time."

Shelly shook her head as tears once again raced down her cheeks. "Is it okay if I go to the restroom?" she asked tearfully.

"I'm sure that would be fine," Callie replied. "Come on, I'll walk with you."

Callie accompanied Shelly to the ladies' room door and then went back to the office, where Mac was once again seated. They spoke to three more waitresses but didn't get any new information to help them fill in the blanks of Melinda's actions throughout the afternoon of her murder.

However, one thing was clear. They needed to interrogate Roger Lathrop and it was something Callie wasn't particularly looking forward to.

"He should be at work now," Mac said once they were back in his car.

Roger had his own insurance business. He worked alone out of an office located a block off Main Street. The tall, blond, attractive man had a reputation as a ladies' man. Callie had never spent any time with him and she doubted he even knew her name. However, she'd definitely heard about his reputation and what she'd heard about him made him unattractive to her.

Besides, her heart was already involved with another man, although that man had no idea how she felt about him. She cast a quick glance at Mac. He looked so handsome even though a frown cut across his forehead and his fingers clenched the steering wheel tightly.

She could only imagine the stress he must be under as the chief lawman for the town with this heinous murder on his hands. He finally pulled up and parked in front of Roger's office. Before he got out of the car, he made several phone calls to check in on the other deputies who were also working on the case.

"Ready to do this?" he asked her once he was off the phone.

"Ready when you are," she replied.

They both exited the car and she grabbed her coat from the back seat and put it on. They were immediately buffeted by the cold wind that had picked up since they'd been in the café. She welcomed the warmth in Roger's office as they stepped inside.

Roger immediately stood from behind a sleek, modern black-and-silver desk. "Sheriff, always a pleasure," he said and walked around the desk to shake Mac's hand.

He then looked at Callie, his blue eyes doing a quick up-and-down even though she was clad in her furry winter coat. "I've seen you around town, but I don't think we've ever officially met." He held out his hand to her.

"Deputy Stevens," she replied and gave his hand a quick shake.

He smiled at her, exposing even white teeth. "Does Deputy Stevens have a first name?"

"Callie," she said reluctantly.

"A pleasure to meet you, Callie. So, what can I do for you both? Need some kind of insurance?" He looked from Callie to Mac.

"Melinda Tyson was murdered last night," Mac said.

Roger's eyes widened and he took a step backward. "You're kidding me, right? This is some kind of a sick joke, right?" He looked at Callie and then back at Mac. "Please tell me this is a joke."

"No joke," Mac replied tersely. "And we need to ask you some questions starting with where you were last night between the hours of eight and midnight."

Roger walked back to his chair, sank down and then gestured them into the two chairs in front of the desk. "I was home."

"Was anyone with you who can corroborate that?" Mac asked.

"I...no... I was home by myself. I closed up the office at seven, then went home and watched some television and then I went to bed." He shook his head. "I just can't believe this has happened."

"What about between the hours of eleven to one in the afternoon yesterday?"

Roger frowned. "Here. I was here in the office all day, although about one or so I drove through Billy's Burgers to pick up some lunch."

"We understand that recently you had a pretty volatile breakup with Melinda," Mac continued.

"Volatile..." His eyes widened again. "Wait a minute... Do you think I had something to do with this? You really think I had something to do with her murder?" He released a hoarse bark of laughter. "My God, you've got to be kidding me." He laughed again and shook his head.

"There's nothing funny about this, Roger," Mac said. "Is it true that you were unhappy about Melinda breaking up with you?"

"Well, I wasn't exactly happy about it, but it wasn't like I was madly in love with her. We'd only been dating about a month or so. I certainly wasn't upset enough to feel like murdering her."

Mac continued to ask questions and Callie watched Roger carefully, looking for any tells that might indicate the handsome blond man was lying.

It was hard to tell, especially as he kept casting his gaze to her in what could only be perceived as flirtatiousness. It was not only uncomfortable but it was completely inappropriate and downright sleazy. However, that didn't make him guilty of murder.

Mac finally stood. "You'll be available if we have any more questions for you at another time?"

"Of course." Roger also got up. "But I can tell you if you think I had anything to do with Melinda's death, then you're barking up the wrong tree." He flashed a smooth smile at Callie. "However, if you want to question me again, please feel free to bring Deputy Callie with you."

Callie expelled a deep breath as they stepped out of the office. "That man is a creep with no boundaries and no social awareness at all," she exclaimed once they were back in the car.

"Yes, but is he a murderer?" Mac started the engine and then turned in his seat to look at her.

"Hard to tell at this point. He looked genuinely shocked when you told him about the murder, but that could be just really good acting."

The conversation was interrupted by Mac's radio going off. "Sheriff, it's Pete. I just thought I'd let you know that last night when Claudia Graham was closing up her shop at around eight, she saw Nathan Brighton doing some work on the store next door. I thought you might want to talk to him in case he saw something important last night."

"Thanks, Pete. You have any idea where Nathan is right now?" Mac asked.

"Sorry, don't have a clue," Pete replied.

"Thanks anyway," Mac said. "We'll hunt him down."

"Surely if Nathan saw the murderer or the body being left last night, he would have called you immediately," Callie said once Mac had hung up.

"You would think so, but knowing he was on the street last night just a couple of hours before Melinda's body was left, means I need to find him and question him," Mac replied. "To be honest, I'm not even sure Nathan has a cell phone. In any case I've never had a number for him. We'll start by going to his house."

"It was awfully cold last night to be working on something so late and outside," she said.

"As far as I know Nathan would take a job in hell if one was offered to him," Mac replied.

Callie laughed. Nathan was the town handyman. He traveled in a rusted old black pickup filled with all kind of tools and equipment for doing almost any odd job anyone would ask of him.

Mac headed back down Main Street. Callie gazed at the clock on the dashboard. It was approaching the time when she'd have to put away her deputy badge and go back on the desk.

"Maybe you need to drop me off at the office," she said. "It's almost time for my shift to begin."

"You aren't going back on the desk," Mac said. "I contacted Dana this morning. She'll be working as a dispatcher through this investigation." He flashed her a quick smile. "As long as you're up for it, you're an unofficial deputy, but you will continue to work only with me."

"Oh Mac, thank you." Happiness filled her. "I swear you won't regret it. I want to learn from you and I'll be the best deputy you could ever ask for."

Maybe…just maybe with enough time he would see her not only as a good deputy but as the loving, caring woman he needed and wanted in his life.

However, first they needed to solve the murder and put a madman away.

Chapter Three

Nathan lived in a very small house on the edge of town. An old barn stood on the property, but it was merely a skeleton of broken boards and a roof that had collapsed in on itself long ago.

The house was definitely not a representation of Nathan's skill as a handyman. The place was badly weathered and begged for fresh paint and the steps leading up to the front door looked positively hazardous.

"It's obvious he isn't here. His truck isn't here," Mac said and drove on by the house. "We'll have to drive around town and see if we can find out where he might be working today."

"I've noticed you haven't mentioned anything about the bird or the hat to anyone we've spoken to. I'm assuming you've told everyone to keep those things under wraps," Callie said.

"Definitely. Aside from the medical examiners, I'm hoping the only people who will know about those things are us and the killer. They will be our secret and if we interview anyone who knows about them, then we'll know we're talking to the murderer."

A chill crawled up her back. "It's hard to believe

somebody here in Rock Ridge is capable of that kind of murder…of any kind of murder," she said.

"I guess this is just a reminder that you never know what kind of rage and darkness exists in somebody's mind. Some people only let you see what they want you to see."

"That's frightening to think about, but I know all you have to do is look at the news from bigger cities to know that's true. I just never believed it would be true of somebody here in Rock Ridge."

"There's no way I believe somebody just blew through town last night and randomly killed Melinda," he replied.

"Not with as many stab wounds as she received," Callie agreed. "It would take a lot for me to believe that this was a stranger killer."

"I'm glad we're on the same page," he replied and shot her a quick smile that warmed her more than the heated air flowing out of his car vents.

"When we aren't on the same page, I'll let you know," she replied.

He released a small laugh. "I'm sure you will."

She looked at him curiously. "Surely you wouldn't have it any other way, right? I mean, if I have a different opinion from yours, you should at least hear me out, right?"

"You're right. I wouldn't have it any other way," he replied. "It's important that we all bounce ideas off each other to make sure we remain open to any and all potential perps. Listening to other opinions is how we don't develop tunnel vision."

They fell silent as he drove up and down several

streets, looking for Nathan's familiar truck. She drew in the scent in the car, a smell of leather cleaner that mingled with his very attractive cologne.

So far, she'd spent over eight hours with Mac and in those hours, he'd said or done nothing to break the crush…or her insane attraction to him.

She stared at his hand on the steering wheel. He had big hands and for a moment she wondered what it would feel like to have his hands caressing her. She could just imagine those hands doing a slow slide down the length of her naked body. A new warmth swept through her, a warmth that flushed her from head to toe.

"There he is." Mac's voice yanked her from her brief, very hot fantasy.

She looked out the car window and saw Nathan's truck parked against the curb up the street. Mac pulled up behind it and cut the engine. She turned around and grabbed her coat from the back seat.

"Why don't you just wear your coat when you're in the car?" Mac asked as they walked toward the attractive ranch house where apparently Nathan was doing some work.

"I hate wearing a coat in a car. It feels too restrictive and overheats me," she explained as she got into her coat.

"Do I have the heater too warm in the car for you?"

"No, not at all. It's just a little quirk of mine," she replied.

By that time, they had reached the house and Mac knocked on the front door. A man Callie recognized from around town opened the door. "Hey, Simon," Mac said in greeting.

"Mac, come on in out of the cold," he replied and opened the door wider for them to step into a small entryway. Simon smiled and nodded at Callie and then looked back at Mac. "Is something wrong?" His welcoming smile faded and worry shone from his eyes.

"No, not at all," Mac replied. "We just need to speak to Nathan and we saw his truck outside."

Simon pointed down the hallway. "He's painting our spare bedroom. It's the second door on the right."

Callie followed behind Mac and when they reached the correct door, he gave a quick knock and then opened the door. The room was empty of furniture and two windows were open to vent the odor of fresh paint.

Nathan looked at them in surprise. "Sheriff, what are you doing here?" Nathan was a medium-sized man, more wiry than bulky. He had a round face and wide brown eyes that exuded an innocence of spirit.

"Hi, Nathan. We have a few questions for you about what you were doing on Main Street last night," Mac said.

Nathan placed his paint roller back into the tray and then looked at Mac again. "I was replacing some rotted wood on the bottom of the door to Trisha's Trinkets. Why? Did I do something wrong?" He eyed Mac worriedly.

"No, but I was just wondering why you were working that late in the evening," Mac replied.

"Trisha wanted it fixed after-hours, so I did it as soon as she shut down her shop for the night."

"And what time was that?" Mac asked.

Nathan frowned. "Around seven o'clock or so."

"And how long did it take you to complete your work?"

"Oh, about a half an hour. Why?" He glanced from Mac to Callie and then back again.

"So, did you immediately leave the area once you were finished with your work?" Mac asked.

"It was too cold and nobody was around to hang out with me, so I went right home," Nathan replied.

"Then you didn't see anyone out and about?"

As she had with Roger, Callie tried to see if she saw any signs of lying emanating from Nathan, but he was difficult to read with his innocent eyes and slightly slack features.

"Do you have a cell phone, Nathan? I thought maybe you could give me your number," Mac said.

"Oh, I don't have one of those cell phones. They seem way too complicated to me. But I do have a home phone. It's got an answering machine and everything." Nathan smiled broadly. "I can give you that number."

It took only a few more questions for them to figure out that either Nathan had seen nothing suspicious the night before or he knew more than he was telling and was responsible for Melinda's murder.

"What do you think?" she asked once they were in the car again.

"Hard to tell," Mac replied.

"No offense, but is Nathan bright enough to pull something like this off? I mean, our killer managed somehow to take Melinda off the streets, go to a place where he killed her and then pose her on Main Street and he got away without anyone seeing him. Nathan seems to be just a little slow. He thinks cell phones are too hard."

"Yeah, Nathan wouldn't be on the top of my list of

suspects. Whoever killed Melinda was smart. It took a lot of planning and calculation to pull this off." Mac released a deep sigh.

"So, what's next?"

"We need to start pounding the sidewalks and talking to people. We need to find out if anyone saw Melinda after her shift ended yesterday or if anyone saw a vehicle or a person in or around the post office between nine and midnight last night." He cast her a quick glance. "You know there's nothing glamorous about a murder investigation."

She looked at him in surprise and then laughed. "What makes you think I'm looking for anything glamorous?"

"Sometimes people watch the shows on television about investigating a murder and they don't realize it's a lot of hard work. It's long hours and walking the streets and talking to people."

"Mac, I want to put in that work. My only goal is to do whatever it takes to put this murderer away," she replied. "Besides, you didn't answer my question. What would make you think I'm looking for glamour?"

"I don't know—you always dress really nice and look a little bit glamorous when you come in to work the desk," he said after a long hesitation.

She stared at his profile as a warm flutter raced through her chest. So he *had* noticed her... He'd really noticed her.

"Thank you for the compliment, but honestly, Mac, if I was looking for glamour, I would have stayed in Kansas City, which has far more opportunities for glamour than Rock Ridge. Trust me, I'm right where I want to be and working with you is exactly what I've wanted to do."

He pulled into a parking space on one end of Main Street and turned off the car. "We'll start here. We need to speak to all the people in the stores and on the street. I want to know if anyone saw Melinda yesterday after her shift or if anyone saw a person or a vehicle lingering around the bench around the time Melinda's body was left there."

As they got out of the car, Callie was still processing the fact that Mac had noticed how she dressed, how she looked when she came into work. The other dispatchers usually wore sweats and sweatshirts, but that just wasn't Callie's style. She always dressed up a bit for work, and she was thrilled that her boss…the man she had a major crush on…hadn't been oblivious of the fact.

For the next three hours they went in and out of the stores, asking questions of anyone they came across. Callie was surprised by how Mac seemed to know everyone. He asked about kids by name and had the ability to put everyone at ease as he spoke to them.

Still, even with his personable approach they came up empty-handed. Nobody had seen Melinda during the afternoon the day before and nobody they spoke to had seen anything around the time that Melinda's body had been found.

It was six thirty when he drove through a hamburger place and they each ordered dinner. Callie was starving, having only had a bagel and coffee that morning and no lunch.

They took their burgers back to the office, where Mac had called a meeting of all his deputies. There were fourteen men who made up the sum of the Rock Ridge law enforcement team.

There were still a few missing from the round tables in the break room. Callie and Mac began to eat their cheeseburgers and fries as they waited for the remaining deputies to show up.

The men were unusually subdued. Mac ate quickly and when all the men were there, he began to speak to them about the murder and what little information they had gleaned that day.

Unfortunately, most of the deputies who had been working that day hadn't come up with any information that would move the investigation forward, either.

It was Deputy Dwight Mayfield who had a new name. "I heard from Derek Bowman that he was making a run to the grocery store last night around eight and saw Ben Kincaid on the sidewalk near the post office."

"Did he say what Ben was doing?" Mac asked.

"Knowing Ben, he was probably talking to the spirits or chanting to the gods of the wind," Johnny said wryly.

Ben Kincaid was definitely the town's eccentric. He not only believed in ghosts, but he also believed that people from another planet walked among them and that there were good spirits and bad ones. Had he believed that Melinda was one of the bad spirits who needed to be killed?

"As you can see, Callie has joined our team," Mac said after a few more questions and discussion among everyone.

The razzing began immediately as they all teased her. But the teasing was cut short as Mac then continued. "You all know what I need from you, and remember that we're keeping the bird and the hat information away from the public," Mac said as he finished up the meeting.

"If that information leaks out, trust me I won't rest until I know who leaked it and that person will be immediately fired. Now, get back on the streets if you're on duty and if you aren't on duty then I recommend you go home and get as much rest as you can. This investigation will require that you're all on the top of your game and since we're such a small force, I may need you all working overtime," Mac finished.

"So, are we on our way to talk to Ben," Callie asked once the men were all gone.

Mac looked at her in surprise. "I just assumed you'd be ready to call it a day. You've been going pretty hard at it since early this morning."

"There's still a potential suspect to interrogate. I'll be through for the day when you are." She got up from the table, threw her fast-food trash away and then grabbed her coat. "Shall we?"

Minutes later they were back in his car and headed to wherever Ben lived. "I've seen Ben before out and around on the streets. Has he always been…uh… strange?" Callie asked.

Mac laughed, the low, deep rumble setting off another wave of pleasant heat through her. "I went to grade school and high school with Ben, and for as long as I've known him, he's been pretty odd."

When Mac got to the end of the main drag, he turned left and then turned left again, taking them out to the very edge of town. He then made a right turn on a gravel road and after ten minutes or so he pulled into the driveway of Ben's house.

"Interesting," Callie said as she looked at Ben's home. There were about a dozen yard lights illuminating not only the small ranch house, but also the entire yard, which appeared to be surrounded by woods.

There were half a dozen trees on the property and not only did dozens of wind chimes hang from the branches, but there were also strange little stuffed figures and other odd items.

When they got out of the car the discordant sound of all the chimes clanging together filled the air. Several lights shone from the inside and an old maroon Buick she assumed to be Ben's car was in the driveway.

Mac knocked on the front door and Ben answered. He was a short man with shaggy black hair and intense green eyes. "Sheriff, don't tell me you got another complaint about the things I have in my yard."

"No, nothing like that," Mac replied. "Can we come in? It's rather hard to hear out here."

Ben hesitated a moment and then opened the door wider to allow them to enter. Inside, things were as strange as they were outside.

There was a futon shoved against one wall and a television was mounted on the opposite wall. That's where all normalcy stopped. The walls were covered with pictures of big-eyed aliens and angry demons. There were statues of angels and strange creatures on the coffee and end tables.

He gestured them to the futon, but Mac remained standing and Callie stayed at Mac's side. "Ben, we won't be here long. I just have a few questions for you."

Ben's eyes were scary intense as he stared unblinkingly at Mac. "Questions about what?"

"I understand you were out and about on Main Street last night," Mac said.

Ben's gaze shot to Callie and then back at Mac. "Is that a crime?"

"Of course not," Mac replied. "We had a body of a murder victim show up on the bench in front of the post office. Since you were in the general area not long before that happened, we were just wondering what you were doing there."

"Ah, that explains it," Ben said with a knowing shake of his head.

"Explains what?"

"I picked up a couple things at the grocery store and had a sudden feeling that something evil was coming to Main Street. I walked up and down the center of the sidewalks and stopped occasionally to say a prayer in an attempt to keep the evil away. Unfortunately, from what you just told me my prayers were too late."

"Did you see anything unusual while you were out there?" Mac asked. Callie wondered if Ben would even recognize anything considered unusual.

The man had a restless energy about him. His fingers moved against each other constantly and a tic appeared at the outward corner of his right eye. Were these things normal or were they an unconscious signal of guilt?

Mac asked him several more questions, but Ben had little to add. According to him he'd been in his home all day the day before until he'd left in the evening to go to the grocery store. He professed not only to not seeing Melinda. He said he didn't even know for sure who she was.

"He is definitely one strange man," Callie said once they were back in the car and headed back to town.

"Yeah, but is he our man?"

Callie heard the weariness and frustration in Mac's voice. She felt some of that herself. After the first day of the investigation, they had nothing to go on. They had some ifs and maybes but nothing concrete to follow up on to find Melinda's murderer.

He remained silent on the drive to her house. She sensed it was the heavy silence of mental weariness. "I'll see you tomorrow," he said once he was parked at her curb.

Without any thought, she reached out and covered one of his hands with hers. "We'll get him, Mac. We're going to get this guy and make sure he goes to jail."

He was quiet for a long moment and then pulled his hand from beneath hers. "That's the goal," he replied.

There was an awkward pause between them and then with a murmured goodbye, Callie got out, grabbed her coat from the back seat and then headed up her sidewalk.

She unlocked her front door and then turned to wave at Mac, who slowly pulled away from the curb. She went inside and tossed her coat across the top of the sofa.

It was stupid to be disappointed that they hadn't solved the murder in a single day. This was going to probably be a marathon rather than a sprint.

Still, she couldn't help but feel a little depressed by the utter lack of any real leads. Even though it had been a long day, she wasn't quite ready to go to bed.

She needed to relax and unwind a bit before heading to sleep.

She stared at the Christmas tree she'd put up a couple of nights before. All the trimmings were in boxes on the floor next to the bare tree. Maybe now was a good time to do a little work to turn it into a real, decorated piece of work.

As she began to string the lights, thoughts of the family she'd lost filled her head. A little over two years ago her father and mother and younger sister had all perished when their car had been struck by a drunk driver.

It was a tragedy that still haunted her and it was what had brought her back to her family home in Rock Ridge. She could have sold the house and moved back to Kansas City, but in the end, she couldn't do it.

Memories of laughter and joyous moments filled this house. It was warm and inviting and Callie could easily envision raising her children here. All she needed was that special man. She'd thought she'd found him in Mac.

However, before she could tell or show him how she felt about him she had to be the best deputy he'd ever had.

Chapter Four

Mac woke at a little after five after suffering sleep filled
with nightmares. He'd dreamed of giant bobtail quail
chasing Callie down a darkened street. It sounded ridiculous, but it had been terrifying. The quail had angry
eyes and sharp beaks and he'd known their intent was
to lodge in her mouth to strangle her to death.

He'd chased after Callie, yelling for her not to
scream, not to even open her mouth at all. He'd pulled
his gun to shoot the murderous birds, but when he shot,
he realized his gun was filled with blanks.

He now sat at his kitchen table with a cup of coffee
and all his notes from the day before in front of him.
He needed to concentrate on the paperwork rather than
the dream and the woman at the center of it.

Still, it was thoughts of Callie that intruded in his
mind. She'd surprised him with her intelligence and
her work ethic...at least on her first day. It was possible she'd pushed herself yesterday in an effort to make
a good impression on him and that work ethic would
change as the days went on.

It wasn't how hard she worked that worried him as
much as it was the evocative scent of her perfume, her

ready, beautiful smile and positive attitude. Even now with a new day dawning his hand still seemed to hold the imprint of her small, warm hand on top of his.

He was definitely drawn to her, but it wouldn't be fair to her for him to act on it, as he knew there was no future for her with him. He was confident that as they worked together, he could keep things completely professional with her.

What he really needed at the moment was something…anything…that would help him solve the case. He finally got up from the table and headed into his bathroom to take a shower.

He'd moved into this small apartment three years before, when his world had exploded and he'd needed to escape the house that held far too many memories, memories both good and bad.

He was comfortable in the small one-bedroom space that was furnished minimally. Besides, he really only showered and slept here. He spent most of his time at the sheriff's office.

A half an hour later he was on his way to work, his mind whirling with suppositions and theories. Why would somebody shove a dead bird into Melinda's mouth? The bird had to be important in the psyche of the killer. But why? He felt like if they could solve that, then they'd know who the murderer was. But how did you solve crazy?

When he'd seen the weather report that morning, he'd learned this unusual cold had settled in for good through the holidays and there were several chances for snow in the coming days. He already longed for the spring.

He entered the back door and stopped in the break

room. Callie sat at one of the tables, a cup of coffee before her and reading something on her cell phone. There were little gaily decorated plastic Christmas trees in the center of each round table.

"Good morning, Callie."

She jumped at the sound of his voice. She shot a quick glance at the Christmas tree on her table and then looked up at him. "Good morning, Mac."

He looked at all the trees and then looked back at her. "What are you, the Christmas elf?"

She released what sounded like a nervous laugh. "I'm just trying to counteract your grinchlike nature."

There was no way he intended to share with her that anything Christmas related brought back bad memories of loss and anger and pain and betrayal.

However, he had noticed over the past year that some of those negative memories had begun to dull and no longer hurt as badly as they once had.

"Are you going to make me pack up all these happy little trees? Are you going to take away my joy, everyone else's joy of Christmas?" she asked. She raised her chin and held his gaze intently.

He had to give it to her; she had more guts than the men who worked for him, he thought. In the past three years nobody had challenged him about his no-Christmas policy.

"No, I'm not," he replied. "Now, I'll be in my office for the next half an hour or so and then we're going to hit the streets once again."

Minutes later he was seated at his desk. There would be few people out and about in town at this time of the morning and in any case, he already had four deputies

actively working the streets. But he knew they'd probably have little to report after another cold December
night.

So far, the evidence they had gathered around the
bench had yielded no clues. He hadn't really expected it
to. Right now, Roger Lathrop was at the top of his suspect list. The smooth insurance salesman had a volatile
history with the victim in the recent past and that made
him a definite person of interest.

Ben Kincaid was a close second, only in that the
man had so many strange ideas and the fact that he'd
been out on Main Street around the time that Melinda's
body had been found.

And there was still a question as to where Melinda
had been killed. According to the autopsy report she'd
lost a lot of blood. So, where was that blood? It hadn't
been around the bench. Was it in somebody's spare
room or had it been washed down a bathtub drain?
Unfortunately, he didn't have any evidence to take to a
judge to get a search warrant for anywhere.

He glanced at the clock on the wall. Seven thirty on
the second day of a murder investigation and already
he felt discouraged.

He would be the first person to say he'd had an easy
run since becoming sheriff seven years before. He'd
been twenty-six years old when he'd become the head
lawman in the small town.

In the past seven years there had been bar fights and
petty thefts, neighborly disputes and speeders. He'd
had one domestic dispute that had tragically ended in
a murder, but other than that he'd never been tested in
the way he knew this murder would test him.

And so far, he felt like he was failing.

At eight o'clock he rose and grabbed his coat for another day of walking the streets and talking to the people of his town. When he went back into the break room several of the deputies who had come off duty were there along with Callie.

They were all involved in a lively discussion about various serial killers of the past. He stood in the doorway and listened to them for several minutes. He was lucky his team was built with strong, intelligent people who all worked together for the same common goal… to live in a town where law and order ruled the day.

"All right, people. Thankfully we aren't chasing a serial killer right now. You men who just got off work need to go home and get some sleep, and Callie, it's time to hit the streets again," he said.

Callie immediately got to her feet and went to the rack to grab her coat. The other men got up more slowly, wearing their weariness after their shifts visibly in their slowness of movements.

"I did some more research last night," Callie said once they were in the patrol car.

"Was that before or after you packed up all those little Christmas trees to bring to work?" he asked with a sideways glance at her.

"It was after. Do you intend to subtly punish me all day for those trees?" she asked.

He released a short laugh. "No, I have far more important things on my mind." In fact, he'd realized the decorations in the office didn't bother him too much. At least when he got home at night there were no items of the approaching holiday there to distract him.

"Why do you hate Christmas so much?"

Her question took him by surprise, but there was no way he intended to answer it. At heart Mac was a very private person. He didn't share personal things about his life with anyone. Besides, Callie was really a stranger to him.

"It's a long story and we don't have time to talk about Christmas or my personal feelings about it right now. I'm far more interested in what you researched last night."

"I did a search for the phrase 'bird in the mouth.'"

"Ha, I doubt that yielded anything," he replied.

"Actually, to my utter surprise I got two hits. The first one was a poem that I didn't really understand and the second one was a short story that was a bit bizarre. I read them both very carefully, but I don't think they have anything to do with our murderer."

"Can you write down the references and give them to me?"

"Absolutely." She pulled a small notebook and pen from her purse and wrote for a minute, ripped off the page and then set it on the console between them. "Maybe you can get something out of them that I missed. I'm just not the literary type. I'm a simple girl who likes my poem to rhyme."

He smiled wryly. "If you couldn't make sense of the references then I doubt I'll have any better luck. I'm just a small-town sheriff and I like my poetry to rhyme, too."

He felt the warmth of her gaze on him. "So, what's on our agenda for today?" she asked.

He released a deep sigh. "Same as yesterday. We talk to people we haven't talked to yet to see if anyone saw anything on the night Melinda's body was left on the bench. I can't help but think there has to be somebody who might have seen a vehicle parked there around that time. We also need to try to find anyone who saw Melinda at any point after she got off work."

"At least it isn't quite as blustery today as it was yesterday," she said. "The more people we speak to, the better our odds that we'll find somebody who saw something."

There was such an optimism in her voice and he found that optimism appealing. He was finding a lot of things about Callie Stevens appealing. He tightened his hands on his steering wheel, as if it might protect him from his own growing lust where she was concerned.

And he definitely had a growing case of lust that was building with every minute he spent with her. Each time he smelled her scent, or listened to the low, sexy sound of her voice, his desire for her grew.

Maybe he should have kept her on the desk. At least that way he'd only see her briefly a couple times a day. But what kind of a man would he be to stop her ambition just because she made him uncomfortable? She deserved to be in the seat next to him. She was intelligent and sharp and had already proved to him that she belonged playing an active role in the investigation.

He was just going to have to get over his attraction to her. However, right now that seemed as difficult as catching a killer.

IT HAD BEEN another long day of pounding the pavement and talking to people. Finally, at seven o'clock they knocked off to have dinner at the café.

"Well, today was a waste of time," Mac said as they sat in a booth toward the back of the café. His eyes were the color of turbulent storm clouds.

"It might feel that way right now, but at least we know now who didn't see anything the night of Melinda's murder," Callie replied. "In the process of elimination, we're making progress."

"Do you always see the bright side of things?" One of his dark brows rose up quizzically.

"It's a flaw of mine," she replied with a half smile. "My mother used to say I could find something positive at a funeral."

To her sudden surprise, a burst of emotion rose up inside her at thoughts of her family. Tears misted her eyes and she quickly stared down at the wooden tabletop.

"Callie, I've never told you how very sorry I am about you losing your family, especially to a drunk driver." He reached out and covered one of her hands with his. "It wasn't fair and it wasn't right and I'm really sorry about your loss." He pulled his hand away but not before she gained strength from the comforting warmth of his touch.

She drew in a deep breath to tamp down the unexpected emotions and then looked up at him. "Thanks, Mac. I won't lie—it was the absolute worst time in my life. But after I got through the initial shock and grief, I realized it was important that I celebrate them instead of mourn them."

The conversation halted as a waitress came to their table to take their order. Mac ordered the meatloaf platter and Callie a bacon cheeseburger and fries. They both opted for sodas.

"That's why Christmas is so important to me," Callie continued once the waitress left the table. "My mother loved the holiday. All my memories of Christmas are of warmth and happiness and love, and that's what I intend to have in my home this year."

"Then I hope that's what you have," he replied. "I'm wondering if we need to reinterview Roger at his home and see if he tells us the same story about his relationship with Melinda as he did before. Some of her friends that we've spoken to have indicated the relationship was more volatile than Roger let on."

She wasn't lost to the fact that he'd intentionally changed the subject. But they were in the middle of a murder investigation and she understood he probably wasn't really interested in her personal life.

"I don't even know where Roger lives," she replied.

"He owns a house right here on Main Street. It's a nice two-story like your place."

"Too bad we can't get a warrant to search it from top to bottom. So far he's the best suspect we have."

"I agree, but I can't go to a judge and tell him we think he might be guilty because almost a month before, he dated the victim. We need something more concrete than that for a search warrant to be granted." His frown returned to etch lines across his forehead, lines that did nothing to detract from his attractiveness.

At that moment the waitress returned with their meals and drinks. "Anything else I can do for you?" she asked.

"No, I think we're good," Mac said. The waitress left to attend to other diners.

"It's obvious from all our questioning of people that

nobody saw Melinda after she stopped working. All I can think of is when her shift ended and she walked outside, there must have been somebody in a car, somebody she would trust to get into their car," she said.

"And the logical person would be Roger," Mac said.

Callie shrugged and then grabbed a fry and dragged it through a pool of ketchup. "Maybe he pulled up and told her they needed to talk…that he was still interested in her and wanted a reconciliation."

"Maybe," Mac agreed. "But we're a small town. There might be somebody else who she'd trust to get into their car. Hell, we don't even know for sure that the killer is a male."

"I just assumed it was a male by the strength shown in the stab wounds," she replied.

"An enraged woman could have made those wounds," Mac said. "We have to keep an open mind with this case."

"But Shelly told us she didn't have any problems with anyone…that she was well-liked among all the women who work here. If I was having an issue with somebody, my best friend would know about it and I believe that would be the case between Shelly and Melinda."

"So, that brings us back to square one. However, I do believe Melinda got into somebody's car outside here and that somebody took her to a place, held her for hours and then killed her."

For the next few minutes, they ate in silence. Unanswered questions whirled around in Callie's head. Who had picked up Melinda after she'd finished her shift here? Was Mac ever going to notice her as a woman?

Where had Melinda been murdered? Was she being stupid to believe that Mac could ever fall in love with her?

They were halfway through their meal when Mac began talking again. "I keep trying to figure out how the killer managed to get hold of a bobtail quail. Birds aren't exactly the easiest creatures to catch and those birds in particular have good camouflage."

"Is there anyone in town who raises birds?" she asked.

Mac shook his head. "Not that I've ever heard about."

"Maybe we should speak to Craig Olson at the pet store," she suggested. "He might know any breeders in the area."

"Dammit." Mac slammed his hand down on the table.

His outburst caused her to jump in surprise. "What?"

He must have realized he'd startled her. He offered her a slightly sheepish smile. "I'm just mad because I didn't think about talking to Craig until you just now brought it up."

"Mac, give yourself a break. It isn't like you've been in your office lounging around and playing video games since the murder occurred. You've been working your butt off." And a fine butt it was, she mentally added.

"I have to say I've been surprised and impressed that you're putting in the hours with me."

"The minute I saw Melinda, I knew I'd work as long and as hard as I could to put away her killer. I hope you'll consider me your right-hand man, or in this case, your right-hand woman."

This time he offered her a real warm smile. "Thank

you, Callie. I appreciate it. I appreciate your thoughts and opinions as this case continues."

She nodded and began to eat once again. Oh, when he smiled at her like that, with his eyes a warm smoky gray and his features all relaxed, she wanted to jump into his arms and feel his closeness.

She wanted to see his sexy, smoky eyes light up with desire for her. She wanted to feel his big strong arms around her. More than anything she wanted him to love her.

Maybe this case and spending so much time with Mac was making her a little bit crazy. She definitely had a crush on him, but a crush was a long way from real true love.

Her thoughts about Mac might be getting away from her because, despite what she had told him about the joys of Christmas, this year she felt a loneliness she hadn't really experienced before.

One day at a time, she reminded herself. One way or another her feelings toward Mac would work themselves out and one way or another she was determined to have a wonderful Christmas even if she was all alone again.

They had just finished eating and were in the process of leaving the café when Allen Wilson bumped into them as they stepped out the door.

"Sheriff…just the person I need to see." Allen grabbed hold of Mac's forearm. Allen's eyes were wide and he was half-breathless. "I… I knew a parking spot would be hard to find in front of the café so I… I parked on th-the other side of the center park and w-walked over. But…there's a dead body in the park."

Chapter Five

Mac's heart crashed to the ground at Allen's words. What the hell? A body in the park? He pulled the man completely outside of the café. "Could you tell who it is?"

"I think it's Candy Waltrip, but I'm not positive," Allen replied, his eyes still big with obvious shock.

"Where exactly in the park is she?" Mac's head reeled with dread.

"You know the bench next to that big oak tree? She's there," Allen said. "I've… I've never seen somebody dead like that before. At first, I thought she was just sitting there, but I got a little closer and her eyes were wide open…just staring and I realized she was…she was dead." He released a deep gasp. "It's bad, Sheriff… It's really bad."

"Allen…" Mac pulled him away from the café front door. "I'm going to ask you a big favor," he said. "If you still intend to go inside and have dinner, could you not tell anyone about this? The last thing I need right now is a crowd to gather around the scene."

"To be honest, I don't feel much like eating right now. I think I'll just head back home," Allen replied.

"You'll be at home if I need to talk to you later?" Mac asked.

"I'll be there."

"Thanks, Allen, and I'm sorry you had to be a part of this." Mac clapped the man on the back. "And I appreciate you keeping this quiet for now."

Minutes later Allen had left and, after grabbing high-power flashlights and protective gear from Mac's trunk, he and Callie began to walk from the café to the park bench Allen had indicated.

"I can't believe this is happening," he said tersely.

"Surely it's not the same," Callie replied. "Hopefully this is the result of some sort of accident or a medical emergency of some kind."

It wasn't the result of any accident or a medical emergency. Mac gazed toward the body in the distance and the first thing he saw was a small Santa hat on Candy's blond hair. He couldn't stop the groan that rose up from the very depths of him.

Before getting any closer, he and Callie stopped to put on booties and gloves and then they approached the body. It wasn't quite the same. Instead of a dead bird in her mouth, Candy held a dead bird in each hand. And yet it was the same.

She wore the light blue T-shirt with the café logo on the front. It was what all the waitresses wore when working there. It was obvious she had been stabbed numerous times and was beyond any medical help.

Mac called all his deputies in. Bright lights were set up and the coroner was contacted. Onlookers began to gather and some of the deputies kept them away while others worked to process the scene. Mac conducted the action, ever aware of Callie at his side.

There was an odd sense of comfort in knowing she was just as shocked, just as appalled as he was and in the fact that he knew she and the rest of his team would do anything possible to help him solve these crimes.

He was aware of Callie watching everything. She directed questions to the deputies and the coroner and took copious notes that he knew she'd share with him later. She showed no weariness; rather her high energy was contagious. She was quickly proving herself to be a ride-or-die kind of partner.

When Candy's body was finally taken away, and the birds had been tagged and bagged, Mac and Callie went over the bench with a fine-tooth comb, hoping to find something, anything, that might point to the killer.

Fortunately, his team had done a good job and there was nothing left to collect. Once again there was also no blood, indicating she'd been killed elsewhere. While his deputies continued to process the scene, Mac and Callie headed back to the café.

Once more, he found himself facing Jimmy in his small office. "I heard that somebody is dead in the park," Jimmy said, his broad features radiating concern.

"That somebody is Candy Waltrip," Mac replied.

"My God, what in the hell is going on?" Jimmy asked and shook his head. "Who in the hell is killing off my waitresses?"

The question caught Mac by surprise. He'd been so deep in his own head about the fact that there had been another murder with the victim having birds at the scene that he hadn't had time to look at the bigger picture that had potentially emerged with this newest murder.

Two dead waitresses. Was it possible the answer to the murders rested here in the café? "So, who have you ticked off lately, Jimmy?" Mac asked. He knew the owner of the café had a reputation for having a pretty bad temper.

Jimmy leaned back in his chair, wiped a hand across his bald pate and frowned. "I had to fire that no-count Ralph Marsten, but that was about three weeks ago. I doubt he could pull together a murder scheme any more than he could figure out how to efficiently work a mop."

"How did he take the news that he was fired?"

"Well, he wasn't happy about it, but he was fond of all the waitresses and I can't imagine him getting some kind of sick revenge on me by killing any of them. He and his wife have been in a couple of times to eat since I fired him and he doesn't seem to be holding a grudge."

"Is there any diner you can think of who might have had an issue with both of the women?" Mac asked.

"None, both of them were well-liked by everyone they waited on. They were friendly, hardworking young women." Jimmy released a deep sigh. "I just can't believe this. I do know this…both of them at one time or another dated that snake oil salesman, Roger Lathrop. Maybe you should talk to that slick creep."

"Oh, trust me, we will," Cassie spoke up for the first time. "Do you know when Roger dated Candy?"

"I think it was right before he dated Melinda. The two used to joke together and say they were members of the Roger the Creep Club."

"What shift did Candy work today?" Mac asked.

"She worked a midshift from ten to two." Jimmy frowned once again. "If either of these women were murdered because of something I said or did, I'll never be able to forgive myself."

"Don't start beating yourself up right now," Mac replied. "We need to solve these murders and figure out what the motive really is." Mac got up with a sense of urgency. "We'll be in and out of here over the next several days interviewing all of your employees. If you think of anything else, Jimmy, please give me a call."

"You know I will," Jimmy replied. He rose from his chair and walked Cassie and Mac out the café's front door.

They immediately headed to the Waltrips' home, where they delivered the news that destroyed another family. Callie was quiet when they returned to the car. He figured she was feeling as bad as he was about the notification they'd just made.

"Where are we going?" She finally broke the silence between them as he headed to the outskirts of town.

"Although my gut instinct tells me Ralph Marsten has nothing to do with any of this, we need to question him so I'm headed to his place now."

"At least we have a bit of direction right now. I can't believe it's just a coincidence that two women who work at the café have been murdered. Somebody has to have some sort of grudge against Jimmy," she said.

"Yeah, tomorrow I intend to push Jimmy harder to think of somebody he's had trouble with," Mac replied. "Jimmy sometimes pops off to someone in a fit of anger and it's possible he popped off to the wrong person."

"I've been in the café when he's hollered at somebody for complaining about his cooking. However, I kind of just assumed everyone took Jimmy with a grain of salt."

Mac tightened his hands on the steering wheel. "But it's possible somebody didn't." He racked his brain to think of somebody, anybody who would harbor such hatred toward the owner of the café.

Had Jimmy somehow stiffed somebody financially? Maybe a supplier or somebody else he did business with? Mac made a mental note to get a list from Jimmy of everyone who he dealt with on that end of the café.

"I still don't know what to make of the birds," Callie said. "The ones Candy was holding in her hands looked like ordinary pigeons."

"That reminds me tomorrow we need to talk to Craig Olson down at the pet shop to see if he knows anyone in the area who raises domestic birds," he said. "We also need to question again all the staff at the café."

"I can't believe we have a second one so quickly after the first," Callie said softly.

He shot her a quick glance. "I can't believe it, either, but here we are."

He turned down a long drive that led to the Marsten home. Ralph and his wife, Rebecca, had lived in the small ranch house for as long as Mac could remember. They had raised their two boys here. Both now lived outside of town, but visited often.

For years Ralph had worked as a janitor at the grade school. He'd retired from that a year ago and since then had been working part-time at the café.

Lights from inside the house shone out into the night

and Ralph's car was parked in front. Mac and Callie got out and headed for the front door.

Rebecca answered Mac's knock. She was a diminutive woman with long gray hair she wore in a thick braid down her back. Her blue eyes widened at the sight of Mac. "Sheriff," she greeted him and opened her door wider to allow him and Callie inside.

They entered into the living room, where Ralph sat on the sofa. He was clad in a royal blue robe and stood to greet Mac with a handshake. He nodded to Callie and then gestured for them to have a seat.

"What's going on?" Ralph asked once they were all settled on the sofa and in chairs.

"Where were you about two hours ago?" Mac asked.

Ralph frowned. "I was right here. I've been home all day… Why?" He looked from Mac to Callie and then back to Mac.

"Rebecca, you can confirm that he's been home all day?" Mac asked.

"I can. In fact, he's been underfoot for the last couple of days," she replied. "Please, Sheriff, tell us what's going on?"

"We heard Jimmy fired you, Ralph," Mac said.

Ralph laughed. "He fired me right after I told him I quit. That man doesn't know how to talk to people. I got tired of him yelling at me that I was slow and stupid. I took it and took it and I finally had enough. Since then, I've just been hanging around home and driving my wife crazy." He cast a fond smile to Rebecca.

"Now, would you please tell us why you're here and asking all these questions?" Rebecca asked.

"Candy Waltrip was murdered tonight," Mac replied.

Both Ralph and Rebecca gasped in obvious surprise. "Oh, that poor girl," Rebecca said. "But why are you talking to us about it?"

"Candy makes the second waitress from the café that has been murdered, so we're questioning anyone who might hold a grudge against Jimmy," Mac explained.

"And you thought I…" Ralph's voice trailed off as he stared at Mac. He then shook his head. "Mac, my life is too damned short to hold any kind of a grudge with anyone."

"That's kind of what I figured, Ralph. But I had to do my due diligence in talking to you." Mac stood.

He'd been doubtful all along that Ralph was capable of committing most any crime. Rebecca wasn't the kind of woman who would lie even for her husband. If she said Ralph had been home the last couple of days, he believed her.

Within minutes he and Callie were back in the car. "I knew that would be a bust," he said as they headed back into town.

"But you still needed to check it out," she replied. "And now we're headed where?"

"Lathrop's place. Even though it's getting late I think it's a perfect time to pop in on him." He cast her a quick glance. As always, he couldn't help but notice how pretty she looked in the illumination from the dashboard. "I'm sure no matter what the time he'll be happy to see Deputy Callie."

"Ugh, don't remind me," she replied.

Mac had to confess, Roger flirting with Callie the last time they'd all spoken hadn't sat well with him. And he consciously didn't want to examine why.

Instead, he thought about the two murdered women… women who were crying out for justice and right now he had no idea how to find it for them.

And with each day that passed, he knew their cries would only get louder in his head.

WHEN MAC PULLED into the driveway of Roger's house, Callie steeled herself for seeing the smooth-talking creep again. Even though she wasn't impressed with Roger Lathrop, she had to admit that his two-story house was quite attractive.

Painted a light gray with darker gray trim, the house also sported two red flowered lounge chairs on the porch that looked welcoming. The place showed way more class than Roger did.

Together she and Mac got out of the car and approached the front door. Despite it being almost midnight, a light shone from the front window.

Roger answered Mac's second knock. "Sheriff, what are you doing here?"

"We need to ask you a few more questions. Can we come in?" Mac asked.

Roger hesitated a moment. "It's awfully late. I was just about to go to bed."

"We were driving by and saw your lights on," Mac replied. "We won't keep you for long." Still Roger hesitated. "Are you going to invite us in or do we have to conduct our interview out here in the cold? Or maybe you'd prefer to come down to the office and answer questions there?"

Roger opened his door to allow them entry. He was clad in a white T-shirt and a pair of navy flannel sleep pants. The living room held a black sofa and love seat and sleek metal-and-glass coffee table and end tables.

An undecorated Christmas tree stood in one corner. On the hardwood floor in front of it several boxes spilled tinsel and a tangle of lights. However, what Callie noticed instantly was a faint smell of bleach in the air.

"Have you been cleaning something?" Mac asked, apparently noticing the same smell.

"Uh, not really. I washed a load of whites a little while ago," Roger replied.

"Your home is very nice," Callie said. "I've always wondered about these grand two-story homes here on Main Street. Would you mind giving me a tour?" She forced a friendly smile to her lips.

"Yeah, I guess I can do that as long as you keep smiling at me like that," he replied and then winked at her.

Callie wanted to throw up, but she kept the smile on her face as he walked them through the front room and into a large, airy kitchen and dining room. The laundry room was right off the kitchen and the smell of bleach seemed to waft in the air from there.

He then took them upstairs to see the three bedrooms and bath. "Thank you for the tour, Roger," she said as they returned to the living room.

"If you're looking for a murder scene here, you're looking in the wrong place," Roger said jokingly.

"What makes you think we'd be looking for a crime scene here?" Mac asked.

"Because last time I met Deputy Callie, I made it my business to find out where she lives. I just happen to know she lives in a two-story house pretty much like this one." He grinned at Callie. "Don't worry, I would never hold the little white lie that you always wondered what a house like this looked like on the inside against a pretty little lady like you."

Despite her irritation with him, she couldn't help the guilty warmth that swept into her cheeks at being called out. It was true that her family home had the same floor plan as Roger's place. It was also creepy that he'd gone to the trouble to find out where she lived.

Roger gestured for them to have a seat on the black sofa and then he sat in a chair facing them. "So, what's going on? Why are you here?" he asked. "More questions about me and Melinda?"

"Actually, we're here to ask you about your relationship with Candy Waltrip," Mac said.

Roger's eyebrows shot up in surprise. "Candy? I don't have any kind of a relationship with her."

"But you had one in the past," Mac said.

"Months ago… Why? Has something happened to her?"

"Who broke up with who when you and Candy stopped seeing each other?" Mac asked.

"It was kind of a mutual thing. We only went out a couple of times and that was all the time we needed to know we weren't right for each other," Roger replied. His eyes widened a bit. "Has something happened to Candy?"

"She was murdered."

Mac's words appeared to punch the wind out of Roger. He slammed back against his chair and expelled a huge gasp. "First Melinda and now Candy?" The shock in his eyes was quickly replaced with anger.

"Don't think you're going to pin this on me just because I dated them both for a little while. Don't pull some kind of rush-to-judgment crap and arrest me because it might make you look like a hero. If you arrest me, that won't stop the killer…because I'm not the damned killer."

"Calm down, Roger. We're not trying to pin this on anyone. We're just in the gathering-of-facts process in the investigation," Mac replied calmly.

"I've told you all I have to say." Roger stood. "I didn't kill either one of those two woman and I'd like you both to leave now. It's way past my bedtime."

Mac and Callie got up and walked to the front door, which Roger yanked open. "If I have more questions for you and you don't want me to speak to you here, then I'll be glad to take you into the office and do it properly," Mac said firmly.

Roger flushed and drew a deep breath, then released it slowly. "That's not necessary. I'll be glad to cooperate in any way I can. You just really shocked me with the news about Candy."

"We'll be in touch," Mac replied and then he and Callie headed for his car.

"It's too late to do any more investigating tonight," Mac said when they were back in his car. "God, I wish there was a bar we could go to and get a drink," he said.

"I wouldn't mind a drink myself," Callie replied. "But you and I sitting in the Red-Tailed Rooster with two women dead would be a very bad look."

The Red-Tailed Rooster was the only bar in town. It was not only a popular place for the hard-core drinkers, but with its large dance floor it was also a popular place for couples to hang out.

"I agree, but nobody can give us a side-eye if we have a drink at my place. Are you up for it or do you want me to take you straight home?" he asked.

"Sure, I'm up for a drink at your place," she replied. She was pleased with his offer and eager to see what Mac surrounded himself with in his personal space.

They rode in silence until they reached the apartment building where Mac lived. They got out and she followed him to the door of his place. He unlocked the door, reached in to turn on a light and then gestured her inside.

The living room was small and held no personal warmth or appeal. There was a gray sofa and chair, a coffee table and television and that was it. There was certainly no sign of Christmas, no photos of family hanging on the wall, nothing to indicate that anyone lived here. To Callie the whole space felt sterile and more than a little sad.

However, there was one clue for her to recognize and know this was Mac's place. The scent of him lingered in the air. It was the scent of minty soap and shaving cream and the familiar woodsy cologne of his. The combination of those smells always made Callie feel safe and oddly comforted.

He led her into his small kitchen, where once again there was no sign of real life except for the single-serve coffee maker and a toaster on the countertop.

"Have a seat," he said and gestured her to the island, which offered two black-and-chrome bar stools. She pulled one out and sat and watched as he grabbed two glasses from the cabinet and then began pulling several bottles of booze out from a lower cabinet.

"I've got gin, whisky and Scotch and I think there might be a bottle of cinnamon schnapps here somewhere," he said. "What's your poison?"

"Do you have a cola?" she asked and he nodded. "Then I'll take that with a splash of whiskey."

"Coming right up." He fixed her drink and then fixed himself a Scotch and soda. He pulled the bar stool around the island so they faced each other.

"Cheers," he said and they clinked glasses.

They each took a drink and for a moment sat in silence. She felt the weight of both the seriousness of what they were up against and the long day they'd just had tugging at her with weariness. She knew he had to be feeling the same way.

He finally broke the silence with a weary sigh. "What in the hell is happening in my town, Callie?"

"I wish I knew," she replied.

"We've got to find this perp before…" He paused as Callie held up her hand.

"Don't even say it out loud." She knew he was about to say they had to find the perp before another murder occurred. The last thing she wanted to believe was that another victim would show up. "Hopefully this is the end of it. Whatever the murderer wanted by killing Melinda and Candy, he got it and that will be the end of it."

"It won't be over until we have him behind bars," Mac replied. He took another sip of his Scotch and then continued. "I can't believe we've had two horrible murders in just three days."

For the next few minutes, they talked about the crimes and compared the way the two women were left to be found. Aside from the difference that Melinda had a bird in her mouth and Candy had a bird in each hand, the victims were virtually the same.

"What do you think about our latest interview with Roger?" he asked.

"I was surprised that he displayed a bit of anger with us. He's still on the top of my suspect list. Even though he acted shocked by Candy's murder I have a feeling Roger can summon up any emotion at any time if it serves his best interest."

"He definitely seems to like you. Would you ever be interested in going out with him?" Mac stared at her intently.

She nearly choked on her drink. "Are you kidding? The answer would not only be no, but hell no."

Mac nodded. "I figured that would be your answer. So, I don't even know… Are you dating somebody else right now?"

"No, since I moved back here, I haven't found anyone I've been interested in dating," she replied and then mentally added, *except you.* "What about you? Why aren't you dating or married to some nice woman? There are certainly plenty of single women in town who would love to be dating you."

"I haven't really been interested in dating since my divorce. I have no plans to ever get married again, so why would I date?"

She gazed at him in surprise. "You're divorced? I didn't even know you'd been married."

"Yeah, I married Amanda Crowley. We were married for a little over two years, but ultimately it didn't work out."

She had a vague memory of Amanda. She was a

dark-haired beauty who had worked at the local women's wear store. In the two years since Callie had been back in town, she hadn't seen Amanda anywhere around town.

"I'm sorry things didn't work out for you," she said. It was the truth. If he'd truly loved his wife and the marriage hadn't worked out, then she was sorry for him. She always wanted love to win. "Is that why you've decided not to ever marry again?"

"Yeah, once was more than enough for me," he replied. He downed the last of his drink in a single swallow. "I'd better get you home. It's late and tomorrow is going to be another long day."

She had a feeling he needed to take her home before he divulged anything more to her about his marriage and divorce. "I'm ready when you are." She slid off the stool and grabbed her coat and purse from where she'd placed them on the sofa as she'd walked in.

She paused at his front door and turned back to face him. "You shouldn't close yourself off to new relationships just because you had a bad one," she said. "Mac, you are too good a guy to spend the rest of your life all alone."

He stood so close to her and his eyes suddenly darkened and flamed with an emotion she'd never seen there before, and it momentarily took her breath away.

And then he leaned down and took her mouth with his. Shivers of both surprise and pleasure swept through her from head to toe. She immediately responded by wrapping an arm around his neck and opening her mouth to him.

She'd imagined Mac kissing her a hundred times in

her dreams, but the reality was far better than anything she could have imagined. His lips were hot and hungry and he tasted of sweet desire and warm Scotch as the kiss continued. He pulled her closer and his tongue slid in to dance with hers.

It all lasted far too briefly before he released his hold on her and stepped back with a deep audible gasp. "I'm so sorry, Callie. That should have never happened." He opened his door and walked outside.

She followed close behind him, the cold night air a slap in her face after the heat of his unexpected kiss. They got into the car and for several minutes they rode in silence, although the tension in the car was palpable between them.

He pulled up in front of her house, parked the car and then he turned to look at her. His eyes were dark and unfathomable. He stared at her for a long moment and then released a deep sigh.

"Callie, in the midst of the stress of these murder investigations you could be a very soft spot for me to fall into and I don't want that to happen. But if that happened, which it won't, you have to understand that it wouldn't mean anything for me. I'm sorry I kissed you. I should have never crossed that line with you and it won't happen again. Now, I'll just say good-night."

"Good night, Mac." She got out of the car and then opened the back door to retrieve her coat. "And just so you know… I really, really liked your kiss," she said and then closed the door.

Chapter Six

That kiss. That damnable kiss kept Mac turning and twisting for what was left of the night. He'd had no forewarning that he was going to kiss Callie until he was actually doing it.

She'd just looked so pretty and he felt as if he'd been thinking about kissing her for the past two years. He tried to tell himself that it had been an unpleasant experience, but he was definitely lying to himself.

Kissing Callie had been beyond wonderful. Her lips had been so soft and filled with a sweet, warm invitation. It was definitely something he'd like to do over and over again. But he wouldn't.

He couldn't allow it to happen again. He'd told her the truth when he'd said she would be an easy, soft place for him to fall. With the stress of the murders so heavy on his shoulders it would be easy for him to want a connection that had nothing to do with murder and death.

And she'd told him she'd liked it. Her parting words to him last night had sizzled in his brain throughout the night. Not that it mattered that she'd liked it. That was just a piece of information to further torment him.

It was just after six in the morning and he now sat

at his desk in his office with the second autopsy report in front of him. He read it, finding no real surprises. Candy had been stabbed twenty-two times.

Again, it was an overkill that screamed of some kind of personal rage. What had these two young women, who worked as waitresses, done to anyone to warrant such horrendous deaths? Who had hated them so much?

Candy also had the same ligature wounds. Albertson still believed the women had been held by ropes and they had struggled against them hard enough to leave bloody wounds behind. How horrible it must have been for them to be tied down and then stabbed to death.

After reading the report, he wrote out duties for his deputies for the day. Along with their regular work, each of them would be interviewing people and checking out alibis to further the murder investigation.

Mac was grateful that his deputies were all smart people who used their initiative and didn't need babysitting from him. He told them what he needed from them and they did the best they could to deliver for him.

This second murder changed everything. The townspeople would demand answers and he wished he had some. There would now be a pall of fear overlaying the town and he absolutely hated that.

At the very least he needed to call a town meeting to let people know what had happened before rumors and false information made the rounds. At seven, he made a few phone calls to set up the meeting for that evening.

At seven fifteen he got up from his desk to head to the break room for the morning briefing. He had a quick moment to wonder how things would be with Callie today. Would they be awkward? Would she want to talk about what had happened between them the night before? God, he hoped not. He just wanted to forget about the whole kiss thing.

He walked into the break room and, despite his desire to the contrary, his gaze immediately shot to Callie. Her eyes sparkled with their usual enthusiasm and liveliness as she smiled at him.

He couldn't help but return her smile, then he cleared his throat and began the meeting. It didn't take him long to hand out the daily assignments and to tell the deputies to let everyone know that he would be holding a meeting at seven that evening in the town hall.

Once the men had all left, Mac sank down in the chair next to Callie and opened up the notebook he'd carried in with him. "At nine, I want to be at the pet store to question Craig, but before then I thought maybe you could help me write up something for the town meeting tonight."

"Of course," she said and to his immediate discomfort, she moved her chair closer to his. "What exactly is it you need to tell people."

"Obviously I need to tell them that two young women have been murdered. I certainly don't want to go into all the gory details, but I also want to dispel any false rumors that might be making the rounds."

"What about questions? Are you planning on taking questions from everyone?"

Mac frowned. "I'd rather not, but I'm afraid if I don't then everyone will think I'm hiding things and the last thing I want is for the people in this town to think they can't trust me."

"Mac, it's okay to tell a few little white lies in the

interest of protecting the investigation," she said. "Besides, if we can anticipate what some of the questions might be then those are the things you address in your report." She placed her hand on the notebook he'd carried in. "Do you mind?"

"Not at all." He pushed the notebook in front of her and handed her his pen.

He watched as she bent her head down and began to write. He steeled himself against the torment of her nearness. If he allowed it, her familiar scent would dizzy him, her body warmth would burn into his brain at the memory of holding her...of kissing her. He consciously refused to acknowledge any of these things. He had two murders to solve and that was where his focus had to be.

Callie wrote for several minutes and then pushed the notebook back in front of him. "Tell me what you think."

He read the three paragraphs she had written. They were a perfect recap of the crimes, minus the information about the birds and the Santa hats, and exactly what he needed to tell everyone in town. "This is great. Thank you," he said.

"Have you thought anything about the fact that both the victims were blondes?" she asked.

"I have," he replied. He was hoping this wasn't the work of some crazed serial killer who would continue to murder until he was caught. He was desperately hoping that whoever had killed Candy and Melinda had a specific motive to kill those specific women and now was done.

"I'm hoping that's a coincidence and not a pattern,"

he continued. "However, I intend to warn the women in this town that they need to travel in pairs or groups until we get this killer behind bars."

"And let's hope they take the warning to heart," Callie replied.

They worked several more minutes fine-tuning Mac's speech for the town hall meeting and once he was confident it said everything he needed to tell the people of Rock Ridge, they stood up from the table and got ready to head out to the pet store.

Callie was quiet on the drive and Mac wondered if she was thinking about their kiss. He hoped not. He hoped that kiss was the last thing on her mind. He certainly didn't want to think about it anymore.

"I still believe it's possible that Roger is our man," she said, breaking the silence between them. "There's something not only sleazy about him, but also we know he has a temper. With him dating both Melinda and Candy, I just can't help but believe he's a number-one suspect."

"I'm definitely leaning that way," he replied, grateful that she was thinking about murder instead of their kiss. "I believe both of the women would have felt comfortable getting into Roger's car after their shifts at the café. Because he works alone in his office, his alibi will be that he was at work, but he has nobody to corroborate his alibis."

"It's possible the nasty breakup with Melinda brought out some kind of darkness in Roger. He apparently takes rejection very hard. And even though he said the breakup with Candy was mutual, we can't know that for sure. Maybe, ultimately, she had rejected him, too."

"If it is him, then I hope he hasn't dated anyone else who might have angered him," Mac said as he pulled up in front of Olson's Pet Palace.

"Let's hope we can get a few answers here," she said as they got out of the car.

The moment they opened the door and walked inside the shop they were greeted by barking dogs in cages. There were also kittens in cages along with rabbits, guinea pigs and hamsters in pens on the floor. Large aquariums held a variety of colorful fish, and rows of items made it easy for people to feed and care for whatever pet they bought.

Craig Olson was in his middle fifties. His dark hair was just starting to turn gray and Mac knew he'd been married to his wife, MaryBeth, for years.

He approached them from the back of the store. "Sheriff," he said with a wide smile. He nodded to Callie and then looked at Mac once again. "Have you finally decided you need a dog?"

Mac laughed. "You know better. I don't have time for a dog. I'm rarely home and it wouldn't be fair for an animal. But I do have some questions for you."

"Okay, fire away," Craig replied.

"Do you know anyone in the area who is raising or keeps domestic kinds of birds?" Mac asked.

Craig frowned. "When you say domestic birds, what exactly are you talking about?"

"Specifically, bobtail quails and pigeons." Mac replied.

Craig's frown deepened as he slowly shook his head.

"I don't know of anyone raising those kinds of birds. I can't imagine why anyone would. Those aren't species anyone wants to buy and they certainly don't make good pets like a parakeet or a cockatiel."

"That's what we thought, but we figured if anyone knew anything about it, it would be you," Mac said.

"Does this have something to do with the murders?" Craig asked.

"Unfortunately, I can't discuss anything about the ongoing murder investigations, but I'm having a town meeting this evening at seven to answer some questions," Mac said.

"Good to know. MaryBeth and I will definitely be there," Craig replied. "Is there anything else I can do for you? You sure you aren't in the market for a sweet little puppy?"

"No…no, thanks, Craig. Maybe when I'm not the sheriff anymore," Mac replied.

"Ah hell, Mac, you're going to be voted in as sheriff until you're ninety years old," Craig said with a laugh. "Everyone in town loves and admires you."

A few minutes later Mac and Callie were back in the car and headed to the café to continue to interview the staff. "Have you ever thought about getting a dog?" Callie asked.

"Not really. As far as I'm concerned getting a dog is right up there with getting another wife or having any kind of deep relationship with a woman. It's not going to happen." He spoke the words strongly…forcefully.

The moment Callie had told him she liked his kiss, she'd subtly told him she would be open to a relationship with him. He needed to make it clear to her that he would never be anything to her except her coworker.

Or maybe he was reminding himself that Callie was strictly off limits because the more time he spent with her...the more he wanted her.

THE TOWN HALL was packed with people, along with the chairs that had been set up for the evening. The raised stage on one end of the room held only a podium where Mac would give an update to the people who depended on him and his team to keep them safe.

Jimmy had provided coffee for all and Danny from Danny's Donuts had carried in dozens of the treats for people to enjoy. Despite the sober events that had brought them all together, everyone milled about, talking and laughing with each other.

Callie and the other deputies stood against the wall to the left of the stage, ready to support Mac in any way they could. Callie had confidence that Mac would do just fine He was as well prepared for this meeting as he could be.

Still, her stomach tightened with nervous tension as Mayor Alex Broadbent stepped up on the stage and walked toward the podium. The mayor was a short, squat man who wore his self-importance in the jut of his jaw and the loudness of his voice.

He was not a favorite among the people at the sheriff's office. Occasionally he would come in and puff out his chest and complain about things they were or weren't doing and then he'd fly back out to throw his weight around someplace else. He had only been voted in as mayor because nobody else had wanted the job.

"People…people," Alex said and raised his hands for silence. "Please find seats and quiet down so we can get this meeting underway."

It took several minutes for everyone to settle into chairs and then a hushed pall descended over the crowd. "As you know we've all been brought together tonight due to tragic circumstances that have recently taken place in our town. Two innocent lives were stolen away and I know we're all grieving their loss and wondering what our law enforcement is doing about it."

Mayor Alex continued to talk for the next ten minutes, speaking about improvements he was hoping to make in the town and all the Christmas celebrations that would occur over the next three weeks. "Starting next week our park will be transformed into the North Pole complete with a Santa to talk to the kids."

Callie frowned in distaste. The mayor obviously had no good sense of timing to be talking about the holiday celebrations taking place in the park where a murdered body had been found.

"Get off the stage," a deep voice finally yelled from someplace in the back.

"Yeah, we came to hear Sheriff McKnight," another male voice cried out. Disgruntled murmurs began to get louder.

Alex laughed and held up his hands once again. "Okay…okay. I hear you. Let's bring out Sheriff McKnight to inform us all about the tragic circumstances surrounding two young women's murders and find out what he's doing about it."

Finally, Alex got off the stage and Mac walked to the

podium. Callie's heart expanded. He looked so handsome and so confident.

Everyone hushed once again as Mac stepped up to the podium. He began to talk about the murders that had taken place. He explained that each of the women had been stabbed and that they had apparently been kidnapped off the streets hours before their murders.

His voice held compassion for the victims and an underlying confidence that the guilty would be caught. He finished by telling everyone that they had leads they were following, but also asking anyone who might have information about the two murders to please come forward.

He was eloquent and spoke with no notes, indicating he was speaking from his heart. This was what the people in Rock Ridge loved about him. He was such a good man and Callie wanted to make him *her* man.

After he finished talking, he called for questions. There were only a few, and those were easy for him to answer. Once the few questions had been answered, Mac told the women of the town how important it was that they not be on the streets all alone until the killer was caught. "No matter what time of the day or night, don't be out alone until this killer is behind bars," he reiterated.

Once it was all over, Mac came down from the stage and mingled with the people for a few minutes and then he and Callie and the rest of the deputies left the building.

The deputies went back to their duties and Callie and Mac drove through the hamburger place for a late dinner and then headed back to the station. It was after ten by the time they sat at a table in the break room.

"Murder investigations are definitely bad for the diet," she said as she unwrapped the bacon cheeseburger and then pulled out her large order of fries from the take-out bag. "I've never eaten as much fast food as I have the last five days."

God, had it only been four days since Melinda's body had been found? It felt as if it had been weeks. The two women haunted Callie at night, invading her dreams with their desire for justice. And Callie desperately wanted to give them justice. But right now, despite what Mac had said about leads in his speech, the investigation was pretty much stalled.

"If you weren't investigating this murder and grabbing late-night fast food, what would you cook yourself for dinner?" Mac asked.

Callie popped a fry into her mouth and chased it down with a drink of soda. "Probably an herb-encrusted chicken breast and some steamed broccoli," she replied.

He raised a dark brow. "Sounds like you must be a good cook."

"I do all right. Most of the things I cook are from recipes my mom made for family meals. What about you? Do you cook?"

His lips turned up into the smile that always shot a rivulet of warmth through her. "As long as the café is open, I'll never go hungry."

She laughed. "That certainly answers my question."

His smile lingered for another moment and then turned into a frown. "When we finish eating, I'd like to go over some things to see if we've missed anything."

"Whatever we need to do," she replied, although she couldn't imagine that they'd missed anything. It felt as if they had spoken to every single person in town, had followed up on the few leads they had and yet were as clueless as they had been following the first murder.

For the next few minutes, they ate in silence. She felt the weight of the long hours weighing on her shoulders, but she would push herself to her very physical and mental limits to help Mac catch this killer.

Once they were finished eating, they opened the notebooks they'd each carried since the night that Melinda's body had been found.

In this respect they had a common work practice of keeping continuous notes in ordinary notebooks that they referred to often.

Mac thumbed through his pages and then stopped on a particular page. "What I want to do again is go over the places where Melinda's and Candy's lives intertwined. We need to make sure we've crossed all those t's and dotted all the i's and that we haven't missed anything."

She turned to the pages in her notebook where she had detailed that particular information. "The biggest one is that they both dated Roger," she said.

"We also know both of them got their hair and nails done at Wanda's," Mac added, referring to Wanda's Beauty Spa, the one place in town that catered to women and beauty.

"But we spoke to everyone who worked there and everyone indicated they found Melinda and Candy friendly and fun," Callie replied and looked down at her notes once again. She looked back up at Mac. "This is a small town. The two went to the same stores, drank at the same bar and hung out with the same friends. We've all checked everything possible, Mac."

"I know." He released a deep sigh and closed his notebook. "I just want to catch this creep so badly."

"That makes two of us," she agreed. "Maybe the town meeting tonight will prompt somebody to remember something they saw on the nights of the murders. Maybe somebody will come forward with some new information we can use."

He smiled at her. "There you go again with that eternal optimism."

"Sorry if it irritates you. It's just the way I look at things," she replied.

"It doesn't irritate me at all," he replied. "Sometimes I wish I had a little more of that cheerful outlook on life."

She searched his features. "You don't believe in the joy of Christmas and you don't have a cheerful outlook on life. What happened that stole all that away from you, Mac?"

She suspected it had to do with Mac's first marriage. She wanted to know the ins and outs of him, wanted to understand what drove him and made him who he was. She wanted him to trust her with his emotions and thoughts, not just about the murders but also about his life.

He released a deep sigh and leaned back in his chair. He stared down at the tabletop for a long moment and then raised his head and looked at her once again. His eyes were dark and turbulent…the color of thunderstorm clouds.

"Three years ago my wife walked out on me on Christmas Eve," he finally said. "I didn't see it coming and she totally blindsided me."

"Oh Mac, I'm so sorry," Callie replied. She wanted to touch him, to pull him into her arms and hold him until the pain in his eyes...in his heart...was gone forever.

He shrugged. "It was a long time ago, but it definitely ruined this particular holiday for me forever."

"Mac..." She reached out and grabbed his hands in hers. "I'm so sorry if she hurt you. I can't imagine any woman foolish enough to ever walk away from you, but don't let her steal your joy of Christmas...all the joy of your life...away."

He briefly rubbed his thumbs across the back of her hands and then pulled his away and stood. "I think on that note it's time to call it a night."

She wanted so much more from him. She wanted to know why his wife had left him. Did he still love her? Is that why he had no interest in another relationship? Because he was holding out hope for some kind of a reconciliation with Amanda?

She didn't ask any of those questions. As she rose from the table a huge weariness slammed into her. Even though it was almost eleven thirty, the earliest she would be home since Melinda had been murdered.

"Maybe something will happen tomorrow that will bring us clarity concerning this killer," she said once they were in his car and he was driving her home.

"I still don't understand why the birds were left with the bodies," Mac replied. "They have to mean something to the killer. Otherwise why were they left?"

"Maybe Roger killed both of the women for breaking up with him and then he left the birds to throw us off track and make us believe some crazy person killed them."

"Or some crazy person with a vendetta against blonde women really did kill them and unless he somehow messes up, we're never going to catch him," he replied.

"There you go with that negativity again," Callie said half-teasingly.

He flashed her one of his sexy half smiles. "You're right. I need to change some of that about myself."

For the first time she saw the lines that dug deeper down the sides of his face, the ones that fanned out from his tired-looking eyes. All of the deputies were feeling the long hours and hard work that had come along with these murders.

They were quiet for the rest of the ride. He pulled up at the curb in front of her house, put his car into Park and then turned to look at her.

"I know we're all running on empty right now," he said. "I don't want to see you at the office tomorrow before nine. Take some extra time to sleep in a little. It's obvious this investigation is going to be a marathon and not a sprint and if we continue to work these crazy hours, we're all going to burn out."

"And what time are you coming in tomorrow?" she asked.

"I don't know. I'll know when I get up in the morning."

"You know you need to take care of yourself as well," she replied. "You're working longer hours than anyone."

"Yeah, I know." He flashed her a tired smile. "I'll see you tomorrow after nine."

She wanted to take his hand and pull him out of the car and into her king-size bed. She didn't necessarily want sex or anything from him. She just wanted to somehow take care of him, to make sure he got a good night's sleep and ate a good breakfast in the morning.

There was a part of her that wanted to take care of him, and there was a part of her that wanted to be cared for by him. She now understood why he hated Christmas and why he'd lost faith in love. Apparently, his breakup with his wife had broken his heart…had broken him.

She wanted to change all that, but as she got out of the car and headed toward her front door, she realized that a romance between her and Mac might never happen.

For the first time since she'd started working for Mac, she faced the fact that the girlish crush she'd had on Mac was transforming into a grown-up woman's love. She also had to face the fact that no matter how much she might want him, he might never love her back, he might never be *her* man.

Chapter Seven

For the next two days Mac held meeting after meeting with his deputies. They went over and over the elements of the crimes, searching for anything and everything they might have missed.

He and Callie beat the streets, talking to the same people over and over again, checking and rechecking whatever alibis they could and trying to ignore the fact that they had no clues, no real leads to follow.

Mac had never worked with a partner before. Despite the fact that Callie intrigued him as a man. In spite of how much he'd like to let himself go and fall into the warm depths of her eyes, accept the sweet fire he knew she might offer, he wouldn't do that.

However, he did appreciate her being an intelligent partner both as a sounding board and somebody who threw out ideas of her own. He enjoyed her company, both when they were talking about the murders or when they were just small-talking about anything other than murder.

Once again, he was driving her home. It was ten thirty after another fruitless day. The silence between them in the car wasn't one that made him uncomfortable. Thankfully, Callie wasn't the kind of woman who needed to fill every silence with conversation and he appreciated that about her.

When he pulled up in front of her house, he couldn't help but notice the colorful lights that shone from a Christmas tree just inside the large picture window. They looked cheerful and inviting.

"Nice tree," he said as he parked at the curb.

"Thank you. After a long day of a murder investigation, it's nice to come home to a pretty tree with festive sparkly lights. Maybe you should get one for yourself. You know…embrace the season and all that."

He released a dry laugh and shook his head ruefully. "You're like a mischievous elf constantly whispering in my ear."

She laughed, the deep, sexy sound sweeping through him on pleasant notes. "You can't blame an elf for trying."

Mac's phone rang, jarring their conversation. He answered on speaker. The caller identification showed that it was Deputy Cameron Royal. "Cameron, what's going on?" Mac asked.

"Sheriff…we've got another one."

Cameron's words sliced through Mac, and Callie grabbed his forearm as if to keep them both grounded. "Where?" Mac asked.

"It's Linda Bailey and she's in front of the bank," Cameron replied.

"We'll be there in five." Mac hung up and threw the car into Drive. He got back on the phone and called in more deputies and the medical examiner.

"Linda Bailey…she's another blonde," Callie said

softly when Mac got off the phone. In Mac's peripheral vision he saw her reach up and touch one of her own blond curls.

Mac's stomach clenched tight and a faint nausea rose up inside him as he thought of Callie in the hands of this madman. She would definitely be the blond-haired young woman who might draw the killer's attention.

Still, right now all he could think about was that there was yet another innocent woman who had been killed.

What in the hell was happening? He was the sheriff in this town and yet he felt as if he'd been dropped into the middle of a horror film where he didn't know the plot and couldn't see the end. He was terrified for his town.

Once again, he was thankful that it was another cold, blustery night and late enough that nobody else was on the streets. However, that didn't take away the sickness inside him.

There was only one bank in town and Linda Bailey worked as a teller there. She was a pretty blonde and Mac would guess her to be in her late twenties or early thirties.

He saw Cameron's car parked at the curb and he pulled in just behind it. Together he and Callie got out of the car, pulled on gloves and booties and then approached the scene.

As with the other two women, Linda's body was posed with a little Santa hat on her head. She had no coat and she was clad in a long-sleeved white blouse and black slacks. The blouse was bloody in several places with what Mac assumed was the result of knife wounds.

At her feet were three dead chickens.

Mac stared at the dead birds and myriad emotions filled his head. Confusion about what the birds meant, horror that another woman had met her death at the hands of a madman and the whisper of self-doubt that had haunted him since his ex-wife had left him.

Are you good enough? The words fluttered in his head and made all the muscles in his body tense. His ex-wife certainly hadn't thought so. The answer was obviously no. Linda made the third woman who had been killed. How many more women would have to die before he could get the perp behind bars?

More deputies arrived and they began to process the scene. As Mac worked along with everyone else, he had no time to entertain any more self-doubts. Maybe this one would yield the clues he needed. Perhaps Linda's death wouldn't be completely in vain and this was the case that would solve all the murders.

Maybe some of Callie's optimism was actually rubbing off on him. He glanced over to where she was talking to Deputy Johnny Matthews. She looked earnest and he appeared…appeared smitten.

A strange emotion swept through Mac. Jealousy? Ridiculous, he scoffed to himself. "Mac, we're ready to take the body," Richard Albertson said as he stepped up next to Mac. "I don't expect any real surprises when I do the autopsy. I'm sure it will pretty much be like the last two."

"Unfortunately, I'm sure you're right," Mac replied.

"Have you figured out anything about the birds?"

Mac frowned. "Right now we don't have a damned clue as to what they mean and why they're being left at the scenes. I think if we could solve that much, we'd be well on our way to making an arrest."

"I hope that happens soon," Richard said.

"That makes two of us," Mac replied.

It took another two hours after Linda's body had been carried away to finish up processing the scene. Linda lived alone in an apartment in the same complex as Mac. Her parents had moved out of Rock Ridge to Kansas City. He would wait until morning to call them, a call he dreaded making.

It was one thirty when he and Callie got to Linda's apartment to have a look around and see if she'd left any clues as to what had happened to her. There had been no phone found with her body, but Mac was hoping to find out what carrier she used for cell service and request records from them. He was still waiting for records from the other two victims.

"Sorry to wake you at this time of the morning," Mac said to Ed Canton, who was the apartment building manager.

"Sorry for the circumstances," Ed replied. "Linda was a good tenant, always paid her rent on time and never caused any problems." He unlocked the apartment door and shoved it open. "If you don't mind, just lock up after you're done."

"Will do," Mac replied.

He and Callie stepped into the apartment and Mac flipped on an overhead light. The living room was attractively decorated with a beige sofa and chair and throw pillows in a bright yellow.

On one wall was a desk holding a computer. Mac immediately went there to see if there was anything on her social media that might be helpful. While he was working with that, Callie disappeared into what he assumed was the bedroom.

Mac did a cursory search on all the social platforms and it didn't take him long to learn that Linda wasn't much of a poster. He was grateful to find a password book in her desk drawer. With that in hand, he closed down the computer and began to pack it up to take with them.

Deputy Pete Taylor was their computer expert. He knew computers inside and out. If there was anything on Linda's computer that might lead them to her killer, then Pete would find it.

He turned as Callie came out of the bedroom. "Find anything interesting?" he asked.

"Nothing, except for the fact that Nathan must be doing some work for her in her closet. It looks like some new shelves have been added and more are ready to be put in."

He finished wrapping up the computer cord. "How do you know that Nathan is doing the work?"

"There's a wooden toolbox in there with Nathan's name carved into the side of it," she replied. "What about you? Anything on her computer?"

"I just did a quick search of her social networking and didn't see anything worthwhile. She also had a couple of texts from several friends that I looked at but they were all about a week old. At first glance I would say she wasn't into the whole social networking thing, but we'll see what Pete can find."

"Sounds good," Callie replied.

They finished searching the apartment and then left

the building. "There really isn't much more we can do tonight," Mac said wearily as he drove to take Callie home. "First thing tomorrow we'll head to the bank to start questioning people."

"And we need to establish a time line as to what she did and where she went yesterday. So far it seems like he takes his victims and holds them for at least six hours or so and then he kills them," Callie replied.

"If Linda worked yesterday then he broke the pattern," Mac replied. "If she didn't get off work until five, then he only held her a couple of hours before killing her." Mac clenched his hands on the steering wheel. Who was this creep and when was he going to make a mistake? "Obviously we also need to speak to Nathan again."

"Maybe this will be the one," Callie said softly. He could hear the weariness in her voice. "Maybe this will be the one that breaks the case wide open."

"If it doesn't, it might be time for me to call in the FBI," Mac replied. "It's obvious now this person is looking and acting like a serial killer and we have no real clues as to his identity."

He hated the idea of admitting defeat, and that was what a call to the Feds meant. It would mean that he and his team couldn't do it, that they didn't have the capacity to solve the crime.

But despite that it would look like defeat to his team…to his town…he also wanted the killing to stop. If it took the FBI to make that happen, then he would be all in. He pulled up in front of Callie's house and turned to tell her goodbye.

Her eyes blazed with a surprising energy in the dashboard light. "Mac, don't do anything rash. Don't give up on your team yet," she said fervently. "Don't give up on yourself just yet."

"Callie, I have to be honest with myself. Three women are dead and we don't have a lead—we don't even have a single clue to find the killer. Maybe the FBI has more tools than we have. All I care about is getting this killer behind bars before another woman dies. If it takes the FBI to do that, then so be it."

"At least wait until we examine all the evidence in Linda's murder. Who knows where the investigation will lead us," she replied. "Mac, you're the smartest man I know. All you need is one little clue, one little break, and you'll catch this killer."

His heart warmed at her words. "Callie, I appreciate the vote of confidence. We'll see what happens in the next couple of days or so."

As he'd done every night since this nightmare had begun, he watched her walk to her front door. And once again the lights from the tree in the window winked and twinkled cheerfully. When she disappeared into her house, he drove home.

Once inside his apartment, despite the lateness of the hour, he was too wired up to immediately go to bed. He sank down on his sofa and his mind filled with the images of the three dead young women and the birds that had been found with each one of them.

The birds had to be at the center of the case. But damned if Mac could figure out how. What did the birds mean to the killer? Was it some kind of a ritualistic kind of thing? He needed to check with surrounding towns to see if they had seen something like this.

He was also concerned because the killer was on such a fast track. He was scarcely giving them time to investigate one murder before another one was committed. What had triggered the killings in the first place?

He released a deep sigh, leaned his head back and closed his eyes. For the first time he wondered what it would be like to come home to Callie's place.

He knew it would be warm and welcoming...like Callie herself. He imagined it would smell like peppermint and cinnamon and vanilla from the candles she burned.

The lights on her tree would create a soft ambience that would inspire peace and tranquility. God, he wished he was there with her right now.

Instead, he was in his cold, sterile apartment and headed into all the dark places in his mind as he dreamed of the murder victims night after night.

Chapter Eight

By eight o'clock the next morning Mac was seated at a desk in the bank interviewing one of the bank tellers and Callie was seated at a desk across the room interviewing another one of the tellers.

Barb Timmons was an attractive brunette in her middle thirties. She openly wept at the news of Linda's murder. "I just can't believe this," she cried and grabbed several tissues from the box on the desk. "She was such a sweet person." She dabbed at her eyes.

Callie gave her a few moments to gather herself together. "When was the last time you saw or spoke to her?"

"Yesterday was her day off, so it would have been when the bank closed on the day before. She and I didn't really hang out so we didn't talk on the phone or text each other unless it had to do with bank business."

"And why was that? Why didn't the two of you hang out?" Callie asked.

"We were just at different places in our lives. I'm married and have a small child at home and Linda is… was…still in the single lifestyle, so we didn't hang out after-hours."

"The last time you talked to her did she mention going out with anyone? Do you know if she was dating anyone specific?"

"She didn't mention anything, and I'm pretty sure she wasn't dating any one person." Barb shook her head ruefully. "I do know she was excited about Nathan Brighton doing some work in her closet. He was installing some shelves and she told me she couldn't wait to put her shoe collection there instead of spread out all over the floor."

"So, you have no idea what she might have planned for her day off?" Callie asked.

Barb shook her head and tears once again filled her eyes. "I… I just can't even believe she's gone. I can't imagine anyone wanting to hurt her."

"If you think of anything, anything at all, would you please give me or Sheriff McKnight a call?" Callie removed one of Mac's cards from her shirt pocket and handed it to Barb.

"I promise I'll let you know if I think of anything," Barb replied.

"Thank you for your time and now you can get back to your regular work." Callie watched as Barb made her way across the bank lobby to her position behind the counter as a teller.

Callie glanced over to Mac, who was now interviewing the bank manager. There was nobody else for Callie to speak with, so she remained seated at the desk waiting patiently for Mac to finish up.

During the last couple of days of her and Mac working together for such long hours, they had shared pieces of their lives with each other.

She now knew he liked his burgers without tomatoes, his steak rare and his eggs over easy. She'd also learned that he liked old rock and roll music, that his favorite season was spring and that when he was stressed out, he rubbed the back of his neck.

He'd told her that like her, he'd had an idyllic childhood. His father worked for the Rock Ridge Fire Department and his mother had been a stay-at-home mom. A year before, his father had retired and he and his wife had bought a small farm about forty-five minutes away. Although he and his parents were close, he'd confessed that he had yet to visit them on their new farm.

She'd talked to him about Lily, the sister she had lost, and had shared stories about when the two were young. He'd been warmly supportive as he'd listened to her talk about her sister and she'd felt as if their friendship had grown deeper with all the conversations they'd shared.

The schoolgirl crush she'd had on him was truly blossoming into something deeper and more grown-up. She was on the verge of being completely and totally in love with him.

And with that love came worry. It was the worry of a woman for her man. What concerned her about him right now was his decision to potentially call in the FBI.

Mac's entire self-identity was that as sheriff of the town he loved. If he wound up calling in the Feds, it would be an admission that he no longer believed in his team…and more importantly that he no longer believed in himself. And if that role as a trusted, confident sheriff was taken away from him, then what would he be?

As she saw Mac stand and hand the bank manager his card, Callie also got up and met him at the front door. Together they walked out of the building and into another cold, blustery day.

"Anything?" Mac asked once they were in the confines of his car.

"Only that Linda was excited about the shelves Nathan was building into her closet. Nobody I spoke to had any idea about what she might have done yesterday on her day off."

"The only information I got was that Linda was a good employee, always on time and never a problem. But nothing about her day-off activities or about anyone who might want to hurt her."

"So, what next?" she asked.

"We talk to Nathan again."

Nathan wasn't at home, but they found him at the café. He sat in a booth alone and offered them both a friendly smile when they approached him.

"Hey, Nathan. Mind if we join you?" Mac asked.

"No, not at all," Nathan replied.

Callie scooted in on the bench seat facing Nathan and Mac slid in next to her. Almost immediately waitress Nancy Weatherby appeared. "Morning Callie... Sheriff," she greeted them. "What can I get for you this morning?"

"Just coffee for me," Mac replied.

"Make that two," Callie added.

"Two coffees," she replied. "Nathan, you doing okay?"

"I'm fine as a fiddle," Nathan replied. "You two should have ordered the pancakes," he said once Nancy had left the booth. "I always get the pancakes because they're so good." As if to prove his point, Nathan took a big forkful of the fluffy cakes.

"We both ate breakfast earlier," Mac said. They made small talk until Nancy brought the coffee and then left the booth again.

"I understand you've been doing a little work for Linda Bailey," Mac said and then took a drink of his coffee.

"Yeah, I've been building some shelves in her closet for her." Nathan wiped his mouth on a napkin and then frowned. "But I think maybe I did something to make her mad at me and maybe she doesn't want me to do the work for her anymore."

"What makes you think that?" Mac asked. Callie took a sip of her coffee and kept her gaze on Nathan.

"Yesterday morning I was supposed to show up at her place to keep working on the shelves, but when I got there I knocked and I knocked and she never came to the door. I tried to call her a couple of times yesterday but I kept getting her voice mail. Then I stopped by there again this morning and she still didn't answer the door, so I figured I'd done something to make her mad even though I don't know what it was." Nathan shook his head and cut into his pancake.

"She wasn't mad at you, Nathan. At some point yesterday Linda was kidnapped and murdered," Mac said.

Nathan gasped, his eyes opened wide and he slowly lowered his fork back to his plate. "For real? Sh-she's dead?"

Mac nodded. "She's really dead. We found her body last night."

"But who would want to hurt her? She was a really

nice lady," Nathan replied. "She was really nice and patient to me. Why would somebody even want to… to kill her?"

"That's what we're trying to figure out," Mac replied. "Did you see anything suspicious around her place when you went there yesterday morning?"

Nathan slowly shook his head. "I didn't, but I wasn't really looking for nothing. I'm sorry." His big, round eyes welled up. "I should have been looking around."

"There's nothing to be sorry about," Mac assured him. "But if you think of anything please call me." Mac withdrew one of his cards and slid it across the table. "I'll also make arrangements with a deputy to get your tools to you sometime later this morning."

"I appreciate that. I can't do much without my toolbox," Nathan replied. "And I guess I need to look for a new job."

Mac stood. "Somebody will be in touch with you about your box. Thanks for your time, Nathan."

Callie slid out of the booth and together they left the café. "I think we'll head back to the office and see what Tim found in the evidence that was gathered last night around the body," Mac said. Deputy Tim Franklin was their evidence guy. Mac made a quick call to make sure Tim would be there to meet with them.

Knowing how busy the big labs were and the time waiting for results was often months, four years ago Mac had sent Tim to school to learn all about gathering and analyzing evidence. Much of their work could now be done with their little local lab while still using the big labs for deeper analyzation and toxicology results.

"So, what did you think about Nathan?" Mac pulled out of the bank parking lot.

"He seemed genuinely surprised when you told him about Linda. I'll say one thing—he would have to be the stupidest killer in the world to kidnap and kill a woman and then leave his toolbox behind for law enforcement to find it."

"I agree."

She watched his fingers whiten as he gripped the steering wheel tightly. "Mac, you need to relax a bit. Otherwise, you're going to have a heart attack before this is over and this little Christmas elf doesn't want to see that happen to you."

His fingers immediately loosened on the wheel and he flashed her a quick smile. "I've never had my own personal Christmas elf before. Shouldn't you be at the North Pole making toys or something?"

"There are elves that make toys and then there are elves who spread joy and happiness. I'm one of the latter," she replied with a grin of her own.

The levity between them only lasted a few minutes, halting the moment he parked in his space behind the sheriff's office. They went in the back door, took off their coats and then met Tim in the small room that held equipment to display photos and a metal table to view evidence more closely.

Callie knew the official evidence room was in the basement and held years' worth of items from crimes that had occurred long before Mac had become sheriff.

Tim was a serious man in his mid-thirties. He was tall and thin and wore thick horn-rimmed glasses that did little to hide the sharp intelligence in his brown eyes.

"What have you got for us, Tim?" Mac asked as he and Callie sat in the two chairs the room held.

Tim shut off the overhead lights and cast a photo onto the viewing screen. "As you can see there is a lot of dirt and several cigarette butts that were gathered in the area where Linda's body was found. I don't believe the cigarettes were left by the perpetrator. They're too old to have been left last night."

"I can't imagine our man setting the body on the bank steps, putting a Santa hat on her head and the birds at her feet and then hanging around to smoke a cigarette," Callie said.

"What else?" Mac asked of Tim.

Tim pulled up another photo of more dirt and something small that was shiny and bright. "What you're looking at here is a fourth of a carat cubic zirconia that probably fell out of a piece of jewelry…possibly a ring or a necklace. It could have fallen out of something last night or it could have been there for weeks. Unfortunately, there's no way of telling."

"Anything else we should know about?" Mac asked.

Tim turned the lights back on. "Nothing."

"Where is he?" A deep voice thundered down the hallway. "I know he's here somewhere. I saw his car parked out back."

Callie recognized the voice… Mayor Broadbent.

"Thanks, Tim," Mac said and left the room. Callie hurried after him. Mayor Broadbent stalked down the hallway and met Mac.

"Sheriff, I need to talk to you right now," Alex said. "I need to know what in the hell you're doing about these murders. Every time I turn around there's another body. I need answers that I can take to the people of this town. Young women are scared to go out of their houses."

"What do you want me to say, Alex? My men and I are out there trying to find answers. We're working long hours and doing the very best we can. I held the town meeting and told everyone in town what was going on," Mac countered.

"Well, your best isn't good enough. I'm holding another town meeting and I need something to say that will help ease the fear," Alex replied. "For God's sake, man. Give me something."

"Right now is probably not the time for you to try to ease the fears of the young women in this town. They need to be afraid, there's a killer out there who is targeting young women and right now we don't know who the killer is."

Mac reached up and rubbed the back of his neck in obvious frustration. "We're doing everything we can but if I were you I'd be damned careful about what you say to alleviate the healthy fear that each young woman in this town should be functioning with right now."

Alex's eyes flashed darkly. "Don't tell me how to do my job, Sheriff, especially when you don't seem to be doing yours so well these days."

Callie watched as every muscle in Mac's body tensed. "Is there anything else you have to say to me?"

"If these murders continue to happen, maybe it means you aren't really up for the job. I wouldn't be surprised if somebody didn't start a recall effort to get somebody else in position who can do the job properly."

"Thanks for the heads-up, and I really appreciate

your support. Now, you're wasting my time and I have murders to solve. So, if you'll excuse me. Callie, let's head back to the evidence room."

Callie turned on her heels and headed back down the hallway the way they had come. She was acutely aware of Mac hot on her heels. Definitely hot—she could feel his anger radiating out from him.

Tim was no longer in the room. Mac flipped on the light and once Callie was inside, he slammed the door behind her. This was the first time she'd seen Mac really angry.

His eyes blazed and his lips pressed together in a thin slash. He paced the small confines of the room a couple of times and then stopped and drew in a deep, audible breath.

"He's a total jerk, Mac," Callie blurted out. "And most of the people in this town can't stand him. He's nothing but a pompous ass and you shouldn't pay any attention to him or what he says."

Mac drew another deep breath and a small smile curved his lips. "Thank you…you took the words right out of my mouth. He is a pompous ass." The smile lasted only a moment and then he frowned. "But the longer these murders keep happening, the more the people will demand answers and right now we still don't have any. I'm failing the people of this town."

"We'll get him, Mac." She walked over to him and placed a hand on his forearm. "Nobody in this town has lost faith in you. The people love you and realize you're working as hard as you can to solve these murders."

She stood so close to him she could smell the scent of his shaving cream and his cologne. She could feel his body heat warming her from head to toe. The muscles beneath her hand slowly lost some of the tension.

The blaze in his eyes transformed into something different than anger and her breath caught in her throat. Was he going to kiss her again? Oh, she hoped so. She'd thought about their last kiss for what felt like forever and she desperately wanted another kiss from him.

He dipped his head toward her, his lips coming within mere inches of her own, and then he suddenly stood straight up and stepped back from her. "We need to get back to work. Let's hit the road."

Callie nearly moaned in disappointment. She'd wanted the kiss she believed he'd been about to give her. However, she wanted to catch this killer before he killed another woman...before he destroyed Mac.

FOR THE NEXT four days Mac and Callie stalked the streets, looking for answers. They had been unable to learn anything about Linda's movements on the day of her death, leading Mac to believe that she had been taken fairly early right from her apartment and before Nathan had knocked on her door. If that was the case, because there had been no indication of a break-in, then Linda had known her killer and had opened the door to him.

In all three cases, Mac believed the victims had known and had trusted their killer. So, who in town warranted that kind of trust? That kind of respect? If he could just figure out that common denominator...

It was now after ten and he was driving Callie home after another long, fruitless day. "Have you considered that our man still might be Roger?" Callie asked, breaking the silence that had lingered between them as he drove.

"Isn't it possible that maybe he killed Linda to throw us off? He killed Melinda and Candy because they rebuffed him. Since those two murders pointed a finger directly at him, maybe he killed Linda and hoped that would take the heat off him."

"At this point nobody is off the suspect list as far as I'm concerned," Mac said. His phone suddenly rang. He stared at it for a long moment. Phone calls at this time of night were never good, especially since he saw it was one of his deputies who was on duty calling.

Mac knew even as he answered the call. There was another one. This time she'd been left in front of the hardware store just off Main Street.

"Dammit," he exclaimed as he hung up the phone.

Callie remained silent as he turned his car around and headed to the scene. He couldn't speak at the moment and he was grateful that she didn't talk, as well.

The last four days had had him hoping that the killer was done. And now…another victim. Dear God, who was behind these murders? What had triggered this killing spree? What did the birds mean? The same questions whirled around and around in his head, questions that had begun with the first murder. And now the count was four dead women and the same questions hadn't been answered.

He felt sick in his very soul. The people in this town depended on him to provide law and order, to protect them so they could sleep easily at night knowing that he and his men were on the job.

He made the call to get everyone to the scene and

within minutes he and Callie arrived at the hardware store. Rhonda Hickson was against the door, a Santa hat on her head and four ordinary blackbirds at her feet.

"What's with these damned birds?" Deputy Adam Cook asked as Mac and Callie approached where he stood on the sidewalk.

"I wish we knew," Mac said with a frown. He looked at the body. It was like he was having a déjà vu moment. The face had changed, but the scene was the same.

Rhonda was an attractive blonde in her mid-twenties. She worked as a night nurse at the small Rock Ridge hospital and now she was dead, her white blouse stained with her own blood.

Blackbirds and chickens, pigeons and a quail… What did they all mean? How was Mac supposed to make sense of nonsense? What did the birds mean to the killer? And dammit, why couldn't Mac or anyone else figure it out?

As they all worked to process the scene, he thought maybe Callie was feeling the same way he was—defeated and lost in a miasma of dark emotions.

He looked over at where she stood out of the way of the medical examiner. She was quieter than he'd ever seen her. She wasn't asking questions, she wasn't making comments, but she just stood, looking as bleak as he felt.

Their eyes locked and hers instantly warmed as they held his gaze. For just a moment he didn't want to think about murders and birds. He didn't want to smell the scent of blood and death.

He wanted this murderer behind bars but at the moment what he really wanted to do was fall into the warmth of Callie, to lose himself in her evocative scent. He wanted to get out of his own head and be in hers, where maybe he wouldn't feel the weight of the murders so heavy on his shoulders for a little while. He wanted to drive her to his place, take her to bed and make love to her. He just wanted to escape into her for a few mindless moments.

With a frustrated sigh, he broke off eye contact with her and instead watched as Rhonda's body was bagged and taken away. By the time the crime scene was completely processed, it was almost two in the morning. Rhonda lived at home with her parents and Mac dreaded another notification of a beloved one's death. But it had to be done now. The last thing Mac wanted was for them to find out about their daughter's death from somebody else.

Despite the lateness of the hour, Callie insisted she go with him to make the notification. It was as difficult as the last three. He delivered devastation with empty platitudes. He gave them utter heartbreak with apologies he knew did nothing to ease their pain.

By asking questions he learned that Rhonda wasn't dating anyone in particular and only had a few good friends from the hospital with whom she socialized.

He and Callie were silent for several minutes as he drove her home. He was grateful for the quiet. He was in a place where he had no words left as his brain whirled with what he needed to do next in order to investigate this most recent murder.

If he didn't find a credible lead or a clue to point to the killer within the next two days, then he was going to admit defeat and call in the FBI. He had to…before another murder occurred.

He pulled up to the curb in front of Callie's house. Instead of getting out of the car, she turned to look at him. "Mac, maybe this will be the one that…"

He held up a hand. "Callie, stop. I don't want to hear any of your cheerleading right now."

He must have spoken more sharply than he intended, for the light in her eyes doused and instead tears filled her eyes. She looked as if he'd stabbed her to her core. "Then I'll just say good-night and I'll see you in the morning," she said.

Before she could slide out of the car, Mac took hold of her arm and held her in place. "I'm sorry, Callie. I didn't mean to hurt you." He released a deep sigh. "I'm just processing so many things in my head right now and we both know we're in trouble. This killer is flying under our radar and murdering women at an incredible pace. The only clue we have is a small cubic zirconia diamond that may or may not have fallen out of a ring or a bracelet, a diamond that may or may not have even come from the killer."

He stopped only because he was too exhausted to continue. He dropped his hand from her arm and rubbed the back of his neck where a bundle of muscles tensed painfully with stress.

"I think maybe both of us need to get some sleep," she said softly. She smiled at him, a bright, beautiful smile that momentarily lit up the darkness in his heart. "Good night, Mac. Tomorrow will be a better day." With that she slid out of the car, grabbed her coat and then headed to her door.

Mac pulled away from the curb and hoped she was right. Tomorrow *had* to be a better day. Maybe this really would be the one that would yield the clues he needed to make an arrest.

For the next three days Mac and Callie and the rest of the deputies worked almost around the clock to find a connection between the victims other than their blond hair. They interviewed all of Rhonda's coworkers and friends from the hospital in an attempt to find somebody who might have a grudge against her.

They learned that Ben Kincaid had been in the area of the hardware store an hour or two before the body had been left. In talking to them, he'd told them he'd bought a new bird feeder so the birds could eat throughout the snowfall. He also spoke again of an evil spirit that walked the streets of the town.

All the deputies and Mac exchanged ideas about the birds but had yet to come up with anything that made any sense.

Each morning Mac thought about calling in the Feds, but he was hoping for something to finally come together before he made the call. There were eleven more days until Christmas and he was hoping to give his town the gift of a killer behind bars.

He had done another town meeting, once again warning all women in the town to stay in pairs or a group whenever they were out and about. Thankfully, the mayor had stayed off his back since their last encounter. The last thing Mac needed was Broadbent to put any more pressure on him than Mac was already putting on himself.

As he took Callie home on the evening of the third

day after Rhonda's murder, he was worried about his "partner." Her eyes appeared less bright than usual and she seemed to have slowed in putting one foot in front of the other. It was obvious the ridiculously long hours they'd been working had finally gotten to her.

"I want you to take tomorrow off," he said to her as they arrived at her place.

She looked at him in surprise. "What are you talking about? We're in the middle of an investigation."

"You definitely need a day off," he replied.

"But…but what are you going to do without me?" Her blue eyes searched his features quizzically.

He smiled at her. "Callie, I'll do just fine without you for a day. Now go, get to bed and I don't want to see you anywhere near the office tomorrow."

"Are you sure?" She released a slow sigh that sounded like utter exhaustion.

"Positive. You need a day off, Callie," he said firmly.

It was only while he was driving home that he recognized not only did Callie need a day off, but he needed a day off from Callie.

Despite all the stress of the murders, he was aware that his emotions where Callie was concerned were beginning to get out of his control. He looked forward to seeing her each morning and he hated dropping her off at her house each night.

She was definitely getting under his skin like no other woman before her had. He didn't even remember feeling like this when he'd first started dating his ex-wife.

Callie was the kind of intelligent woman he'd always imagined himself with for the long haul. There was no question he thought she could be his soft place to fall. And he also knew she cared about him.

He felt that caring each time she touched him and he yearned for her touch far more than he should. In fact, he was falling in love with the beautiful blonde whose smiles warmed his heart and who continued to sneak in bits of Christmas into the office. His little Christmas elf was working some magic.

He didn't want to be in love with Callie. He didn't want to be in love with anyone. After his first marriage he told himself he would never trust a woman again. More than anything right now he wanted to catch a killer and more than anything right now he had to figure out how to not fall any deeper in love with Callie.

Chapter Nine

It was a little after ten o'clock when Callie opened her eyes to the midmorning sun filtering in through her bedroom curtains. She started to jump out of bed, but then remembered and instead snuggled deeper beneath the blankets and released a small sigh.

As much as she hated to admit it, she'd needed the day off.

The long hours had drained her and she'd definitely needed the extra sleep and time to recharge. The past two days she'd been so tired she'd felt as if she were walking through sludge. Not only was her body completely exhausted, but her mind was, as well.

She felt as if she'd been thinking about murder forever. She knew Mac intended to call in the FBI in the morning if nothing broke today. He'd given them all the last couple of days to come up with something… anything…that would move the investigation forward. And they'd all failed him.

The birds left at each murder scene haunted her dreams. If they could only figure out what they meant. They were obviously part of the killer's ritual and meant something important to him.

At least now the women in town had taken Mac's warning to heart. As soon as the darkness of night fell, the streets emptied of people. During the day if women were out and about, they were always with a friend or in a group. They all were taking their safety very seriously and hopefully making it impossible for the killer to take another victim.

That was the only reason Mac had put off calling in the FBI. However, Callie knew tomorrow morning he was probably going to make that call. Hopefully the FBI with their more sophisticated tools would be able to crack the case.

No more thoughts about murder today, she chided herself. It was her day off and she intended to spend it doing things that made her happy.

With that thought in mind, she finally pulled herself out of bed and headed for a shower. Forty-five minutes later she sat at her kitchen table with a cup of coffee and a piece of toast. She finished off the toast and then as she drank the rest of her coffee, she made a list of the people she wanted to buy Christmas presents for.

Normally by this time of the month she'd already be finished with her shopping and the presents would be wrapped and ready to go. But normally she wasn't involved in a murder investigation.

She always bought gifts for the other dispatchers and she also had a few friends she usually bought for. But she hadn't had much to do with her friends lately. She also wanted to find something really special to give to Mac.

Mac. Her heart expanded with thoughts of him. There was no question she was falling deeper and deeper in love with him even though she wasn't sure how he felt about her. There were times she thought she saw love for her shining from his beautiful gray eyes, and then there were other times when she felt as if he intentionally shut her out.

She finished up her list, determined that she wasn't going to think too deeply about anything today, and then got up. She rinsed her cup, tucked her list into her purse and then put on her coat.

By the time she got outside, the early-morning sun had given way to a steel-colored sky that portended snow. She hadn't watched any weather forecasts lately, but she definitely smelled snow in the air.

She smiled. There was nothing she loved more than a white Christmas and if it snowed now and the temperatures remained below freezing then she'd get her wish.

Her smile immediately fell away. Her first hope was that by Christmas the killer would be behind bars and the fear that had possessed the small town would finally be gone.

She walked briskly down the sidewalk, grateful that her home was walking distance from the downtown area. The first place she intended to go was Janie's Stuff and Things, a quaint little shop that carried a little bit of everything beautiful, fun and unique and was owned by one of her good friends.

She hoped nobody got offended seeing her out and about today doing shopping in the middle of the murder investigation. Surely most of the people would realize that everyone deserved a day off. Besides, Janie was one of the friends Callie had loved to hang out with before her life changed with the murders.

She entered the shop and the scents of peppermint and evergreen and sugar cookies greeted her. It was the heady scents of Christmas and that instantly filled her with the joy of the season and with the desire to shop for special presents for special people.

"Hey, Callie," Janie greeted her from behind the cash register counter. "Or should I say Deputy Stevens?" Janie added teasingly.

"Oh, stop," Callie replied with a laugh. Janie walked around the counter and the two women hugged.

"I know you've been working practically day and night. What, did Sheriff McKnight finally give you some time off knowing that he was working you to death?"

"He's not working me to death. These murders are. I have today off, but tomorrow I'll be back at work as usual."

"So, how is it working with him?" Janie asked curiously.

Callie instantly felt a blush warm her cheeks and before she could say anything Janie grinned and winked. "Ah, so it's like that," she said. "Tell me the truth—have you slept with him yet?"

"No," Callie replied firmly, the heat in her cheeks growing hotter. "And why would you even ask me something like that?"

"Because I know you've always had a mad crush on him and you're two single consenting adults, so why not?"

"We've had a few more-pressing things on our minds lately," Callie replied. "But I don't even want to think about that right now. I'm here to shop."

"Good, you know I'm always willing to take your money," Janie replied with a laugh. "I'll just let you get to it. Let me know if I can help you with anything."

"Thanks, Janie. I'm just going to wander for a little while and look at all the treasures." And there were lots of treasures.

She found pretty little trinket boxes with pink jeweled, old-fashioned telephones on top and placed one for each of the dispatchers into her little shopping basket.

As she walked around the store, she felt herself relaxing like she hadn't in the past few weeks. Seeing all the unique and fun things the store offered, along with the cheerful Christmas music playing overhead, fed her soul.

She found most of the presents she needed but unfortunately found nothing right to buy for Mac. What did you buy for a man who seemed to want for nothing, a man who had no hobbies and was a workaholic?

From Janie's she stopped into the coffee shop and had a mug of hot chocolate with whipped cream. She sat at a window seat and people-watched as she enjoyed the hot drink.

She now couldn't imagine why she'd ever wanted to move away from this small town. Her parents had teased her and said she'd eventually tire of the big city and want to come home. She wished she had come home sooner. She wished it hadn't been their deaths that had brought her back.

And she desperately missed her younger sister. Lily had been three years younger than Callie. She'd been the typical pesky little sister, but despite her peskiness, the two had been very close. And now she was gone forever, thanks to a drunk driver. Callie shoved these sad thoughts away.

It was after four when she finally returned to her house. It had been a successful shopping day even though she hadn't found a gift for Mac.

As she made herself dinner, big fluffy snowflakes began to fall outside the windows. She ate and watched them fall, glad that she was inside the warm confines of her home for the night.

After eating a bowl of soup and a salad for dinner, she went upstairs and changed out of her jeans and blouse and into a soft fleece jogging suit. She went back downstairs and into the living room. She turned on some Christmas music and then sat on the floor next to the sparkling tree to wrap the presents she had bought.

Several times throughout the day she'd thought about calling Mac to see how things were going, but she'd decided not to. Surely he would have called her if anything with the case had broken loose and she didn't want to bother him by contacting him.

Once the presents were all wrapped, she built a fire in the fireplace, made herself a cup of hot cocoa and then curled up beneath a soft blanket on the sofa.

Holiday music continued to play as she stared into the flames that danced in the fireplace. Once again thoughts of her parents and the sister she had lost intruded into her head.

She had so many happy Christmas memories with them and as she sipped her hot drink, she allowed those remembrances to play freely through her mind.

Tears filled her eyes and she swiped at them angrily.

She had sworn to herself that she wouldn't grieve for them, but rather she would celebrate them.

As memories of her family slowly ebbed away, thoughts of murder filled her head. She hoped the killer was behind bars by Christmas. She wanted to celebrate the holiday with no thoughts of murder in her brain. And she wanted Mac to be free of the stress and weight this killer had placed on his shoulders.

She finished her drink and then leaned back and closed her eyes and let the music wash over her. She had definitely needed today to refresh and recharge. She was now eager to get back to work tomorrow. And she was definitely eager to see Mac.

She was just about to get up and head to bed when one particular Christmas song played. Her eyes snapped open and her heart began to beat a rhythm of excitement. Was it possible?

Could it be an answer to some of their questions about the murderer? She threw off her blanket and hurried up the stairs to where her computer was on a desk in her bedroom.

For the next half an hour she did some research and jotted down her findings in her notebook. When she was sure of what she had, she called Mac.

He answered on the first ring and she didn't even give him a chance to greet her. "Mac, can you come over to my place right now?"

"Callie, it's almost ten o'clock and there's two inches of snow on the ground. What's going on?"

"I don't want to go into it over the phone. Please come here… It's important. I swear you won't be sorry."

"This better be good," he replied and then with a muttered goodbye, he hung up.

Immediately doubts began to fill Callie's mind. Was it good? Had she found a clue to the case or was she only deluding herself? Could she be wrong? She grabbed her notebook and headed back downstairs. She desperately hoped she was right because if she was, it would be the first thing that made sense in this whole horrendous case.

AFTER HEARING THE forecast for six to eight inches of snow, Mac had been in contact with all his deputies. Tonight they were all on traffic duty. There were always the fools who thought they could drive through the snow, fools who found themselves stranded on the side of the road or crashed into another vehicle. If they got eight inches of snow the whole city would shut down and the only vehicles moving would be the snowplows.

The last thing he needed was to be heading to Callie's house, but there had been a simmering excitement in her voice that definitely had him curious.

He was so used to having her around almost every minute of every day and he hated to admit that he'd missed her presence next to him today. In fact, it bothered him that he'd missed her as much as he had.

It made him want to gain more distance from her. And yet here he was in the middle of a stalled murder investigation on a snowy night rushing to her home.

When he pulled up in front of her house, the lights from the tree sparkled outward and reflected beautifully on the new fallen snow. Even though he was curious as to why she had called him here, he was reluctant to go inside because he knew he might like being in her space.

He pulled up in her driveway and parked and wondered again why she'd called him here. "Only way to find out is to go inside," he muttered to himself.

He got out of the car and approached the front door. The snow was coming down even faster now. Before he could knock on the door, she opened it. "Mac, come on in." She opened the door wide enough for him to step inside.

She looked beautiful and comfortable in a soft pink hoodie and matching jogging pants. She led him from the foyer into a large living room. A fire snapped and popped in the fireplace and everywhere he looked there were Christmas decorations. It was exactly the way he'd imagined it to be…exuding warmth and invitation. He shrugged out of his winter coat and laid it on the top of the beige overstuffed sofa.

"So, why am I here?" he asked.

"Please, have a seat." Her eyes sparkled with what appeared to be excitement as she gestured him to the sofa. She joined him there, sitting so close to him he could feel her body heat.

"Are you going to tell me why I'm here?" he asked.

"Absolutely. I think I've figured something out about the murders. Mac, it's not about the birds."

"What do you mean?"

"We've been trying to figure out what the birds meant and we've believed the murders were somehow about the birds. Now I don't believe the birds mean anything other than a manifestation of trauma."

"I don't understand. What's changed your mind?" Mac looked at her quizzically.

"'The Twelve Days of Christmas'… Do you know the song?" she asked, that shine of excitement still in her eyes.

He frowned. "Not really… Isn't it something about five golden rings?"

"Before you get to the golden rings there are colly birds and French hens, turtle doves and a partridge in a pear tree," she replied.

She reached out and took both of his hands in hers. "Four colly birds… They are blackbirds, Mac. I looked it up. Three French hens…three chickens. Then there's two turtle doves, which was two pigeons, and finally a partridge, which is like a big quail. The murders are not about the birds, Mac. They're about Christmas. Somehow, I believe thoughts of Christmas triggered our killer. Somebody out there hates Christmas as much as you do and that's how we'll find him. He's following the song."

Mac tried to digest what she'd just said. Was it possible she was right? Was it possible the birds weren't what was driving the murders, but rather it might be something traumatic that had happened at Christmastime that had triggered the killer?

An edge of excitement danced through him and he squeezed her hands. "Maybe this is the break we've been waiting for."

"It's definitely a new path to investigate," she replied. "We're really going to find him now, Mac." To his surprise she leaned forward and wrapped her arms around his neck. "I swear we're going to get the bastard," she whispered into his ear.

He needed to distance himself from her. He couldn't think when she was so close to him and yet even as he processed that thought his arms enveloped her.

She'd brought him a new lead to follow, but it was getting late on a snowy night and there was really nothing that could be done tonight about it.

He loosened his arms from around her as she reared back from him. He thought she intended to move completely out of his arms, but she stopped moving backward and suddenly her lips were right in front of his.

"Mac." She said his name softly and with what sounded like a deep yearning.

"Yeah?" he replied, just as softly.

"Are you going to kiss me?" Her eyes were sparkling blue pools that he could drown in.

"I might." A white-hot desire seared through him, a desire he'd been fighting against since last time he had kissed her.

"When will you know if you're going to?" Her tongue made a quick dash across her upper lip as if in anticipation.

That single evocative action broke him. "I know right now," he murmured just before his mouth took hers.

It wasn't a soft, tender kiss; rather it was something hot and wild as their tongues immediately swirled together. She tasted faintly of chocolate and a fiery desire.

Her arms tightened around his neck as she leaned into him. Her full breasts pressed against his chest and, despite the danger alarms that rang in the back of his head, his arms encircled her and pulled her even closer against him.

The kiss seemed to last forever and yet didn't begin to satisfy the ravenous hunger in his soul for her. He ended the kiss only to slide his lips down her slender neck. He felt half-dizzy with his desire for this woman…for Callie…and he consciously refused to listen to any more alarms that went off in his head.

"Mac," she whispered softly and once again he thought he heard a deep yearning for him in her voice. She leaned back just enough for her fingers to go to the top button of his shirt.

He sucked in a deep breath as her gaze held his. Blue fire…and he felt himself falling mindlessly into her flames. She unbuttoned his first button and then leaned forward to kiss the bare skin she'd uncovered. Another button…another kiss. More buttons unfastened until she could push his shirt off his shoulders.

She unfastened his gun belt and took it off and laid it on the sofa next to them. She then leaned back from him and pulled her hoodie over her head, exposing a pretty pink bra and full breasts he definitely wanted to touch. She stood and reached out a hand to him.

Someplace in the back of his mind he knew if he took her hand wonderful things would happen…things he would probably regret. But right now, regrets were the last thing on his mind.

He was lost in Callie, lost in her scent, her warmth and the sweet essence of her very bright soul. He placed his hand in hers. She pulled him off the sofa and led him to the throw rug in front of the fire.

He pulled her into his arms, loving the feel of her

bare skin against his. Their lips once again met in a searing kiss that rivaled the heat cast out from the fireplace.

When the kiss ended, she sank down to the rug and pulled him down along beside her. "Mac, I want you to make love to me," she said, her voice low and sexy.

All thoughts of anything else fled his mind. His blood surged through his veins and his want…his need…for her was the only thing in his head. Still, he tried to maintain some semblance of himself.

"Callie." He reached up and gently pushed one of her curls away from her face. "I've told you I don't want a relationship."

"I just need to know, do you want me?" Her gaze held his intently. "Do you want to make love with me right now in this moment, Mac?"

"There's nothing else I want to do more right now," he replied honestly.

She smiled at him, that beautiful smile that toasted his insides even more than they already were. "Then what are you waiting for?"

He gathered her into his arms once again and as they kissed, his hands stroked up and down her back and then finally stopped at her bra fastener. Her heartbeat mirrored his own, fast and frantic. In his haste to unhook her bra, his fingers became clumsy.

After a moment or two of fumbling, she reached behind her and unhooked it. She shrugged it off her shoulders and suddenly he was holding her warm, full breasts in his hands. Her nipples were pebbled into hard peaks and as he ran his thumbs across them, she moaned.

His lips followed his hands. He licked and sucked

as she writhed beneath him, torching his desire even higher. Her fingers clutched at his shoulders as she continued to moan with her pleasure.

She suddenly rolled away from him. In one graceful movement she took off her pants, leaving her in a wispy pair of black panties.

"Now you," she said half-breathlessly.

He didn't hesitate. He first took off his shoes and socks and then shucked his khaki slacks, leaving him clad only in his black boxers.

The flickering light from the fire loved her features, painting them in a soft golden glow. He gathered her into his arms once again and it wasn't long before her panties and his boxers went the way of their other clothing.

He held her against him, her bare skin warm and inviting against his own. She shifted to his side and once again his tongue teased the tip of her breasts at the same time his hand caressed down her hip.

He was fully aroused and ached with his need, but before he let himself go, he wanted to give her as much pleasure as possible. As his hand moved toward her very center, she rolled over on her back and parted her legs to welcome the intimate touch.

As he dipped his head to taste her lips once again, his fingers danced over her moist and heated skin. She moaned once again and rose up to meet his touch. He quickened his pace as she reached down and grabbed his hard length. He pushed her hand away, afraid that he would lose it too soon.

And then she was there. He felt the shudders that raced through her as she cried out his name over and over again. She fell back against the rug, panting as her eyes gleamed with gratification. That gratification lasted only a moment and then she reached down to encircle his shaft once again. "Take me, Mac. I want to feel you inside me."

Her words nearly broke him. He moved on top of her and hovered there, momentarily staring deeply into her eyes. The blue depths bewitched him, shining not just with sexual eagerness, but something deeper and even more captivating.

Slowly he entered her, groaning with the exquisite pleasure that instantly overtook him. Her warmth surrounded him tightly and immediately he began to stroke in and out of her. She gripped hold of his buttocks, urging him to move faster and faster.

He complied and felt himself quickly reaching his climax. Thankfully before he did, she moaned, her muscles all tightened and then with a shuddery sigh she melted.

That was all it took for him to reach his limit. His climax exploded from him, quaking through him with a force that left him weak and boneless.

When it was finished, he collapsed alongside of her, waiting for his panting breaths to return to normal. Beside him, Callie was breathing unusually fast and seemed to be waiting for her normal to return, as well.

She finally rolled over to face him and placed her hand on his chest. "You are so beautiful, Mac," she said in a half whisper.

He smiled at her. "Thanks, but the real beauty in this room is you." He tried not to focus on the regrets that were already forming in the back of his head. He ran a hand through her soft blond curls and released a deep sigh. "I probably need to get up and get out of here."

"Why don't we get up from here and go upstairs to my bed." She cuddled closer against him. "It's probably still snowing outside, Mac. There's nothing more you can do tonight. Spend the rest of the night here with me."

Oh, it was so tempting. She was so damned tempting. Gracefully she got to her feet and once again she held out her hand to him. And once again he knew that if he took her hand he'd be breaking all the promises he'd initially made to himself where she was concerned.

Still, he took her hand and stood. In for a penny...in for a pound, he thought. Besides she was right; there was nothing he could do about the investigation tonight. She put on her panties and he pulled on his boxers and grabbed his gun from the sofa and then together they went upstairs.

Her bed was covered in a peach-colored spread with matching accent pillows. Floral pictures hung on the wall. The top of the dresser held bottles of perfumes and an earring stand.

The room looked feminine, but also as equally warm and welcoming as the living room had been. "There's a bathroom right here," she said and pointed to a doorway in the bedroom. "And there's another one right down the hallway."

"I'll head to that one," he said.

Once in the bathroom he washed himself off and then pulled his boxers back on and stared at his reflection in the mirror over the sink. "What are you doing, man?" he asked his reflection. But the man in the mirror had no answer.

There was a window over the tub and he leaned over to get a peek outside. There appeared to be about four inches of snow on the ground and it was still coming down. It was not a night for man or beast to be out and about.

Besides, the thought of sleeping next to Callie, instead of him sleeping in his bed all alone, warmed his heart in a way it hadn't been warmed in a very long time. And that scared him more than a little bit.

Maybe it was time he remind her that in the long run none of this meant anything to him, that this night was an outlier and something that would never happen again.

Still, it was difficult to hold on to that thought when he walked into the bedroom and saw her sitting in the bed and clad in a pink, sexy little top.

She smiled and patted the other side of the bed. "In, Sheriff McKnight. I know how much you need to get some good sleep."

He got into the bed…the soft bed that seemed to envelop him. He released a deep sigh as his aching bones and muscles relaxed into the mattress. It was only when he was completely relaxed that she leaned over and gave him a tender kiss on his cheek.

"Sweet dreams, Mac." She then turned and shut off the light on her nightstand, plunging the room into darkness.

"Good night, Callie," he replied. He decided he needed to have a talk with her in the morning and explain to her that this had all been a mistake. Even with this weighing heavy on his mind, and the fact that the investigation had suddenly taken a new twist, he was asleep within minutes.

Chapter Ten

Callie awakened spooned against Mac's body. His arm was slung around her as if to keep her in place and snuggled tight against his big, warm body. She knew he was still soundly asleep because he snored lightly.

She didn't want to awaken him and in any case she wasn't inclined to move. She wanted to revel in his body warmth and in the familiar smell of him. Their love-making the night before had been everything she'd dreamed about.

He'd been a tender, yet commanding lover. He'd made sure she found her release before he allowed himself his own, which made him a generous lover.

Surely last night meant something to him. He had to have feelings for her, feelings that were bigger than mere lust. She had no doubts about her feelings toward him. She was in love with him. She wanted to wake up every morning in his arms. She didn't want to be his deputy; she wanted to be his life partner.

His snoring halted and his body tensed, letting her know he was awake. She found herself tensing up, wondering how he was going to handle the morning after.

He pulled his arm from around her and rolled away. "Good morning," he said as he sat up.

She turned over to gaze at him. "Back at you. Did you sleep well?" He looked so hot in her bed with his bare chest golden in the early-morning light that drifted through her window.

"I can't remember when I slept so well," he replied. He threw off the blankets and stood. "But duty calls and I need to get to the office." He walked over to the window and peered out.

"How does it look out there," she asked, although she was more interested in the view inside. He was clad only in his boxers, and she couldn't help but admire his physique. His shoulders were so broad and his stomach and hips were slim. His legs were long and muscled. He took her breath away all over again.

"A bit nasty," he replied. "Looks like we got about four and a half or five inches of snow." He turned back to face her. "Thank God you live on Main Street, which I'm sure by now has been cleared off."

She sat up. "Let me fix you some breakfast before you head in to the office."

"I appreciate the offer, but I need to get out of here. Don't get up on my account. I'll just head downstairs and get out of your hair. I'll relock your door when I leave."

Before she could say anything else, he walked out of the room. Minutes later she heard her front door open and then close. She flopped back on the bed and released a deep sigh.

Now she knew how he intended to deal with the morning after. He didn't intend to deal with it at all.

He'd basically pretended that nothing had happened between them the night before.

She glanced at the clock on her nightstand. It was a few minutes after seven. At least he got a good night's sleep, she thought as she sat back up and got out of bed.

She padded into the bathroom and got into the shower. As the water beat down on her, she continued to think about Mac. Even knowing how he'd acted this morning she wouldn't take back a single minute of their time together.

If nothing else ever happened between them she would have the memory of making love with Mac forever etched in her heart, in her very soul.

With the loss of her family, maybe she was trying too hard to fill the loneliness in her life. Maybe she had to realize that where Mac was concerned, she was chasing a dream that would never come true.

She turned off the shower water, got out and dried off and then dressed in her uniform. As she strapped her gun around her waist, she shoved Mac out of her mind. Instead, she turned her thoughts to the murders they had to solve.

If she was right, and she truly believed she was, the next murder would have some form of five golden rings left at the scene. However, with this new information she was hoping they could catch the killer before he acted again.

With this thought in mind, she ran down the stairs, pulled on snow boots and her coat and then left her house to walk to work. It was Sunday morning and with a lack of people on the streets and the new fallen snow, there was an unusual hush. Her boots crunched the snow beneath her feet, providing the only sound in the air.

As she drew closer to the back door of the sheriff's office, her thoughts turned to Mac once again. At some point in the day would he talk to her about what had happened between them last night?

If he didn't, she had to maintain her professionalism. Their personal life was one thing, but they had a killer to catch and with the new information they had new paths to investigate. That's where her focus needed to be.

When she walked into the break room nobody else was there. She hung up her coat and then went down the hallway to Mac's office. She knew he was there because his car was parked out back.

She knocked and heard him say for her to come in. She opened the door. He was seated at his desk, paperwork before him and a deep frown across his forehead.

"Good morning again," she said and sank down in the chair facing his desk.

"Yeah, good morning," he replied.

"What has that deep frown on your face?"

"If these killings are happening because something traumatic happened to our killer at Christmastime, then I'm trying to figure out how we investigate that."

"Maybe the first thing we need to do is revisit the people on our suspect list and see if they've done anything to decorate for Christmas. If the perp hates the holiday, then surely he wouldn't do anything to celebrate it."

"Despite all of our investigating we only have the same suspects that we had with the first murder." His frown grew deeper. "We've got Roger, who had reason to get revenge against two of the victims. Then there's Ben, who was seen in the area right before two of the bodies showed up."

"And Nathan, who was on Main Street when the first body showed up and then was working for Linda Bailey, who was another victim," she added.

"Aside from those three, no other suspects have come to the surface," Mac replied.

"So, we focus our energy on those three. We recheck their alibis for the times of the murders. We go hard at them and either find our man if he's one of the three, or we completely get them off our suspect list."

He nodded. "I studied the lyrics of 'The Twelve Days of Christmas.' We now know the next thing is five golden rings. When the stores open today, we need to see if we can find out who might carry cheap golden rings."

"Mac, I truly believe we're on the right track now," she said.

For the first time since she'd walked through his office door he smiled. "I do, too. All we have to do now is wait for the stores to open. Between it being Sunday and all the snow, they won't open for another couple of hours. In the meantime, we can probably catch all our suspects at home this morning."

Callie stood and returned his smile. "Then come on, partner. Let's get going."

He stood and grabbed his coat from the back of his chair. Together they walked down the hallway. He paused just outside the break room while she grabbed her coat and then she followed him out the door and to his car.

"We now have four time lines of the murders and when the victims were posed on the street, so we need to check alibis for all four of the times," Mac said the minute they were in the car.

It was obvious he had no intention of addressing what had happened between them the night before. He apparently intended to pretend it had never happened.

He got on his radio and contacted Glen Malick, who was in charge of the road crews. He arranged for Glen to clear the roads to Nathan's and Ben's places. Like Callie, Roger lived on Main Street and so the road to his place was already plowed and salted. They headed there first.

"As I recall Roger had a Christmas tree up when we talked to him the last time," Callie said. "What we need to find out is what he really thinks of Christmas."

He flashed her a quick glance. "I'll leave it up to you to delve into lover boy's mind. I'll stick to grilling him about the alibis."

"Gee, thanks," she replied drily. "I have a feeling being in Roger's head for too long would make me want to throw up."

Mac laughed, the warm sound breaking some of the tension she'd felt wafting from him since they'd awakened together that morning.

Thankfully, the road crews had done their job, making it relatively easy to get to Roger's house. "You two again?" Roger said the moment he answered Mac's knock. "What now?" He glared at Mac with unabashed anger.

"Can we come in or are you going to have us conduct our business on your front porch?" Mac asked.

Roger stepped back from the door, allowing them to enter. "Wow, what a beautiful tree," Callie exclaimed as she walked over to the tree that sparkled with multicolored lights and held glittery miniature ornaments in the shapes of dogs and cats clad in Santa suits.

"Thanks," Roger said, his tone warming up a bit.

Callie turned back around and smiled at him. "You must love Christmas to have such a wonderful tree."

"Christmas is okay. Honestly, though, I put up the tree and all the trimmings because it's all kind of a chick magnet." He winked at her. "If I get a woman in here, the Christmas stuff shows I have a sensitive side."

Roger's "sensitive" side wasn't showing minutes later as Mac grilled him about his alibis for the days and nights of the murders. Rather he became angry and hostile.

"How in the hell am I supposed to remember exactly where I was on all those dates?" Roger asked emphatically. "I can tell you where I wasn't. I wasn't anywhere near the victims. I didn't kill those women. I've never killed anyone in my entire life."

Callie believed him. There was a passion in his eyes that spoke of truth telling. Besides, surely the guilty party would have their alibis ready for the asking.

Roger might be smarmy and without much of a moral compass when it came to women, but she didn't believe he was their killer.

Mac finished up the questioning. "You guys are killing my love life," Roger said as he walked with them to the door. "Every woman in town is steering clear of me now because you keep questioning me about these murders."

"The good news is I think we're done with you for now," Mac replied. He apparently felt as she did, that Roger wasn't their man.

He confirmed that once they were back in the car. "Initially I thought he was our best suspect, but now I'm just not feeling it," he said.

"I agree. Roger might be many things, but I don't believe he's a killer."

"So, we'll pop into Ben's next. Hopefully by now the road crews have cleared the roads to his place."

They rode in silence. She could smell his cologne in the small confines. It was a scent that had made her feel safe and protected throughout last night. She wished he'd say something about what they had shared the night before, but if he didn't want to talk about it, then she didn't want to make him uncomfortable by bringing it up.

Her relationship, or lack thereof, with Mac flew from her mind as they pulled up outside Ben's house. Ben was clad in all-black winter gear and was up in one of the trees. As Mac and Callie got out of the car, Ben pointed a rifle at them.

WHAT THE HELL? Mac froze and desperately hoped Callie had done the same. His hand itched to get his own gun out of the holster, but he was afraid the movement might make Ben shoot him.

The air snapped with a dangerous energy. "Ben, what's going on this morning?" Mac yelled.

"Evil walks the earth," Ben shouted back. The barrel of his rifle pointed first at Mac and then at Callie. "I have to be on guard to keep the evil away from me and my home."

"Ben, you know me. I'm not evil…and neither is Deputy Stevens," Mac replied. "Why don't you come down from there so we can have a little chat."

The gunshot exploded, sending birds flying from all the other trees in the area. The bullet whizzed by Mac's ear. Mac immediately crouched down and motioned for Callie to do the same. "I don't want to have a chat," Ben yelled.

Mac's heart beat a thousand times a minute as his blood rushed to his head. He'd never seen Ben so fired up before. At the moment he was both unpredictable and dangerous.

Right now, Mac had reason to arrest the man. He'd shot at a sheriff and that was against the law. But first he had to somehow get Ben out of the tree and disarmed.

He also wanted to protect Callie and the only way to do that was to make himself the bigger target. Tentatively he rose up once again, holding his breath to see if Ben would fire on him again.

"Ben, tell me what I can do to help you," Mac stated.

"Nothing can help me. The bad spirits have me in their sights."

For the first time Mac wondered if Ben was on some kind of medication…some medicine that he'd perhaps stopped taking. It appeared he was having some kind of a psychotic break. Had he killed the women while in the clutches of some form of madness?

"I can help you fight the bad spirits, Ben. If you come down and talk to me, we can fight the spirits together."

Ben was quiet for several long moments. "What do you know about fighting bad spirits? You're normal— you probably don't see the shadow people that are all around me, just waiting to suck the life out of me."

"You're right, Ben. I can't see the shadow people, but that doesn't mean I can't help you. Come down so we can talk and I can tell you in more detail how I can help you."

Mac held his breath, waiting to see what the man would do. Ben once again pointed his rifle in the direction of Callie. "What about her?" he yelled down.

"I can promise you that she is a good spirit. She's full of light and love and hope and all things beautiful. She can help make the bad spirits go away. Trust me, Ben. She can help, too."

The three of them remained frozen in place for several tense moments and then, finally Ben began to make his way down the tree.

"Can I have the rifle?" Mac asked once Ben was on the ground.

Ben caressed the rifle's stock and his green eyes gazed intently into Mac's. "This is a special rifle that kills bad spirits."

"If you give it to me, I promise I'll take good care of it," Mac replied. He was aware of Callie standing up on the opposite side of the car.

Ben continued to hold Mac's gaze and Mac held his breath. Finally, Ben handed the rifle to him. "Callie, can you come here so Ben knows you're his friend, too?" Mac's voice was even and calm.

Callie joined them, and smiled at Ben. "Hi, Ben.

Remember we met before? Deputy Stevens is kind of a mouthful, so you can call me Callie."

Mac was grateful that she appeared soft and warm and friendly. It was just what was warranted for the situation.

He felt the tension waft from Ben as the man stared into Callie's smiling eyes. "Do you mind if Callie holds your special rifle?" Mac asked.

Ben tensed once again and adrenaline shot through Mac. He had no idea if Ben would cooperate or not. At this point he didn't even know if Ben had another gun on him. Ben gave a curt nod and Mac handed the rifle to Callie.

"Ben, I'm afraid I'm going to have to arrest you now," Mac said. He reached for Ben's arm, but Ben twirled away from him and took off running.

"Dammit," Mac muttered as he raced after Ben. He cursed himself for speaking out loud what he'd intended to do. He'd figured if he could get Ben held down at the jail for the next twenty-four hours, they could either figure out if he was the killer or if he simply needed medical attention.

Ben maneuvered around the trees like a slithering snake, dodging easily the feeders and wind chimes and other strange items that hung from the trees while Mac cursed and bumped into the hanging things as he worked to keep Ben in his sight.

He feared what might happen if Ben managed to slip away from him. Obviously, Ben was suffering a great amount of paranoia. Mac worried about what that paranoia might make Ben do. Had it made him kill four innocent women?

Despite his snow boots, Mac slid down to one knee and then hurried back up again. His breaths came in deep pants, the cold air aching in his lungs.

Suddenly a figure jumped out at Ben and took his legs out from under him. Callie. She'd apparently come from another direction and got just in front of Ben to take him down.

Before Ben could get to his feet, Mac reached him and grabbed him at the same time he pulled out his handcuffs. "Thanks, partner," he said to Callie, who had gotten to her feet and now held her gun pointed at Ben.

"No problem," she replied and smiled that beautiful smile that always lit up something inside him.

Ben had begun to sob as Mac got him into the cuffs. "Ben, it's going to be okay," Mac said as gently as he could. "We're going to take good care of you."

Callie holstered her gun and then placed a hand on Ben's shaking shoulder. "Ben, bad spirits can't get into our jail. In fact, they can't even enter the sheriff's office at all."

He looked at her with tear-filled eyes. "Are you lying to me? Is…is that really true?"

"It's true," she replied. "You'll be safe in jail until we can get your home safe for you to come back again."

Ben held her gaze and then slowly nodded. "Okay."

Mac did a quick pat down of Ben and discovered a large knife in one of Ben's pockets. "That's special," Ben explained. "It kills bad spirits that come around me."

Mac placed the knife in an evidence bag. Once again,

his heart beat a little quicker. Was it possible the knife was the murder weapon? It appeared clean, but if it had been used to stab the four women to death, then hopefully the lab would find any trace of blood that sealed the deal.

Ben remained docile as they got him into the back of the patrol car and then checked into jail. Throughout the ride Callie continued to talk to Ben in calm, soothing tones. Mac admired the fact that she'd read the situation correctly and was acting accordingly. Once Ben was in jail, they returned to the car.

"Damn, I forgot to check to see if Ben's front door was locked," Mac said. "He specifically asked us if we'd make sure it was locked. We need to go back and make sure the door isn't unlocked."

"What are you going to charge him with?" Callie asked.

"If he isn't our killer, then I probably won't charge him with anything," Mac replied. "I can hold him for up to twenty-four hours before I either have to charge him or cut him loose." He glanced over to her and then back on the road. "That gives us twenty-four hours to catch this killer."

"Great, just what we need…more pressure," she replied drily.

"Keep in mind, we don't have a search warrant. However, I do intend to go inside and see if I can find some medication or the name of a doctor who might be able to see Ben while we have him in custody."

"He definitely needs some help," she agreed. "Nobody should be that afraid."

"He's always been strange, but this is something different than strange. I think he's had some sort of a psychotic snap."

"Do you think we found the murder weapon?" she asked.

"If that knife stabbed those women, then the case is solved. I don't think it's out of the question that Ben might have seen the women as bad spirits and attacked them. But we don't stop investigating until we know for sure that Ben is our man."

When they got back to Ben's, sure enough his front door was unlocked. Callie remained at the front door while Mac went inside to check for any medication he might find.

The first thing he noted was there was no sign of Christmas anywhere in the place. He made his way through the living room and into the bathroom. A peek in the medicine cabinet yielded several bottles of medicine. Mac pocketed the bottles and then walked into the bedroom.

Unlike the living room with its odd statues and wall hangings, this room was pretty sterile, just holding a twin bed, a dresser and a nightstand. There was nothing hanging on the walls and there were heavy black curtains covering the single window.

On the nightstand Mac found two more bottles of medication and pocketed them, as well. As he walked back to the front door, he gazed all around him. Nowhere did he see a sign that four women had been killed here.

Still, he couldn't discount Ben's current mental state. He still believed it was possible the man saw the women as evil spirits and so he'd killed them. Ben had plenty of land around his house where he could have taken the women and stabbed them to death.

"No sign of Christmas in there," he told Callie as he got back in the car. "But I have a pocketful of medicine bottles that need to be sorted out. We'll head back to the office and I'll see if I can make contact with the prescribing doctor. Once that's done, I'll call Nathan and see if he'll meet us at his home."

Minutes later Mac was in his office and on the phone to a Dr. Tony Georgino, who was the doctor on all the prescription bottles. Mac explained Ben's behavior and the doctor immediately believed Ben was off the medication he was prescribed for anxiety and schizoaffective illness.

When Mac told him Ben was a suspect in the murder of four young women, the doctor immediately came to Ben's defense. "I have been treating Ben for the past six years. In my professional opinion Ben doesn't have a homicidal bone in his body. However, if it would help, I could drive in and see Ben sometime late this afternoon."

"That would be great," Mac replied. "Maybe you can give me some insight that I need."

They made arrangements for the doctor to meet Mac at the office at four o'clock. Mac hung up the phone but remained seated at his desk.

He only had a little bit of circumstantial evidence with his three top suspects. Beyond that there was no evidence to point to anyone else. Roger had fallen off their suspect list, leaving Ben and Nathan at the top.

His head filled with all the details of each and every murder. They had spent so much time spinning their wheels about the birds. Now he believed the murders had to do with Christmas. The bodies had been posed with Santa hats on their heads and an enactment of "The Twelve Days of Christmas."

As he thought of Ben firing the rifle at him, he couldn't help but wonder if Dr. Georgino might be wrong. Maybe the doctor didn't know about how much his patient might have deteriorated. Maybe he didn't realize that throughout the last couple of months Ben's obsession with who he perceived was evil had turned deadly.

Then his thoughts moved from murder to Callie. She'd surprised him, both with her takedown of Ben, and then in her display of utter compassion for the man. She had to have known the knife they'd found on Ben made it even more likely he was their killer and yet she had been soft and gentle with him.

He was in love with her. In another lifetime he would have asked her to be his wife and he would have been incredibly happy to be planning a future with her.

However, his fear was greater than his love. He'd known his ex-wife, Amanda, since grade school. When he'd married her, he'd believed she was a good woman with a compassionate and giving heart. But ultimately, she'd shocked him with her utter ruthlessness. She'd not only walked out on him, but she'd also gutted him in the process.

How was he to know Callie wasn't the same? How could he trust that things would be different with her? Sure, Callie might have a crush on him now, especially after him making love to her the night before, but ultimately he would bore her or disappoint her and things would crumble and turn ugly between them.

He'd taken a chance on love and marriage once, but it didn't matter how much he cared about Callie; he just wasn't willing to do it again.

Last night he'd given her a false signal. By making love to her, by then sleeping with her in his arms, he'd definitely given her the wrong impression. He was sure he'd given her the signal that he was all in on having a relationship with her. And before this night was over he needed to let her know that wasn't the case.

Chapter Eleven

Mac was silent as they drove to Nathan's place. Callie had thought he'd be in a bit of a celebratory mood with the potential killer behind bars.

The knife that Ben had on him had been big enough, wicked enough, to be the murder weapon. Time would tell, but right now Callie was feeling very optimistic about it.

There was no way for them to know the depths of Ben's paranoia. It was very possible that what had driven him to murder were what he perceived were evil threats to him. Maybe when he was interviewed later with his doctor they could find out what might have happened to Ben around Christmas that had made him identify with the holiday song.

However, Mac apparently wasn't feeling it. His silence felt heavy and too thick for her to penetrate with idle conversation. She had never felt such distance from him before and she wished she could see into his brain to see what was going on with him.

When they arrived at Nathan's place his truck was parked in the driveway, letting them know he was waiting for them. He stepped out on his porch as they got out of their car.

"Good morning, Nathan," Mac said.

"Almost afternoon," Nathan replied.

Callie followed Mac up the drive to the porch. "We've got a few more questions for you today. Can we come in?"

Nathan hesitated a moment. "Okay, but today wasn't cleaning day so it's kind of messy inside." He opened the door to allow them inside.

It apparently wasn't cleaning month, Callie thought as she stepped in and looked around. The small living room–kitchen area smelled of garbage. There was no Christmas tree or holiday decorations.

The table was piled high with food wrappers and take-out containers. Clothes covered the only chair in the room, clothes that she couldn't tell if they were clean or dirty. She and Mac sat on the sofa and Nathan pulled in a chair from the kitchen and sat facing them.

"Did you get your toolbox back?" Mac asked.

Nathan nodded. "Deputy Caldwell brought it to me."

"So, what are you working on now?" Mac asked.

"Nothing right now. I'd set aside a couple of days to finish up in Linda's closet but…" His voice trailed off.

"I see you haven't decorated for Christmas," Callie said. "Do you plan on putting up a tree?"

Nathan gave her a winsome smile. "Nah. I figure Christmas is mostly for kids, and since I don't have a wife or kids, there's really no point in putting up a tree."

"How long have you been here in town, Nathan?" Mac asked. "What is it, six…seven years?"

"Actually it's almost eight," Nathan replied. "I lived in Kansas City all my life and when my parents were gone I decided to take off in my rusty truck and see the world."

Mac laughed. "Rock Ridge isn't exactly an exciting place to live. Why here?"

"My truck broke down just out of town and so I ended up staying a couple of days for it to get fixed. Everyone was so nice here. I liked it here…so I stayed." Nathan smiled. "It's a good place to live."

"It isn't so good right now with a killer on the loose," Mac replied. "And speaking of that…" Mac began the line of questioning into Nathan's alibis for the times of the murders.

Once again Callie focused on Nathan's facial features, trying to discern if he was a liar or not. However, he appeared genuine as he tried to answer Mac's question to the best of his ability. And once again she didn't really believe Nathan had the mental acumen to pull off the murders.

It was after one by the time they made their way back to town. Most of the stores had opened although there weren't many people out and about.

It was the perfect time for her and Mac to hit the stores to see if they could find the five golden rings the killer might be using next. If they could figure that out, then maybe there would be a record of who bought them.

They went into store after store, hunting for the elusive golden rings, but the only place they found them was in the jewelry store for three hundred fifty dollars per ring. A little pricey for five to be left at a murder scene.

"It's possible the killer ordered costume rings off the web," Callie said as they headed back to the office to meet with Dr. Georgino. "I'm sure there's all kind of party places that sell cheap rings as party favors or whatever."

"With the knife we found on Ben, I should be able to get a search warrant not only for his property, but also all his phone and banking transactions. If he ordered rings online, then we'll find out," Mac replied.

Dr. Georgino was an attractive middle-aged man with black hair, dark eyes and a warm personality that Callie guessed served him well in his profession. He greeted both Mac and Callie warmly. "How's my patient?"

"We're hoping you can tell us," Mac replied. "I had him brought up to the interview room so you can speak to him and perhaps make some assessments. I can't allow you to be with him alone given his unpredictable actions earlier."

"I understand that," the doctor said.

"Then let's go see Ben," Mac replied.

Callie was disappointed that she wasn't invited to sit in for the interview. Instead, she went into the break room. Nobody else was there. She grabbed her purse and pulled out a couple of dollars to buy herself a soda and a bag of roasted peanuts from the vending machine.

As she sank down at the table and began to munch on the peanuts, her thoughts went over everything that had happened that morning.

She'd been terrified for Mac when Ben had shot at him. She'd been afraid Ben would shoot again and again and Mac would be killed. She really believed they now had their killer behind bars.

The knife that Ben had on him had cinched it for her. With the belief that it was finally over washing through her, a huge weight lifted from her shoulders.

Would Mac now send her back to her desk job? She hoped not. She hoped working the murder cases with him had shown him that she had what it took to be a great deputy. Of course her real dream was to be his wife. But she'd felt his distance from her all afternoon and her hope of being his woman…of him being her man…was slowly diminishing.

She could love him to death, but it didn't matter if he didn't love her back. Certainly their time together over the past two weeks had been so intense with both the highest of highs and lowest of lows. Was it only the stress of the job that had driven Mac into her bed? She didn't want to believe that. In fact, she didn't believe it.

She'd caught him gazing at her on more than one occasion with a softness in his eyes. Beyond the lust he obviously felt toward her, she believed in her very heart and soul that he was falling in love with her. She just hoped he was willing to embrace her love and everything she wanted to bring to his life.

The minutes ticked by and she remained alone in the room and deep into her thoughts. She didn't know how long she remained there before Mac finally walked into the room.

She immediately got to her feet, but he motioned her back down and then sank down in the chair next to hers. "Dr. Georgino just left."

"And?"

"He wants to institute a 5150 process."

Callie raised an eyebrow in surprise. "A seventy-two-hour hold due to mental issues?"

Mac nodded. "He was surprised by the depth of Ben's psychoses…specifically his paranoia. He believes Ben has been off his medication for months and immediately put us on notice as to what Ben needs while he's in our custody."

"So, here's the important question—does the doctor believe Ben is our killer?"

"Before talking to and seeing Ben today, Dr. Georgino believed there was no way Ben could kill anyone. However, after seeing Ben today, he admitted that he couldn't rule it out."

"Hopefully within the next seventy-two hours we'll get forensics back on the knife and we'll be a hundred percent positive that we've got our man."

She leaned forward and placed her hand on his shoulder. "I believe it's over, Mac. I think we have the killer behind bars and the town is safe once again."

He leaned back in the chair and her hand fell away from him. He rubbed the back of his neck and released a deep sigh. "I hope it's over, but in the meantime I have Deputy Roark running background checks on Roger, Ben and Nathan."

"The one thing I'd like to know is what ultimately triggered Ben. I mean, I know it was his mental illness that probably had him kill those women, but why the birds? Why did he identify with that particular Christmas song?"

Mac shook his head. "We may never know the answers to everything." He stood. "And now you're off duty for the day and I'll take you home."

She looked at him in surprise. "But it's only five thirty," she protested.

He smiled. "Welcome to a regular shift."

She got up, walked over to the coat rack and grabbed her coat. She turned to look at him once again. "Are you sure you want me off duty so early? Surely there are still things that need to be done."

"Whatever needs to be done can be done tomorrow. I'm letting several of the others go home on time tonight. We have a viable suspect behind bars. We have seventy-two hours to prove beyond a reasonable doubt that he's our killer and tonight we can all take a breath and then get back hard at work in the morning."

She nodded. "You're the boss." She followed him outside and to his car.

Was it just last night that they had been in each other's arms? Dear God, with everything that had happened today their lovemaking felt as if it had happened months ago.

However, when they got back into the small confines of his car, his scent washed over her, bringing back once again the wonder of being in his arms.

They rode for several moments in silence, but it wasn't the comfortable quiet they occasionally enjoyed. Rather this was the charged silence of things unsaid.

Callie had waited all day to see if Mac would bring up their lovemaking so they could discuss how they each felt after the experience, but now it was obvious he had no intention of bringing it up. So, she would.

She couldn't go to sleep without knowing exactly where she stood with him.

He pulled up in front of her house and parked. He turned to gaze at her and in his eyes she saw that softness, that something that made her believe he was in love with her.

"Mac, before we say good-night we have to talk about the elephant in the room," she said.

Immediately his eyes darkened and shuttered against her. "I didn't think there was anything to talk about. I've been clear to you that I'm not looking for a relationship. Last night was wonderful, but it shouldn't have happened."

"But it did happen and it was more than wonderful," she replied. "I… I'm in love with you." The words falling from her lips surprised her. She hadn't meant to let him know just yet how she felt about him. But now the words hung in the air between them.

He shifted in his seat and looked out the front window, obviously uncomfortable. He released a deep sigh and then gazed at her once again, his eyes still dark and impossible to read.

"Callie, the last couple weeks have been intense, and we've spent a lot of time together. Emotions have run high for the both of us, but I think you're now misreading your own feelings."

She stared at him and then released a dry laugh. "Please don't try to undermine my feelings, Mac. I know how I feel about you. I'm in love with you."

He winced, as if he found her words painful. "Don't love me, Callie. You deserve to love a man who can return your love with his whole heart. I don't have a heart that loves. Save your love for somebody who does. And now I think it's best if we just say good-night."

She searched his features for several more moments, seeking some form of softness, some way in beneath the armor he seemed to have drawn around himself. She found none.

"Good night, Mac," she said. "I'll see you first thing in the morning." She got out of the car and opened the back door to retrieve her coat. "She must have done some number on you," she added. She closed the door and headed up the sidewalk and fought back tears of disappointment…of utter heartbreak.

After a night of crying and cursing her heart for falling in love with a man who she believed loved her, but refused to act on it, she was ready to head back into the office.

With a credible suspect behind bars, she wondered whether Mac would put her back on the desk, or keep her as a deputy. If he was now uncomfortable to be in her presence, the best thing for him would be to put her back on the desk, where he only had to have contact with her a couple of times a day.

He'd certainly never promised her a permanent position as a deputy. She'd known all along he'd only appointed her as one because of the situation he'd found himself in with a killer on the loose.

She shoved all these thoughts out of her head and instead steeled herself for seeing Mac again after the conversation they'd had the night before. Opening her door, she stepped outside into the bright sunshine.

She immediately saw Nathan's truck parked at the curb and Nathan on the ground, hunched over and holding his ankle. "Nathan, what happened?" she asked as she took several steps toward him.

"I was on my way to Jason Donovan's house to do some work and I thought I had a flat tire. I parked to get out and look and slipped and twisted my ankle."

He looked like a pathetic little boy sitting in the snow with a stocking cap askew on his head and his eyes filled with hurt. "Can I call somebody to help you?" Callie asked.

"I don't have anyone to call," he replied. "I just need to get in my truck and go home." He tried to stand, but fell back in the snow. "Could you just help me to the driver's door?"

Callie hesitated a moment and looked around. There was nobody out on the snowy streets at this time of the morning. She felt no real threat from Nathan. She'd always believed he wasn't bright enough to pull off the murders.

She touched the butt of her gun to assure herself and then approached where Nathan sat. When she reached him he threw his arm around her shoulder and moaned slightly.

With her help he managed to get to his feet and together with him leaning on her they got to the driver's door. He turned back to her. "Thanks for your help, Deputy Stevens," he said.

He made a quick movement and something sharp stuck Callie in her thigh. "Ouch... What...?" She looked down to see a hypodermic needle. She looked up at Nathan in surprise.

His eyes were no longer innocuous, but rather filled with a sly cunning. She fumbled at her side, wanting to pull her weapon, but it felt as if she was moving through sludge.

Her vision blurred as Nathan grabbed her gun from her holster. Her heartbeat slowed despite the fear that filled her.

Her muscles refused to work with her brain and her knees suddenly weakened. She felt herself falling, but Nathan caught her. He picked her up in his arms and carried her to the back of his pickup.

Danger. Oh God, she was in danger. Nathan wasn't on Mac's radar anymore. Nathan began to hum "The Twelve Days of Christmas" song, chilling her to her bones.

She fought to stay conscious, but she was completely boneless and a frightening darkness crept in. Nathan placed her in the bed of the truck and then covered her with a blue tarp.

Help me! The words screamed in her head. As the darkness overtook her, her last conscious, horrifying thought was that she was going to be the five golden rings… She was going to die.

Chapter Twelve

The brief conversation with Callie last night had played and replayed in Mac's head all night long. He'd felt her love for him pouring from her. He'd wanted to pull her into his arms and kiss her all night long. He'd wanted to tell her that he was deeply in love with her, but he hadn't. He couldn't.

The blow Amanda had delivered to his heart that Christmas Eve when she'd walked out on him had forever scarred him. He'd been truthful when he'd told Callie he had no heart to give her.

She deserved to have a man who could love her with all his heart and soul. She deserved so much more than what Mac could give her.

It was just after six when he sat at the kitchen table and drank a cup of coffee before going into work. His mind raced with thoughts, both about the murders and about Callie.

Did they have the right man in jail right now? Had Ben committed the murders while in a fugue state due to him going off his medication and becoming trapped in a depth of paranoia about evil spirits?

How would things go with Callie when she came in

this morning? Would she be embarrassed by her profession of her love for him the night before? Would she be hurt and wear that hurt in her beautiful eyes? God, he wasn't sure he could stand that. The last thing he'd ever wanted to do was hurt her.

He recognized that he was guilty of giving her mixed messages. He'd told her he wasn't interested in a relationship and yet he'd touched her in loving ways, and he'd kissed her and made love with her.

He stared out the window where the rising sun reflected red and orange on the snow. He hoped he heard from forensics today that the knife taken off Ben was the murder weapon. That would seal the deal on Ben's guilt and the young women in the town would once again be safe.

With this thought in mind he finished up his coffee and then pulled on his coat as thoughts of Callie returned to his mind. If he knew her as much as he thought he did, then she would come in first thing this morning with her head held high.

He couldn't help but smile with this thought. She had more strength, more spunk than any other woman he had ever known and that was part of what he loved about her.

He got to the office and went directly to his desk. He needed to check his email to see if any reports had come in. Unfortunately, there was nothing. He'd have to be patient and in the meantime he'd make sure his deputies were still questioning people about the murders.

Even though he'd pretty much written off Roger and Nathan as suspects, that didn't mean that more questioning might not turn up another suspect. They also needed to begin to build a case against Ben if he was their man.

They needed to find out what his actions were on the date of every murder. Any alibi he had for the days and nights had to be checked and rechecked.

He was vaguely surprised when eight o'clock rolled around and Callie still wasn't in. He held his morning meeting with all his other deputies and once they all had their assignments they left.

Mac put his coat back on and got into his car. He wanted people to see him out and about. He needed them to know that he was still working on their behalf. He drove up and down the streets, making notes of areas that hadn't seen a snowplow yet.

It was after ten when he returned to the office, shocked that Callie still hadn't come in. It wasn't like her. Even with the conversation they'd had the night before, it wasn't like her to avoid him. It definitely wasn't like her to blow off work.

He finally called her, but the call went to her voice mail and he hung up. A half an hour later he called her again with the same results, but this time he left her a message. "Callie, where are you? I figured you would already be here. Call me back and let me know what's going on." He hung up, dissatisfied with the message and with the fact that she wasn't answering her phone.

Had the fact that he'd told her he had no heart to give her somehow broken her? God, he hoped not. He couldn't imagine seeing her without the sparkle in her eyes, without that optimistic smile on her face. Surely she was stronger than that. Dammit, he knew she was stronger than that. So, where was she?

It was just after eleven when the faint niggle of worry he had about her became too big to ignore. He got back in his car and headed over to her house. He parked in her driveway and headed for her front door.

Nothing appeared amiss. He knocked on the door loud enough for the neighbors to hear. No reply. He knocked again. "Callie, come to the door," he yelled. Still no response from her.

He waited several minutes and then headed back to his car. Maybe she was inside the house and just not answering any calls from him. With this thought in mind he headed toward Janie's Stuff and Things. He knew from idle conversation with Callie that she and Janie were close friends.

He wasn't one to put his personal business on blast, but the truth was he was worried about Callie and just needed to know she was okay. Hopefully Callie would answer a call from her friend.

The store was open even though there were few people out and about on the snowy sidewalks. The moment he walked into the store he was surrounded by Christmas, which immediately evoked thoughts of Callie and her home.

"Sheriff." Janie greeted him with a warm smile. "Fancy seeing you in here. Are you looking for a special gift for somebody?"

"Actually, I'm hoping you would do me a favor." He hesitated a moment, wondering if he had completely lost his mind. Still, all he wanted was to know that Callie was okay. "Uh… I know you and Callie are good friends. Have you talked to her at all today?"

"No. Why, is something wrong?" Janie immediately appeared worried.

"She hasn't come in to work today and she didn't call in to say she wasn't coming. I went by her house and knocked, but she didn't answer. I've also called her several times but she isn't answering my calls." The words fell out of his mouth faster than he could edit himself.

"We…we had a conversation last night that might have upset her, so she might not want to talk to me right now so I was wondering if maybe you could call her and make sure she's okay. Surely she would answer your call."

Janie grabbed a black purse from behind the counter and pulled out her cell phone. "No matter what happened between the two of you, it's not like her to blow off work. Callie has always been the utmost professional when it comes to her job."

Janie opened her phone case and punched a button that would ring Callie. Mac waited, hoping…praying… that Callie would answer and he'd know she was okay.

However, the phone rang several times and then went to voice mail. Janie frowned. "Let me try her again." Janie punched the button again and got the same result. "I'm sorry, Mac. Maybe she's busy with something or in the shower. I'll keep trying her."

"Thanks, and could you let me know when you hear from her?"

"For sure. I'll call and let you know," Janie replied.

As Mac left the shop, the alarm bells that had been ringing about Callie grew louder. What if they had the wrong man in jail? What if Ben wasn't the killer?

A vision of Callie filled his head… Callie with her

blond curls... Callie who was the perfect fit for the killer's victimology.

As he got into his car he hoped and prayed that he was wrong, that Ben was their killer and Callie was someplace safe. However, as he drove back to the office the alarm in his head screeched.

One way or another he had to find Callie. If what he feared was true, then he only had a matter of hours before she would be stabbed to death and left someplace on the street with a Santa hat on her head and five golden rings on her fingers.

CALLIE CAME TO in bits and increments. The smell hit her first...the dank scent of earth...the noxious smells of blood and death. Her mind worked to make sense of it. Where was she?

She cracked open her eyes and fought through the fog in her brain. She was in a root cellar of sorts. She opened her eyes wider despite a headache that rolled across her forehead.

There was a workbench against one wall, shelving on the other wall and she was on a bunk bed. The workbench held a lamp that illuminated the area. She started to get up and realized her arms and feet were tied to the bed.

Sheer panic screamed through her. What had happened? How had she gotten here? Oh God...what was going on? And then she remembered. Nathan and his pretense of a hurt ankle.

Oh God, she'd been so stupid. She'd fallen for a ruse she should have never fallen for. She hadn't believed he had the acumen to be the killer, and yet here she was.

She strained against the ropes that tied her wrists to the bed frame. There was no give. She attempted to move her legs, but the rope around her ankles held tight.

She spied a pile of coats and purses in the corner of the room. They were items that belonged to the murdered women and her white winter coat was on top. The sheet beneath her felt stiff and as she moved her body to one side and peered down at it, she saw the reason for the stiffness. Blood…old, dried blood. They'd wondered where the killing place was and now she knew. Panic once again soared through her and she kicked and pulled against the binds that held her until she was breathless.

Where was Nathan now? She looked toward the slanted wooden door. The next time she saw him would he come down with a knife in his hand, ready to stab her to death?

A deep sob welled up and exploded out of her. She was in trouble. When she hadn't shown up for work that morning had Mac just figured she was avoiding him? After their conversation the night before had he believed she was mad at him and that's why she hadn't come in to work?

Did he even know she was missing? Another sob escaped her. Was anybody even looking for her? She didn't want to die. She didn't want to be another victim.

Tears chased each other down her cheeks as she frantically tugged at the ropes. Somehow…some way…she had to escape. She had to get off of the bed and out the door.

She couldn't depend on anyone to find her, especially if they didn't even know that she was missing. Somehow she needed to save herself, but at the moment she wasn't sure how to do that.

She had no idea what time it was, but she knew it was only a matter of hours before Nathan would come at her with a knife. If nothing changed, then she knew she was on a countdown to her own death.

With that thought in mind, she began to scream for help…hoping and praying that somebody would hear her cries.

BY THE TIME he got back to the office, Mac was frantic. His fear for Callie was a living, breathing thing inside him. He put all his deputies on alert to be on the watch for her and then he hit the road again.

The first place he drove was to Roger's insurance company. Roger's car was parked out front and as Mac slowly drove by he could see Roger inside the office.

On his drive to Nathan's place, he tried to call Callie again and got the message that her voice mail was full. That only sent his fear for her higher. Where could she be? He couldn't believe she was just out walking around the snow-filled streets of the town or hiding out in her house.

He believed it was quite possible that the serial killer who had terrorized the town now had Callie in his clutches. His stomach muscles clenched tightly at the very thought.

When he got to Nathan's place the man's truck wasn't there. Mac returned to town and drove up and down the streets until he found Nathan's vehicle parked at the curb of Jason and Margaret Donovan's house. Mac got out of his truck and hurried to the front door. Jason answered. "Is Nathan here?" Mac asked before Jason could even greet him properly.

"Yes, he's doing a little work in our kitchen. Is there a problem?" Jason asked.

"What time did he get here today?" Mac asked.

Jason frowned. "I'm not sure, I think it was around nine or so. Is there a problem?" he asked again.

"No, but do you mind if I speak with him?" Mac asked.

"Of course not... Come on in." Jason opened the door wider to allow Mac entry. He followed Jason through an attractive living room and into a large, airy kitchen. Margaret was seated at the table with a cup of coffee in front of her and Nathan appeared to be changing the hardware on the cabinets.

"Margaret," he greeted her.

"Good afternoon, Sheriff," she said in obvious surprise.

"Hey, Nathan, how's it going for you?" Mac said.

Nathan offered him his usual smile. "Can't complain," he replied.

"I was wondering if you saw Deputy Stevens this morning?" Mac watched the man carefully.

"Deputy Stevens?" Nathan looked at him with what appeared to be confusion. "Why would I see her this morning? Was I supposed to see her?"

"No, I was just wondering if you had. She seems to be missing," Mac replied.

"Missing?" Margaret looked at him worriedly. "Is it possible...? Do you think...?"

"I don't know what to think, but we're actively searching for her now. I just figured Nathan was probably up and around earlier this morning so he might have seen her."

"Sorry, but I didn't see her anywhere around," Nathan replied.

"Then I'll just be on my way. Thanks, folks." Mac hurried back to the front door and to his car. As he drove away, a lump of despair filled the back of his throat.

Nathan would have been his biggest suspect, but he was in a kitchen changing hardware on cabinets instead of holding Callie somewhere to wait for killing time.

She walked to work every morning. She would have been vulnerable to being kidnapped off the street. Why in the hell hadn't he been picking her up every morning to make sure she wasn't exposed to a killer?

And if not Roger or Nathan, then who? The investigation had yielded no other suspects. He didn't know where to begin to find her. But dammit, if he had to break down every door in the entire town, he would do it to get to her.

According to the previous four murders, the women had been killed between the hours of seven and nine in the evening. It was now almost two. That gave him and his team five hours to find her before she'd be found dead and posed on the street.

Chapter Thirteen

Callie didn't know how long she screamed before she ultimately stopped. She finally realized if she was being held someplace around Nathan's house, then there was nobody around to hear her cries for help.

Minutes ticked by…agonizing minutes that ticked off her very life. She had no idea what time it was, but it felt as if hours had gone by.

She continued to tug and pull at the ropes until she felt the warmth of her own blood, to no avail. There was nothing she could do but wait for Nathan to return. As she awaited her own death, her head filled with myriad thoughts.

At least in death she would be reunited with the family she had lost. She would once again feel her father's strong arms around her and her mother's loving kiss on her cheek. She'd throw her arms around her little sister and hold her until they were both giggling.

However, as much as she loved her family and as much as she wanted to be reunited with them some day, she wasn't ready for it right now. She wanted to live to get married. She wanted to know the joy of childbirth and being a mother.

She'd been hoping for more time to make Mac realize they belonged together and that whatever had happened in his past had nothing to do with the never-ending love she had for him. She truly believed it was just a matter of time before he'd realize he could trust her and embrace not only the love she had for him, but also the love she knew he had for her.

But time had run out for her...for them. Tears once again blurred her eyes, tears of hopelessness, of loss. She would never again hear the wonderful sound of Mac's deep laughter, or fall into the soft gray shades of his eyes.

She wouldn't know anymore the wonder of being held in Mac's arms, the complete joy of him kissing her. She would never have the pleasure of making love with him again. And she wept uncontrollably at these thoughts.

She didn't want to die this way. It was going to be an excruciating way to die. She was going to be stabbed over and over and over again. She could only pray that the first stab killed her, that she wasn't alive or conscious for additional stabs wounds.

How frightened the others must have been to be tied down and know they were going to be stabbed to death. They hadn't even known it was because they were blondes and fit the victimology of a disturbed man.

Finally, she had no more tears to shed. Her wrists and ankles burned and hurt and she was exhausted by her efforts to get free.

She must have fallen asleep for the sound of snow crunching beneath footsteps awakened her. Every muscle in her body froze as the cellar door creaked open, footsteps sounded on a couple of the stairs and then the door fell shut.

Nathan walked down the stairs and turned to look at her. It was Nathan and yet it wasn't Nathan. Gone was the slight emptiness in his eyes and the cheerful smile that usually played on his face.

Instead, his eyes were filled with a shrewdness and his mouth was a slash of tight-lipped anger that only made her fear flame hotter.

He stared at her for several long, heart-pounding moments. "Ashley, why won't you ever die?" he finally said. "I've tried to get rid of you over and over again, but you keep reappearing."

"Nathan, I'm not Ashley. I'm Deputy Stevens… Callie… Remember me?" She forced a smile. "I'm Callie and I don't know Ashley."

"Shut up," he snapped. "I don't want to hear anything coming out of your lying mouth. I want you to shut up and listen and understand exactly what you did to me."

He began to pace in front of the bed. His short, quick steps, along with one of his hands racing through his hair over and over again, spoke of his deep agitation.

He stopped again in front of her and held out his hand. She was surprised to see a wedding band on his finger. It was a gold band with tiny diamondlike chips all around it. Callie knew he was missing a chip… It had been found at a murder scene. But nobody else knew that.

"You gave me this ring and promised before God and all our friends that you would love me forever. You remember that, Ashley? You remember all the promises you made?" He spoke deceptively soft.

"Please, Nathan. I'm not Ashley."

His unexpected slap to her face instantly made her cry out in pain as tears filled her eyes. "I told you to shut up. You can't fool me, Ashley. It was bad enough that you broke our wedding vows and divorced me. But then you killed my son." He practically screamed the words at her.

Despite her pain…in spite of her fear… Callie looked at Nathan in surprise. She needed to know what exactly had happened to Nathan that had turned him into a cold-blooded killer.

"Nathan, tell me, how did your son die?" she asked and then winced as she waited for another slap to her face.

Instead of slapping her for speaking, he began to pace once again. "You know how he died. You were the one responsible."

"Let's talk about it, Nathan," she said softly. Not only did she want to know what had happened, but she also wanted to keep him talking for as long as possible. Even though she knew she was entertaining false hope, she wanted to believe that somebody…anybody…might rescue her in time.

"You know what you did, Ashley. After you left me, we shared custody of little David and you had him for Christmas Eve. You put him in a bathtub and then you answered a phone call. While you chatted on the phone, our little boy slipped under the water and drowned. His safety wasn't as important as your damned phone call." Anguish filled his voice. "He died while you were on a damned phone call."

"Oh, Nathan, I'm so sorry." A deep sadness swept

through her at his story…for his pain. "Nathan, I'm so sorry for your loss." So, he'd lost his son on Christmas Eve. That explained Christmas being his trigger. What about the song? "What's important about 'The Twelve Days of Christmas' song?"

He stopped pacing and glared at her. "Don't you remember anything? That damned song was playing in the background when you called to tell me my son was dead." His hands clenched and unclenched at his sides.

So, now she understood all the dynamics of his crimes. She comprehended the overkill present with each victim. What she somehow needed for him to understand was that she wasn't his ex-wife… She wasn't his Ashley, who he apparently thought needed to be punished by death.

"Nathan, I'm so sorry about what happened to you. I'm sorry your wife left you and I'm sorry your son died in what sounds like a tragic accident," she said, trying to keep her panic out of her voice. "Nathan, please look at me. I'm not your wife. I'm not Ashley."

"You lie," he screamed. He twirled around from her and grabbed a knife from the top of the workbench. Her breath caught in the back of her throat. "You keep lying to me over and over again. I keep killing you but you come right back again. You're a damned demon woman and you have to be killed once and for all."

He stabbed the knifepoint into the bench, making Callie jump and release a heart-stopping gasp. "You killed my little boy and for that alone you have to die. I hear him crying in my dreams, I have nightmares about him being under the water and not being able to breathe. I watch him die night after night while that damned Christmas song plays over and over again."

"Nathan, killing me isn't going to make it stop. You need help, Nathan. You need to talk to a doctor. He would help you realize that killing Ashley over and over again isn't working for you. It isn't helping you with your grief." She tried to keep her voice calm, despite her need to scream.

He stared at her for a long moment, causing her breath to catch below her ribs and making it impossible for her to breathe. He grabbed the knife once again.

"You don't understand. I have no other choice. I have to stop the nightmares. I have to make it right. My little boy needs justice and killing you is the only way he'll get it." He turned his wrist over and looked at his watch.

He gazed back at her, his eyes dark and dead. "It was eight o'clock when I got the call that our son was dead. You have an hour and a half to ask for atonement and to pray for your sins. Then the knife of justice will come for you."

He placed the knife back on the workbench and then reached into his pocket and pulled out a handful of little bright golden rings, making her gasp painfully once again.

He stared down at the rings, put them back in his pocket and then headed toward the stairs. "Nathan... wait. Just let me go, Nathan. I'm not Ashley. Please just let me go," she said, begging and pleading.

He whirled back around, anger once again flashing in his eyes. "I've told you over and over again to shut up. Now I'm going to make sure you shut up."

He grabbed a roll of duct tape from the workbench,

ripped off a couple of pieces and then pressed them
tightly against her mouth. As he walked up the stairs she
screamed against the tape. He reached the top, opened
the door and stepped out and then slammed the door
shut behind him.

IT WAS JUST after six and Mac was frantic. Nobody had
seen Callie all day long and Mac was absolutely convinced she'd been kidnapped and was now being held by
the killer. He knew time was running out for her. What
he didn't know was the identity of the killer.

All afternoon his deputies had been out knocking
on doors in search of their fellow deputy. They had
checked out empty sheds and barns seeking the place
where women had been held and then murdered. They
found nothing.

It was as if Callie had disappeared into thin air. But,
dammit, she had to be somewhere. He now sat in the
break room going over everything and waiting for a few
of his deputies to check in for new orders.

He didn't know what new orders to give them. Find
Callie. That's all he wanted—that's all he needed. He
couldn't imagine never seeing her smiling face again. He
couldn't stand the thought of never hearing her
laughter again. His fear was so great for her it filled
his chest almost to the point that he couldn't speak.

He loved her and the thought of her being murdered…stabbed to death…caused a wealth of grief to
bring tears to his eyes. He felt so helpless.

What little evidence they had, had been gone over
a million times. The hunt for additional suspects had
yielded nothing. The tears raced faster from his eyes

and he angrily swiped at them. Now wasn't the time for
him to get emotional or break down. He needed action.

Dammit, where could she be? Who was holding her
with the intent of killing her? The minutes ticked by…
ticking down to Callie's death. He consciously shoved
his grief aside and once again focused on the paperwork before him.

Roger and Nathan had been two of his leading suspects. But both of them had worked all day. When
would they have had time to kidnap Callie and hold
her someplace all day long?

He supposed one of them could have kidnapped her
the moment she'd stepped out her door that morning.
That person could have taken her somewhere and then
left her to go to work to establish an alibi.

He wasn't sure why his thoughts kept returning to
Nathan. He wasn't even sure the man was capable of
committing these crimes, and yet Mac kept going back
to him.

Johnny came in, his face as troubled as Mac's
thoughts. "Nothing," he said and threw himself into
the chair next to Mac's. "I checked half a dozen sheds
and any building that might be the hidey-hole place of
the killer. Where could she be, Mac?"

"God, I wish I knew," Mac replied. "I have this ticking clock in my chest and once it ticks down to deto-
nation it's going to rip a huge hole through my heart."

Johnny looked at him for a long moment. "You know
she's crazy about you."

"I'm pretty crazy about her, too." The words fell from
Mac before he could edit himself. He released a deep
sigh. "But it doesn't matter how I feel about her if we

don't find her in time." His chest tightened, making it difficult for him to draw a breath.

He glanced toward the window where dusk had fallen with night soon to follow. The clock inside his head ticked louder. "Maybe we should run by Roger's and Nathan's places and check in with them again," Mac finally said.

"Whatever you want, boss. I'd love to go put the squeeze on sleazy Roger and I know all the deputies are behind you in whatever you need from us," Johnny replied.

"Sheriff," Deputy Andy Roark said urgently as he entered the breakroom, "I think I got him." He handed Mac a printed piece of paper. "This article appeared in the *Kansas City Star* almost eight years ago."

Mac looked at the copy with the headline: "Christmas Eve Tragedy." The article talked about the drowning death of a four-month-old baby. The mother, twenty-five-year-old Ashley Morton, had put the baby in the tub for a bath and unfortunately, she'd turned her back to take a phone call and when she turned back to attend to the baby, he had drowned. Ashley was newly divorced from the baby's father, Nathan Brighton. There was a photo of Ashley. She was an attractive blonde.

All of Mac's muscles froze. It was Nathan. He looked at Johnny. "Get all the men together and meet me in the Halloway driveway." The Halloways' home was the closest to Nathan's. "Nathan should be home by now. We'll meet and formulate a plan to go in without risking Callie's life."

They all moved at the same time, heading for the exit and to their own cars. Nathan. It had to be Nathan. The tragic event in his past at Christmastime had triggered him into a killing spree. And Callie was his next victim.

He drove faster than he'd ever driven before, thankful there was little traffic on the roads. He pulled up in the Halloway drive and then waited for his men to arrive, praying that they weren't already too late. God… they had to get to her in time.

ONCE AGAIN, SHE HEARD his footsteps approaching. Her heart beat so rapidly she felt nauseous. She began to weep, knowing it was time. He was coming to stab her to death. She couldn't help but pray that the first wound killed her quickly. She didn't want to live through twenty-five or twenty-six stabbings.

The door opened and as Nathan closed it behind him, she thrashed on the bed trying with all her power to break free. She screamed once again, the screams trapped in the duct tape that held her mouth closed.

Nathan walked into her view. His eyes were dark and simmering with what appeared to be suppressed rage. "It's time, Ashley…time for my son to get his justice. You should have never put our little boy in the bathtub and then turned your back on him to talk on your phone."

He stepped close to her, his face mere inches from her own. "Who was on the phone, bitch?" he screamed. "Who was more important than our baby boy? Who called you that was so damned important that you had to talk to them instead of taking care of our son? Was it your boyfriend? Huh? Was that who it was, you bitch?"

He backed away until he hit the worktable behind him. "Hopefully you won't come back again. Once I kill you, I hope you stay dead. I need you to stay dead once and for all."

His words only torched her terror higher. Within minutes she would feel the agony of a knife piercing through her. She now realized intimately what the other victims had experienced in the minutes before their deaths. Her heart cried out not only with her own horror, but with theirs, as well.

"You made me have to do this," Nathan continued to rage. "It's all your fault that I have to kill you. You should have never turned your back on my little boy. He was the best thing that had ever happened to me and once he was gone my whole life fell apart."

He whirled around to the workbench. He grabbed up the knife once again and then turned to face her. "I loved you once, Ashley. I loved you with all my heart. But you left me. I could hate you for that alone, but I really hate you for not taking care of my child. I hate you… Do you hear me? I hate you."

He raised the knife and Callie tensed. As if in slow motion she watched the knife come down and then stab into the side of her stomach. Excruciating pain seared through her. She screamed and then gasped against the tape over her mouth.

She was dying. Her mind worked to comprehend the fact that at this very moment she was being murdered by the very serial killer she had sought to find.

The knife stabbed into her again. An agonizing pain once again fired through her and she felt the warmth of the blood leaving her body. Tears wept from the corner of her eyes and she prayed for unconsciousness… for a quick death.

He raised the knife and was about to stab her again when a faint knocking sound stopped his knife movement. He threw the knife on the workbench and hurried up and out of the cellar.

Callie continued to weep with pain and the horrifying knowledge that he'd be back to finish the job.

Chapter Fourteen

Mac knocked on Nathan's door. He'd decided to come in soft with just Johnny by his side, rather than storming the house with all his men. However, those men were now scattered in the woods around Nathan's place just waiting for Mac's call for them.

The darkness of night had fallen, making Mac aware that every minute counted. He knocked again, harder this time, and finally Nathan came to the door.

"Sheriff," Nathan greeted him with his usual wide-eyed innocence. "What are you doing here?"

"I'm here for Callie," Mac replied. All his senses were working overtime. He shot a glance around. The bedroom door was open, but he didn't sense anyone in there. He sniffed the air, but didn't smell a trace of her perfume. He heard nothing that would indicate a woman was in the house and struggling to get free.

"Callie? Why would you think she's here?" Nathan asked, an eyebrow quirked up in confusion. "Did she tell you she was coming here?"

Mac knew with certainty Nathan was their man. He had Callie hidden away someplace. Were they too late? Is that why Mac didn't feel her spirit, her essence anywhere?

"Nathan, cut the crap. We know everything. We know about your son and we know you killed those women. Now, where is Callie?"

The innocence in Nathan's eyes disappeared and instead a dark madness filled them. Before Mac could guess the man's next move, he turned and raced toward his bedroom. He crashed through the window and disappeared from sight.

"Dammit! Call the men," Mac yelled to Johnny as he raced for the bedroom and then dived through the broken window. Once he got to his feet, he turned on his flashlight and shone the light around him to get his bearings.

He immediately spied a root cellar door in the back of the house. Callie. He knew she was down there. He also saw a padlock on the door. His emotional side told him to get to her, but his intellectual side told him to go after the killer, get him under arrest and get the key to Nathan's lair.

There was nothing he could do for Callie right now, but if Nathan somehow managed to escape, then a killer would be on the loose. Mac raced after Nathan. Thankfully between his flashlight and the moonlight spilling down from overhead he could see the man racing for the trees in the distance.

Mac's heart beat frantically as he ran faster than he'd ever run in his life. The faster they got Nathan in custody, the faster he could get to Callie.

Were they too late? Had Nathan already killed Callie? Oh God, he couldn't think that way. Nathan reached the tree line and Deputy Cameron Royal jumped out from behind a tree trunk and slammed Nathan to the ground.

Mac raced to where the two men grappled on the ground. He grabbed one of Nathan's arms and jerked the man to his feet. Rage filled Mac as he thought about what Nathan had done to the victims…to Mac's town. He got Nathan into handcuffs.

He wanted to smash his fist into Nathan's face. He wanted to shoot the man a dozen times, but what he wanted more than anything was the key to the root cellar.

"Where's the key?" Mac was vaguely aware of his men closing in around them. "Where's the damned key to the root cellar?" Nathan merely grinned…a wicked, sick smile.

Mac reached into Nathan's left pocket and found nothing. He checked his right pocket and found a key ring with dozens of keys on it.

"Get him out of here," he said to Cameron. "Take him to jail and out of my sight."

Mac ran, along with half of his men, for the cellar. Mac's heart pounded so hard he felt half-nauseous. She had to be all right. She just had to be. When he reached the root cellar, his fingers fumbled through the keys, seeking the one that would unlock the door.

He tried three small keys before he found the right one. The padlock released and Mac threw it to the side. He yanked open the door and instantly smelled the scent of blood and death and knew that this was Nathan's killing place.

He ran down the stairs and stopped at the bottom. Callie was tied to the frame of the twin bed. Her eyes were closed, her face pale as death, and her khaki blouse had blood on it.

Oh God, he was too late. He nearly fell to his knees as a deep grief pierced through him. She was gone. She'd been stabbed to death.

And then he heard it…a soft moan. "Call for an ambulance," he yelled up the stairs.

"Callie." He ran to her side. "Callie, honey. We're here and you're safe now. Can you open your eyes for me?" How badly had she been hurt? Was she dying right now in front of him? "Callie…please open your eyes and look at me." He pulled the tape off her mouth.

She moaned once again and then he was looking into her beautiful blue eyes. She stared at him for a long moment. "Am I dead?" Her voice was a slow whisper.

"No, honey. You aren't dead and we're going to get you out of here," Mac replied.

"I hurt, Mac. He stabbed me and I'm dying but I… I need to tell you that I'll love you through eternity." Her eyes drifted closed again.

"Callie… Callie stay with me," Mac cried. He looked at Johnny, who had come down the stairs behind him. "See if you can find something to cut her loose," Mac said.

Johnny moved to the workbench. "There's a big knife here with blood on it."

"Find something else to use. That's our murder weapon," Mac replied tersely. Johnny found a second knife and handed it to Mac.

Callie's wrists were bloody from her obvious struggles against the ropes. The sight made Mac's heart squeeze tight. As he worked on the ropes that bound her, he continued to call her name, but she appeared to be unconscious.

He was scared to death. Were they really too late after all? Once he got the ropes off her he feared that any attempt to move her might do more damage. He had no idea how many times she'd been stabbed.

Thankfully, at that moment two paramedics came down the stairs with a stretcher in their hands. Mac and Johnny went upstairs so the two men could work to bring Callie up and to the waiting ambulance.

Mac's heart banged hard against his ribs. All the love he had for her flooded through him. All he wanted right now was for her to be okay.

The minute she was loaded into the ambulance, Mac got into his car and followed the blue-and-red swirling lights on top of the emergency vehicle as the siren released its loud song.

Tears burned at his eyes…tears of stress and the relief that finally the killer was behind bars. Mostly his tears were for Callie. Was she going to survive this horrendous day and night? Or in the end would she be just another victim of a serial killer?

"No," the word exploded from his lips. She had to be okay. She just had to be.

When they reached the hospital, the ambulance disappeared into its bay and Mac pulled into the closest parking space in front of the emergency room doors.

He sat in his car for a moment, wrestling to get his emotions under control. The last thing he wanted was for any of his men…anyone at all…to see him weak. But his love for Callie made him weak. He finally got himself under some semblance of control and then left his car and hurried into the emergency room waiting area.

Lana Albright was behind the receptionist desk. She

was in her mid-fifties and had worked as the nighttime receptionist for as long as Mac could remember. "Lana, they just brought in Deputy Callie Stevens. Can you tell the doctor on call that I'm waiting here for an update on her condition?"

"It's Dr. Washburn on duty tonight and I'll go back and let them know you're out here." She immediately got up from the desk and disappeared behind a door that read No Entry.

Mac was glad it was Dr. Eric Washburn on duty. He was an older man and Mac trusted his expertise completely. Mac sank down in one of the green plastic chairs, nerves racing through him.

Was she going to be all right? She hadn't regained consciousness as they'd loaded her into the ambulance and that had scared the hell out of him.

He had no idea just how many times Nathan had stabbed her. Thank God he'd knocked on Nathan's door when he had. A minute or two later might have really been too late for Callie. He wasn't sure now that it hadn't been too late.

He buried his face in his hands, another wave of grief stabbing through him. He couldn't imagine never seeing her bright smile again, never hearing her optimism ringing in her voice. He just couldn't imagine not having her in his life ever again.

The sound of the emergency room door whooshing open caused him to sit up. Johnny looked at him worriedly. Johnny and Adam Cook entered. "Any word on her condition?" Adam asked worriedly.

Johnny sank down on one side of Mac and Adam sat

on the other side of him. "Nothing yet," Mac replied. "Nathan locked up tight?"

"He is, although I really wanted to beat the hell out of him for what he'd done," Adam said.

"That makes two of us," Mac said.

"Uh…make that three," Johnny replied with unbridled anger in his tone.

"All I care about now is Callie's well-being," Mac said.

"That's what everyone cares about," Johnny said. "We've got to get back on the roads, but we wanted you to know that we're all worried about Callie." The two men stood.

"If you call me and let me know how she's doing, then I'll let all the deputies know because they're all concerned about her."

Minutes later Mac was once again alone in the waiting room. He wasn't surprised the other deputies were worried about Callie. It just reminded him that Callie had touched everyone with her warmth and bright spirit.

The minutes ticked by…agonizing minutes that turned into one hour and then two. What was happening? What was taking so long? How many stab wounds had she received?

Finally, Dr. Washburn walked out. Mac leaped to his feet, his heart hammering in his chest. "Dr. Washburn, how is she?"

"She had one knife wound that thankfully missed all vital organs. However, the second wound stabbed into her spleen, forcing me to perform an emergency splenectomy. Other than that, she was also suffering from shock and loss of blood."

"But she's going to be okay?" Mac asked.

For the first time Dr. Washburn smiled. "Barring any complications, she should be just fine. It will take her about six weeks to fully recover from the surgery and be ready again for active duty, but she's resting peacefully."

"Can I see her?" Mac asked.

"She'll be groggy from the anesthesia and I certainly don't want her to be stressed."

"I just want to peek in on her." Mac desperately wanted to see her and assure himself she was really okay.

"She's in room 110."

Before the doctor could say anything else, Mac was hurrying down the hallway to Callie's room. When he reached it, he stopped in the doorway.

The room was in semidarkness. She looked tiny in the big bed with white sheets pulled up around her and an IV drip connected to one arm. Her blond curls formed a halo around her head and she appeared as if she were sleeping peacefully.

She'd been through hell and back in this single day. *I'll love you through eternity.* Her words played and replayed in his mind. She'd believed she was dying and had used her last breath to tell him that.

And now he was going to have to figure out what he was going to do about that, but in the meantime, he had a murder scene to process and a case to build to make sure that Nathan went away for the rest of his life.

CALLIE JERKED AWAKE, flailing her arms and legs in an effort to get free from the ropes before Nathan could come and finish her off. It took her only a moment to realize she was fighting against an IV line in her arm and tangled sheets around her feet.

She sagged back against the mattress as she realized she was safe. A glance out the window let her know it must be around noon. Noon of what day? Not only was she disoriented as to day and time, but also to find herself in the hospital.

She closed her eyes again and tried to remember what had happened. Snippets of memories began to fire off in her mind. Nathan, screaming in her face and then stabbing her. She still felt the pain of his stab wounds.

There had been a knock…and then Mac crashing down the stairs…and then…and then nothing. It was obvious from where she was now that she'd been saved.

So, what damage had she sustained? Her wrists and ankles burned, but she couldn't see how badly they'd been hurt because her wrists were wrapped up in bandages. Her stomach also hurt. How badly had Nathan damaged her before she'd been rescued?

She opened her eyes once again and raised the head of her bed a bit. At that moment Dana Johnson walked in. Callie had met nurse Dana when some of the hospital staff had come to the sheriff's office to brush up CPR skills with everyone.

"Ah, good. You're awake," Dana greeted with a bright smile. "How are you feeling?"

"Okay, I guess, although I'm having some pain."

Dana moved to her side with a machine that held everything necessary to take vitals. "On a scale of one to ten, how would you rate your pain level right now?"

"Maybe about a seven," Callie confessed.

"Let me get these vitals and I'll speak to the doctor about some pain meds. He'll be in later to speak to you, but in the meantime, we should be able to make you more comfortable."

Dana left and then returned about ten minutes later with pain meds that she inserted into Callie's IV. Almost immediately Callie's pain eased up and her eyes drifted closed.

She must have fallen asleep because the next thing she knew a woman came in serving her lunch. She introduced herself as Wendy. "There's a grilled chicken sandwich and a nice cup of soup for you," she said. "But if you need or want anything else, you just let me know. You're a real hero and it's my honor to serve you."

"Wendy, I'm no hero. The real hero in all this is Mac and his team of hardworking men," she replied. And when was she going to see Mac?

After lunch a procession of flowers began to be delivered. There was a huge, beautiful bouquet from the mayor's office and another one from her fellow deputies. She even got one from the Rock Ridge Garden Club, which she didn't know existed. Each time the door to her room creaked open she was hoping she'd see Mac.

Finally, the doctor came in. "How's my patient this afternoon?" Dr. Washburn asked.

"Okay, but I'm curious what's happened to me. I have a lot of pain in my stomach."

Dr. Washburn nodded and then went on to explain about the two stab wounds she'd suffered and the need for him to take out her spleen.

He answered all her questions and she was dismayed to learn she'd be out of commission for about six weeks. "When can I go home?" she finally asked.

"Given no complications, we'll see about kicking you out of here tomorrow afternoon," he replied.

"That would be great." She was already longing to be in her own home and on her sofa.

"I'll check in with you tomorrow and we'll see where we're at."

After the doctor left, Callie found herself napping off and on. All she really wanted now was to see Mac. Did he not intend to check in on her? That thought caused a pain to shoot through her that had nothing to do with a splenectomy.

Dana checked in on her several times and some of the deputies stopped by to see her. And then dinner was served. The evening meal consisted of a thick slice of meatloaf and mashed potatoes all smothered in a dark gravy. There was also corn, a roll and a bowl of mixed fruit.

As she ate, night slowly descended outside the window. When she was finished eating and her tray was taken away, she leaned back against her pillow and turned on the television. Even though she had nothing in particular she wanted to watch, she just needed something to take her mind of Mac.

The night before she'd truly believed she was going to die and she'd mourned over the fact that she thought she'd never see him again. She'd truly believed he had deep feelings for her, so why hadn't he come to check in on her?

Then he was here, standing in the doorway of her room as if she'd conjured him there by sheer thought alone. "Mac," she said softly. She quickly muted the television.

"Hi, Callie." He came into her room and sat in the

chair closest to her bed. "I checked in with the doctor several times during the day and he told me you were doing well."

So he did care. He had checked in on her. Her heart lifted and filled her with warmth. "I'm doing okay and I'm hoping to go home tomorrow." She searched his features and saw the lines of exhaustion that radiated out from his eyes. "How are you doing?"

"Better now that I know you're okay and Nathan is in jail. We've spent the day processing his lair. Oh, I brought you something." He reached into his back pocket and withdrew her pink wallet and her key ring.

He set them on the table between them. "Unfortunately, your purse and coat are now in evidence, but I got your wallet and keys because I know what a pain it is to have to get back identification and credit cards and your car and home keys."

"Thank you, that was very thoughtful of you." She wanted him to touch her…to reach out and hold her hand or kiss her forehead. But she could feel a distance from him.

"At some point I need to get a statement from you," he said. "I know you'll need a ride home from the hospital when you're released. How about if I pick you up and take you home and I'll get an official statement then."

"That sounds good," she agreed. She had suffered one of the most traumatic nights of her life and she'd hoped Mac would swoop in today and proclaim his undying love for her. But it was obvious that wasn't going to happen.

He told her about the events of the night before, of finding the old article in the newspaper that had led them to Nathan's house. He explained how they'd confronted Nathan and he'd run. Thankfully they were able to get him under arrest but tragically not before he'd murdered four young women.

They spoke for a few more minutes, the conversation rather stiff and awkward and he finally stood. "I need to get back to the office. I've got tons of paperwork waiting for me there."

"Mac, don't work too late. You have to be exhausted. With Nathan behind bars you can take a moment to breathe." Despite her own physical condition, she worried about him.

He smiled at her, the first real smile since he'd walked into her room. "Thanks, Callie. Call me tomorrow and let me know if you're going to be released and when."

"I will." He started to walk out. "Mac," she said, stopping him in his tracks. He turned around to look at her. There were so many things she wanted to tell him. About loving him...about wanting to spend her life with him... "Never mind," she finally said. "I'll talk to you tomorrow."

A look of relief crossed his handsome features and then with a nod, he was gone.

She pulled her sheet and the thin blanket up closer around her, suddenly cold with the absence of Mac in the room. Nobody would ever make her believe that Mac didn't love her. Even though he'd been distant with her just now, there had been moments when she'd seen that love shining from his eyes.

She had no idea where she stood as a deputy right now, but more importantly she didn't know if Mac was going to open himself up to accepting her love for him and acknowledging his love for her.

Her hope had been to get the killer behind bars by Christmastime and they'd managed to do that. Now her biggest hope was that Mac would tell her how much he loved her and he'd come home to her house for Christmas.

Chapter Fifteen

Callie sat on the edge of the bed waiting for Mac to arrive to take her home. It was just after noon and the doctor had already released her. She plucked at the hospital gown decorated in tiny little blue flowers.

Her clothes had been cut off her the night before, leaving her no choice but to wear the gown home. She also had no coat and no shoes to wear home. Still, she was grateful to leave the hospital behind even though she was still in a fair amount of pain.

Right now, she was just anxious to see Mac again and find out what his mood was with her today. She desperately hoped he was the Mac with soft gray, unguarded eyes and that sexy grin that always tugged at her heart.

"Look who I found coming down the hallway," Dana said as she came into Callie's room pushing a wheelchair in front of her.

Mac followed behind her, a brown blanket thrown over his shoulder. "Are you ready to get out of here?" he asked Callie.

"Definitely. Is that really necessary?" she asked and pointed to the wheelchair.

"Absolutely," Dana replied. "All our surgery patients

get the excitement of riding in our chariot to the exit door. Come on, girlfriend. Have a seat."

Once Callie was in the wheelchair, Dana handed her one of her flower arrangements to carry and Mac draped the blanket around her shoulders. "You're going to need this to go outside in the cold," he said.

As he pulled it closer around her, she caught the familiar scent of him in it and she wanted to keep it wrapped around her forever. "Mac, if you don't mind, could you grab the other flower arrangements while I push her out?"

"No problem," he agreed.

Once they reached the hospital exit door, Mac told Dana and Callie to sit tight while he stowed all the flowers in the back seat of his car. He then left the passenger door of his car open and came back inside.

"Dana, thank you for taking good care of her," Mac said and then leaned down and scooped Callie out of her chair and into his arms. She immediately wrapped her arms around his neck.

Despite her pain and the cold as he stepped out of the door, a rivulet of warmth swept through her. His scent surrounded her and she had to fight the impulse to lean into him.

He lifted her into the car seat and then released her. She pulled the blanket more closely around her as he walked around the car and got into the driver's seat.

"How are you feeling this morning?" he asked once he'd pulled away from the hospital.

"I still have a little pain, both in my wrists and ankles and in my stomach."

"I wanted to kill him," Mac replied and she saw his

fingers tighten on his steering wheel. "I so wanted to smash his face in."

"I would have loved to slap him a couple of times myself." She released a deep sigh. "But it's all over now. I survived and you got the killer and the town is safe again."

He shot her that sexy half grin that always half melted her heart. "There's that optimism."

She grinned back at him. "I foresee great days ahead. All I have to do is heal for a little while." She gazed at him for a moment longer. "Will I still have my job when I get better?"

"Of course you will," he replied immediately.

"Uh…which job? Will I be back on the receptionist desk or will I come back as a deputy? I mean, I know I fell for the oldest ruse in the world with Nathan, and that ended up with me being his latest victim, but up until that time I thought I was a good deputy."

"You were a great deputy and I'd love to have you back in that position again. You more than proved yourself and when you're back on your feet, I look forward to swearing you in." He flashed her a quick smile.

"Thank you, Mac. I can't tell you what this means to me," she replied, even though she was hoping for far more from him.

When they got to her house, he asked for her house key and then once again scooped her into his arms. He carried her into the house and gently set her down on the sofa.

"I'll be right back," he said. It took him two trips to get all the flowers in and on her kitchen table. The last thing he did was plug in the lights on her Christmas tree and then he returned to where she'd stretched out on the sofa and sat in the chair facing her.

He pulled out his notebook and set his phone on the coffee table. "Callie, I hate for you to have to re-visit everything that has happened to you, but I need to get an official statement from you. Can you do that for me now?"

"I can."

"Do you mind if I record you?"

"Of course not." She watched as he opened the ap-propriate app on his phone and then her statement began. She started from the time she'd stepped out of her house to go to work and then seeing Nathan seated on the curb.

She had managed to keep all thoughts of Nathan and what she'd endured at his hands out of her mind. But as she went through things with Mac a wealth of emotion began to rise up inside her.

The abject fear she'd endured, the terror of her own impending death and the grief of never seeing Mac again, all of it rose to the surface. When she'd finished telling him everything that had happened, to her hor-ror, she began to weep.

"Ah, Callie, don't cry," he said softly. "Crying is only going to make you hurt more."

"I...ca-can't help it," she said with choked sobs.

She buried her face in her hands as the emotional pain of what she'd been through met the physical pain of her very recent operation. She hurt both inside and out and at the moment she couldn't control her tears.

Then he was on the sofa next to her and pulling her into his arms. She wrapped her arms around him and buried her face in the crook of his neck. He stroked up and down her back and whispered soothing words that slowly began to calm her down. Even after her tears stopped, she remained with her face pressed into the hollow of his throat.

His familiar scent smelled like safety...like love. Her love for him welled up inside her, filling all the spaces in her heart and sweeping away the fear that thoughts of Nathan had created.

"I love you, Mac, I love you so much and if you look deep in your heart, I believe you love me, too." The words tumbled from her, words she hadn't planned on saying in this moment, but she had been unable to keep inside.

He immediately not only sat back from her, but also he stood and moved to the chair once again. "Callie, I told you from the very beginning that I was emotionally unavailable for a relationship." He didn't look at her but rather gazed at some point just over her head.

"Mac, look into my eyes and tell me you aren't in love with me," she said. She wanted this...him...so badly. She wanted a future with Mac. She wanted to have his babies and grow a family with him.

His gaze finally met hers and in the soft gray depths, she believed she saw love. "I am in love with you, Callie," he finally confessed, causing her heart to soar once again. "But that doesn't change anything."

"Why?" she asked in confusion.

He frowned, and raised a hand to knead the back of his neck. His hand dropped back to his side and he released a deep sigh. "When I told you about Amanda leaving me on Christmas Eve, I left out some things."

He got up from his chair, as if unable to sit still as he spoke about his past. "I knew Amanda and I had issues. She hated my job and she wanted a bigger social life than what we had." He began to pace back and forth in front of her sofa. "Two weeks before Christmas Eve, she told me she was pregnant."

Callie looked at him in surprise. Did he have a child with Amanda? Was he afraid Callie wouldn't accept a child of his with another woman? She wouldn't care if he had a dozen kids. She would love them all because they were a part of him.

"When she told me she was pregnant, we promised each other we'd do whatever it took to have a good marriage," he continued. "I cut back on my hours at work and we started going out more."

He paused and drew several deep breaths. "And then came Christmas Eve, when she told me she was leaving me because I wasn't good enough for her, because I bored her and would never be man enough for her. But the real killing blow was she told me she'd had an abortion because I wasn't good enough to be a father to her baby."

His voice broke, letting Callie know just how emotional he was as he told her about this horrid piece of his story. "Oh Mac," she said softly.

He looked at her, his eyes the turbulent gray of storms. "She killed my baby, Callie. She preferred to kill the baby than have me be the father. Doesn't that tell you anything?"

"Yes, it tells me your ex-wife was a selfish, hateful woman and you should be glad to be free of her," Callie replied as she got up from the sofa.

"Well, it tells me that I'm not good enough, I'm not interesting enough to be in a long-term relationship, and in any case I don't ever want to be in a position for a woman to hurt me like that again." He shoved his hands in his pockets as she approached where he stood.

"Oh Mac, she obviously didn't love you the way I love you. I find you fascinating and I know you're a good man…a man who is good enough to be loved." She stood so close to him she could see his individual dark eyelashes, she could almost feel his heartbeat against her own.

"I want you to love me, Mac. I want to marry you and have your babies. I want you to move in here and call this your home. Oh Mac, if you love me even one-tenth as much as I love you, we'll have a happily-ever-after kind of relationship. All you have to do is fully open up your heart." She leaned into him, needing…desperately wanting…him to wrap her in his arms.

Instead, he took a step back from her. Once again his gaze shot just over her head. "I'm sorry, Callie."

"So, you're going to allow a woman's actions from three years ago to stop you from enjoying Christmas… to stop you from ever having a loving relationship again." Emotion clawed up inside her.

He took another step away from her and her heart plummeted to the floor. "Let me know when you're ready to come back to work," he said.

She stared at him. "So, the only difference between you and Nathan is you aren't a killer. But the two of you are just alike in hanging on to a past trauma and not moving past it. I love you, Mac…but I feel sorry for you."

"I'm sorry, Callie," he repeated and then he turned and walked out the front door.

Tears burned at her eyes, tears that began to chase each other down her cheeks. She went back to the sofa and collapsed as deep sobs began to escape her.

She wept for what might have been. She'd truly hoped that by Christmastime, Mac would be home... here with her and ready to build a future together. That's what she'd wanted from Santa, the gift of being together with Mac.

She'd wanted him to hold her while the lights twinkled on the tree and holiday music played. She'd wanted to feed him a Christmas feast over which they could talk about their future plans. She'd wanted to make love to him at night and for him to be the first thing she saw in the mornings.

Now those dreams lay shattered at her feet. However, one of her dreams had come true. She would return to work as a deputy. But that success felt hollow compared to what she had lost.

She didn't know how long she cried. She finally got up and took one of her pain pills, knowing it would help take away some of her physical pain, but there was nothing she could take, nothing she could do to take away the emotional pain of Mac walking away from her love.

CALLIE SLID THE stuffed turkey into the oven and then closed the door. It was the day before Christmas and she'd decided to do all the cooking for her holiday dinner today for the meal tomorrow.

The house already smelled of cinnamon and apples from the pie she'd baked earlier. She still wanted to make sweet potatoes with brown sugar and cinnamon. On the menu was also a corn casserole with cream cheese, mashed potatoes and gravy, and a cranberry salad.

She'd used her mother's recipes and thoughts of her family flitted through her mind. Physically, she'd felt a little better with each day that had passed. Emotionally she still ached and thoughts of Mac continued to make her cry.

With the cooking all under control, she decided to take a break. She made herself a cup of coffee and then sat at the kitchen table. She stared out the nearby window where the sky was a dark gray that reminded her of Mac's eyes. The forecast was for snow so it was definitely going to be a white Christmas.

Under different circumstances she would have considered it a near-perfect Christmas. There would be snow and good food on the table. She'd survived a serial killer and landed the job she'd wanted to have.

But for it to be perfect Mac would need to be here with her, celebrating their love. She heaved a deep sigh as it began to snow. Mac had called once to see how she was doing and the brief conversation had been incredibly awkward.

Hopefully by the time she returned to work the awkwardness would be gone. He'd be her boss and nothing more. She had about five weeks to stop loving him, but she didn't even know how to begin to do that.

It continued to snow off and on all afternoon. By six o'clock the kitchen had been cleaned, the food was all put away and she had changed into a pair of red pajamas with little snowflakes.

She fixed a fire in the fireplace, made herself a cup of hot chocolate and then stretched out on the sofa to enjoy the sight of her Christmas lights filling the room and the holiday music playing overhead.

The last time she had looked there was about four inches of snow on the ground. Tonight, children everywhere would be waiting for Santa to fly with his magical reindeers to their homes.

Once again tears filled her eyes. She knew she had to get over Mac, but she'd never loved anyone like she did him. She missed him. She missed seeing his handsome face and talking to him about anything and nothing. She missed the sound of his deep laughter and…she could go on and on about the many ways she felt his absence.

The evening slowly wound down. She finished her hot chocolate and thought about going up to bed, but before she could put action to thought, her doorbell rang.

Who would be on her doorstep at this time on a snowy night? Her heart beat an accelerated rhythm as she got up from the sofa. She opened the door to see Mac standing on her doorstep.

Her breath caught in her throat at the same time she steeled herself. He could be here for any number of reasons and she wasn't about to get her hopes up only to have them dashed again.

"Mac," she said as she opened the door to allow him entry.

"Hi, Callie. Do you mind?" He shrugged out of his coat and placed it on the back of the sofa.

"What's up?" she asked as she returned to her spot on the sofa and he sank down on the chair facing her.

Just looking at him broke her heart all over again. "How are you feeling?" he asked.

"Better with each day that passes." She couldn't read him. Surely he hadn't stopped by on a snowy night just to check how she was doing, but there was nothing on his features that gave her a clue as to why he was really here.

"That's good to hear," he replied.

An awkward silence descended. "Mac, it's Christmas Eve and it's snowing like crazy outside," she finally said. "Why are you here?"

He released a deep sigh and looked down at the floor. "I…uh…was wondering if you still feel the same about me."

"You mean am I still in love with you? Oh, Mac, my love for you isn't shallow enough to change in a few days. I'm probably going to love you for the rest of my life."

"I've done a lot of thinking in the last couple of days. I've been so scared about loving you, about believing that we really could have a happy future together." He finally looked up at her, his eyes the soft gray of a dove's wings. "I was so afraid I would never be enough to make you happy, Callie. But what I've realized over these past few days is that my love for you is bigger than my fear."

Hope exploded inside her. Still she remained on the sofa, afraid to fully embrace her hope.

He stood from the chair and approached where she sat. "Callie, I've been such a fool. I'm so in love with you and I can't imagine my future without you in it. I need my Christmas elf. I need the woman who makes me think, who makes me laugh and makes me believe that we can have a forever love."

"MAC." SHE FINALLY stood and he pulled her right into his arms. When he kissed her, the kiss spoke of passion and dreams and a future filled with love.

Callie's heart expanded as she realized finally her holiday was complete. A serial killer was behind bars. The lights were twinkling on her tree, snow was falling outside her window and her man had really, truly come home for Christmas.

* * * * *

UNCOVERING COLTON'S FAMILY SECRET

LINDA O. JOHNSTON

Of course, again and as always, this story is dedicated to my dear husband, Fred. I also once more want to thank all the other authors in this enjoyable series, as well as Carly Silver, our wonderful editor for the Colton books.

Chapter One

Now what do I do? thought Madison Colton. He just went inside—I'll stay out here. She stood on the sidewalk in the downtown shopping district of Kendall, Michigan, ignoring the small but flowing crowd around her—not far from where she had been this time last week.

But for a very different reason.

At the moment, she watched the door to a coffee shop, waiting for that man to come out. The person she had come to Kendall to see. And observe closely. Just in case her imagination had a sliver of reality to it.

She had been lucky. She'd seen him already today, not long after her arrival, near where she had seen him before. That was on the next block, across the street, and he had come out of the bookstore there.

She had followed him. Unobtrusively, of course. His goal appeared to have been a chain drugstore a few blocks away. He was only inside for a few minutes and came out holding a bag, then headed back in this direction. He'd stopped in a couple of other shops on the way, and she'd waited for him each time.

At least she wasn't attempting to find a wedding gown here in Kendall right now. That was why she had come last week.

Now, he was in this café. The idea of caffeine sounded good to Madison, but she didn't want to mess things up by getting too close. Not yet.

She wanted to watch him awhile before...what? Confronting him? Not likely. She couldn't exactly walk up to a stranger and challenge him just because he reminded her of her father who'd been dead for twenty-five years. But hopefully she would decide soon what to do.

She knew she appeared very different this week. Which might not be necessary—or it might be very necessary. A kindergarten teacher among a family of mostly law enforcement, she was the last person who'd be expected to be doing this. She certainly hadn't expected it herself.

Yet here she was. Not that she was likely to need to look different, but she felt comfortable in her kind-of disguise—large black sunglasses and a big sun hat, over her charcoal sweatshirt and black jeans, along with similarly dark-colored athletic shoes—not the kind of outfit she wore most days. Not as a teacher in her hometown of Grave Gulch, about a two-hour drive from here. But today was Saturday—and last Saturday was when she had been here before, to visit the bridal shop on the other side of the street and about a block down.

Then, she had been dressed up, wearing a lacy blouse and flowing skirt, because it had felt appropriate for her goal here.

That had been Madison's intention when she had made her appointment there. Before seeing that picture of the dress in *Lake Country Brides* magazine, she had begun wondering if failure to find the right dress had meant something. Something she hadn't wanted to think about. But this dress? She had fallen for it immediately.

To prepare for her upcoming wedding to dear Alec, a teacher at the same elementary school.

That had been then.

And now? Well… She'd been thinking about the gown and more. Hard. Especially after her serious conversation in the car on the way home with her cousin and dear friend Grace Colton. The conversation that had made her question… Never mind. The questions had already been there about Alec, though she hadn't wanted to think about them. And she also didn't want to think about them now.

But what had happened then, what—who—she'd thought she had seen, had caused her to skip the appointment, without explaining it to Grace, who'd assumed it was because Madison didn't really want to marry Alec—which, she'd realized, was actually true. Oh, as they'd walked along, Madison had made herself laugh as she mentioned to Grace that her imagination was in overdrive, that she thought she'd seen someone resembling her long-dead father, then went on to talk about what she was seeing in store windows or otherwise, not indicating she was fixating on that illusion in her mind. And the sudden pain it had caused.

She didn't want Grace to think she was delusional. Was she? Well, she hoped to find out. She hadn't bought the dress then, and that wasn't the reason she was here now. But now she'd returned in this probably unnecessary disguise.

Around her, people continued to walk by, so she backed up toward the curb to get out of the way. To her left were two parents with kids at their sides, and the younger child, a little girl, appeared kindergarten age. She pulled at her mom's arm for attention, and her mother laughed and shook her head. Madison figured she knew what it would be like to teach that insistent child.

Madison always suspected that she'd chosen to teach young kids as a result of wishing her own family had been different when she was younger—like, that it had included her father.

When she looked away, a young couple slowed in front of her as they held hands and stared into each other's eyes. "We're almost there," said the girl, a pretty blonde with flowing hair. "You can't come inside with me, you know. It's bad luck. But I'll see you later. For now—let's hurry to the shop so I won't be late."

"Of course," said the guy, smiling at her, twentyish, somewhat handsome, with short but shaggy facial hair.

Madison couldn't help smiling herself. Wryly. She suspected this couple was heading for that bridal boutique, and she wished them well. But her own regrets started pouring through her once more as she stared at the door of the coffee shop.

Ever since last Saturday, she had been thinking a lot about why she'd not chased down the man, chastising herself about it while refusing to ignore the highly unlikely possibility of what she'd thought she'd seen. *Who* she'd thought she'd seen.

Was it possible? No way. And yet…she had to be certain.

She'd had to find the person who had triggered this absurd obsession, see him again, so she could wipe it permanently out of her mind. Not that thoughts of her growing up without a father around would ever completely stop eating her alive inside.

But even though she had spotted that man again here

in Kendall, she'd put off doing what she needed to: talking to him.

Maybe this was all wrong. She considered pulling her phone from her purse and looking at the picture she'd taken last week—very surreptitiously. She had pretended to talk to someone on her phone but had instead snapped a photo.

One she had looked at often since then. Studied. Analyzed.

And still not been certain.

Well, how could she be, without talking to that man? Asking him questions?

Today, that changed.

But so far…well, she had to continue her observation first. It all seemed so potentially surreal…

Even though she had come all this way, and she'd actually seen that person again, she'd told herself more than once to forget it. Forget who she thought he looked like. Forget her absurd impulse to check it out like this, in disguise, and just go home.

After all, just standing here, ignoring people's glances, watching that door… It now felt weird. She was thinking way too much. She needed to take hold of herself, her emotions, go home and get back to her normal life.

What she'd imagined had to be impossible. Just a result of her own ridiculous thoughts.

Her father was dead, after all. He had been for years. The man she'd followed could not possibly have been him. His resemblance to her brother was totally a figment of her imagination—despite that photo she'd taken, and studied…and not dared to show to her mother.

But… Well, for now, she'd wait till she saw him leave the coffee shop and follow him one more time—even knowing this was all a farce, a way she'd allowed herself to avoid the real issue in her life.

Her urge to end her engagement to Alec.

Thanks, Grace, she thought, recalling their conversation last week. She found herself twisting the engagement ring on her finger now and made herself stop. Again. Her stomach churned the way it did when she'd talked with Grace—and her cousin reminded her that happened a lot when she tried to visit bridal salons. But while Grace had focused on her assumption about getting cold feet, the question Madison attempted not to deal with was *Did she really want to get married?*

Okay, maybe she wasn't madly in love with Alec. But there was no one else, she was getting older, and he checked the boxes for a perfectly nice life with a husband and children.

And yet...

The chill air penetrated her thoughts, and she tucked her hands into her pockets. There wasn't a lot of traffic, yet she smelled a bit of car exhaust.

Near her, a couple of young boys dashed away from their parents, yelling and pushing each other. Madison reeled in her urge to catch up and gently scold them. She wasn't in her classroom now.

Instead, she turned slightly and watched as the minimal traffic passed both directions. Main Street, of course.

But this was getting ridiculous. He might stay in there all day. People kept sending her curious glances, and no wonder.

Maybe that was the place to start chatting with him, after all.

But when she tried to rev herself up to go into the

coffee shop, its door opened. There he was! He had a medium-sized cup of coffee in one hand and the bag he had gotten before in the other.

She maneuvered in the small crowd and began following him again. Fortunately, he walked at a relatively slow pace, and she did the same, trailing him only slightly, on his right side.

He wore a red plaid woolen shirt over jeans. His outfit last week had been somewhat similar, loose and casual.

But it wasn't his clothes that had drawn Madison's attention. It had been his height, his somewhat familiarly muscular build. And, mostly, his face.

She wished she could just stop him, stare at that face, assess it thoroughly. It still appeared as she'd thought last week: intense eyes beneath shaggy black brows. Blue? Yes. She could tell from the picture she'd taken, though she wasn't close enough to see those eyes now. But he did have a high forehead. Dark lashes. Lips that were rather narrow. Pale skin. A somewhat-pointed chin. Ears that hugged his head. His hair was rather light but she saw dark roots in her photo, as if it had been dyed. And...

Okay. Analyzing all his features wouldn't do her any more good today than it had before. The thing that was important was that this guy looked like her brother, Bryce Colton. A lot like him—if Bryce was maybe twenty-five years older. There were some lines and wrinkles in his face.

But heck! To her, he appeared like her brother's doppelgänger despite the difference in age and hair and eye colors.

Was she imagining it? That was what she had come back here to find out. And now, here he was again, not far from her.

What was she going to do about it?

She had an urge to sidle up to him. To talk to him. To ask him a slew of questions.

But not here. Not at this moment.

Next store he went into, though, she'd do it. She hoped he would return to the bookstore. That block, at least, was around the store where she had first seen him today. Did he work there?

She decided to let him get a little ahead and follow him. See if the bookstore was his goal this time. If not—well, wherever he went into, she'd go talk to him there.

She just hoped he didn't get into a car and drive away. No, despite her procrastination out of fear, or whatever, she wanted to talk to him. Needed to talk to him.

And why did she care?

Because he looked so much like Bryce, even with the different hair and eyes…perhaps most importantly, he also looked like the pictures of her long-dead father, Richard Foster, that their mother had kept all these years.

Of course. Richard Foster, who'd had no similarly aged brothers or cousins who might resemble him, had been the love of her mother's life, even though the childhood sweethearts had never married. He'd been a soldier then and frequently shipped out. But he had spent time with Madison's mother when he was home on leave, and he had managed to father Verity's three children: Madison, Bryce and their sister, Jillian.

Their parents had planned to marry when he finally was sent home…but that never happened. He had been killed in action. Their mother had always teared up telling that story, and no wonder. Her description of their dad indicated he had been a wonderful, caring, good-looking man who was eager for his last tour of duty to finally end.

But he had never come home. He had died overseas. *Allegedly.* Was it possible this man actually *was* their father?

He couldn't be. She knew that. Official notice of his death had been provided by the military, and his remains had been sent home to his parents. And yet…

On a lit pedestrian signal, the man crossed Maple Street, at the intersection, to the next block of shops directly across from the bridal boutique. Madison went that way, too. He then appeared to prepare to cross Main Street at the same intersection, but instead, he pivoted and headed into the nearest outlet, a liquor store. Madison went in, too, following him.

What kind of alcohol did he like, this man who so looked like Bryce? Madison knew that Bryce was a beer fancier. And it seemed highly appropriate that this man also headed to the area where crates of beer bottles were stacked.

But he didn't buy any. Maybe he'd changed his mind, or who knew why he'd come in here? But he had a short call on his cell phone. Then, after talking briefly to a clerk who'd asked to help him, he was soon back out on the sidewalk.

With Madison behind him. Without trying to talk to him. Yet.

Where was he going? Should she stop him, after all? But she hoped that watching where he went would help her find him again in the future. That took precedence.

He headed into the small pharmacy next door. Madison did, too, watching him out of the corner of her eye as she fiddled with her purse so anyone watching might think she was looking for a prescription or a list of things to buy.

He didn't stay in there long, either. In fact, his arm nearly brushed hers as he left. He didn't seem to notice her, which was a good thing. But she certainly noticed him.

There were still quite a few people on the sidewalk when they returned outside, but the guy eased himself into the crowd so Madison had to as well. Then, after glancing toward another store, he turned and headed toward the street, but not the signals at the intersection.

There weren't any cars going by just then. Instead of returning to the corner and waiting, the man started jaywalking, right in the middle of the block, as if heading toward the bridal boutique.

Madison realized she might appear too obvious if she followed him that way. But she felt she had no choice. Not if she wanted to be certain of knowing where he went. She wasn't sure what she'd say if the man asked why she'd followed—but she did so anyway, taking a step down at the curb and walking across the smooth paved street.

He walked briskly, and so did she. A light changed, and cars began moving in their direction, worrying Madison, but she fortunately reached the next curb and stepped up, breathing a sigh of relief as she looked around and saw the man continue in the direction of the boutique. She prepared to follow again.

And then—

"Ow!" she exclaimed and pivoted to look at whoever had grabbed her arm.

"You're under arrest," a voice growled at her. She turned to see a man flashing a US Marshals badge.

She stared at it for a moment to memorize his name on the ribbon it was attached to: Marshal Oren Margulies. Then she looked up at him. He was tall, wearing a gray sports coat over slacks. Dark, windblown hair matched his facial hair that formed a mustache and slight beard. He glared at her with deep blue eyes, his lips puckered in apparent anger.

Glaring at her? Angry with her? Why the hell did this guy feel anything at all toward her—and why was he trying to arrest her?

This was one of the few times in her life that she greatly regretted not having any of her law-enforcement family nearby.

"Why are you arresting me?" she demanded in a hiss. "What's the charge?"

"Jaywalking," he responded curtly. He handcuffed her, her arms in front. *Handcuffs?* Then, his hand on one arm, he led her back down the street toward the intersection.

She wanted to scream, but she was in such shock she couldn't even speak as they passed the few shoppers on this part of the sidewalk. Parked at the end was a navy SUV with the US Marshals logo on it.

That made Madison feel slightly better. He apparently wasn't just kidnapping her off the street. Right? But still—what was happening? And the man who resembled Richard Foster had now disappeared. Could she ever find him again?

As the marshal opened a back door and manipulated her inside, cuffing her to a seatbelt buckle, she got her voice back.

"Why the hell would a marshal arrest an American

citizen for jaywalking?" she demanded, knowing she sounded as furious as she felt.

How could she make this marshal let her go? And how would she locate the man she'd been following once she was free?

OKAY, SO THIS woman was clearly angry. Oren understood why. He'd caught and arrested her, though not exactly for what he'd told her.

But he wanted some answers himself.

Outside the back of the SUV now, he whipped around and stared back inside the open door, watching her squirm on the seat with her cuffed hands to one side. He'd noticed as he cuffed her that she wore a ring on her left hand.

"Why were you following that man for the last couple hours?" he demanded. "Were you stalking him?"

"What?" Her voice squeaked. Odd, but Oren found her surprisingly attractive, even with that strange outfit she wore, complete with large dark sunglasses beneath an oversize hat. But her face beneath it was smooth and pretty, what he could see of it. He wondered what color her eyes were. And her hair... Some waves of red spilled out from her hat. "I...uh, I was... How would you even know I was around here for a couple of hours?"

"The man you were following told me. He works near here, saw you walking around for a while, then said you definitely started following him. A woman in disguise. Right? *Were* you following him?"

"I... I was doing some shopping, and... I was looking—"

"You were looking. For hours? That's what I was told. When I got his call, I had to drop everything to investigate. So I was looking, too. And saw you, watched you for a while."

"But...why?" Her head shook, as if she was puzzled.

He was getting nowhere. Enough of this. He had to do his job: protect Wes Windham at all costs. Oren needed more information. He stepped back into the SUV and grabbed her compact black purse.

"What are you doing?" she demanded. "Give me back my property."

"After I check your ID," Oren said. He'd have to call the information in to headquarters, to have them run her name.

"It's none of your business who I am," she spat. "This is all a farce. Let me go now."

But he removed her wallet and looked at her driver's license. Her name was Madison Colton.

Colton? "Why is the name Colton familiar?" Oren said softly, thinking aloud.

Colton. He definitely needed more information, both about her and about what she had been up to.

Oh. Right. Colton. Dread settled in the pit of Oren's stomach as he recalled how he knew the name. The witness he was protecting had had some connection to the large Colton family. And the fact this woman was one of them—well, it could mean danger to his subject, if this meant he'd actually been found. Others could wind up at risk, too.

In any case, this was the kind of situation he'd become a marshal to deal with: witness protection in any kind of circumstance, no matter how unusual, no matter how odd.

Sure, he'd handled plenty of other situations since he became a marshal, although none with a potential suspect as beautiful—and apparently determined—as this one. Most had been closer to his headquarters in Grand Rapids. Coming to Kendall like this? Well, he would go wherever he was needed. But would this set of circumstances have a happy ending—with the man under his protection remaining safe?

That would depend on why this woman was following him and what Oren could do about it.

This gorgeous, clearly opinionated woman.

Well, Oren might even enjoy himself as he questioned her further. But one way or another, he would continue to do his job, and do it well.

And keep his witness safe.

Chapter Two

This was unbelievable. Madison just sat there, itching to somehow ditch these handcuffs. Itching to run away. Under arrest for jaywalking? By a US Marshal? Why here? Could the Kendall Police Department help her?

Maybe she should call Bryce. He was an FBI agent, after all.

This marshal apparently recognized the name Colton. That, at least, wasn't a big surprise, since most of the family was in law enforcement.

But could there be any other reason the Colton name was familiar to him?

She could ask, but—

Well, maybe she was thinking too much, even now, and probably not clearly enough. Talking about this situation might be a lot better, more productive. Apparently, jaywalking or not, her arrest was somehow involved with her following that man who'd called the US Marshals Service for help. Maybe she could just give this marshal an explanation—modified or not—as to why she might have appeared to be following him. But how would she phrase what seemed to be impossible?

The whole thing made no sense. Jaywalking? Not stalking? Sure, this marshal might have assumed she was following that man, since that was what he asked, so why arrest her instead on a different charge?

She'd figure out what to say as she spoke.

She tried to fake a smile toward the marshal who remained outside, regarding her from just beyond the SUV's open door. Her purse was now on the floor. He'd put her wallet on top; possibly he could grab it again, or so it appeared. In case she tried to run away? Or to keep her identification close to him?

"The thing is…" she said. "Well, what I was doing might have looked a little strange, wandering these streets for a while like I did. I live in Grave Gulch. I'm sure you saw that on my license. I came here last Saturday because I wanted to go into the bridal boutique—" she pointed to the shop near where the car was parked "—because…because there was a dress there I wanted to try on. I'm engaged, you see."

She watched his face. It was a good-looking face crowned by wavy dark hair, enhanced by trimmed facial hair, but she shouldn't notice such things. He probably didn't give a damn, but… Well, there actually was a change in his expression. It had been somewhat neutral as she'd complained and yelled at him and all, but now he looked…a little angry.

Because she was engaged? Because she was talking?

Still, she continued. "The thing is, I'm kind of second-guessing getting married, thinking about what it would be like to spend the rest of my life with my…fiancé. We're both educators. I teach kindergarten. We see each other a lot at school, but I'm still deciding if more is a good idea."

She elaborated because she'd seen another change in this Oren's expression. But why was she blathering that way about her engagement? She needed to approach her explanation about why she was following that man another way.

"So you're around kids all the time," he cut in.

"That's right." Did he have any kids? Was he married? She couldn't see his hands from here, but she hadn't noticed a wedding ring—which didn't necessarily mean anything, anyway.

Why had he asked about kids? He was off on a tangent like she was. But did she give a damn?

"Interesting," he said, not sounding particularly interested at all. "But I'd rather hear about why you were following that man."

"Maybe," she said. "But…okay. It's ridiculous, I know, but let me tell you why I came back here this week." She inhaled but kept on talking. "I'm not a cop or otherwise in law enforcement. Even so, I tend to be observant. Kindergarten teachers have to be, after all, to keep an eye on the kids. So last week when I was here and outside that bridal shop—well, as I said, it's ridiculous—but I happened to see a man who looks like my younger brother, Bryce."

She was telling the truth, although she knew it probably sounded absurd.

But, looking down at her cuffed wrists, she continued, "The thing is, the man I saw looked like Bryce thirty years or so older, or how I'd imagine he'll look. Also like some photos our mother has of our father, but also thirty years or so older than those pictures. He was killed overseas in combat years ago. And, well, it's impossible of course, but I wanted to try to find that man again. Look at him. And, if my opinion didn't change, talk to him, so I could get over this idea and get on with my life and not think about it again." Maybe. Unless she wasn't delusional, after all. "I saw him go into the bookstore then, and he went into it earlier today, too. Maybe he reads a lot. But—well, after all this time, no matter what or who I saw, Richard Foster can't possibly be alive."

Madison suddenly stopped talking as she saw Marshal Margulies's expression shift. He'd looked annoyed and dubious before but to—well, she didn't exactly know what it was now, as soon as she had said her father's name.

She couldn't help it. "Okay," she said, "what's going on? Do you know that name?"

He didn't reply. Upset, she forced herself to stand as much as possible in the rear seat of this SUV. Enough of this. She had an urge to jump down, slam herself into this Oren and run away.

To get out of this terrible situation.

Right. With handcuffs on.

But she needed answers, this marshal's cooperation, his release of her. Something. She was scared of this man having control over her the way he did.

Still nothing. Although, instead of looking straight at his good-looking face that irritated her, she found herself glancing over his shoulder. Toward the boutique and the used bookstore beyond.

And there was that man again. Amazing! Or not. He exited the bookstore with a bag in his hand and handed it to one of the people on the sidewalk. Then he ducked back inside.

"He's right there," she breathed. "Beyond part of the crowd on the sidewalk and going in and out of the bookstore—again. He's the man who called you? Please tell me why, what you know about him. And please, let me go talk to him!"

OKAY, WHAT NOW? Oren didn't turn to look in the direction Madison faced. He knew where she meant. And she might well have seen the current subject of his witness-protection services.

Wes Windham. The man had been Richard Foster, before.

Oren needed to stop this all, right now, before it became any more complicated. Any more dangerous to Wes—or himself.

And so, he would appeal to her better judgment—and offer her a deal. If she promised to leave right away, not mention any of this to anyone, he would let her go.

He closed the back door of his SUV, then went around to the other side and got in. He gestured for her to settle back into her seat, and he sat beside her. She immediately leaned toward him, eyes wide, brows raised as if she was filled with hope about what he'd say.

She even thrust her handcuffed hands slightly toward him, resting them on her knees, as if reminding him what she wanted: to be released.

Well, it wouldn't—couldn't—be that easy.

"Look, Ms. Colton," he finally said.

"Madison," she corrected with an eager smile, as if trying to become his friend and thereby get him to do as she'd asked.

"Madison…" he echoed, a lot more gruffly. He considered telling her to call him Oren—but Marshal would be more appropriate, if she called him anything at all. "You're right that there's more going on here than you breaking the law against jaywalking."

The happy, expectant expression on her face melted a bit into annoyance. "So tell me what's going on," she said.

"That's the thing. I can't—or at least probably not

enough to satisfy your curiosity. But you should understand this if you talk at all to your relatives in law enforcement about what they do. If I describe all I know about that man, as you asked and, furthermore, let you go talk to him—well, I'd be risking not only his life but yours, too."

"But why? How?"

She wasn't giving up. And she was pushing him for answers he'd already hinted he couldn't provide her.

"Never mind. But it's true. Let's just keep you both as safe as we can, all right?" He didn't wait for her answer. "You need to get out of here, return to your home in Grave Gulch and forget you ever saw that man, no matter who he looks like—or doesn't. Otherwise, well... you're actually risking a lot of lives, not just your own and his. Got it? If you agree to head home right away and never speak about this, I'll uncuff you and let you go. Do we have a deal?"

He watched her lovely face for a few moments and wished he could read her mind. Her mouth pouted, her red eyebrows arched a bit more over her amazingly green eyes, and Oren wished for a moment that he could take her into his arms and try to convince her with a sexy but meaningless kiss.

Which he, of course, wouldn't do. He had to stay professional. Remote. And, hopefully, convincing.

And it had been a while since he'd kissed any woman. He'd had a few relationships, sure, but they'd gotten nowhere, and he was glad to remain on his own.

Her shoulders finally slumped, and she looked down at her wrists. "Okay," she said. "I really wish I knew what was going on, but I know from my own family that when someone expresses concerns like that, other people need to listen. And so I'll listen to you. I won't talk about this, even to my family, since I understand what you mean. Please remove these cuffs, and I'll go to my car, which is about a block away. Then I'll drive home. I'll give you my contact information, though, so you can let me know if things ever change and you can give me more information about this. Okay?"

"Sure," Oren said, figuring he'd just tear up the paper. Or not. He'd never contact her again…no matter how tempting it might be. And he certainly wouldn't keep her informed about anything regarding the person he was protecting.

Could he trust her to do as she'd said—never speak about this and just drive home? Well, he couldn't keep her here forever, despite the fact he'd claimed to have arrested her. He certainly couldn't take her to his office.

No, he would let her go—and he'd keep an eye on her as long as he could. And assume she would talk, despite her promise, so he would have to deal with that possibility with his subject.

He first pulled the key from his pocket, then reached over and uncuffed her, temporarily feeling the warmth of her hands. He again had an inappropriate urge, this time just to hold those hands for a minute, allow himself to imagine what it would be like to spend more time with this beautiful—but difficult—woman, touching her more, in even less appropriate ways…and her touching him back, with no cuffs on.

He shrugged off that idea as he unfastened the manacles, and she reached into her purse, wrote down her information and handed it to him.

"Thanks," she said and stood in a crouch in the back of the SUV. After thrusting the card into his side pocket,

Owen exited his car, then went around, opened the door on her side and held out his hand to help her out.

"Now, where is your car?" he asked.

"Just around the block there." She pointed in the opposite direction from the bookstore, and Oren glanced that way, wondering what vehicle this beautiful teacher drove.

Bad decision. As he looked away, she started running along the sidewalk, ducking between the pedestrians.

In the direction of the bookstore. Where else?

"Stop!" he shouted, running after her. He wasn't surprised when she didn't obey, though. He, too, jammed his way through the shoppers, many of whom had turned to watch Madison run. They wound up getting even more in his way, damn it.

He didn't want to charge into anyone and knock them over. That would slow him, maybe even stop him.

But how was he going to stop Madison, keep her from reaching that store?

MADISON DIDN'T EVEN glance toward the bridal boutique as she dashed by as fast as she could in the crowd. The name over the door she targeted was Books of Kendall, and large picture windows showed filled bookshelves on both sides of the entry.

She knew she had done something really wrong. She had lied to a US Marshal. But how could she possibly stay away from the man in the bookshop before she could confirm he wasn't her father? How would she deal with that for the rest of her life? What would she tell her siblings?

So Madison didn't stop. She pushed the metal-framed glass door open and hurried inside, unsure where Oren was behind her. Probably close. She just hoped she saw the man right away in here.

Which she did. There didn't appear to be any shoppers in the store as Madison glanced down the nearby aisles. But just ahead, near a counter where there were a couple of cash registers, that man had stopped.

Madison stared at him. Oh, yes, he did look like her brother—amazingly so. Sure, their hair and eyes were different colors, but his blond looked partly dyed, and some parts of him indicated age, like the gray strands in his hair, as well as the wrinkles on his face. But everything else, even the somewhat-muscular build, the way he held himself, his hands that held a book—they also seemed really similar.

Before she said anything, though, she realized he was staring at her, too, his mouth agape as if...as if he, too, recognized her. That wouldn't be possible, even in the unlikely event the guy was her father. They hadn't seen each other in twenty-five years, and she'd just been a child then. Not to mention, Richard Foster had been presumed dead.

But hell, Madison had been told by so many people, and she recognized it herself. She really looked a lot like her mother, except that her hair was red, not blond.

He's staring at me because I look so much like my mother.

What should she do? What should she say? Should she leave?

She heard a noise behind her that didn't sound like any crowd murmurs of customers that she'd anticipated in the shop. She turned.

Oren stood right inside. Yes, he had followed her. No big surprise.

But she had done what she'd promised *not* to—come here to see the man she had been looking for. She hadn't spoken with the look-alike. Not yet, at least. But Madison knew Oren wouldn't be at all pleased with her.

Why did she care? Because he was in law enforcement, like much of her family?

Because he was so good-looking?

Of course not. But what was he going to do? Right now, he just stood there, shaking his head. He then pivoted, turned the *Closed* sign around on the door and locked it. Her heart thumped. There was no turning back now.

Chapter Three

Oren attempted to hide his angry scowl. This wasn't at all the way he wanted things to be. Not only had Madison lied to him and slipped away when she had promised to drive off—for her own safety, even. But she'd run straight here and dashed into this used bookstore, where the subject of Oren's witness-protection assignment now worked—using his new identity, of course. But he was still in jeopardy, and this woman's actions might endanger others, too.

At least the moderate-sized shop, fairly organized with books and somewhat musty-smelling, had been empty when they'd entered, despite the abundance of shoppers on the street on this fall Saturday. He didn't even see the owner. Nor did he see other clerks, although there weren't many. But how would he get Madison out of here while keeping this witness safe?

Only… Well, unless he resorted to taking control as a domineering marshal, which wasn't the worst thing but might not get the ultimate result he wanted, Oren had no choice at the moment except to watch. Right now, the man under Oren's protection, whose current identity was Wesley Windham, stood near the cash-register counter, fists clenched at his side, still staring at Madison—and more. Trembling, his eyes welling, Wes said, "You look…you look so familiar to me. Like someone I once knew. Only…only your hair is so beautiful and red, like— Are you…my daughter?"

And here was that potential consistency, Oren thought. Could it be true?

Madison appeared highly emotional, too, also with tears in her lovely green eyes. She leaned on a nearby glass-topped counter that had books shelved below, and she looked straight into Wes's face. "I think so," she whispered hoarsely. "If you're Richard Foster."

Wow! It was true—probably. He remembered more about the Colton name now. Richard Foster had left behind a girlfriend, Verity Colton, and three young kids.

The guy's smile appeared wistful, almost sad. "That hasn't been my name for twenty-five years."

"But why?" Madison burst out, taking a step toward him, then stopping herself—which was good, because Oren would have had to do it for her, otherwise. "Why didn't you…why didn't you come see us during all that time? Or at least contact us, visit when you weren't on duty in the military or whatever? We missed you—my mother, my brother and sister…me. We thought you were dead. Mom was told you'd been killed in combat."

And, after all that time, what was it about him that she had recognized? She'd mentioned that he resembled her brother, who was undoubtedly near her age. But what about this man looked similar?

This wasn't the time to ask, though. In fact, Oren stepped forward to try to stop the conversation. This man wasn't Richard anymore, not while he was in witness protection, and to bring back that identity could bring back a lot of danger.

But to Madison, this *was* Richard, and while all of them were together, Oren would have to get used to thinking of him that way, too, and not only as Wesley—which was how he knew him. He would have to continue to refer to him, to think of him, as Wesley when Madison wasn't involved.

"Look," Oren said. "No matter who you each think the other is, we need to stop this and separate right now. This is too dangerous. Let's leave, Madison." But she didn't move. She still watched that man.

"Believe me," Wes—no, *Richard*—said, looking at the floor and not toward Madison, "I would have been there if I could. But you see, I stayed away to protect all of you. Myself, too."

"What do you mean?" Madison's tone seemed chillier now, as if she didn't believe him. It would have sounded a bit odd to Oren, too, if he hadn't known at least some of the background. Richard's life had been threatened, and even after all these years he could remain in peril.

Richard looked back up at her. "Please, come over here." He pointed to a circle of chairs used for book clubs. Oren attended now and then to make sure the people there did not appear to present a threat to Richard who, as an employee, was frequently around during the late hours the store remained open for the meetings. Even though his office was in Grand Rapids, Oren visited here often to ensure Richard was doing okay.

In some ways, he hoped to engage in whatever conversation they were going to have. He found Madison amazingly lovely.

Right or wrong, Oren would continue to do all he could to protect his subject. It was his job. And right now, that protection could be even more vital, since Wes's true identity had become known.

Oren took a seat facing the door so he could look outside and make sure no one attempted to get in, although he could understand if people wanted to come and buy some books.

They'd have to wait until later, though.

Right now, he was interested in what Richard had to say, even though he knew at least some of it.

The other two sat down beside each other, to Oren's right. Richard clasped his hands together but looked straight into Madison's face.

"My dear little Madison," he said, his voice choking. "It was…it was horrible. All of it. You see… Well, it happened the night I last came back from overseas. I was on the way to see your mother and you kids just for the weekend, the way things always seemed to work out, but I never got there. I—I witnessed a murder right on the outskirts of Grave Gulch."

"What?" Madison exclaimed. "Who? What happened?"

Oren considered ending this conversation, but then, he'd known what would come out if father and daughter got to talking.

"I didn't know either of the men involved, but… Well, it was so strange. I had stopped to run into a fast-food place for some coffee before I headed to your mom's house. It was fairly late, but the restaurant was still open. I parked under a light near the end of the almost-empty lot, and there was an open area just beyond the curb. I heard some guys yelling at each other right there, so of course I had to look. They both held guns. I was freaked out and was about to get back into my car when one shot the other. I must have made a sound, because the shooter turned and looked straight at me." Richard's voice had risen even as it turned gravelly. "I'll never forget that face—and unfortunately, the guy must have realized that. And he stared right back, memorizing my face as well."

Madison grabbed her father's hand and held it to her face. "Did he shoot at you, too?"

"Yes, but he missed, and I managed to get back in my car and drive away—fast. And I zigzagged so he'd have a hard time following me. When I stopped, it was at a busy gas station across town. I parked and hid behind the building and called 9-1-1. And then…well, it all got even stranger."

Oren knew this part of the story, too, although he listened as Richard told his daughter. The killer had turned out to be a gunrunner the feds had been after for a while. After local authorities went to the place Richard described, found the body—the victim was dead—and chased down and arrested the shooter, the US Marshals then took Richard Foster into protective custody. They needed him to confirm the identity of the perpetrator.

"The thing is," Richard continued, "the feds came right away and took me into their custody, too, so I never did get a chance to go see your mom and all of you. It was for my protection, they said. Not contacting you at all was also for your protection. The feds then insisted that I testify against the shooter in a closed grand-jury hearing. His name, by the way, was Louis Amaltin."

"How awful!" Madison exclaimed. "And it wasn't fair that you couldn't contact your family. We didn't have a father because of them."

"As it turned out, it was fair. Very fair. Safer for me, and safer for all of you."

Madison's head was shaking. "But how?"

"The good thing," Richard responded, "was that my testimony helped to get the gunrunner convicted. But that damn killer yelled right there in court that he'd find out my identity and kill my entire family and then rip the witness—*me*—to shreds. And of course…well, yes, he was in custody, sentenced to prison for the rest of his life, but what if he got out? Or had accomplices who were still free who would do as he asked?"

Richard stood then, pulling his eyes away from Madison. He began pacing in the center of the circle formed by the chairs. Madison joined him, taking his hand as he continued talking.

"I was scared, Madison. Very scared. I was young then and wanted to live. And absolutely to make sure your mom, you and your brother and sister—my kids—lived, too."

Oren maintained his seat and kept watching them and the window beyond them.

Yes, he'd been helping in Richard's protection for a while. He knew the basic story.

But even Oren had to admit to himself that Richard's description, and his apparent scared and sad state of mind, hacked at his emotions.

The upshot of it was that Wesley—Richard, then—had further attracted the feds. They agreed to provide him with additional protection in exchange for that testimony. For one thing, he'd gotten them to make a deal with the army to announce that he was presumed dead overseas. And then he went into witness protection.

"I did it to protect Verity—your mom. And you, and your brother and sister. I swear it, Madison."

"I understand...sort of," she whispered. "But...what's going on now?"

MADISON REALIZED SHE should be happy with herself, even thrilled, that despite how ridiculous, how impossible, it had seemed, she'd been right.

She had seen, and recognized, her father.

Still alive? In witness protection all this time?

Unable to contact the woman he had promised to marry all those years ago—and their children?

She wanted to grab him and hug him. And smack him.

She realized she was in shock. She had to calm down. Figure out a way to deal with this.

Figure out how she would connect with this man in the future.

Or not.

First things first, though. She moved around Richard—she could hardly think of him as *Dad*, at least not right now—and planted herself in front of him, stopping him from continuing to circle and forcing him to look at her.

She glanced then at Oren. Unsurprisingly, he was watching them, his piercing blue eyes seeming to dig inside her—and her father—as if he was attempting to listen to what was really on their minds.

The fact that this marshal was so good-looking, even sexy, was totally irrelevant. Especially since he had attempted to force her to leave without even meeting this man who apparently really was her father. By *arresting* her, of all things.

She looked away from Oren now and back toward

Richard. "Okay, then," she said as he stared down at her with a puzzled expression, but she refused to look away. She was the one who was surely the most confused, after all, not him. "As you can imagine," Madison said, "I'm worried for you—and for Mom and Bryce and Jillian. Are we all still in danger? Could that gunrunner still come after us—that Louis Amaltin? Is he still in prison?"

If they weren't just confronting each other here, Madison realized she would do what she nearly always did: research on her smartphone for information she was seeking. Looking up the name *Louis Amaltin* online, for example. She would do that later. But for now, she wanted to hear what her father told her.

Couldn't he have come out of witness protection long before, while Amaltin was in prison?

He didn't answer. Instead, he turned away from her and sat down on the chair farthest from them. What was going on? What was he thinking?

Madison suddenly—or not so suddenly—wanted to hear it all.

She approached him yet again and also sat down. She considered reaching for his thin hands, holding them, encouraging him to look at her once more and provide more answers. At least he faced her.

"Please. We really do need to know if we're in danger," she said, although if they were, wouldn't they have gotten at least a hint of it long before now?

He looked in her face at first, as she'd wished, and then down again at his hands. "You—we—should all be fine now," he said. "Maybe, although I still worry... The thing is, Amaltin was killed in prison five years after I testified against him. He had a life sentence."

Madison couldn't help gasping, pain—and sorrow—

Linda O. Johnston

39

rocketing through her. "You mean he died, what, twenty years ago? And you knew about it and still didn't contact Mom? Or even get out of witness protection?"

She glanced toward Oren. He was clearly providing some of that protection, or he wouldn't have told her to go home and stay away from Richard—her father. But Oren's bland expression didn't change, and he once more looked over her shoulder toward the display window and the door into this store.

Why? Was there still some danger they simply weren't telling her about? There had to be, somehow, or why would Oren be watching over him? Were they going to tell her?

Darn it. She wanted to go kick Oren in the shin or even someplace more sensitive, somehow get his attention. Sure, he looked sexy—a whole lot sexier than Madison ever found Alec, unfortunately—but he was annoyingly remote when she still needed answers.

"Look, Madison," her father finally said. "It's a bit complicated. Maybe…maybe I could have come out of protection a while back, even now—but it's been so long. I'm a different person now than who I was way back then. I'm no longer in the military and haven't been for ages. For a long time I stayed away, mostly for Verity's protection, since I wasn't sure what would happen. But I got so used to my new life, even as a bookseller here. And, well, rational or not, that murder scared me a lot. Changed me. I did a lot of checking into gunrunners like Amaltin, and arms dealers like that seldom work alone. Sure, he was dead, but he was bound to have some associates, and I figured there would still be animosity toward me for outing Amaltin and getting him sent to prison. More than animosity. And so—I just stayed away."

Madison's turn to look away, not stare Richard in the face. Protecting her, her mother and her siblings—or just himself?

Or maybe he just got used to having no responsibilities to anyone and just didn't want to come home to his family. Would he ever admit that? Unlikely.

She just felt sad now, and tired. And sorry she had even started this.

She just wanted to go home, to her house, and life, in Grave Gulch.

"I get it, Richard," she said sadly to the man who had fathered her all those years ago.

And who, no matter what his rationale, had wanted nothing to do with her and the rest of her family.

"Like I said," he responded, "I barely know the name Richard anymore."

"I get that, too," she said, then stood up again. She glanced at Oren, who was watching her. He was protecting Richard—or whoever—from her, maybe, as well as other people.

Well, they wouldn't have to worry about her any longer.

"It's been good to meet you," she lied, "but I think I'll just head home now."

And never see him again, most likely. It was better that way.

But he said, "Just so you know, the identity I adopted twenty-five years ago is Wesley Windham. That's the name I've answered to for ages. And…well, I'll be here if you ever want to talk more about the past, and if your brother and sister want to meet me."

Oren interrupted. "Forget that. Bad idea."

But Madison chose to ignore him. "And our mother? What if she wants to see you?"

Richard—no, *Wesley*—grimaced. "Sure," he said anyway. "It would be good to see her again."

Yeah, right.

But just in case, it wouldn't necessarily make sense to drag her mother here, or at least not until they had discussed all this. Or her brother and sister, either. "Let's exchange phone numbers so we can talk sometime before any of us come for a visit, okay?"

"No," Oren said. "You need to stay out of each other's lives."

But Richard said, "Good idea." He reached into his pocket as Madison reached into her purse, and they pulled out their cell phones. "What's yours?"

Madison told him, and he entered the digits into his phone. In moments, her phone rang, and she captured his number, adding his name as a contact: *Wesley*. That was all. Not *Richard Foster.*

Not *Dad.*

Then it was time for her to go. She considered just saying bye, waving over her shoulder and leaving quickly. But maybe she should buy a book here. Right. On what? What to do when your dead father reappears?

Or how often to get in touch with your dead father?

Or— Enough. She'd certainly tell Bryce and Jillian what had happened. Probably their mother, too.

Would Alec have any interest?

She certainly hadn't been thinking a lot about him today, and she doubted he'd care much about what she'd been going through.

Another reason that maybe she should end...

No reason to think about that now.

"Okay," she finally said, noting that Oren, too, was standing, although he hadn't approached them. He was frowning, though. "I'm on my way home now. Nice meeting you, Wesley." She could have bitten her tongue after that, but on the other hand, her words had come out with the sarcastic tone she'd intended.

He didn't seem to care. In fact, he came up to her again and took her hands in his. "I can't begin to tell you how glad I am to see you again, Madison. And yes, please, let's keep in touch."

"Like I said," Oren interrupted again, "stay out of each other's lives. Look, you can both use me to communicate with the other. That'll be safer."

Maybe so, but Madison felt certain her father would start calling her daily. *Sure.*

"Time to leave." She waved over her shoulder and headed to the front door.

She was glad that Oren accompanied her to the door. He'd apparently locked it before, and she didn't want to struggle with it.

As she anticipated, he pulled in front of her and turned the switch that unlocked it and turned the *Closed* sign back around. Before he opened it, though, he turned back to Wesley.

"Okay, I know you're going to do whatever you want. Well, I'll be back here soon. And you already have my number."

"Right," Madison's father said, and he waved at both of them.

Madison hurried through the door. There were a few people waiting outside for the store to open again, and they used the opportunity to pop in.

Madison maneuvered around them, heading down the sidewalk to where she had parked her car.

To her surprise, Oren stayed at her side.

"Look, Madison," he said to her, "I know this had to be difficult. I think we need to talk about the situation, including more about why Wesley remains in witness protection, at least sort of. And why I don't think you should stay in touch. And, well, here's what we'll do. I'll drive you home right now to Grave Gulch, in your car."

"Really?" As ridiculous as it sounded, Madison appreciated the idea. She didn't particularly want to be alone right now. She needed someone to talk to. And this man, as difficult as he'd come across, well, she really wanted to talk to him about what he knew. And what he didn't know. She assumed he wanted to accompany her to make sure she actually left town and ended up a distance from the man he was protecting. But—

"How will you get back here?" she asked, assuming he wouldn't want her to drive him back. "Isn't this where you live?"

"No," he said. "I sometimes work here, but my headquarters is in Grand Rapids."

Which made it sound even worse. "Then, how will you get back there?"

"I've been working with some trainees who need new assignments. I'll have one bring my car from here to Grave Gulch and another come pick that trainee up and take him back home. And don't argue with me about it. That's what's going to happen."

Madison had already learned that arguing with Oren didn't get her very far. And this time, she liked what he was proposing.

Still, she made herself sound irritated as she responded, "Well, okay then, I guess. You can drive me home, Marshal."

"Yes," he said. "I can, and I will."

Chapter Four

Madison's car was a small white sedan—appropriate for a kindergarten teacher, Oren thought. She'd parked it around the corner, in front of a small candy shop.

They didn't talk much as they walked there, although when they first passed the bridal shop Madison had mentioned, Oren's mind swam with questions. Who was she marrying? When? She apparently hadn't gone inside either last week or this week, so she hadn't found the dress she wanted there—not yet, at least. But maybe she was looking other places, too. Maybe she had already found her perfect dress elsewhere.

And why did the idea of this lovely but difficult woman getting married annoy the heck out of him?

"Here we are," Madison soon said and took a key fob from her purse. She aimed it toward the car and pushed a button. Oren heard the doors unlock.

He headed first to the passenger's side, where he pulled the door open for her and stood there, his briefcase in his hand. He'd gotten it from his car before going toward Madison's vehicle.

Madison had headed toward the driver's side, perhaps by habit—or maybe to irritate him. He'd already told her he would be driving, after all.

Partly for her safety. Her mind was surely in turmoil after all that had occurred that afternoon. Not to mention that she might be in danger now, having met and talked with Wesley Windham.

And him? Well, he wanted to spend additional time with her. Just to learn more about the situation concerning her father, he assured himself. It wasn't appropriate for him to feel attracted to her, even though he did. After today, it wouldn't matter. He might see her again, but infrequently. And hopefully not just the two of them together.

If they were together, he'd quiz her more about her family and her missing father. Not that she'd have much new to say about Wes. But she might be able to supply more background that could be useful to Oren and the US Marshals Service. Or not. They already had a lot of information about Wes and the situation that led to his being in protective custody, and Oren had reviewed the files in depth after taking this assignment over from another marshal who had recently retired. Some of those files were even on the computer that he had with him, though not all of them. As far as he'd been able to tell, not much had gone on with Wes recently. He'd been under their protection for a lot of years, after all.

And Wes had contacted him because he'd seen someone following him—Madison. Were there any other people to be concerned about now? The threats were deemed minimal, but he still remained under their protection.

"Ready to get in?" Oren asked, still holding the passenger door for her.

"Oh, that's right," she said after standing a few moments staring at him. "This is something new," she said. "I don't think anyone else has ever driven my car since

I got it, except mechanics when I've brought it in for some minor work."

"Well," Oren said, "in case you're worried, I'm not only a marshal, I'm also a damn good driver."

Madison laughed as she slid inside. "You'd better be."

His turn to laugh, although he grew serious again as he got into the driver's seat.

"Do you know where we're going?" Madison asked as he carefully pulled onto the street. There was some traffic around them, but not much. Kendall was fairly quiet, even on a Saturday.

So was Grave Gulch, a couple of hours away. Oren might live in Grand Rapids, but he had good reason to visit the small city of Grave Gulch as often as he could, thanks to family ties.

His parents also lived in Grand Rapids. He was close to his mom. His dad, too, very unlike Madison's situation. He could only imagine what she felt like now. But his sister lived in Grave Gulch, like Madison, and he hoped to see her soon.

He didn't need to focus on their destination as much now as on the woman in the car with him, who had already gone through some pretty emotional moments this day.

"Well, I do know how to get to Grave Gulch," he replied to Madison. "You'll have to direct me to your place once we're there."

To her home, he assumed. Not to the school, since this was Saturday. But that would be that. Maybe they could share a meal at a nearby restaurant before he left, hopefully at his sister Olivia's deli, while he waited for his ride home…or not.

But if he was honest with himself, he realized that

wasn't the only reason. Though she wouldn't be wrong to despise him for what he'd done—tried to keep her far from the man who'd actually turned out to be her father—Oren was coming to like Madison. Maybe too much.

But he admired her attitude. Her gumption in ignoring what she had promised him, a marshal, an officer of the law, to drive out of town fast when he'd first agreed to release her from his irregularly achieved custody. And she'd dealt with the fact he'd arrested her in the first place and ignored it afterward... Well, yeah. That was admirable, even if it was irritating and potentially dangerous.

Anyway, he was interested in seeing where she lived, would remember it, might even drive by it now and then to check on her well-being when he was in town, but that would be it.

After all, she was hardly likely to do anything to endanger Oren's charge, Wes—yes, he could still think of him as Wesley and not Richard after their last conversations with the guy—who just happened to be her father.

Her father. She was being so quiet now. Thinking about that? Overthinking?

"Hey," Oren said, partly to start a conversation, and partly because he really wanted her response to what he was going to ask. "I can imagine what a shock all of this has been for you. And—"

"No," she said. "I bet you can't imagine it. Not really."

"Then, tell me."

Maybe he couldn't completely relate to her situation, but he had worked with many people in WITSEC—witness protection—and had learned a lot about them and how they felt about missing their families if they were relocated or even had to fake their deaths. But he was coming to care about Madison and would be glad to hear more about what she was thinking. They had just stopped at a traffic light before getting onto the highway toward Grave Gulch. He turned briefly to look at her and was somewhat surprised she was looking at him.

"I'm not sure that's a good idea," she said. "I don't know anything about you or your family, but...well, okay. Here's some of it. I grew up a Colton, as I mentioned, which is a large family with lots of branches, in Grave Gulch and elsewhere. But we were a bit different from most of the rest. Colton is our mother's last name. Our father—Wesley, now—never married her, as I also mentioned, although I guess you could say they were engaged."

The light had changed. Oren drove forward. He noted that Madison grew quiet. Thinking about her own engagement? Oren really wanted to hear about that, but this wasn't the time to ask.

"So what happened?" He had some idea from their earlier discussion with Wes, but he still wanted to hear more from Madison's perspective.

"I was pretty young back then, though I was the oldest of the three of us kids. Twenty-five years ago, when our father supposedly died, I was only five years old. Bryce was three, and Jillian was two. None of us really knew what was going on then, of course."

"Of course," Oren affirmed. "Not at that age. But—"

"But we learned more as we grew up. Our mom always talked so lovingly about our dad. From what we gathered, he had enlisted in the military but came home on leave as often as he could."

And they obviously didn't care about any embarrassment that might accrue to those kids as they grew up.

Oren didn't get the impression that Madison was upset about her parents not being married, only that their dad had stayed away for so long.

That was definitely different from Oren's experiences growing up, with family around. His parents had been wonderful. Still were. They'd taught him and his fantastic sister all sorts of traditions that they sometimes still engaged in today.

Hearing about Madison's childhood only made him appreciate his own situation even more. And also caused him to vow he'd never abandon his kids if he ever had any of his own.

"So your mom was okay with it?" Oren asked to keep the conversation going. They had reached a four-lane road, still without many cars on it. It would take them most of the way to Grave Gulch. They seemed far from civilization out here, with tall elms, maples and other trees lining the highway, nearly leafless this late in the year.

"That's what she told us later. She said they always planned to marry but had decided to wait till our dad finally left the military, which she said he'd intended to do right around the time…the time she was notified that he'd been killed in action. She'd believed it, of course. So did his parents, apparently, who were sent what were supposedly his remains and had them buried. They stayed in touch with her for a short while, but they made it clear to my mom and her parents that they didn't believe in having kids out of wedlock. So the only grandparents we saw often as kids were my mother's folks—more Coltons."

He couldn't help wondering what it had been like for

Madison, growing up in that family but not really part of her father's family, whoever they were. The Fosters, of course. But—

"Were your dad's family members in Grave Gulch?" Not that it mattered under those circumstances.

"No. They were in a nearby town. And when we were in our teens, we heard they died in a car accident, so my brother, sister and I wouldn't have gotten to know our grandparents on that side very well, anyway."

"What a shame!" Oren exclaimed. What a tough childhood, even if her Colton family did remain close. He was aware of some rather difficult situations relating to the Coltons in Grave Gulch during the last few months or so, though. For one thing, the former police chief had been a Colton but had resigned because of some things that had gone wrong in the department, and that hadn't been all.

But did her father know his family was gone? Wasn't that a good reason to get in touch with his kids? Oren knew he'd be tempted to break his protection to do so... but Richard Foster?

Apparently not.

MADISON COULD UNDERSTAND Oren's interest in her family, even now. They got into the news a lot, partly because of tragic occurrences in Grave Gulch. Some of it related to apparent corruption in the police department beginning when her cousin Melissa had been police chief, and even more. And then there'd been things that happened in the past, when her father supposedly died—and instead wound up in witness protection. The somewhat sordid situation helped to explain some things in the life of the man Oren now protected. Nothing in the news, or what her mother had been told, explained why her father had stayed away after the convict who'd threatened him and his family had died. But Wesley had provided his own absurd story about that.

Definitely absurd. But she forced herself to tamp down any anger as it began to rise inside her. What good would it do?

Still… Would she be able to forgive him for avoiding them for so long?

Well, Madison didn't want to think about any of that right now. She was also done talking about it for the moment. Except…

"There's a lot I don't understand yet about my father and what happened to him and why he didn't contact us. And right now one of the things that make me curious about it is…you. Why are you marshals still protecting him after all these years?"

Madison didn't look at Oren's face as she asked the question, and that felt difficult. She found the marshal too worthy of her stares. She rarely saw such good-looking guys, not at the school where she worked, the neighborhood where she lived or elsewhere. His strikingly masculine features enhanced his dark facial hair… Oh, yeah.

And her fiancé? Well, he wasn't bad-looking, but he wasn't that good-looking, either. *Ordinary* was the word that came to her mind when she searched for one.

Still, he was a respected third-grade teacher with a normal family. Maybe that was a reason she had been attracted to him. But that wasn't a good reason to stay with him, with nothing else.

And right now she didn't want to search for anything related to Alec.

She drew her gaze from Oren and watched the road ahead.

Sure, she had driven the opposite direction earlier, but she hadn't focused on the roadway except to the extent needed for safe driving.

Today, her mind had been focused on her motivation for making this trip: finding the man whose appearance had kick-started the chaos in her mind.

"Well," Oren said, "we're still protecting your dad for the same reasons we were when the marshals all those years ago recruited him to testify in the case against that gunrunner Amaltin, although there hasn't been much going on with Wesley or his long-ago case for most of those years. But once we take on an assignment, our service stays on it, or returns to it, anytime the situation requires it."

"And my learning my father is alive presented one of those situations?" Madison asked.

"Well, we knew who he was, of course, and the Marshals Service changed his identity for his protection. But the fact you suspected, and now know, that makes our focus on his case necessary again."

Madison felt her body tense up. "But you don't need to protect him from me. I might be angry with him, but I'd never hurt him."

She saw Oren glance toward her, then return his attention to the road. Didn't he believe that?

Fortunately, he apparently did. "I figured that. Now that I've met you and gotten to speak with you, I'll be able to tell my superiors that I don't think you present a danger to our subject, even though he let us know you were following him. But…your knowing about him and potentially accidentally referring to it could become a reason he could be located again. There's always a possibility you could unintentionally endanger him."

Ouch, Madison thought. Well, she'd be careful—but Oren continued before she could reassure him. "Apparently the people who worked on the matter long ago did buy into your dad's concerns that the gunrunner he outed and helped to send to prison had associates. Some of those associates might still be around even now. And though it's unlikely they even know your father is alive, or have an interest in going after him now, it never hurts to play things safe."

"Got it," Madison said, which wasn't exactly true. On the other hand, if she was in her father's position, she might feel relieved that help was always over her shoulder.

After all, someday she might need to be protected from something in her life coming to the attention of bad guys who wanted revenge… She almost laughed aloud at that ridiculous idea.

But it obviously wasn't ridiculous to her father. Or to the Marshals Service.

Okay, she really had been thinking too much about all this.

She liked this man, despite having just met him—and despite the fact he'd arrested her.

Though, it still seemed a bit strange that he was driving her home and she was enjoying it.

They would be alone together in this car for at least another hour and a half. She'd been doing most of the talking so far.

It was his turn.

"So," she said, "tell me a little about you. I gather you live in Grand Rapids."

"I do now, thanks to my job, and I really like that city. It's where I grew up."

He looked a few years older than Madison, so even if they had grown up in the same place, they wouldn't necessarily have met in school or somewhere else.

"Is your family still there?" Madison asked.

"Yes. My parents still work there, too. But my sister is now in Grave Gulch. And now I visit her as often as I can. We're Jewish, and Olivia opened Bubbe's Deli there. She named it in honor of our late grandmother."

"Really?" She'd passed Bubbe's Deli, she was sure, but she didn't think she'd ever eaten there.

But the idea of this great-looking guy Oren having a sister in her town, one who owned a restaurant... Madison wanted to know more.

"Where is the deli located?" she asked. "And what does your sister serve there?"

"It's downtown and called Bubbe's Deli because *bubbe* means *grandmother* in Yiddish, and our grandmother—who's no longer with us, unfortunately—introduced us to some wonderful Jewish classics. My sister Olivia now has a lot of them on her menu."

Oren was smiling broadly, clearly proud of his sister and grandmother and their heritage. Madison smiled back. She loved her family but hadn't learned anything that special, at least in terms of cooking, from them.

Family loyalty, though? Yes, she had learned about that while growing up, thanks to things that had occurred in other branches of the Coltons. There'd been an unsolved murder case way back that had caused a number of family members to go into law enforcement, partly to protect each other.

Then there was her father…

Madison glanced at a road sign ahead of them. They seemed to be making good progress toward Grave Gulch. Traffic wasn't too bad, and she figured all the cars traveled at the somewhat generous speed limit or better.

She realized that her time with this man would soon be over. That was a good thing. Wasn't it?

Somehow, she didn't think so. Despite how they had met and their interaction with her father—well, she liked Oren.

And once he dropped her off at her house and his ride arrived, they were unlikely to see each other again, or at least not much…unless he decided to show up each time Madison decided to visit her father.

If she ever did again.

Although, she figured she would at least go to Kendall with company, to introduce her brother and sister to Wes and to possibly observe their mother's reaction on seeing him again.

But for now, time to return to the conversation they'd been having.

"Okay," she said. "I've got a feeling a visit to Bubbe's Deli is in my future. Tell me more specifically some of the food your sister serves there."

"Well, it's kind of standard deli stuff, including knishes, matzo ball soup, corned beef and pastrami sandwiches on rye bread and more."

"Sounds good! Only, well, I've never had matzo ball soup. What is that?"

"Great stuff. Chicken broth and large matzo balls, which are dumplings mostly made out of matzo—un-

leavened bread that's typically used at the Jewish holiday Passover. The texture and seasoning are excellent.
One of my faves at my sister's restaurant."

"It really does sound good. I'll have to give it a try."
She was serious, only it might feel odd to visit this marshal's family restaurant. Would she introduce herself to
his sister? Probably not. Why should she?

But sampling the food there did have some appeal,
and if she ever saw Oren again she could talk to him
about that—and less about her father. Maybe.

"Good idea," Oren said. He didn't look at her now as
he spoke but into the sideview mirror. "Maybe we can
go there tonight."

Wow! She hadn't meant her discussion of the place
and its food as a hint, but the idea of going there not just
to check it out but with Oren along sounded great.

"Maybe so," she said, hoping it worked out.

But why did Oren keep looking into the mirror that
way? Madison turned and saw some cars behind them,
but everything seemed okay.

Didn't it?

Chapter Five

What the hell was going on? A black SUV seemed to
keep approaching them, then falling back in their lane...
and then speeding around those other cars and nearly
catching up again. But not quite.

Oren probably hadn't noticed when it began. He was
mostly keeping his eyes on the road in front of them,
then glancing over toward Madison as much as seemed
safe while they talked.

Maybe he was imagining things. Could be the driver
was just trying to speed a bit, then changing his mind.

But each time he seemed to change his mind when
he reached their car. There were other vehicles ahead
of them, so the driver could have approached the ones
in front, then fallen back. But that wasn't happening.

At age thirty-seven, Oren had been in law enforcement over a dozen years. He had learned a lot—and he
could tell something here definitely wasn't right. Should
he speed up to get far ahead of that driver? But this car,
though it drove well, wasn't exactly built for speed. That
was one reason he'd stayed in the right lane.

Should he slow down? No. That would make it too
easy for that other driver to reach them, if that was what
was going on. While that tactic would definitely suss

out whether they were his target, they might get hit or forced off the road.

And even though he was armed, Oren wouldn't attempt to use his weapon with Madison in the car unless it became absolutely necessary.

"What's going on?" Madison demanded. "What's with your driving, Oren? Are we okay?"

"Yeah," he said, hoping that wasn't too much of a lie. "Just hang on."

As Oren pondered more how to handle this, he noticed an exit just ahead with a short road leading uphill to some service stations. Maybe that was what he should do: wait till the other car was near them, then veer suddenly onto that roadway, at an angle, and fast enough that the other car couldn't follow.

He realized then that Madison had stopped talking, too. He didn't want to attempt to voice his concern, but he did want to warn her that things were about to change.

"Need to get off this highway for a minute" was all he said as they approached the exit, going a little more than the speed limit. He hoped they appeared to be heading forward beyond it—but instead of passing the exit he yanked the steering wheel to the right, and the car headed up the exit ramp.

"What's going on?" Madison cried out again. Out of the corner of his eye, he could see her gripping her seat with both hands, but he didn't have time to tell her.

Though Oren had hoped otherwise, the other vehicle veered toward them rather than staying in its lane, then exited up the ramp, too. Oren heard the squeal of tires on pavement as drivers behind them stomped on their brakes.

What was *with* that guy? Why was he driving that way?

Despite the exit only having one designated lane, the other car, now speeding, pulled up beside them, then slammed sideways.

Oren felt the impact on his side, which pushed him the other way and dug his seatbelt into him, juddering his ribs.

"No!" Madison screamed.

Oren swore and kept his hands on the steering wheel as he regained balance. An accident? No way. He needed to take control of the whole situation.

Of the other driver.

Only, as Oren turned to look at the guy, he saw that the jerk, now right beside them, had a rifle pointed toward them. For an instant, Oren stared straight at him. He seemed young. Did he appear familiar? There was something about his eyes that did somehow, though Oren couldn't figure out who he was thinking of. Dark eyes. Intense. Furious. And, yes, familiar.

Hell, that didn't matter. So what if he'd met their would-be murderer before if they wound up dead?

As Oren quickly accelerated and jerked the steering wheel, the guy took a shot at them, the sound exploding. Thanks to Oren's maneuvering, though, he missed hitting Madison's sedan—or either of its occupants. But that wasn't enough. Oren had to respond, but his weapon was too small to be of much use, especially against a rifle and while they were moving. He ignored the panic that rose within him and yelled at Madison to stay down.

One good thing about that ramming was that it had partially turned Madison's car so it was sideways on the exit road; their pursuer was aimed up the hill. Oren couldn't quite see its license number, but the plate was Michigan blue and white, and had a *B* and a *7* on it.

Now, instead of stopping or veering to speed up the hill, Oren turned the steering wheel again so they were aimed back down the hill they had just come up.

That gave them some advantage over the other driver, who couldn't turn his fast enough.

Oren sped back down the road, going the wrong way. Fortunately, no other cars on the highway had followed them up this ramp. Oren accelerated as they reached the highway again and entered the road at the exit, turning so they were headed back into the flow of traffic.

Oren glanced at Madison to make sure she was all right and still hunkered down. Fortunately, she looked okay.

He looked in the side-view and rearview mirrors. He glimpsed the other car—maybe attempting to follow them but not successfully, far behind them, thank heavens.

Oren didn't know what that was all about. Something to do with Madison meeting her father? But why? He intended to find out. Without stopping or playing into that weapon-toting lunatic's hand. Which meant calling 9-1-1 was out of the question. If they stopped to talk to the local cops who responded, their attacker might find them more easily—even if Oren had armed authorities attempting to help him.

Still speeding, weaving his way around the cars that had wound up ahead of him, he called his office in Grand Rapids. Deputy Marshal Jon Lettier answered. "What's up, Oren?" he asked. Nice guy, but this wasn't the time for pleasant conversation.

"Some bad stuff," Oren replied and briefly related what had happened, including a description of the car that had hit them and where they were. He also explained why he hadn't called 9-1-1. "But I'd like you to contact the state police to see if anyone reported seeing the supposed accident out here on the highway—any onlookers from other cars, or even our attacker reporting the damage to his vehicle. Have them send a patrol to check out the area, too, and hopefully find the other guy. Also, please call Wes Windham to make sure he's okay, in case this has something to do with him. There's something strange going on here."

"Got it," Jon said. "You okay?"

"Yeah, at least for now. I'm leaving this area, though, so give the authorities you talk with my number. I'll provide them with a description of the other car, but I wasn't able to make out a license number, just part of it."

"Okay, I'll let the state police know what happened. The Grave Gulch PD, too—that's where you're heading, isn't it? I'm sure they'll check into things but I'll tell them not to stop you. And you stay in touch with me. You hear?"

"I hear you," Oren acknowledged. Would he keep Jon informed about everything? Or the local authorities? Not likely, unless that driver was immediately found and apprehended.

He doubted that would happen. Things were happening too quickly. Were too strange.

And the fact he had been able to see the driver and perhaps recognize him? Or at least get an idea…

"Thanks," he said, finishing the conversation. "Talk to you soon." He pressed the button to hang up.

"Okay, Oren." Madison spoke demandingly from beside him. He could tell from her hoarse tone that she'd been crying. Maybe still was. "I didn't want to interrupt while you were talking to, well, whoever it was on the phone, but what happened? Do you know what that was about?"

Oren had an urge to put his arms around her and hug her to soothe her, but of course he didn't. "Not really, but—"

"I know it may be far-fetched, but could it be related to my dad, and the fact that I found him here, and... Well, I don't know."

"Neither do I," Oren said. "But it does seem ridiculously coincidental that this occurred on the day you just happened to trail and find Richard Foster." A thought struck him now about why the guy with the gun had possibly looked familiar. He would have to check whenever they had an opportunity to stop and he could use his laptop.

He surely didn't really resemble the pictures Oren had seen of Louis Amaltin. But what if Oren's impulse had been correct and the shooter had been a relative?

"Unless, of course," Madison continued, "you're being attacked as a marshal. Are you involved in some other dangerous case now? Could they have been after you?"

To soothe her a little, Oren responded, "Could be." But that was a lie. None of the other matters he was currently working on had struck him as particularly dangerous: tracking down assets seized by a federal criminal by illegal activity, working out a new identity for a woman about to go into witness protection...

Sure, there could be perilous aspects to both of those situations, but nothing had seemed especially stressful.

"Then, what are you doing? Shouldn't you stay involved in whatever cases you're working on and just leave me alone?"

He glanced over toward her. Her face appeared pale; she looked highly distressed.

"I'm doing exactly what I should be doing. I'm not going to leave you till I'm sure everything around you is okay."

Her shoulders appeared to relax a little. "Thank you," she said softly.

Fortunately, there were no surprises during the rest of the drive. Oh, Oren did see a fleet of three bright blue Michigan State Police cars, lights flashing, heading in the opposite direction across the highway: a good thing. They were probably the result of Jon's call. Maybe, if their attacker was still behind them, he'd exit more quickly, or at least act as a normal driver with the state police around—assuming his car hadn't been damaged enough to make it conspicuous.

Oren glanced often at the other vehicles around them and their drivers, but no one appeared to be checking him out, as some might if they'd seen the incident.

All seemed okay as they reached the outskirts of Grave Gulch.

"Are you going to take me right home?" Madison's voice sounded hoarse. Was she nervous about being left alone soon?

She should be, Oren thought. "Not yet," he said. "I need to make a stop first."

Which was true. He'd come up with an idea where to go for now to park and get into his briefcase and check out the file he was now itching to see. Fortunately, he knew Grave Gulch well enough to know where one of its main parking lots was located, near the shopping district in the center of downtown. The lot was three stories high and fairly long, and a lot of workers at the local businesses, as well as their customers, parked there.

Right now, Oren just needed a place to keep watch over his surroundings while he did what he needed to, and he grabbed the ticket from the machine as he entered, which made the automatic gate in front of him rise.

He would keep Madison with him in the car, of course, observing their environment closely.

"What are we doing here?" Madison asked. Her voice sounded stronger now, which Oren considered a good thing. But was she going to argue with him?

"I just need to look at something in my files without being out in the open where we can be seen easily. It won't take long."

"But—"

"When I'm done, I'll check again with my contacts, and if all seems all right we'll head for my sister's deli for dinner. Okay?"

"Maybe, but should I call one of my relatives in law enforcement to come here to help?"

Interesting possibility, Oren thought, but it might just make them more obvious. "Not at the moment," he said. "Maybe later. But we should be fine in this garage."

"I—I guess so," she said, sounding uncertain. "But how long is this going to take?"

"Not long," he promised. He backed into a space in an area that wasn't particularly crowded so he could watch the parked cars and the ones that passed by, as well as the people in or walking around them. He soon got out and examined the damage to the side of the car. Not pretty, but not too bad, either.

Madison joined him, touched it and sighed. "Fortunately, I have insurance," she said.

"Good. But please don't report it till we've had some opportunity to try to find the guy who did it."

"I'll wait for a little while, but not long." She got back in the car.

He opened the rear door on the driver's side so he could pull out his briefcase, sitting on the back seat since the steering wheel wouldn't give him as much space to use his laptop,

An idea had come to him about who their attacker resembled. Was it feasible? Heck, he'd seen something similar today as Madison recognized the man who was her father twenty-five years later. Maybe that had led to him coming up with this totally ludicrous idea.

But what if it was real?

Just in case, he was looking up the information he had on that gunrunner, Louis Amaltin, against whom Wes— Richard then—had testified. Oren hadn't known Foster twenty-five years ago, of course, but at least some of the files the Marshals Service kept were quite broad and intense, including photographs of all parties involved. And he had studied them in depth when he had taken over Wes's protection in Kendall.

He found what he was looking for. It amazed him— but it shouldn't have.

"Can't you tell me anything about what you're doing?" Madison was leaning through the gap between the front seats, staring at him. Her brows were knit over her green eyes, and she looked as worried now as she had several times earlier today.

Should he? Maybe. She should know at least part of this, and he would have to find a way to keep her safe since, if he was right, this did involve her.

"Okay," he said. "How would you like to hear something really ironic?"

She seemed to stiffen, yet she managed a small smile. "More ironic than finding my father alive after all these years?"

"In a way, yes, since I'll need to dig in even harder to make sure he stays that way."

"What is it?" she demanded. She appeared so frightened again that Oren had an urge to return to the front of the car and take her into his arms, hold her protectively tight.

As if that would also take care of her father.

"Well, that gunrunner he testified against all those years ago—"

"Who's dead, right?"

"Right. He was a married man back then when he was captured and incarcerated. Louis Amaltin had a young son, who perhaps looks like him now. I don't know that for certain, of course, but the man who ran into us before and shot at us—"

"You're not going to say he looks like Amaltin before he died and could be his son, are you? And he somehow tracked my father down, despite his being in witness protection, learned I was his daughter and tried to hurt me? Boy, you're right. That would be ironic." She shook her head, and her red hair bobbed gently around her face. "Especially after all the recognition from the past that's already gone on today."

"Exactly. That is what I was going to say. But that's not all."

The slight amusement in her expression seemed to melt back into fear, as maybe it should. "Tell me," she said.

Once again, he wished he was holding her tightly to

him, in protection…and, ridiculously, because he was beginning to like this brave woman a lot.

"Well, consider some more irony. But it's also an explanation why that guy came after us, assuming I'm right and he's Amaltin's son."

"Please tell me," she urged again.

Oren did reach out, and Madison thrust her hands between the seats.

He took them into his own and said, "Would you believe that today is the twentieth anniversary of when Amaltin was killed in prison?"

AMONG OTHER DUTIES as a kindergarten teacher, Madison helped her students begin to read.

But she didn't attempt to teach them literary techniques at that age—like irony.

Yet, as she and Oren had talked, so much of what had gone on today struck her as the opposite of normal, everyday living. Discovering a dead father was alive. Apparently reminding that man enough of her mother decades ago that he recognized she was his daughter after all these years. And now this: the son of the person her father had helped to put in prison where he'd died, chose an anniversary of that death to find and try to kill the witness's daughter…

Weird. Yes, ironic. And it all made her worry about what would come next, since a lot of it involved deaths or assumed deaths. And the man who had wanted to kill her and apparently Oren, too, was still on the loose.

How had he found where she was? And why had he come after her and not her father?

Unless… "Oren, is my father okay?" she said, turning to him in the back seat.

"You're sharing my thoughts," he said. "I'm going to hang out with you, of course, but I've got a call to make before we head to dinner."

She didn't know who he spoke with a minute later, but she figured it was someone else from the marshals' office. He told whoever it was that he had already called the office and requested that someone be sent to Kendall to keep an eye on Wes Windham until his return. Now, he wanted to be sure that person was on the way—or, preferably, already there. "I'm in Grave Gulch," he continued, "and want to do more work here. I'll be out here at least until tomorrow, so I'd like whoever's now on the assignment to contact me... Right. Yes... What's that? Who... Call me back."

He hung up. Then stared straight ahead.

"Is something wrong?" Madison asked. "I mean more than we've already experienced, and—"

"I don't know." Oren's voice was sharp. "I think so, but... Well, something's going on, and they're apparently just learning about it in my office. They'll let me know more soon." He looked over at her. "So, are you ready for dinner?"

Chapter Six

So what was going on now? Oren worried about the hub-
bub at the office for the entire drive from the parking lot
to Bubbe's Deli. Something was going on. Jon had made
that clear before hanging up. Oren needed to learn more.

Oren also needed to learn more about Amaltin's possible son apparently having found Madison. How?

The deli was only a few blocks away. Oren liked the
way downtown was set up, with long four-lane main
streets of a mile or more organized in a grid. Lots of
retail places one or two stories high, as well as taller
buildings containing other kinds of businesses and even
the Grave Gulch Police Department were located in the
center of town.

He liked the town well enough to consider moving
here to be nearer his sister—but this wasn't where his
job was. Plus, their parents were in Grand Rapids.

It had been a couple of weeks since Oren had last visited, which was why he paid attention—a little—to what
he was seeing of the town.

And he paid attention to his passenger. Despite what
they'd gone through on this road trip, she now seemed
more relaxed than she had since he'd met her. Pretty

lady. Worth watching, especially when she didn't appear so stressed.

But too involved in things she only partly understood.

Mostly, though, as he drove his mind buzzed around the phone conversation he'd just had with Jon—a much more intriguing and potentially upsetting conversation than the others they'd recently had. Maybe it wouldn't seem so bad if it had been completed. But the part that had occurred had definitely stirred up Oren's mind. Still did. Especially because Jon had ended their conversation by saying a couple of other calls were coming in then that he had to deal with. Sounded like bad stuff, he'd added, and hinted it might involve Oren's assignment. But Jon didn't have enough information to fill Oren in yet. He'd promised to call as soon as he could. Oren certainly hoped so.

"I think I'm finally zeroing in on where the deli is," Madison said from beside him. Her tone sounded excited, happy—totally different from what Oren was feeling. "The thing is, I've seen it, maybe even noticed it, but it's close to some of my family's favorite restaurants that we've been frequenting for years. When I'm out for meals it's usually with other people I'm close to, and around here, where the food is generally good and I'm used to it, I rarely try to suggest something different."

What restaurant does your fiancé like best? was the question that stomped through Oren's mind, but he didn't ask.

He didn't care.

Did he?

Certainly not now. There were too many other things on his mind that were more important.

"There!" Madison exclaimed, pointing through the windshield. "Right?"

"That's right," Oren said, and in fact they were only a few storefronts away from Olivia's place now. Which was fine.

But when was he going to get the rest of his phone call?

He came here frequently enough that he knew where to park despite the area along the curb being full: in the lot behind the deli. He drove around back and up the short driveway. A couple of empty spaces were marked *Staff*, and he pulled into one of them.

"Are you a staff member?" Madison asked.

"Close enough. My sister isn't going to disown me for parking here. She never has before. And we won't be here very long."

"Of course. Quick dinner. That's all." The somewhat-sad expression on Madison's face almost made Oren smile. Did she want to stay with him longer? He definitely wanted to see more of her. To protect her, that was all.

Or was he just trying to fool himself?

Whatever. He faced the steering wheel as he pushed the button to turn the engine off. "Okay," he said. "Let's go in." Although he usually told Olivia in advance when he was coming to town and visiting the deli, Oren hadn't today—not surprising, considering all that had happened.

They could have gone in through the back door from the parking lot, but Oren had an urge to give Madison the best view of the place, and that would mean entering from the door to the sidewalk at the front. There was a narrow walkway between the deli's building and the

Italian restaurant next door, and that was the way he led Madison—him in front, just in case the dangerous sleazebag who'd come after them earlier that day was waiting for them. Highly unlikely for many reasons. If he was still around, how could he guess where they were heading? But Oren wasn't taking any chances that he could avoid.

The deli had a second floor, which Olivia used for her office. Oren wondered if one of the places Madison frequented with her family and friends was the Italian restaurant, but he didn't ask. He wanted to take her hand to lead her along the narrow walkway but decided that wouldn't be appropriate. The paving was flat, and she was unlikely to stumble, anyway. Plus, if she did, she could reach out to one of the buildings to steady herself.

The area was busy. It was nearing six o'clock, a popular dinner time, although the deli tended to be crowded for another hour, then would wind down as the evening wore on till it closed at nine o'clock. Oren had often stayed around late enough to check that out. Then he would sometimes stay overnight in Olivia's spare bedroom in her house nearby. The drive home to Grand Rapids took a couple of hours.

For now, he just stood at the window, looking into the front area where the electronic cash register sat on a counter to the left, along with a credit-card reader and some candy for sale in the glass case below.

Across from it was the takeout area where specialized deli food was prepared to go: warm slices of corned beef, roast beef and pastrami sold by the pound, rye bread, knishes, gefilte fish and more.

Or people could order full sandwiches and matzo ball soup to go. Delicious stuff, as far as Oren was concerned.

He often took some with him when he returned to Grand Rapids. But he always enjoyed eating here, at one of the deli's many tables, and sometimes with Olivia sitting down to keep him company.

From out here, he couldn't show any of that to Madison. He led her inside. "Just so you know," he said, "this place has some great Jewish-style food, but it's not kosher. We appreciate our heritage, of course."

"I can't wait to try some," Madison said, which made Oren feel good. She certainly had the right attitude. He preceded her inside.

Olivia was there at the cash register. She trusted some staff members enough to handle customers' payments, but she seemed to enjoy handling that herself when she could—and getting the opportunity both to thank people who were leaving and to greet those who were coming in.

Olivia had big blue eyes and untamed black hair, complemented by her round earrings.

He gestured for Madison to join him at the counter so he could introduce them. He couldn't help noticing his sister's curious expression as she looked from him to Madison.

"Good evening," he said. "Madison, this is my sister, Olivia. She owns this special place, and you're about to get one heck of a good dinner."

"Hi, Olivia," Madison said, stepping up to the counter. She waved slightly as she smiled.

As Olivia smiled back, though more tentatively, Oren said, "And Olivia, this is Madison. She's helping me on a case."

That was brief and ambivalent enough to get Olivia wondering, Oren knew, but it was all he felt comfortable saying right now about the situation.

"Nice to meet you, Madison," Olivia said, then turned again toward Oren. "Go ahead and take one of your favorite booths at the back," she said.

"Fine," he responded. "Hope you'll come sit down with us for a while."

"Maybe a little later," Olivia said. "And I hope you enjoy your meal." She was looking at Madison again, her expression still curious, but Oren put his arm around Madison's shoulders and gently led her down the restaurant's main aisle toward the conglomeration of tables and booths he liked best.

They were soon seated, and at Madison's request Oren made some suggestions about what to order. He wasn't surprised that she chose a bowl of matzo ball soup. They'd talked about it earlier, and he'd expressed how much he enjoyed the delicious taste of this delight that Madison had never eaten before.

He ordered some, too, but just a cup, which meant a smaller matzo ball, and a pastrami sandwich. Their server was Sally, a delightful woman who'd waited on Oren many times before, and she promised to bring them both some water right away.

As she left, Oren's phone rang. "Sorry," he said to Madison, pulling his phone from his pocket. Seeing Jon's name displayed, he knew he had to talk. He pressed the button to answer. "Hi, Jon," he said.

"You ready to hear some awful stuff?" the deputy asked him.

"Lay it on me," Oren growled.

MADISON WISHED SHE knew what was going on.

Oh, she'd known Oren was expecting a phone call. He'd seemed frustrated before when his last conversation had ended abruptly and he had indicated it would continue sometime later. And he wasn't happy that it wasn't immediately.

Well, the time had apparently come.

He didn't look at her, just at the table. The waitress brought their water, and Oren grabbed his glass and took a swig as he listened. Madison figured he wished it was something stronger. Did they serve alcohol here, at the deli? Should she order him some?

"So where is she now?" Oren was asking. He scowled unreservedly—although the difficult expression did nothing to change how handsome the guy was. He glanced up at Madison briefly with angry blue eyes but looked away quickly, as if he didn't really want her to know his mood.

But Madison wanted to know what was being said on the other side of the conversation. She leaned forward on her pale red seat at the booth near the deli's back wall.

"At least she's still alive," Oren continued. "Right?"

The question shocked Madison. Who was *she*? What had happened to her? Or was Oren referring to Madison herself?

At least the answer must have been positive, since Oren said, "Fine. I'm not far from that hospital now. I'll head right there."

Hospital? That added to Madison's desire to learn more and made it clear he wasn't referring to her, although the reference to a hospital suggested *she* was still alive.

Whoever he spoke with must have responded negatively. "Okay. Glad you guys are already on it, of course, and I don't want to stress her out even more. But I want to hear everything that's learned from her as soon as possible. Got it?"

Apparently that person did get it, since the conversation soon ended, just as Sally placed their meals on the table in front of them. Good timing, Madison thought. Or not.

She wanted to hear everything that was on Oren's mind now.

But the guy was apparently not only a good federal marshal, he was a good actor, too. He put the phone down on the table beside him and looked up at the server, appearing pleased and relaxed. Or at least that was how Madison read him. "Thanks, Sally," he said. "It all looks delicious, as usual."

"I'll tell your sister you said so," said Sally. Her grin reflected amusement, and she looked fond of the guy she'd just served. It appeared genuine, not just because he was her boss's brother.

"Yeah, you do that," Oren said.

Sally winked, then walked away.

"She seems nice," Madison said, hoping to begin a conversation with Oren. "Now, tell me what was going on in that phone call."

"Yeah," he said. "I will. But not here and not now." He leaned across the table toward her. "I'm not just going to drive you home later," he said. "And I hope your sofa is comfortable."

"What!" The word came out a lot louder and sharper than Madison intended. But she also suspected what Oren now planned.

He wanted to stay the night with her, in her condo.

Good thing Alec didn't live with her. But there were a lot of reasons for that. What was going on?

Nothing positive. That was for certain.

Although the idea of being with this appealing but

difficult man overnight somehow got Madison's juices flowing. Bad idea.

She wanted to reach across the table and strangle the marshal when he moved his gaze away from her and pulled his cup of soup closer to him on the laminated-wood tabletop.

Instead, she said, "What makes you think I'd welcome you at my place? Maybe your sister would let you stay with her. And—"

"Does your fiancé live with you?"

"No, but—"

"Okay, all the more reason for me to join you. And, if you want to hear what my conversation was about, you need to let me hang out with you at your place, at least for tonight. In fact, even if you don't want to hear, you're going to let me stay there. Things are going on, and you appear to be right in the middle of them. I need to—"

Before he could finish, his sister joined them. Olivia wore a short silvery dress that Madison admired. She approached Oren's side of the booth and gestured with her hands for him to move over.

He grinned at her and obeyed, leaving Madison disgruntled and wanting to shout at the man. Tell him to stop playing games with her.

Tell her now what was really happening.

But he'd already implied at least some of it. Was she in danger somehow? She certainly believed so, after they'd been rammed and shot at.

How else might she be in the middle of what was going on, a subject of his earlier, clearly complicated conversation?

"Hey, bro," Olivia said, then turned her head. "And hey, Madison. Have you ever eaten here before? In any case, what do you think of our matzo ball soup? Have you eaten it other places? Do you make it at home?"

Madison had the impression that Oren's sister wasn't just asking about her opinion of the soup, here or elsewhere. She might have been attempting to get a little info on Madison's background.

Madison didn't want to get into it. Yes, she was a Colton, but maybe no one would recognize her, since she wasn't in law enforcement, and she certainly didn't want to bring up the connection.

Olivia's arrival at their table, and her questions, did manage to divert Madison's attention, at least a bit.

"This is my first time here," she said, smiling at Olivia. The Margulieses shared good family genes, Madison thought. "And I really don't frequent delis like this anywhere, although that might change after this meal. I might even try cooking my own, as you suggested. I'd heard good things about matzo ball soup before, but nothing I heard is anything like the real thing. It's wonderful!" Madison knew she was laying it on a bit thick. She didn't *need* to impress Olivia or try to make Oren's sister like her. But she had, in fact, tasted the soup and some small bites of matzo ball, and she'd really enjoyed it.

"So glad to hear that," Olivia said. Then she turned back toward Oren. "Good to see you," she said, "but I wasn't expecting you." Did Oren usually tell her when he wanted dinner at her deli? "Can you tell me what brought you here?"

"Nope," Oren replied, his voice a lot lighter than it had been before when he was talking to Madison about the phone call with contents he'd refused to reveal.

"Then, tell me at least, is it good stuff—" Olivia shot a quick glance toward Madison "—or marshal stuff?"

"I'll let you guess," Oren said. Madison figured that answer told Olivia what she wanted to know. If it had been *good stuff*, surely Oren would have told her. And what kind of good stuff? Was she asking if Oren and Madison were on a date?

What did she feel about that? Madison couldn't help thinking about Alec. Maybe if she'd already broken off their engagement... Well, did she really want to go on a date with Oren? But they had other reasons, scary ones, to be together right now.

"Got it." Olivia then turned her head, scanning around them. The place was crowded. And people who'd been sitting at a booth near them were standing now, looking toward the front of the place—maybe ready to pay and leave.

She figured that was what Olivia thought, too. Oren's sister stood. "Got to leave you here now, but let me know if there's anything I can do for you, okay?" She looked first at Madison, but her gaze landed on her brother.

Was she inviting him to stay longer? Maybe even spend the night at her house? Or was Madison reading too much into her words?

"Sounds good," Oren said. "See you again in a bit."

Olivia slipped away, preceding her customers down the walkway toward the front of the restaurant.

"Hope you weren't just trying to say nice things to my sister," Oren said. "Do you really like the soup?" He'd finished his cup and had just taken a bite of his sandwich.

"Definitely." Madison spooned off another piece of matzo ball.

"Good," he said. "We should finish up as quickly

as we can, though. It's getting late, and I want to go to
your house soon."

"Sure," Madison said. The bit of matzo ball seemed
to stick in her throat, and she swallowed hard.

She had the impression that Oren wanted to get her
away from other people, to the privacy of her home, as
fast as possible. Most likely because of that phone call.

Well, good. At this point, she wanted to get out of
here, too. Go somewhere that Oren would be willing
to talk to her.

Reveal all.

What was going on?

Chapter Seven

The drive to Madison's place didn't take long—a good thing, Oren thought. She lived in the better part of town—not surprising since she was a Colton, despite not being a member of what he believed to be the most affluent branch of the family.

As she gave directions, she told him they wouldn't pass the grade school where she taught kindergarten, though it was nearby. It was in Grave Gulch West, the more affluent area of town, but she didn't think that made a difference in how well her kids learned.

Oren appreciated her position on that.

"Fortunately, most of my students have families that are thrilled when their kids do well in classes, even starting as young as kindergarten. And it's always a delight when I get a student struggling with learning issues who I can help to point in a better direction."

Oren liked the sound of that, too, and the sweet sound of Madison's enthusiastic voice.

He also liked that they were talking about something other than the phone conversation that hung between them like a ticking metronome holding explosives.

He nevertheless kept looking around for that car that had hit them before—and observing all others, too, in case the fiendish, dangerous driver had obtained another one. And if so, maybe even stolen it, judging by the kind of person he seemed to be.

Which Oren knew even more about after his most recent conversation with Jon—that he would soon be discussing with Madison. Like it or not. But he had to, for her safety. He'd notify the cops soon about what was going on—even sooner, if he saw anything worrisome.

"Make a right turn here," Madison said from beside him. They were already in a nice residential area. One side of the street held small but attractive homes. There were larger buildings on the other side that Oren assumed were apartments or perhaps condominiums.

He followed Madison's directions, and they soon pulled into a driveway on an adjacent street. Madison told him to continue till its end in a nearly full parking lot.

"I take it you live here," Oren said as he parked in the spot Madison indicated was hers. The structure was three stories high and appeared to be made out of an attractive shadow-gray limestone, with balconies for each unit.

"That's right. Second floor. It's got a view onto the street, and it's also easy to walk up the stairs, although there is a small elevator in the building that mostly the people on the third floor use."

And it was in fact easy, both to get into the building— although fortunately, Madison did need to use a key so it wasn't open to the public—and to walk up the flight of wooden steps covered with black, designer stair treads to help prevent people from falling, Oren assumed. But he was disappointed to see no security cameras.

They soon reached the second floor and once more

she used a key to open the door to the hallway. Good. There was at least some security here.

Just in case— "Do you own your unit?" Oren asked as he followed her. "And does anyone else like a manager have a key?"

"Yes, I own my unit. We all do. And no one has a key other than us and whoever we give one to. We do have a condo association that takes care of the essentials like landscaping, cleaning the common areas and all that. And in case you're asking about security, too, yes, we pay for a security company to patrol the area sometimes."

Oren had to laugh. "Was I that obvious?"

"What do you think?" Madison countered.

She had the last unit down the hall, on the left. Oren figured there were ten units on this floor, five on each side.

They were soon inside Madison's place, and she closed the door behind him. He wasn't at all surprised that it was well decorated, with attractive multicolor area rugs on the wooden floor and furniture in the living room in complementary colors of lavender, beige and deep pink.

"Nice," he said, as she led him into the kitchen. Also nice, with a tile floor and silvery appliances, as well as a square wooden table with four matching chairs.

Okay. Good. He was paying attention to other things besides what was on his mind. *Madison.*

Till just then, at least. "So, let's talk," Madison said after placing her purse on a stool near the stove. "Have a seat. Oh, and I gather that what you have to say isn't pretty, so would you like a beer?"

He looked into her sparkling green eyes. She seemed amused. Well, that was a good thing for now.

He doubted she'd feel the same way once they'd talked.

"That sounds good," he said, "if you'll join me."

"Of course." She pulled two bottles out of the stain-less-steel refrigerator: a nice, dark amber beer from a popular high-end brewer. She also got a couple of beer steins from an upper cabinet near her sink and pulled a bottle opener from a drawer. She soon handed Oren a full glass, then waved toward the table. "Have a seat," she said. "And I'm going to take a swig first to get my-self warmed up for what you're going to say."

Oren wanted to laugh, but he couldn't. "Good idea." He pulled a chair from the end of the table and sat down. She sat across from him, and they both drank a little beer. It was cold, and as tasty as Oren had anticipated.

"So tell me," Madison said.

Oren realized he had been delaying not only to pro-tect her but to protect himself from relaying to her the current circumstances that were even more miserable than he had anticipated—even after their attack on the way here and his assumption about who the guy who'd come after them was.

No, after *her*. That guy had vengeance in mind, and Oren had to assume that Madison was his target.

But not his only one.

"Okay," Oren finally said. "Here's what I was told by someone else in my office. And it's pretty ugly. After discussion with some other law-enforcement agencies, including around here, they've learned that someone bribed a newly hired records clerk in my office to grab some files and give them to him. Turned out the clerk looked over those files herself, and after she told him a little about the contents, the guy said she should meet him here in Grave Gulch with them to get paid off."

"And does that guy happen to be the one who ran into us and aimed his rifle at us, the son of that gunrunner?"

Oren hadn't been attempting to hide anything from Madison, but he appreciated her intelligence in latching right on to what he hadn't yet said. "Yeah, his name is Darius Amaltin. His father's name was Louis."

"And the connection to us—whatever he was looking for in those files—did that happen to be my father?"

"Exactly. Darius hadn't been able to figure out before where Richard Foster was or how to find him. But those files had at least some of what he needed."

Madison took another swig of her beer but continued to look Oren straight in the eye. Those green eyes of hers could drive him to distraction if he let them. But he wouldn't.

"Our father had been safe before thanks to you and your witness protection," she said. "I appreciate that even more now. But why did Darius want the clerk to meet him here?"

"I gather she told him something, but not everything, about the Grave Gulch connection she saw in the files. He'd already hinted he didn't want to pick up or pay for the files in Grand Rapids or be anywhere near our Marshals Service offices, considering what he had in mind," Oren told her.

"So what did he have in mind?" Madison asked. "Nothing good, I'm sure."

"Absolutely not," Oren said. "You see, that foolish clerk has been in the hospital here in town for a few days. Will be there a while longer before she's arrested for what she did, but at least she's recuperating."

"Recuperating?" Madison's voice was raspy.

"Yeah." Oren didn't particularly like his own angry

tone, so he cooled it a bit as he continued. "Darius met her in a motel room in Grave Gulch to pay her off and get the files—or just to get the files. Once the clerk turned over what she'd brought, he shot her in the head—didn't pay her, of course—and fled with them."

"Shot her in the head?" Madison had paled, and her long fingers now cupped her face as if she otherwise couldn't hold up her own head. "And she survived? Thank heavens. But—"

"Yes, and though she's now still hospitalized, she's able to tell her story. Beyond what the clerk—her name is Nita—had told him to get him here, Darius learned enough in those files not to directly find the man in protective custody he was after but to become aware the man had had several kids here in Grave Gulch, and not just one—and he's been watching all of you, I gather, for at least a few days. He didn't mention any other relatives of yours, at least, like your mother. But your brother and sister are in this town, too, right?"

Madison nodded, and he saw tears in her eyes. She clearly feared not only for herself but also for her siblings. "Bryce and Jillian are both around here, at least now, so Darius can probably find them, too. Bryce is an FBI agent. And Jillian is a relatively new crime-scene investigator for the Grave Gulch PD. Our mother lives here as well. This is a good place for Darius to accomplish at least part of his horrible goal—hurting our father by doing something to us before…before killing him, I guess. Isn't that it? I'd imagine Darius didn't know where he was before. But why did he zero in on me? How would he have known…? By following me—well, I may have led him to our father." Her head fell forward, so she seemed to be staring at the table, and Oren had an urge to go over to her and give her a hug.

Bad idea, of course, so he sat still. "For one thing, a schoolteacher would probably be easier for him to get to than an FBI agent and a member of the local police force. Plus, you were apparently the first one to leave town. After Darius checked you all out and didn't see any of you hanging out with your father, and neither did he recognize anyone here in town as being Richard Foster, he must have decided to follow any of you who left town in case you were about to visit your dad—like when you went to Kendall, at least the second time. And who did you see there? The exact person Darius was after."

Madison drew in her breath. She was clearly crying, even as she took another long swig of beer. "Then, I did lead Darius to him." She seemed to choke on the words as she looked at Oren. "Is my dad still okay?"

"I'm sure he is, at least for now," he answered.

"That's good, at least. But I'm so sorry. If only I'd known... I'm glad in a way that he did come after me instead of my father, but why did he do that to me—and you, too, unfortunately?"

"My guess is that you're right," Oren said, "and he wanted to kill you or one of your siblings or your mother, or maybe even all of you, so your father would suffer pain like what he might have been feeling all this time since his own father was killed in prison. I'd imagine, now that Darius has disappeared again, that he is still after you, and maybe Bryce and Jillian, too, and possibly your mother. And assuming I'm right, after he's done with all of you, he'll go after your father. But I learned some good news on that front in my call. Your dad's been moved into a safe house in Kendall now."

He couldn't help it. "Mind if I grab another beer? And would you like one, too?"

"It's fine if you take one. And yes, please, bring me one as well. And—well, how did your fellow marshals in your office learn all this?"

Oren stuck his head in the refrigerator and soon returned to the table with the two bottles that he'd already taken the caps off. He poured one first into Madison's nearly empty stein, then filled his own.

"Well, after the clerk, Nita, disappeared, the deputies checking into her situation discovered some files were gone. She didn't have any family in Grand Rapids, so there was no way of checking into her more that way. But they got in contact with me because the missing files involved a case I recently took over when the former marshal on the case retired."

"My father, in witness protection," Madison piped up immediately.

"Exactly. And I'd already noticed in those files, when I'd gone through them, that the twentieth anniversary of Louis Amaltin's death in prison was coming up. The idea of my having the case on such an important anniversary was sort of interesting to me, but I hardly thought that date meant anything. The gunrunner's death in prison. A shame, but so what? Only, what if the son wanted to get his hands on the witness who helped to convict his father—and his family—partly because of the anniversary?"

"What had Darius been doing all this time—waiting for this anniversary to start killing people? Or had he done bad stuff before?"

"I don't know for sure," Oren said. "I was told a little bit about him in my phone conversation about the injured clerk. Apparently Darius had skirmishes with the law before and had seemed very determined, to the officers involved, to accomplish whatever he'd begun. And there were some indications that he'd mentioned being furious because of the death of his father."

"This is all so strange," Madison said, shaking her head so her red hair swished gently around her face. Oren had an even stranger urge now, after his thought about hugging her, to go close and gently sweep that hair back and stroke it with his hands…

No way. Sure, she was beautiful, and he didn't have anyone in his life now. Didn't want one. Relationships never worked out for him. He'd tried enough in the past.

One woman he'd been interested in had also wanted to become a marshal—and she'd dumped him for one of his superior officers, which seemed even more inappropriate.

Then there was the lovely accountant who neglected to tell him she'd been married before and had a child. He wouldn't necessarily have minded the kid—only the fact she'd tried to hide it from him.

There was also another woman who just seemed very nice and sweet and sexy—but they had just grown tired of one another. Otherwise, he dated, spent the night with some women, but didn't find any he wanted to get closer to.

And Madison? Well, nothing could come of any attraction to her. She was part of the important case he was now handling.

He forced his mind back to where it should be. "Yeah," he said, "the entire case is strange, and where it stands now… Well, my job now is to protect people, you included. I want to meet with your law-enforcement relatives and the local chief of police tomorrow at the police station, if that's possible, and talk to you about how to deal with the situation, including regarding your mother."

"Oh, good," Madison said. "I'm worried about all of us, and Mom in particular. And how she'll be when she learns… Well, I'll be glad to discuss what to do."

Oren nodded, understanding her concern, of course. He continued. "I gather, from the research I've done and records I've looked at, that the interim chief right now is Brett Shea. With your sister Jillian's connection with the local police, and yours with her and your brother, I want your help to try to set up that meeting. Okay?"

Oren was surprised at the sudden dubious look that marred Madison's beautiful face. "I'll call Jillian, and Bryce, too, of course. I'm fairly sure I can get them to meet with us, and hopefully Jillian will be able to arrange for Brett to join us. Not my mom yet, though, till the rest of us have talked first. And I'll ask Jillian to set it up at the station tomorrow—unless the interim chief says otherwise. I've got cousins who work there, too. But there have been a lot of demonstrations at the station recently, thanks to some things that have been going on in the department, one person's actions in particular, and—"

"I've heard about that," Oren said. "A forensic scientist who was part of the force doing some pretty nasty things, right?"

"Right. And there is serial killer Len Davison on the loose, too. And—well, it's getting late. Let me start my calls, and we'll see what we can arrange."

"Fine. And I've already seen what a nice couch you have there in your living room. It looks comfortable enough for me to spend the night right there."

"As if I had a choice," Madison said, but her beautiful red eyebrows were raised apparently not just in skepticism, but in amusement, too. "And I do have a spare bedroom, so if you have to stay, you could use that."

"You're right," Oren said in a light voice in return. "You don't have a choice." Unless, of course, she wanted him to hang out in her bedroom with her... No. That wasn't going to happen, even though the very thought made his body start to react. And she was *engaged*.

Inappropriate. And even the thought of what they could do together might distract him from what he really needed to do here.

"And thanks for offering me the spare bedroom," he continued, "but I'll sleep on the couch."

He didn't mention why he had to stay, or why he chose the couch, but he was certain that Madison knew. He was going to protect her. And hanging out in an extra bedroom might mean he wouldn't hear if there were any problems in the night.

For now, he'd hang out with her till her bedtime. And before that, he wanted to participate in any of the calls she made to her siblings, too, to make sure, even though members of his department had already been in touch to warn them as well.

Chapter Eight

This was all so frightening. And it had been that way from even before she had met the man who had in fact turned out to be her father.

No, at least some of it had started at the time the man who was now with her, who said he still intended to protect her, had arrested her for jaywalking. *Jaywalking*.

That thought should have made Madison want to laugh again. Instead, considering all that had happened since, and all that could happen in the future, whether or not Oren was with her… Well, she almost wanted to cry.

But she wouldn't. She would stay strong. She would act perfectly normal as she spoke with her sister and brother so she could help to protect them. And they could all protect their mother.

She hoped. It crossed her mind that if she'd been closer to Alec, maybe he could have helped her deal with her difficult situation. But she didn't even want to tell him about it. Right now, she had an urge to call Grace, not because she was a cop but just to have someone else to talk to about all this absurdity. Even more appropriate, maybe, because Grace had been with her when she had first seen the man who had in fact turned out to be her father, though Madison had pretended to laugh it off then. But Grace would be a good one to talk to now, since she had gone through some rough stuff recently—as well as finding the right man in her life.

Madison wouldn't call her now, though. Nor would she phone her mother. She and her siblings would need to discuss letting Mom know what was going on, and taking care of her, when they met.

"Okay," she said to Oren now. "Let's do it. I'll call my sister, Jillian, first about setting up the meeting at the police station and getting the interim chief to join us."

"Let's see how it goes," Oren said. "If there's a problem, maybe I can help as a member of the federal Marshals Service."

"Wow." Madison managed a smile. "If there is a problem, maybe I can temporarily join the local county sheriff's department. It may be the only law-enforcement arm around here that we don't already have represented."

Oren laughed, then said, "Okay, I agree—with your starting the calls, not becoming a sheriff's deputy." He grew serious immediately. "Just so you know, it's fine for you to warn your sister and brother about the potential danger they face, but they've already been told some of it. They were called by one of our deputies, who gave them no details but told them they were potentially being stalked by someone who intended to harm them and others in their family, so they should be very cautious. That may not be unusual for Coltons, but at least they were forewarned."

"That's good, I guess," Madison mused. "I was going to call to warn them, but since they've already had a heads-up, and they're both in law enforcement, they'll know how to protect themselves. But it'll be a whole lot better for them—and me—once we've discussed it in more detail tomorrow and they know what's going on."

"That's what I figure, too," Oren said. Madison liked the way he looked her straight in the eye and nodded. "You'll all come out of this just fine, if I have anything to say about it."

"Or do about it," Madison responded with an attempt at a smile. "I already have the impression you're all about action."

"Exactly."

"But as I've already indicated, I'm also concerned about our mother. Do you know if Darius is after her, too?"

"He mentioned only you and your siblings when he stole the files and shot Nita, so hopefully not. But we can't be certain, of course."

Madison ended that part of their conversation by putting her phone on the table in front of her and swiping the screen on. She pressed the phone icon, looked under recent calls and pushed Jillian's name.

Then she put it on Speaker. She doubted this conversation would contain anything personal, and it might help to have Oren join in.

"Hi, Madison? Are you okay?" Jillian answered right away. "I had the strangest, even scariest, conversation before with a deputy marshal and wanted to discuss it with you tonight, but I was told to wait till around now to call you, if I intended to. And you can be sure I'm not happy about it. In fact, I nearly called you, anyway."

Why would the deputy Oren mentioned tell her that? Madison glanced across the table at him, but he shrugged as if he was puzzled, too.

"Have you talked to Bryce?" Madison asked. Would their brother have been told the same thing?

"Yes. He asked me to set it up as a conference call when I did get in touch with you. Should we add him to this conversation?"

Madison looked at Oren, who nodded.

"That sounds fine," Madison said. "And just so you know, I have someone with me now who'll also be participating. His name is Oren Margulies, and he's with the US Marshals Service."

"Hello, Jillian," Oren said before Jillian could question anything. But Madison, knowing her sister, figured there was a lot going through her mind.

They soon had Bryce on the line, too. Like Jillian, he seemed irritated he'd been told that not only could his life be in danger but also that he'd get more information tomorrow.

But Madison was glad that the result of this chat was to confirm that her siblings did know something was going on and were taking care of themselves. And that they'd all get together tomorrow to discuss it in a meeting at the police station. That was confirmed, too, after Jillian left the call to get in touch with Grave Gulch Interim Police Chief Brett Shea. The plan was to get together at nine in the morning.

"Do you know what's going on, Madison?" Bryce asked while they waited for Jillian to return.

"Kind of," she replied. "And I've already agreed to wait to discuss it till tomorrow, so don't try to get me talking about it now, except to tell you to be careful and stay safe tonight." She glanced at Oren, who had just finished his second stein of beer. He nodded his agreement with her, and she rolled her eyes.

Jillian soon returned to the call. "It's all set," she said. "We'll meet at the station at nine."

But— "With all those demonstrations, will we be able to get in?" Madison asked.

"Not sure there'll be any tomorrow, but I've been able to enter the building, even during the worst of them," Jillian said. "From what I gather, now that our cousin Melissa is no longer the acting police chief, things are calming down a bit. But give me a call if the front entrance seems blocked, and I'll let you in through one of the rear doors."

"Got it," Madison said. They soon said their goodbyes and hung up.

And there they were, she and Oren. Alone in her condo that night. Together, yet not together.

She was much too attracted to the guy. She knew that. But it could largely be because he'd been protecting her. Never mind that he'd arrested her earlier.

He rose across the table from her. She had an urge to join him and give him a good-night kiss—maybe one that could lead to something a lot more fun.

But that wasn't going to happen, she chided herself. How could she even think such a thing? Sure, she might be questioning her relationship with Alec, but they were still engaged.

But that was the point. She might not even consider kissing Oren if all was right between Alec and her...

She stood up, too. "You may be sleeping on the sofa, but you might as well be comfortable. I'll show you where my extra pillows, sheets and blankets are, and you can grab whatever you like. Towels, too, so you can use the bathroom out here." Fortunately, although it was more of a powder room, it contained a small shower.

"Sounds good," he said, and she first walked to the refrigerator, where she got him a bottle of water.

Then she showed him where everything else was. "I assume we should get up tomorrow morning around seven thirty or so, since it's Sunday, not a workday. I'll set my alarm. I have the fixings for breakfast, so we can eat right here. And—"

"And thanks for all this." Oren held the water bottle in his left hand as he drew closer to her in the kitchen. "And don't tell me to sleep well. I'll sleep as much as I can, but I'm used to this kind of thing, believe me. The slightest noise will wake me up."

She understood he was attempting to make her feel at ease, allow her to sleep that night, and she appreciated it. She appreciated *him*.

"Thanks," she said and realized her voice was hoarse.

Oren was right in front of her. He put the water down on the table, and before she could get sensible and retreat to her room, he moved toward her, and she was in his arms.

His body was hard against her—and so was the particular part of him below that made all lingering vestiges of sensibleness in her fly away. She held him close, and in moments they were engaged in a kiss.

His touch was hot, strong, enticing, and she enjoyed the feel of his rough facial hair against her face. She had an urge to pull back just long enough to tug him down the hall and into the bedroom.

But fortunately, one of them still remained sane: him. He pulled back and looked down at her with his sexy blue eyes.

"Good night, Madison," he said hoarsely. "Sleep well. There's nothing to worry about tonight. I'll make sure of it."

Nothing but her sanity, Madison thought as she wished him good-night, too, and headed to her room.

As she got ready for bed, she kept reliving that kiss in her mind, over and over, her body reacting even without Oren's presence.

It didn't seem right that she'd gotten so close to the man who was protecting her—and yet also it felt very right.

And when she finally got beneath the lacy beige coverlet on her queen-size bed, she realized that despite all she had gone through that day and her current worries about the man who wanted to kill her family, she was falling asleep and appreciated the presence of the dedicated—and handsome—marshal who she'd no doubt would do as he'd promised and keep her safe.

And only when she was nearly asleep did she realize she'd come home but hadn't yet called her fiancé.

Well, she'd get in touch with Alec tomorrow. After she'd had her important meeting with her siblings, Oren and the cops.

And do what she needed to do—finally break up with her fiancé.

OREN WOKE SEVERAL times that night, as he'd programmed himself to do. He pulled off the sheet he'd thrown over himself on the sofa and walked around, taking his phone off the charger he always kept with him and using it as a flashlight.

He listened at the front door. He looked out windows. He walked down the hall, pushed open the door slightly and peered into Madison's room, ignoring his impulse to do more.

He'd already done enough. That kiss was uncalled

for...no matter how much he had enjoyed it. He was here as a professional, guarding her.

And she was engaged. Well, at least all appeared to remain fine in her home.

And Oren wondered where the hell Darius Amaltin was and hoped all Madison's family members were also safe.

He woke on his own around seven thirty, as planned, and heard Madison stirring. He showered and got dressed, and as he exited the bathroom he found her in the kitchen cooking breakfast: a cheese omelet and toast plus coffee. "Hope it's okay," she told him, and it was a lot more than okay.

She'd made breakfast for him, as if he'd spent the night for something beyond her protection. They'd shared a kiss. He would just have to keep in mind even more that he was here on an assignment. Nothing more.

At least they didn't spend much time eating that excellent meal. He knew Grave Gulch well enough to get to the police station without directions, but that didn't keep him from glancing toward Madison often. She'd dressed in an outfit he assumed she also taught in, a pretty, pale green dress and brown shoes with low heels. Professional enough for a meeting at the police station.

And him? Well, he hadn't picked up the change of clothes he kept in his car before they'd left, or dropped in at his sister's house to pick up clothes he kept there, so he still wore the same gray sports coat, shirt and slacks he'd had on yesterday. He'd slept in his underwear—and fortunately hadn't seen Madison all night, to tempt him to take them off.

Up till now, they'd mostly just talked about nothing,

like what a nice day it was for autumn in Grave Gulch. But as they neared the station, Madison said, "I gathered from what you said yesterday that you're aware of the protests that have been going on around here."

"Olivia has kept me informed. I understand they're partly about recent police misconduct."

"It's more than just that. Some people are protesting the supposed corruption of the local police department since a forensic scientist there, Randall Bowe, had apparently been creating or destroying evidence, maybe thanks to bribes, so sometimes even murderers have gotten off scot-free. And there's Len Davison, and some people have accused my cousin Grace of an unjustified shooting, even though she's been cleared. The public's not happy about that. Me, neither. Anyway, better go slow here." Madison leaned toward the windshield. "I know Jillian said the protests seem to have stopped now that our cousin Melissa is no longer in charge of the police department, but we should still be careful."

"Oh, that's right. The rookie cop who was accused of inappropriately shooting was a Colton, and so was the former police chief, right? And you're a Colton, too. Will the protesters come back if they know you're here?" He kept his tone light. He was joking, after all.

"Let's hope not," Madison said dryly. "Besides, Melissa and Grace aren't the only Coltons on the police force. There are a lot of them—certainly not including me. But the idea of so many Coltons appears to rattle a lot of people. And some have blamed Melissa for the misconduct of that forensic scientist."

"Any idea why so many Coltons got into law enforcement?" Oren couldn't help asking.

"I understand it was because a family member was

killed in a still unsolved murder years ago—Amanda Colton, who was then married to my uncle Geoff. It prompted a lot of the family to spend their lives seeking justice, even if they couldn't achieve it for Amanda."

"Interesting," Oren said.

They had reached the station, no slowed vehicles or protesters in sight, and Oren pointed that out to Madison. "Thank heavens," she said.

Oren pulled into a parking lot near the front of the station, telling Madison to remain in the car till he came around for her. But would someone with a goal of killing people visit a police station with that in mind?

Besides, Darius didn't know about this upcoming meeting—did he?

Oren soon opened Madison's door and watched as she pivoted, admiring her lovely legs as she exited the vehicle. "Thanks," she said.

Oren continued to look around, including at the station. It was a nice building, one story, made out of stone and clearly antique. Quite a few people were heading into or out of the station but not congregating as if in a protest. A good thing.

He resisted the urge to take Madison's hand to lead her to the door. Instead, he followed her. She soon had her phone at her ear, and he assumed she was calling her sister to let her know they'd arrived so she could meet them and take them to wherever the meeting was to be.

"Great," she soon said. "We'll be there in a minute."

MADISON HAD VISITED the lobby of the Grave Gulch Police Department a few times, mostly to meet Jillian for dinner after both had finished with their jobs for the day. Jillian's ending time varied more than Madison's, since the obligations of a crime-scene investigator could change at any minute, whereas a kindergarten teacher generally had a more predictable schedule, including any after-school meetings with her students and their parents, plus her preparations for the next day. And occasionally, Grace joined them.

Madison therefore knew what the greeting area of the police station looked like and usually appreciated this delightful building that had been constructed way back in the 1850s—when she wasn't about to have a meeting about the danger to her family.

Behind the gated front desk were other desks for some of the department's employees.

At the moment, a group of three people she assumed were civilians stood at the front desk. She also saw a few uniformed cops in the greeting room and others inside the open enclosure. She tried eavesdropping after she heard one of those nearby say the word *protesters*. Best she could discern, they were relieved that whoever the protesters had been, they weren't around any longer, though they still hung out sometimes at other places nearby, like around city hall and the courthouse. "They're still demanding justice for that missing forensic scientist Randall Bowe's crimes," one of them said.

"No big surprise," said another.

But Madison couldn't listen any more. That wasn't why she was here. She wondered where their meeting would be held and wished Jillian had let her know. She turned toward Oren, ready to ask if he'd ever been here before, but she saw Bryce walk through the door they'd entered from. She grinned. "Hi, bro!"

FBI agent Bryce was dressed professionally for the meeting at the police station, in a black suit, beige shirt and red tie. "Hi, sis." He gave her a hug.

Madison always considered Bryce a nice-looking guy. Now, under the circumstances, she found herself pulling back and staring, comparing him in her mind with the man she'd discovered was their father Richard Foster, now known as Wesley Windham. Bryce gave her a puzzled frown as she continued to regard him. Same shape of eyes beneath shaggy brows. A high forehead. Dark lashes. Lips that were a bit narrow. Fair skin. A somewhat-pointed chin. Ears that hugged his head.

She knew her mind was repeating all she had thought about when she'd viewed Wes in person and in the not-so-great photo she'd taken of him last week. But yes, her brother did look a lot like their dad, though with darker hair and eyes, of course.

Bryce pulled away. "What's going on, Madison?"

"Something amazing," she replied, "and scary." She then noticed Oren just behind Bryce, watching them. "For now, though—" she motioned for Oren to join them "—Bryce, I'd like you to meet Marshal Oren Margulies. Oren, this is my brother, Bryce. It's thanks to him…" She let her voice taper off. She'd no doubt Oren would know what she meant.

"Hi, Bryce." Oren had joined them and now held his hand out to the agent, who shook it.

"Hello, Oren." But then Bryce looked back to Madison. "So tell me what's going on."

"Not out here," she said, and, fortunately, that was

when Jillian hurried from a door behind the reception area toward them.

Jillian's hair was light brown and a lot longer than Madison's. And though Madison was reasonably slim, Jillian was even more slender. Madison admired her, though she refused to be jealous of her younger sister. Jillian was twenty-seven.

"Hi, all of you!" she exclaimed as she reached them. She looked from Madison to Bryce, then toward Oren, obviously realizing that, whoever he was, he was part of this group. "Come with me. Chief Shea is meeting us in one of the conference rooms."

Motioning for them to follow, Jillian led them first to the front desk, where she spoke to the uniformed officer in charge. After they showed their IDs, the gate was unlocked, and Jillian led them to one of the original wooden doors, which she opened, and then she waved for them to go inside. "I'll let the chief know we're all here—right?" She glanced again at Oren, then looked at Madison.

"Fine. This is Oren. I'll explain when Chief Shea gets here." Madison joined Bryce and Oren as they sat down at the long wooden table at the center of the room. "So you're a fed," Bryce said to Oren. "What do you do in your job?"

"A lot." Oren grinned as he glanced toward Madison, who'd taken a chair beside him. "Protecting people, arresting people—"

That made Madison laugh—and feel glad she could find her arrest humorous now.

"I think Oren will be the one who'll talk most here," Madison said. "He's got the background. I'm just a newcomer to the situation, and in a way so are Jillian and you."

"But—" Bryce interrupted.

He was interrupted, too, as Jillian came in with Brett Shea.

"Okay, all of you," the interim chief said. "What the hell is going on?"

Chapter Nine

Nice introduction, Oren thought. But the man who approached and clearly thought himself in charge glared at the three siblings, then stopped his gaze on Oren. And yes, he was in charge, in this location and under these circumstances.

Interim Chief Shea was maybe early thirties, five or six years younger than Oren. He looked fairly rugged, though, as if he'd seen some pretty nasty things in his life in law enforcement. He was tall, with reddish hair and blue eyes he didn't move from Oren. He of course wore a uniform with a badge, nameplate and lots of stripes, as well as the obligatory belt with tools and a gun.

"What's going on, Jillian?" Brett said. "You told me there's a dangerous situation in town but didn't tell me anything about it. Who'll explain, so we can figure out how best to handle it?"

"That would be me," Oren told him smoothly. "I'm Oren Margulies of the US Marshals Service. Of the three members of the Colton family who are here, the one who knows most about what's going on is Madison, and she's in the most danger."

"Really?" Jillian bent down near Madison's chair to give her a hug. Her hair brushed her sister's shoulder.

"Please tell us more about what's happening," she said, looking at Oren, "and how we can keep Madison, and ourselves, safe."

"He's about to do that," Madison said in a soft and somewhat-confident voice that made Oren want to hug her, too. Of course he didn't, but he managed to smile at her while her sister sat back down. But then Madison said, "Just let me start off, though. It's something my brother and sister and I never imagined." She looked at Bryce first, then Jillian. "Our father is alive."

"What!" Jillian rose again.

"Okay," Bryce said through gritted teeth. His fists were clenched on the wooden table. "Get this story started." He looked at Oren, who could only imagine what emotions must be rushing through both of Madison's siblings.

"I should probably have invited Grace to be here, too, since she was with me when…when I first saw him. I'll make sure she hears about it."

Madison described what Oren already knew. She first told them about seeing someone who looked much too familiar on her first visit to Kendall—familiar enough that she returned. She didn't mention what had brought her to that town in the first place—looking for a wedding gown—which Oren found interesting. It even gave him a little zing of pleasure that she wasn't talking about that part of her personal life, even to her family.

She then described how she met the man, without mentioning Oren's arresting her to keep her away, which he appreciated since it wouldn't help with what they were attempting to accomplish. "He recognized me, too, kind of," Madison said with tears in her eyes. "He thought I looked like our mother, but with my age and red hair he knew it was me. And when we talked… Oh, yes, he's our father."

"Then, why hasn't he been in touch with us all these years?" Bryce demanded. "I don't see much reason to have anything to do with him after he deserted us and Mom."

"I'd better let Oren explain, including why we're in danger." Madison looked at him with her watery green eyes. Oren's urge to hug her increased, but of course he stayed where he was. He had a story to tell.

And Oren wanted to make that story as concise as possible but also wanted to ensure that the siblings and interim police chief had enough detail to understand. He explained how he'd been put in charge of a man in protective custody of the Marshals Service when his predecessor retired. The subject's name was Wesley Windham—formerly Richard Foster.

Without stopping at the gasps and exclamations of Jillian and Bryce, he looked at Brett. "Richard Foster was the father of these three."

He went on to explain how Foster had been in the military and had witnessed a murder on his final trip home. He'd helped to identify the killer and been recruited to testify at his murder trial. The perp, Louis Amaltin, had been sentenced to prison. He'd threatened Foster with revenge, thanks to his cohorts who were still free, so that was why Foster/Windham was put into protective custody and now lived in Kendall, Michigan.

"I think he decided to stay far away from all of you for your protection, which is required due to the danger I'm about to describe," Oren said. Bryce and Jillian appeared skeptical, which he understood. He explained that Amaltin had been murdered in prison, but of course all his colleagues still posed a threat, so Wes Windham remained in protective custody.

Was that a solid reason for him never to contact his family? Oren hadn't been too sure of it before, but after what had just gone on with Madison and him and the attack they'd endured, he now figured it had been a good decision for Wes's sake.

"Amaltin had been married and had a kid," Oren continued. "Amaltin's murder occurred exactly twenty years ago now, and his son, Darius Amaltin, apparently wants revenge on Wes by killing his family first, then maybe coming after him. He attacked Madison already." At her siblings' respective additional gasps, he explained what had happened on the road driving to Grave Gulch, letting them know he'd stayed with Madison to keep her safe. "And I can't help believing that he'll probably come after one or both of you, too, followed by Wes, although he fortunately hasn't mentioned your mother."

"Is that miserable jerk here in town?" asked Brett. Of course the local police chief would want to know that.

"Don't know for sure. But he's been here and knew how to find Madison as a result of bribery and attempted murder." He described how the foolish bribed clerk had been found.

"That's horrible," Jillian exclaimed. "And oh, Madison, I'm so glad you're okay. Bryce and I have been trained in ways to keep us safe, and we can always call on our colleagues for backup. But… Well, we also need to figure out the best way to inform, and protect, Mom." She turned toward Oren. "I know you'll be concerned about our father, since he's your assignment. But, please, can you continue to help keep Madison safe?"

Oren nodded. "I have colleagues in Kendall protecting your dad," he said. "For now, Madison is my assignment. I already figured she's in the most danger of you siblings, since you two have law-enforcement backgrounds and he's seen her. Madison may get tired of seeing me around, but for now, at least, she's stuck with me." He realized that might sound too personal, so he added, "Good thing she's got a comfortable sofa that I tested last night while also doing rounds. And I'll be working on ways to get Darius captured while Madison's in safe environments. I'll have to check on security at the school where she teaches, of course."

"What about when she's with her fiancé?" Jillian asked. "He's just a teacher, too. Darius might use him as a tool to get to Madison."

"No," Madison said softly. "I've been worried about Alec, of course. I think this might be a good time to break off our engagement. He doesn't need to be involved."

"At least for now," Bryce agreed.

Oren was interested that Madison didn't respond to Bryce's remark. Maybe she did just want to protect the guy.

Or maybe she actually wanted to end the engagement for personal reasons. He tried not to feel too happy about that possibility. It was none of his business.

"I'm not thrilled that all this is going on in my town," Brett said, "but we'll stay in close touch."

"Sounds good," Oren said.

"Thanks for letting me know," Brett responded.

"Us, too," Jillian said. Her head was cocked as she looked at her sister, and that long hair of hers dangled down one side. She was attractive, too. She didn't wear a ring, so maybe she was available, unlike engaged Madison.

But he really didn't care about Jillian's marital status. Of course, he didn't know Madison well, either. But something about her really attracted him.

Yeah, his interest in her continued to grow. That was highly inappropriate. Besides, he'd had those three go-nowhere relationships in the past that had soured him on anything more than casual dating. He now knew that attempting to settle down with one woman wasn't for him. But Madison was in danger. She had already been recognized and attacked. He would do his job and safeguard her—and nothing else. He knew better than to cross the professional line.

He turned to their FBI-agent brother. "So Bryce," he said. "You're a fed, too. Anything you can do to help your family?"

"I'll notify my superiors, of course. Have them check on those Amaltins and their background, see if there's anything we can do to add to the search and investigation. Do my best to protect my family, too."

"Sounds good." Oren rose from his chair. Being in the police station had to be good and safe. But he'd accomplished what he needed to here, so it was time for Madison and him to leave. Although she might want to spend more time with her family. If so, he'd have them nail down where they were going and what they were planning to do. And otherwise? "So Madison," he said, "what would you like to do now?"

Like, are you ready to go into witness protection till the cops bring in the guy who wants to kill you?

He wouldn't ask that now, though, in front of her family.

"I'm fine with heading home now," she responded.

But Oren shot a glance at Brett and found the interim chief was looking at him.

"There's something else I want to talk to you about first, Margulies," Brett said. "You, too, Bryce. Please come to my office. We can leave Madison and Jillian in this room. They'll be safe here, inside the station, but the thing I need to discuss right now doesn't concern them."

Really? What could it be? Oren shot a glance at Madison, and though her eyes widened in obvious surprise, she said, "That's fine. Jillian and I can catch up a little more. We haven't been spending a lot of time together lately."

So it was apparently settled. Curious about what Brett intended to talk about, Oren pushed his chair back under the table as the other men in the room did the same thing.

"Thanks," Brett said to none of them in particular. "Gentlemen, please follow me."

MADISON COULDN'T HELP wondering what it was that the interim police chief wanted to discuss with the marshal and the FBI agent. Cop stuff. Or law-enforcement stuff.

Something he didn't want to talk to his own employee, Jillian, about.

For now, Madison watched the three men leave the conference room.

"I wonder what that's about." Jillian moved so she was sitting beside Madison in the chair Oren had just vacated.

"So do I," Madison responded. "Maybe Bryce will tell us about it later." Or Oren would tell her—maybe.

"Guess that'll depend on what it is, and whether the chief says it's okay to mention it. If it was, he might as well have just talked about it here while we were all in the same room together."

"You're right." Madison smiled. "In any case, it's good to see you. What's going on in the world of crime-scene investigation?"

She liked how Jillian grinned, her eyes sparkling. "Nothing much that's new, although a rookie like me certainly learns a lot daily." She laughed. "And let me suggest again that you get into some kind of law enforcement like our brother and me."

"Oh, I'm just fine as a kindergarten teacher. I like working with kids, seeing their progress and all."

And I want to have kids someday, too, Madison thought. That was one reason she'd gotten engaged to Alec. Still...

It was as if Jillian read her mind. "So I guess you'd better do whatever's necessary to warn Alec about what's going on, too. I gather you didn't find the ideal wedding dress on your trips to Kendall. But finding our father instead? Wow!"

"Wow, indeed," Madison agreed. "And I didn't spend much time—" *no time at all, in fact* "—checking out dresses in that shop I told you about. And now, I'll really be worried about Alec. As I've said, maybe I should end things with him. I could let the world know so that horrible Darius person will leave him alone." She paused. "I think it's time to break up with Alec anyway, for lots of reasons." That all sounded a bit hollow. She knew it. But Jillian probably wouldn't accuse her of insincerity about Alec or anything else. She'd undoubtedly support whatever Madison decided.

"I've wondered about that," Jillian said. Interesting. Was it that obvious?

"But with Bryce and you and Mom," Madison continued, "I'm afraid I can't do anything like that to keep you safe. We'll have to figure something out. Your being in law enforcement doesn't mean that miserable man can't hurt you. And our father…"

"Amazing that you actually met him. We'll have to go to Kendall with you someday soon. You'll have to introduce all of us."

"That's what I'm hoping," Madison said, "as long as we're all protected from that dangerous creep Darius."

As she hopefully was, thanks to Oren.

OREN FOLLOWED THE other men from the conference room into the large, enclosed entry area. There were a bunch of other people around there, mostly uniformed cops, and he also heard voices from beyond the reception divider. He figured this place was always busy.

Brett led them through the ornate door at the far left corner, then closed it behind them. "Please have a seat." He walked around them and sat in a large chair at the desk that must be his.

"So what can we do for you, Brett?" Bryce asked.

"Well, I mostly want to bring another fed, Oren, up to date on that situation you're aware of, Bryce, and I'll update you, too, since there've been some recent changes. Very recent. Like, ten minutes before our meeting in the conference room."

Interesting, Oren thought. He felt oddly proud that he was going to be given whatever information Brett was about to relate. Sure, he was a fed, but his marshal status didn't put him in charge of much besides the assignments he was given.

So what was this about?

First thing, Brett asked, "Are you aware, Oren, of the demonstrations that have been going on around this station, as well as other landmarks in this town, like city hall?"

"Yes, somewhat. Madison talked about them on our way here. I guess she talked to Jillian about them, too, who told her things seemed to have calmed down, at least right here."

"True." Brett sat back in his chair, locking his fingers behind his head. "And do you know what they were about?"

"I think she said the main cause was that a forensic scientist who worked for the police department was purposely modifying some evidence and how it was evaluated. The community is angry and worried about both the evidence tampering and the inmate releases, plus a recent surge in citywide crime." Most likely justifiably, Oren thought, but he didn't say so.

"Exactly," Brett said. "We've been trying to chase the scientist down and bring him in, but good old Randall Bowe has been hiding. Even our best resources haven't located him yet."

Oren nodded, wondering where this was going. He glanced beside him toward Bryce, who was nodding. "I'm not sure what the Marshals Service can do to help," Brett continued, "but I figure your knowing what's going on can't hurt, and if I think of any specifics I need from either of your agencies, I'll be sure to let you know."

"Thanks," Oren said, although that depended on what Brett was talking about and what he'd need.

Brett started describing how the situation had changed a short time ago. Turned out he had gotten a phone call just before the meeting from Baldwin Bowe, the brother of Randall and a ghost bounty hunter, who used mercenary tactics to find people. Baldwin had told Brett that Randall had finally answered the burner-phone number he'd given to Melissa. The cops had supplied that information to Baldwin.

Baldwin had apparently told Brett that the phone conversation had been weird and difficult. According to Baldwin, Randall had ranted in his ear for two minutes or more, talking about everything from how their parents had always liked Baldwin better, and how their dad was a cheating louse, and that everything was everyone else's fault, not his.

"Baldwin told me he'd asked Randall where he was," Brett said, "and tried to get his brother to meet with him, but Randall hung up on him. Baldwin said he's going to try to figure out where Randall might be hiding, and if he can help catch him, he will. But in the meantime, he's after another fugitive in his bounty-hunter capacity, so he won't have a lot of time to chase his brother at the moment." Brett paused. "So if either of you has any suggestions about how to track Randall down now, let me know. I'll have our techs look into tracking the location of that burner phone, of course, but my suspicion is that Randall will stay far away from it now, at least for a while."

"Good guess," Oren said. "Anyhow, nothing comes to mind at the moment, but I appreciate your letting me in on this, and I'll ponder what might be advisable to do next. I'll run it by some appropriate people in my department and let you know if they've any suggestions."

"That's what I hoped," Brett said. "Glad I briefed you on this. We need to find that guy before anyone else is injured or killed as a result of him—and also to prevent our department from looking any worse for keeping him on staff as long as we did."

Chapter Ten

The meeting of the men was apparently over. Or at least that was what Madison figured when first Bryce, then Oren trooped back into the conference room. In a moment Brett joined them with a black Labrador retriever beside him on a leash, who looked at the people in the room and sniffed the floor. Cute, Madison thought. She'd heard that the interim police chief had been a K-9 officer, and now she believed it.

They all sat back down, with Oren beside her again after Jillian moved across the table once more.

"Everything okay?" Madison asked. Did their meeting have to do with the Amaltins? She hadn't thought so, but were Jillian and she being protected from whatever it was, for some reason?

"Fine," Oren said, nodding his head toward Brett, who was glancing around the table. And then he said softly, "I'll tell you about it later."

Which made Madison feel a little better. At least she'd learn about whatever it was that drove Brett to talk to the two feds around here, even if it was the person who was putting her in the most danger.

If so, she most certainly wanted to know what was going on.

"Okay," Brett said, once more taking charge. He leaned across the table in Madison's direction. "I'll notify some of my subordinates about what's going on and let them know to keep an eye out for anything in town that indicates Darius Amaltin has paid us a visit. I don't really want to find out, and I doubt any of you do, either."

Maybe one person here—*me*, Madison thought.

"But not everyone needs to know the details," Brett continued, "unless there is some indication of further criminal activity."

"Sounds fine to me," Oren said from beside her. "But all you Coltons had better be careful and keep an eye out for your own safety, too—yours and your mother's." He looked from Jillian to Bryce and then back to Madison. With her, he winked as he nodded. She interpreted that to mean he was going to be keeping an eye out for her safety, as he'd already promised. Which she appreciated, of course.

But she intended to be damn careful, too. And to observe the world, and their surroundings, deeply enough to try to keep Oren safe as well. Darius had undoubtedly seen Oren driving her car, even if he didn't know who the marshal was then. But he could have learned more since.

All five of them stood and walked toward the door. "You're going to keep in touch with us, aren't you, Madison?" Bryce asked, only it seemed more like a demand than a question.

"Of course. And I expect the same from you, too." She looked from her brother to her sister and then looked again at Brett as well as the dog by his side. She resisted going over to pet it, since she understood police dogs generally needed to be left alone except by their human partners. "I'm hoping this includes you, that you'll let us know if the Grave Gulch PD learns anything about that Darius, like where he's staying and what he's planning next."

"To the extent it's necessary to protect any or all of you, absolutely." Brett's blue eyes were narrowed, his lips tight in a positive grimace as if he was making a vow by his words.

And maybe he was. But that didn't mean that Madison and her siblings or their mother or Oren would remain safe from Darius's wrath.

"Maybe we should meet here and talk again soon," Jillian said. Madison wondered whether a rookie CSI could set up this kind of meeting that included the interim chief and others.

Brett said, "Maybe so. Let's see how things go, and we can coordinate something in a few days if it makes sense."

Oren nodded, and since he apparently believed it made sense, so did she.

Especially if it kept all of them safe from what Darius had attempted to do to Oren and her on the drive here, or from anything else.

"Ember, come," Brett said to the dog, and the black Lab stayed at his side as they left the room.

As the meeting broke up, the three siblings also committed to get together again soon, though nothing definite was decided there, either. And soon, Madison and Oren were walking back to her car outside.

Madison could practically feel the tension in the marshal beside her as he kept watch around them.

Well, she might not have the law-enforcement background, but she was used to watching her surroundings, too...mostly to make sure kindergartners weren't getting into trouble. But now she likewise kept an eye on her surroundings, including the police station and everyone she saw while she was inside, and everyone on the street and sidewalk.

Would she recognize Darius Amaltin if she saw him? She hadn't gotten a good look at him when he'd shot at them, and if the police had found his picture on his driver's license or in their system, she hadn't seen it yet. But most likely he'd be watching them, so she kept her eyes open for anyone who seemed to be observing others around them—or, most especially, them.

Fortunately, nothing. She hoped she wasn't missing anything obvious, but at least Oren's degree of stress didn't appear overwhelming, although he was definitely observant. But that wasn't all that was on her mind. Portions of her conversations with her siblings came back to her. The timing might not be perfect, but she had things she needed to do.

Like call—

Her cell phone rang in her pocket. She guessed who it might be, mostly because she'd just been thinking about calling Alec.

She glanced toward Oren, who had a curious look on his face just as they reached her car.

Oren opened the passenger door for her, and she slid in, then answered the call. "Hi, Alec," she said, attempting to sound cheerful.

She wasn't about to tell him what was going on with her. But she did want to…to make things right between them. Right, in the way she had just been pondering and had sort of discussed with Jillian. This wasn't a great time to do it, though. And she didn't want to do it on the phone.

Especially when Oren slid into the seat beside her.

"Hi, Madison," said Alec. "What's going on? I haven't heard from you. Did you buy that dress you were so excited about? Are we one step closer to the wedding?"

Of course she had told her fiancé about her trip—no, *trips*—to Kendall and talked about the boutique. Otherwise, they might have seen each other on one or both of those Saturdays.

"Um…no. It wasn't quite right." *Because I've decided I don't want to marry you, no matter what I wear,* she thought. A small twinge of guilt shot through her but she shrugged it off. Alec would be better finding someone he loved and who loved him too.

"Okay. I get it. But I want to see you. Can we get together for dinner tonight?"

"Dinner? Tonight?" she said aloud so Oren could hear, even though it shouldn't be his business. But her going somewhere without him *was* his business right now. "I don't…" She happened to be looking around again, mostly so she didn't meet Oren's eyes. An idea came to her. "Could I call you right back? I have a thought about getting together, but I need a couple of minutes."

"Okay," Alec said, though he sounded miffed. "Call me right back, then." And he hung up.

Madison turned to Oren. "I do… I do want to get together with my fiancé tonight." She left it at that for the moment just to see his reaction. He knew she was engaged. She had a sense that he had more in mind than just protecting her.

"Okay," he said, and he sounded totally neutral about it. Was she wrong? He hadn't done anything to signal any more interest in her, but she'd felt it, anyway.

Or was that wishful thinking by a woman doubt-

ing her feelings about her fiancé? Whatever it was, she
needed to be fair to Alec.

"Here's what I have in mind. See that coffee shop?"
She pointed to the coffee shop across from the police
station. It was an ideal place to meet Alec, a place they
could talk at one of the side tables and still be near the
protection of the police station.

"Yeah," Oren said. "Are you having a craving for coffee?" He said it as if he didn't believe in the possibility,
so Madison decided to play with him.

Craving? The word caused her to react. Coffee craving? Yes. But surely…she couldn't have one for Oren,
too.

She made her voice soft, maybe a little husky. "Oh,
yes. A definite craving. One I can't ignore."

"Then, let's go get you a cup." Okay. Oren wasn't
buying into it. "I wouldn't mind some, either, though I
don't need it."

Madison laughed. No more games. Not right now.
"Neither do I, really. But…" She grew quiet. "As you
no doubt figured, that was my fiancé on the phone. He
wants to get together with me tonight. We haven't really seen each other much lately except at school, and
what I want to talk to him about can't be said there."
She looked at Oren pleadingly. "We mentioned having
dinner together, but instead I'd rather go right across
from the police station, so we'd be safe, and grab coffee that I can leave with if the conversation is as bad
as I fear—"

"I get it," Oren said. "Yeah, call him back. I'm fine
with your setting up a date with the guy right there and
right now."

IN FACT, OREN liked the idea more than he should.

He wasn't certain what she'd been up to while they talked about coffee, but he chose not to go there.

More importantly, she was going to dump that guy, end her engagement. Or at least that was what Oren gathered.

Of course, he could be wrong. She might decide to fling herself into his arms and profess love forever.

But at least in a coffee shop there couldn't be much physical about it.

He definitely didn't want his imagination to take over.

If she did dump the guy, all the better. Oren would have no responsibility, real or assumed, to protect the man she otherwise might have married. And if word got out to the world that they were no longer an item, Darius would likely have no reason to threaten the ex-fiancé. *Alec*, was it?

Oren thought of the kiss he'd shared with Madison, as he'd started to do a lot. But no way was that a harbinger of things to come. After his prior relationships with women that had all fizzled… Well. He particularly thought of Anabel, the woman who'd wanted to also become a marshal. He'd thought at first she might be the one…but she hadn't been. So—no more dating. Not now, at least.

He would remain Madison's protector. That was his job, so he'd have to be near her. A lot…

Madison called Alec back. Oren checked some things on his own phone as she talked, since he didn't really need to eavesdrop.

Madison ended her call, then looked at Oren. "Alec will be here in about ten minutes. I want to go into the coffee shop and pick out as private a table as possible. Would you like to help?"

"Private and safe," he stressed. "Yes, I'll be happy to help make that decision."

He walked beside her toward the coffee shop. That involved crossing a street, which they approached about halfway between traffic lights. "Care to jaywalk?" Madison asked him, grinning.

"Hey, like I said, I'm in law enforcement. I have to follow the law—unless I'm after someone who's breaking it."

"Then, how about if *I* jaywalk again?"

He wanted to laugh and thought about how Madison made him smile a lot. Much more than any other woman... Well, so what?

And in fact, it wasn't a big deal. But the light changed, and cars drove down the street both ways. Not a good time to jaywalk. "I think we'd better go to the corner and obey the light," he told her.

"Guess so. You win, Marshal." She was the one to laugh.

Once inside, he helped Madison choose a table in a corner toward the back, in an area that didn't appear particularly popular. He took a table for himself even farther down that row so he could watch Madison and her date—he hated to think of this meeting that way, but the guy was her fiancé, after all—and also the front of the place and its wide window.

Madison sat down also facing the front, which meant her back would be toward Oren. That would be fine. It would give Oren more opportunity both to watch for unwelcome people—one in particular—entering the place, and also see the expressions on Madison's guy's face as she told him whatever she intended to tell him at their meeting.

To leave her alone was what Oren assumed. But that could change, of course. Alec could convince her he was the world's gift to women, particularly her, and get her to change her mind.

As much as Oren despised that idea. It even made him grit his teeth now as he left Madison at her table and headed toward his own.

Unlike a lot of chain eateries, this one had servers who came to the tables to take orders. Oren had noticed that as soon as they entered, so he felt comfortable maintaining his place there. A young lady in long, skinny pants and a bright shirt came over almost immediately, and he requested a large black coffee. No food. He figured that, if all went as he hoped, he'd have dinner with Madison later, probably stopping for takeout on their way back to her place.

The person they were waiting for was just entering the shop. Oren assumed the guy walking through the door was Alec, since as soon as the waitress left her table, Madison half rose and waved in that direction.

The guy, who had a mustache and glasses, smiled and waved back, and soon Alec had joined her, with a small hug and kiss.

Then Madison and Alec began their conversation.

Oren wished he could hear it, but he studied Alec's face, hoping to be able to figure out what was being said. But he'd also thought of a couple of things to talk to Brett about, so he made a quick call to the police captain as he watched.

And tried not to think too hard about the conversation he was observing and the lovely woman who'd ini-

tiated it—nor his own somewhat inappropriate hope that
Madison was, in fact, ending her engagement.

"HI, MADISON!" ALEC said enthusiastically as he joined
her at the table.

He gave her a hug before sitting down, and she sort of
hugged back. At least his kiss was brief and not heated at
all. Alec didn't hesitate at all in ordering his rich, fancy
latte. Madison asked for a large decaf.

When the server was gone, Alec continued. "So tell
me what's going on. I understand you didn't find the perfect wedding dress on your trips to Kendall. Have you
found one someplace else? Where? Or if you haven't,
where are you looking next?"

Madison made herself smile as Alec spoke so enthusiastically. He looked like the teacher he was: short,
medium-brown hair that had begun to recede at his forehead and a matching mustache. His glasses were large
and black-rimmed. When he smiled, he revealed perfect
teeth that he'd told Madison were the result of a lot of
dental work while he was in college.

Heck, he was a good guy. An okay-looking guy.

But essentially, he was just fine. Although he wasn't
nearly as handsome as Oren, that was irrelevant. And
he certainly didn't kiss as wonderfully as Oren. But that
wasn't why she was going to talk to him now. Even if
the other stuff hadn't been going on in her life, ending
their relationship just seemed the most appropriate thing.

"Well, I haven't…" Madison began in response to
his questions and managed to say she'd checked the in-
ternet for other ideas, which she had. A couple weeks
ago. She was glad when the server placed their drinks

on the table in front of them. "That was fast," she said, then thanked her.

Madison watched as Alec immediately tasted his latte, seeming to savor it as he moved his lips and tongue around the disposable cup. She resisted shuddering as she watched his disgusting action. "Thanks," he then told the server. "Tastes great."

Good. She figured he'd send it back and demand another, otherwise. It wouldn't be the first time. He seemed to feel more masculine and in charge if he sent food back after it was served, which Madison found rude.

When the server left, Alec leaned over the table toward Madison. "So tell me what's next." He smiled broadly.

Madison took a sip of her decaf. Okay, she knew what she was going to do. What she had to do. But how much should she tell him?

Nothing beyond the most necessary, she figured.

"Alec, there's something I need to tell you."

The smile on his face disappeared, and his brown brows lowered behind the frame of his glasses. "That sounds serious," he said and took another sip of his drink as if it had been spiked with alcohol, which he loved.

"It is," she said, staring down at her coffee. But that wasn't right. She needed to look at him as she said this, and so she did, looking right into his pale brown eyes. They appeared curious. And worried. She took a deep breath and continued. "Alec, I'm really, really sorry. But I'm ending our engagement. I don't want to marry you."

His expression shifted, reflecting surprise. His eyes moistened, though no tears fell. Fortunately, he didn't stand or holler at her, either. He just sat there, looking at her.

What was he thinking?

"I understand, Madison," he finally said, his voice soft. "I think that's for the best. I don't think marrying each other would be good for either of us."

Really? Madison tried hard not to breathe a huge sigh of relief or yell out a *yay!*

"I'm so glad you understand" was what she said, then wondered a bit at the pang of sorrow that went through her. He wanted out of it, too? That was good, but still…

What he said next made her feel even worse. "The thing is, you know I like you a lot. A whole lot. You're pretty and sexy and sweet. Nice. A smart teacher. But… Well, I really don't love you, Madison, and I don't think you love me, either."

Shock somehow shot through her. He didn't love her, either? He'd never given any indication…

And yet *she* was the one breaking things off. She hardly imagined she'd feel any hurt, yet somehow she did.

Not a lot, though. Ecstatic love forevermore was hardly the reason she'd entered into an engagement with him. But she wanted kids someday, and Alec had seemed like he'd be a good dad.

Not that she would tell him that now. She wouldn't even mention the fact that her life was in danger and that, by booting him out of her life, she could be eliminating that danger from his.

"No," she said in response. "I'm really sorry, Alec, but I don't love you, either. You're really a nice man, and I like you. I admire you and your teaching, but still…" She removed her engagement ring and handed it to him.

"Okay, then." He rose, stuck the ring in his shirt pocket and picked up his latte. "We're in agreement. A good thing. We'll see each other in school, of course, but that'll be it."

"Right," Madison said, a little surprised at the new pang of regret that ran through her—but didn't last long. She was free!

Except for all the dangers around her. And her need to be near another man who was a whole lot more attractive to her, someone she didn't dare get close to, even assuming he had any other kind of interest in her.

"So, see you tomorrow, friend," Alec said as he started away, aiming a small wave at her.

"See you tomorrow, friend," she said in return, then watched her ex-fiancé leave the coffee shop.

She was free! She felt relieved but also guilty as the thought of her kiss with Oren zipped through her mind, even though it really had nothing to do with her breakup with Alec, except maybe in her own mind.

Well, she apparently hadn't hurt Alec's feelings, and that was a good thing. But she was surprised at her own pang of sorrow suddenly being alone and not having a current chance at a wedding and kids and...

She vowed to thrust it aside. Quickly.

Chapter Eleven

Interesting, Oren thought, taking a sip of his cooling coffee.

As that guy Alec left, Oren had been able to hear their last words to one another. They'd called each other *friend*.

Which indicated that Alec had been okay with Madison dumping him. That made Oren want to smile. It was therefore unlikely the guy would give Madison a hard time later.

Oren hadn't been able to eavesdrop on what was being said at Madison's table, of course, thanks to the distance as well as the place growing busier and therefore noisier. But though he'd been prepared to pop over and try to cool any arguments down, there hadn't seemed to be any, and Madison had handed back her engagement ring.

An unwelcome thought went through Oren's head as he watched Madison watch the man leave. How would he react if Madison and he became an item and she dumped him?

Not that they would get together that way. But if they did, he felt sure his reaction, if she ever tried walking away, would be anything but calm and friendly.

Not that he'd ever hurt her. But his attitude would undoubtedly be furious and hurt and—

Fortunately, before he could overthink this nonsense any further, Madison turned at the other table and looked at him.

"I'm done here," she said just loud enough that he could hear her over the noise of other nearby patrons.

"Okay." He stood. Reaching her side, he said, "I'm going to get my cup topped up. Would you like more?"

"Yes, please." She handed him her cup.

She was so calm. So quiet. He wondered what she really was thinking. Even though she was the one to end that relationship, was she sorry about what she'd done now?

He took their cups to the counter, and the smiling barista filled up both of them. After he returned to the table and handed Madison's back to her, he sat down across from her and said, "How about if we pick up some dinner on the way back to your place?"

The expression she leveled at him seemed contemplative. Surely it was no surprise that he intended to stay with her again that night. "That sounds fine," she said. "I just wish I didn't have to impose on you that way."

"It's no imposition," he assured her. "It's part of my job." He realized how unfriendly that sounded and added, "Besides, I'm happy to do it to keep you safe."

"Thank you." Her voice sounded a bit hoarse, and she cleared her throat. "And maybe I can help to keep you safe, too."

He laughed. "Of course." He liked her attitude—even though he doubted there was much she could do to help him that way.

She certainly couldn't do anything to keep his heart

safe when she was the one who was endangering it…
Forget that. Thinking about having some kind of real
relationship with her made him feel warm and fuzzy—
and mad at himself for even considering it.

They soon left the place and walked to her car. Oren
scouted their surroundings but saw nothing and no one
that worried him. He helped Madison inside the car once
more. After he got into the driver's seat, they discussed
where to pick up their food and decided on a pizza place
halfway between where they were and Madison's condo.

Once they reached the restaurant they had to wait
about ten minutes, but after that it was straight on to
Madison's. Still, nothing on the way got Oren overly
concerned, though he remained watchful.

Soon, they were sitting at her kitchen table. They'd
already had their coffee, of course, but she again offered
Oren beer or wine, which he declined that night.

"I don't know what you have in mind for tomorrow,"
Madison said as she served pizza from the box, "but I
need to get up early and head to my school. Tomorrow's
a kindergarten day for me." She grinned, and he returned
it, glad that she appeared relaxed and far from depressed
after what she'd just gone through.

"I guess it's a school day for me, too, then," Oren said,
also smiling, as he ate his first slice. For the next few
minutes, as they both ate, Madison described generally
what a school day was like for her: when she reported to
her classroom, when her students began arriving, what
she anticipated working on with them tomorrow, how
their recess generally was handled.

Her workday sounded interesting, certainly different
from his. He appreciated how she must be around those
kids. Sounded so sweet…

Oren had already intended to hang out in the area and walk through the school as often as made sense. He'd arrive with Madison and get her to introduce him to the principal so his presence wouldn't be a problem, although he'd want her to be discreet about describing why she needed a lawman with her for now. He'd ponder that and suggest before they got there what she should say.

And of course he would be outside observing when Madison took her students out to the playground for recess.

He felt sure he'd enjoy watching her, seeing what she did. He regretted it wasn't appropriate for him to join them.

After they were done eating, Madison excused herself. "I'll hang out in the living room now, but after our earlier discussions I want to call Jillian and tell her about how things went between Alec and me. You can eavesdrop if you wish. But I think it's only fair to say my sister really liked the idea of me ending things with Alec, how well it worked out. Although..."

"Although?" Oren prompted. Was there something else she'd spoken with Alec about? Some other issue that they hadn't resolved?

Something else he needed to protect her from?

"Although," she finally continued, her red brows raised and her mouth somewhat pursed, "our mother loved the idea that I was engaged. She was helping to plan the wedding. She liked Alec well enough, too. She's not going to be happy, and I want to talk to my sister about how best to let our mom know that it's over."

Well, Oren thought, he might feel good about Madison's ending her engagement, but maybe not everyone would feel the same way. Hopefully, whatever her mother said wouldn't make Madison rethink what she'd done.

MADISON SAT ON her comfortable lavender living room couch, her coffee cup on the end table beside her despite it being cool and nearly empty. But she didn't care. She was talking to her sister, her cell phone at her ear, and the conversation was emotional.

Admittedly a lot more emotional than her discussion with Alec had been.

She knew Oren sat on one of the fluffy beige armchairs across from her, but she mostly watched her lap as she talked.

She felt warm, protected, happy with him watching over her the way he was. Maybe that wasn't a good thing—but it was the way things were at the moment.

"I thought you'd be talking ecstatically," Jillian was saying. "You did tell Alec that you no longer wanted to marry him, didn't you?"

"Yes. And I didn't mention any possible danger but explained the truth, that I just didn't think it would work out." Madison paused, then said, "Which was actually fine, since he said he didn't love me, either. And I have to admit that hurt my feelings, even though it was the best response he could have given me. And I didn't need to tell him the real reason I'd gotten engaged to him was just to have someone there so I could have kids someday."

Jillian laughed, and out of the corner of her eye Madison noticed Oren stand. By the time she looked at him, he'd turned his back on her and approached the window a few feet behind his chair. He probably was checking the front yard to make sure no one was there who shouldn't be, but Madison wished she could have seen his face at her admission to Jillian. Would he have laughed, too? He couldn't possibly care about how Alec felt, let alone how she felt.

But she was surprised at how much she cared about what he was thinking.

But then her conversation with Jillian grew even more emotional, as it shifted from her dumping Alec, with his happy consent, to the fact that Madison now had to tell their mother. No more Alec, whom their mom had liked.

No more wedding, though the idea of having one had made Verity Colton ecstatic.

"Let's get together with Mom for dinner tomorrow," Jillian suggested. "We can have a delightful girls' night out, then let her know about…about Dad. And more, including the danger she could be in, too, and that she's also being watched by cops. Okay?"

"Sure," Madison said. "That's a great idea. And you'll be there, too, so that may take at least some of her emotionalism off me regarding Alec."

"Or not. But at least I'll be able to try to act as a buffer."

"Thank you, thank you, thank you," Madison told her sister.

"And I'll even call Mom to set it up. How about six o'clock? That's a good time for dinner."

"Six is fine with me." Madison noticed Oren's head move from side to side as he apparently continued to scan the yard. Was that really a good idea? She didn't have the living room brightly lit, but there was some light behind him that would give away the fact someone was looking out the window. If Darius was there, Oren could be in danger.

Time for her to protect him?

"And I have a good idea where to eat tomorrow," she told Jillian as she rose and approached Oren. Drawing up to him, she bumped him slightly with her shoulder, and he aimed an irritated, and maybe quizzical, glare toward her that surprisingly set her pulse racing. She waved for him to follow her away from the window, which he did. "My new friend Oren introduced me to one really nice restaurant here in town that we haven't frequented, Bubbe's Deli."

"Your *new friend*?" Jillian asked. "You mean that marshal who's protecting you?"

"Exactly," Madison said, watching that very marshal's expression change to bemused. Or maybe *amused*. "We went there for dinner, and I really liked the place. It would probably be good to introduce Mom to it, too. And it's arranged well, so we can get a booth in the back where it's quiet, and we can have an emotional, and maybe even loud, conversation without, hopefully, bothering other customers."

She didn't mention how much she'd liked the food and meeting Olivia—and that she was now wondering whether the rest of his family was so warm and caring. Maybe she'd find out one of these days.

"Sounds good to me," Jillian said. "I'll call Mom now and tell her what we're doing, though not the reason, of course. If there's a problem, I'll let you know. Otherwise, let's touch base tomorrow to finalize plans."

"Great," Madison said. They exchanged a few more sisterly comments, then ended the call.

As she pushed the button to hang up, Oren said, "Really?"

"Yes," she said. "Why not?"

"Why not, indeed? Now, I think I'll take another walk around this place outside, then get ready for bed."

Madison felt her insides plummet. "Do you really need to do that? If Darius is out there—"

"I'll be careful. And I'm sure you're aware I'm armed. I want to make as sure as possible that he's not going to attempt to get in here tonight."

Madison sighed. "I understand, but—"

"No *but*s." He gave her a glare that dared her to contradict him again. She wouldn't. But she'd be damn worried. "I'll be back in soon," he continued. "I'm sleeping on your sofa again, in case you had any questions about that."

"Nope," she said. "You know you're welcome to choose the guest bedroom, but I figured you, my brave marshal protector, would choose the same accommodations as last night." Not her bedroom, unfortunately...but she didn't want to distract him while he was watching over her. And she figured that she'd be prepared to call the GGPD if anything appeared to go wrong.

"Exactly," he said. "And we can say good-night here and now so I won't have to bother you when I come back inside."

"Fine."

They were standing at the side of her living room, much farther from the window, which made Madison feel relieved—for the moment. But Oren was going outside. He'd likely be even more in danger there than while standing at the window—or maybe not. In either case, Madison was worried for him, and not just because he was her protector. And she was the one Darius seemed to be after.

She liked Oren, appropriate or not. She didn't want to see him hurt. Period.

But she knew she wouldn't be able to convince him to stay inside. Sure, it was his job. But she gathered that bravery was who he was.

She had an urge to throw herself into his arms for a good-night kiss.

Instead, she figured she would indeed get ready for bed—but she would listen for his return. Maybe glance out the windows often herself—carefully, of course. And then, if all went well, that would be the best time for a relieved kiss goodnight.

First, though, she called Grace, who'd been the first to hint that Madison should dump Alec. Unsurprisingly, Grace was delighted.

Plus, she mentioned that she hoped Madison would find her true love someday soon—as she recently had, with Camden Kingsley.

Sounds good, Madison thought. *Someday. Maybe.*

And she ignored the image of Oren that passed through her mind.

"Hey, we need to get together again one of these days," Grace said. "Maybe even get some more Coltons to join us."

"Sounds good," Madison said but didn't want to plan anything right now.

Especially not with Oren outside looking for the man who wanted to kill her.

WHERE THE HELL was the guy now? Not that Oren wanted to run into Darius here, in this nice residential community, when it was late and fairly quiet except for the sounds of a TV or radio now and then. And dark, although the condos here had outside lights both on the buildings and on poles, mostly somewhat dim.

The air was cool and humid. Maybe some rain, or even snow, was in the forecast.

Walking slowly and carefully, remaining attentive, Oren stayed in the shadows as much as he could, in the lawn areas in front of and behind the buildings. He ducked in and out of the parking areas, too—although they were lit.

No sign of him. No sign anyone but Oren was out here creeping around.

Could it really be as safe as it felt? Most likely not. Darius had surely done his research. He undoubtedly knew where Madison lived. He hadn't shown up here last night, either. But Oren had no doubt the murderous son had something else in mind around here.

Did he now intend to kill only the man he blamed for his father's death? Maybe he'd dashed back to Kendall.

If so, other deputies were in charge there, taking care once more of Wes, in protective custody.

And here? If Darius's original plan still filled his mind, Madison's siblings could be on the guy's radar, too. Of course, they knew it now. And they were both in law enforcement, so hopefully they'd be damned careful and also be watching.

And their mother? The woman the former Richard Foster had apparently promised to marry all those years ago—after having three kids by him?

Darius probably knew about that, too, since he'd apparently done his homework about the family and followed, then attacked, Madison.

Well, Brett knew about it, too. And Brett had promised some police protection for Verity Colton, which

Oren assumed would include patrol cars passing frequently through the neighborhood where she lived.

The mom they would probably have dinner with at Bubbe's tomorrow evening—an idea that made Oren shake his head. Too many connections between his family and Madison's that way—though he doubted Darius would go after any Margulies because of it. Unless, of course, he decided to kill Oren to get him out of the way so he could get to Madison.

Not going to happen.

And it appeared that nothing was going to happen tonight, or at least not now. Oren decided it was time to return to Madison's condo.

Which he did, still carefully, still watching everywhere around him.

He'd borrowed Madison's key to come out here, and now he used it to get back into the building. Once inside, he listened. Some voices emanated from the nearest unit, a man and woman, too soft for him to hear what they were saying, but they sounded calm. He kept listening nonetheless as he headed up the stairs. He could no longer hear those voices once he reached the top, and he heard nothing else.

He walked around the second-floor hallway, both looking at the rows of doors and listening. Still nothing seemed out of line, although he again heard what sounded like TV shows through a couple of them.

Soon, he used the key to reenter Madison's place. Her hallway lights were lit, but he didn't hear or see her.

He did knock on her door, though. "I'm back, Madison," he called.

"Everything okay?" she responded.

"Seems that way. Everything okay here?"

Her door opened, and she entered the hallway—wearing silky gray pajamas that shouldn't look sexy but did.

"I think so," she said, blinking. He saw that the light inside her bedroom was dim, so the brighter hallway illumination probably bothered her eyes. "Just remember I need to get up around six thirty tomorrow." She frowned at him as if making sure he understood how important that was.

Of course he remembered it. He'd probably be awake anyway, but just in case he'd set his phone's clock. "I will," he said. "Good night."

"Good night." Before he could react, she took a step toward him and kissed him very quickly on the lips, then turned and headed back into her bedroom, shutting the door behind her.

Leaving him much too sexually charged for such a minimal encounter. But of course, nothing would come of that.

Yet he felt caring. Too caring. Wanting to at least give her a good-night hug, too.

Silently, he wished her a good night's sleep, though he'd of course get up often to make certain all remained okay.

When that alarm went off the next morning, Oren was already awake. Maybe that wasn't surprising, since he'd gotten up at least five times during the night. Checking out the unit.

Checking on Madison, in her bedroom. He seldom heard her breathing deeply. Was she as awake as he?

He'd refrained from doing as he wished: talking to her. Going inside. Giving her an even better good-night kiss. And maybe more...

Nope. He was a marshal on duty. That was all, no matter what his instincts goaded him to do.

He'd probably get tired during the day, but at least they'd be around a lot of people at the school.

Not only would he have Madison introduce him to the principal and whatever security they had around there, he'd request that the principal get whatever passes he needed to patrol the school grounds.

He wouldn't get into detail, of course, but he'd let any security folks know there was a chance Madison might have an issue. Nothing major, he'd indicate. Otherwise, if it sounded bad, they might wonder why she'd even come to school that day and potentially put kids in danger.

Which in a way was a good question. But they didn't really know if or when she was in danger, where Darius might be, or what, if anything, he had in mind.

Now, Oren did as he had yesterday morning: rose, showered, got dressed. He'd run his clothes through Madison's washing machine before heading to bed last night, draping himself in a bath towel before it was all done.

Maybe today his car would arrive, and it contained a change of clothes. Or maybe he'd be able to drop by Olivia's to pick up a change of clothing he kept there. He'd be seeing his sister that evening, after all.

She'd understand he was just doing his duty by hanging out with Madison. Protecting her. Despite his undeniable attraction to her.

Chapter Twelve

Everything started out well that Monday at school. Madison got there when she wanted to, early in the morning—after Oren and she both grabbed a quick breakfast of cereal and coffee at her house, then left when she said it was time. Oren acted like she was in charge for a change, which she was. Even so, he was clearly the marshal who protected her, and she appreciated it. She appreciated *him*—for that reason and maybe too many others, like his kindness, his willingness to hang out with her even on her workday, his sexiness... but she hardly even knew him.

As she expected, he also observed everything around them as they headed to the school.

Of course she looked around, too. Even though she didn't have his law-enforcement assessment skills, she considered herself fairly intuitive. She'd recognized her father, hadn't she?

Fortunately, she didn't see anything—anyone—noteworthy here now, either.

She'd gotten tired of Oren being her chauffeur, so that morning she insisted on driving them to their destination—it was her car, after all—and parked in her usual area behind the school.

"Nice," Oren said as he looked at the building before they walked inside. Madison had to agree. Like other notable buildings in Grave Gulch, this school had been here for a while and had been well designed many decades ago. It wasn't especially fancy, but it was two stories high, and there was attractive concrete scrollwork decorating the outsides of the windows on the brick building.

Her kindergarten classroom was on the first floor, which worked well since her young students didn't generally have to use the stairs. Madison led Oren there first thing so she could lock her purse in her desk and check the laptop she left there to confirm her lesson plans for the day. Nothing stressful, but a lot that kids could learn while having fun. That was her primary intention.

Meanwhile, Oren walked around the room, surveilling it, she assumed, including looking out windows along the far wall from different angles.

And she watched his many angles. Who knew that his intense observation for her protection would seem so sexy?

Okay. Enough of that.

Although being on the first floor was good for the kids, Madison wondered if she should be worried about it for her own safety that day. It would be easier for someone from outside to see in and get inside and...

And nothing. Today would be fine.

"Are you ready to introduce me to the principal?" Oren said as she looked up from her laptop.

"Sure." She led him down the hall, saying hi to other teachers she saw who were just arriving.

Including Alec, who seemed nice and friendly—and relieved? Or was she just reading that into his happily brief greeting?

Alec also shot Oren a curious look.

She laughed internally. Oren was the current guy in her life—but not for the reasons Alec might be thinking. If only... Forget that.

She led Oren to the far end of the hall on the first floor, where the school's offices were located. They entered the outer room. The principal's assistant wasn't there yet, so Madison knocked on the door behind the desk that led into the principal's office.

Madison expected Principal Nelson to call out and ask who was there. Instead, the door opened, and the principal looked out.

"Good morning, Madison," she said. "Something on your mind?" She looked toward Oren, who remained behind Madison.

"Yes. I'd like to introduce you to Marshal Margulies of the US Marshals Service—" she gestured toward Oren "—and let you know why he's here."

Principal Mae Nelson aimed a curious stare in his direction, then gestured for them to join her inside.

It was a nice-sized office, with a desk in the middle and file cabinets along the side, all organized and neat, which Madison always considered representative of who Principal Nelson was.

Mae, an African American woman in her forties, was pretty, with long wavy black hair with some gray in it pulled back in a braid down the back of her neck.

And she was one smart, excellent administrator.

"Okay," Principal Nelson said. "Sit down and tell me what's going on."

Before she could speak, Oren said, "I'm just here as a precaution today, Principal Nelson. There are some issues going on in another town that might remotely affect Ms. Colton here, so I'm just keeping an eye on her to be sure there are no problems in Grave Gulch. And I most certainly won't allow anything to happen here at an elementary school. So far, there's just been a rumored consequence of something that went on long ago that had to do with Ms. Colton's family, so we're just being extra cautious. I've followed up with GGPD, and they recommended I tail Madison for now. I asked Madison to introduce me to you so you'd know why this strange guy who's definitely not a kindergartner will be hanging out around the school, including in her classroom."

Madison watched as Oren pulled his badge from his pocket and showed it to the principal, who studied it for a few moments.

Madison was glad to see Principal Nelson smile. "No, I wouldn't consider you a kindergartner, Marshal." But the smile morphed into a frown. "Can you guarantee that nothing will go on here, that no students are in danger?"

"I don't generally like the word *guarantee*," Oren said. "And I have no reason to think this person will target any students. But I can guarantee I'll do my damnedest to protect everyone here, and I'll have the ear of the local cops if anything goes wrong—which it shouldn't."

The principal rose and folded her arms in front of her. "What is this really about?" she demanded.

"A case we thought was pretty well closed ages ago, but since it isn't completely closed I can't discuss it, other than to request that you be careful and let me know if anything around here appears different from usual. Okay?"

"Yes, it's okay," Principal Nelson said. She accepted Oren's business card, then aimed her concentrated gaze toward Madison. "And you'll let me know if anything goes wrong." It wasn't a question.

"Of course," Madison agreed.

"Would whatever this is stay away from here if Madison also stayed away from here?" Principal Nelson asked Oren.

"We couldn't be certain," he said. "But my being here keeping an eye on things should help."

"I hope so."

Madison's classroom was still empty when she and Oren returned to it, but this was near the time that students began to arrive. Almost immediately, Cora, a classroom aide, popped in and said good morning. Madison was glad to see her. The aides provided whatever help was needed fast, ran errands and accompanied young kids who needed to use the restroom.

Today, in particular, Madison wouldn't have wanted to send any of her students on their own.

"Hi, Madison," Cora said.

"Hi, Cora." Madison turned slightly. "I'd like to introduce you to Marshal Oren Margulies. Nothing to worry about but he's watching over the school for the moment because of a potential security issue." Her assistant knew about the Coltons and their involvement with law enforcement. She also knew to keep any curiosity to herself. Madison might tell her more later but didn't need to now.

Dressed in a smock over her shirt and slacks, Cora was youthful and energetic and full of smiles for the kids. Madison thought about warning Cora to keep watch around the school since the aide would be wandering around a lot. She started to tell Oren about the aides, but kids began entering before she had a chance to get his opinion whether she should have given Cora a heads-up about watching for anything different at the school. She figured she could always ask Oren to accompany Cora or any others when they escorted the kids. But then he'd be leaving her alone…

Better that he ensured the kids were okay.

The kids each greeted her with "Hi, Ms. Colton." They all removed backpacks when they reached their assigned seats, chairs with desk arms. The backpacks went underneath after they took out a notebook and set of crayons.

All fifteen of them were soon there. Time for lessons to begin, including learning more letters by reading and printing, and counting the items in pictures in some books. Plus biology discussions about various animals.

Madison kept an eye on Oren when he was in the room, but he left often. Had he seen anyone he shouldn't? But he gave no indication of it.

She was so glad to have him there—for her protection, and everyone else's. She knew she was lowering her eyes and smiling too much when he happened to look at her.

She got a brief chance to talk with him during recess, which occurred about an hour and a half into the class. "Don't stay out here too long," he told her as they stood at the side of the playground where Madison and Cora kept an eye on the kids playing on swings and slides. "Limit your recess time as much as you're able. Not sure, but I thought I saw…you know. In the distance, walking away fast. Still…"

Really? He'd possibly seen Darius? She hustled the class back inside not long after that—and hoped that everyone, including her and Oren, would remain safe. At least there it was easier to keep an eye on everyone.

Everything went fine that day, including lunch. She was glad when the class was over and the kids either went home or into school childcare. She remained in her classroom, making notes about all that had occurred and plans for tomorrow. She also called Jillian, leaving a message at first. Her sister soon called her back.

"Of course I didn't say why," she said to Madison, "but Mom is delighted with the idea of meeting for dinner tonight. Bryce will be joining us, too."

"Great!" Madison really was glad she'd be able to get together with her family, though she didn't look forward to telling her mother what she had to about her engagement, let alone the possible danger. "Are we all just meeting there?"

"I'm picking her up, but Bryce and you—and Oren, I assume—can get there on your own."

"See you then," Madison said. She knew it would feel somewhat odd to have Oren there at a family dinner, but his presence was definitely needed.

She would feel just as glad to have him there as she'd liked having him around all day.

OKAY. HE MIGHT have been mistaken, looking so hard for Darius that he believed he'd seen him in the distance when he hadn't.

But in any case, Oren intended to be damn careful, keep watching even more.

The figure he'd seen had been across the street from the fenced playground, standing behind a parked car. He'd appeared to be looking toward the school and the students—and Oren. But he hadn't remained there after leveling a glare in the marshal's direction.

Oren didn't believe he had imagined it. He was hardly

an imaginative person. Still, he'd been carefully attempting to scrutinize their surroundings in case Darius was around, and maybe he'd seen characteristics in that guy that actually weren't there. It could have just been a local resident, or even a parent, glancing at the school for no inappropriate reason.

He kept up his inspection of the area for the rest of Madison's school day, also watching when any of her students left her presence. He accompanied the aide often when she walked a kid to the nearby restroom.

He sort of enjoyed himself. He hadn't thought it would be fun to hear the enthusiastic, high voices of kindergarteners as they got excited when Madison praised them for achieving something, like reading a word or counting some pictures.

He'd thought now and then about having kids of his own. Rather liked the idea. But so far all the relationships he'd begun had gone bad so he couldn't count on it.

He definitely wasn't going to ponder what it would be like to marry Madison and have kids with her. Sure, this kindergarten teacher would be a good mom.

And right now, he was also uneasy.

Not just because he thought he might have seen Darius around here, in this environment where peace should reign, but also because he hadn't been able to verify it.

Or even go look for his target.

Darius, or whoever he'd seen, had been too far away and had quickly disappeared from his vision. Too quickly. Going after him would have been futile.

Staying here, keeping a protective eye on Madison and everyone around her made more sense.

But that uneasiness…

He was glad when her school day drew to an end,

several hours after her students had gone. She'd had a couple of meetings with other teachers, touched base with Principal Nelson once more and spent time on her computer, evaluating kids and planning lessons for the rest of the week. Or that's what she'd told him.

But finally, around five fifteen, she stood up from her desk in the classroom and started walking toward him. Oren had just taken his most recent patrol around both the interior and the exterior of the school.

Now Madison said, "I'm going to close things down in about five minutes. Are you about ready to leave?"

"Sure," he said. And was he ever.

He knew that Madison had made arrangements to have her sister show up at Bubbe's with their mother and meet their brother there around six o'clock. Oren recognized he might find it enjoyable to watch those Coltons together over dinner. The family and its closeness were well-known.

His sister would be there, too, so he'd also have someone around.

Meanwhile, he had taken time now and then to contact his colleagues in Kendall and at the home office in Grand Rapids.

The deputies now assigned to Kendall had assured him all was peaceful there. Nothing new in Wes's existence for the moment. Of course, he was only working in the bookstore part-time now that he was back in full-time protective custody.

"Okay," Madison said, "let's go."

"Am I driving this time?" Oren asked as they shut the door of her classroom behind them. "I know the way to Bubbe's best."

"I'm sure I can find it." Madison looked up at him

as they walked, the expression on her pretty face confident. And he had no doubt that she could, too. "And I'm driving. I don't want my family seeing me riding in my own car with someone else behind the wheel—especially now, when part of the reason for this get-together is to let my mom know Alec's out of my life."

When they started out, Oren, as passenger, noticed Madison drove a longer way to get to the deli than he would have, and he told her so. Her expression from the driver's seat seemed more amused than sorry for the error. And it wasn't an error, as it turned out.

"I know. But I'm taking a slightly longer way to avoid passing by the school where my mother teaches. I just want to meet them there, not trade waves on the way."

"Got it." Oren wasn't surprised. Madison knew her way around Grave Gulch. "I'll just be quiet and let you drive."

"No need to be quiet," Madison responded, and for the short distance to the deli they did talk, mostly about her school and teaching—and Oren continued to enjoy being in Madison's presence and just talking with her.

When they arrived, Oren told Madison to park in the employee's space they'd taken last time.

Olivia would be glad to see him, he figured, as well as happy to get to serve their party of five that night.

Oren just hoped it would be a pleasant, quiet meal, despite the fact that Madison was going to tell her mother she was no longer an engaged woman.

How would Verity Colton react to that?

And to the fact that Madison had seen her father, if she hadn't already told her mother—and he didn't think she had.

And the potential resulting danger.

How would Madison's mother take the news?

This could wind up being a very interesting evening.

Maybe even more than he imagined, since, after Madison shut off the car, she scanned the parking lot. "Don't see them here, but they could have parked anywhere," she said.

And before Oren could agree, she maneuvered over the console between them and planted a quick but much-too-enticing kiss on his lips. "Wish me luck," she said without explaining why she thought she would need it. And then she got out of the car.

Chapter Thirteen

Okay, so why had she done that? Madison didn't even look at Oren as they walked around the restaurant to the front. She'd kissed him. And enjoyed it. And regretted it—sort of. They weren't in that kind of relationship. Although it had been one hot, enjoyable kiss… What was he thinking now?

And her? Well, she did it to kind of boost her courage. Not that she wasn't happy to be getting together with her family. She loved them. But she figured her mom wasn't going to be thrilled about no longer having the fun of planning a wedding and would have no hesitation about letting Madison know.

And Madison would have to mention having seen, and talked to, her dad. What would her mom think about that? How would she react?

Oren would be there with her. Protecting her, though not from her mother. And not being a love interest the way Alec had been. Of course, her siblings knew Oren's role in her life, but she'd also have to explain it to her mom. Even more important, she had to warn her to be careful.

But surely Darius, now that he'd started after Madison, wouldn't try to include other family members in his horrible plot, except the main focus of his anger, her father.

Would he?

She certainly hoped not.

They'd reached the end of the walkway between the two restaurants, and now Oren gently held her back as he scrutinized the street and sidewalk. His hand was on her arm. If she turned, maybe she could stand straight against him and—

No. She didn't want to distract him, no matter how much she enjoyed his touch.

"Okay," he soon said. "Let's go in."

Oren had told Madison he'd already called his sister and she was reserving a table in a back corner. Madison's family should therefore have a good place to get together and talk—and eat some of the food Madison had enjoyed so much when she was there before with him.

Madison saw Jillian walking toward them along the sidewalk, and with her was their mother. Madison dashed forward, arms out to give her mom a big hug.

"Madison!" Verity Colton exclaimed. "So glad to see you, dear." Her mother hugged her back, then pulled away and looked her up and down.

Madison was still in the dress she'd worn to school that day and figured her second-grade-teacher mother was, too. Mom's was a navy blue that went well with her short, platinum blonde hair. Madison studied her mom's features, thinking how she'd often been told that they resembled each other—most recently, of course, by her father. Madison didn't always see it, but their lips, noses and cheeks were similar shapes, and even their eyebrows arched somewhat alike. But Madison's hair was red, of course, and she wore it long, unlike her mother's almost pixie cut.

Did they actually look much alike? Well, it didn't really matter. They must resemble each other well enough for her dad to recognize her after all these years…

"So how are you doing?" her mom asked. "I know Bryce is joining us too, but I don't see Alec. Is he coming?" Mom's gaze had left Madison and was now aimed straight at Oren.

"Let's go inside and get our table," Madison said, not wanting to attempt to explain anything now, out here, and without a glass of wine in front of her.

Jillian broke into the conversation. "Good idea." Then she leaned toward Madison and added more softly, "Everything okay?"

"Hope so," Madison replied, but she knew that her attempt at a smile didn't get very far.

Her mother stopped and looked at Oren. "Hello," she said, her tone cool. "I'm Verity Colton, Madison's mother, and Jillian's, too."

"I know. Nice to meet you. I'm Oren Margulies. My sister owns this deli, and she's saving a table for us."

That was enough explanation for now, Madison thought. But it was time for her to get this going. She hurried to Oren's side, careful not to even brush against him slightly. "Mom, Jillian, come on." And she led even Oren into the restaurant.

"Hi, Madison. Welcome," greeted Olivia. "And you too, bro. Your favorite large table in the back is all yours this evening."

"Thanks, sis," Oren said.

"Yes, thanks so much, Olivia," Madison echoed her

appreciation, then added, "We're expecting one more person this evening, Bryce Colton. He should be here soon."

"Like now," said a familiar voice from behind Madison. She turned to see her brother—right behind her. They exchanged hugs. "And hi to you, too, Marshal," he said to Oren, who shot him a smile and a lopsided salute which he returned.

Made sense, Madison thought. It felt natural, having Oren the marshal there, with her FBI agent brother.

In moments, Oren led them all through the deli's middle aisle toward the back, where there was an empty table for six in the corner, which they wouldn't completely fill. The tables around it were mostly occupied, and a hum of conversations filled the air.

So did an aroma of delicious food. Madison thought she caught the slightly spicy scent of warm corned beef.

Madison ordered matzo ball soup, of course, as well as coleslaw. Some of the others also chose soup, but mostly sandwiches were on their radar, including corned beef and pastrami, either on rye or challah. Madison didn't pay a lot of attention to who ordered what, except she did notice, and wasn't surprised, that Oren chose corned beef on rye. It was a choice that tasted good, and Oren undoubtedly ate it here a lot.

Once they ordered, their mom stood and raised her wineglass. "Time for a toast, everyone. You all have a new baby cousin." Her gaze lit on Madison, who figured that was a not-so-subtle hint that her mother hoped she'd have similar news soon. Verity explained, though, that her brother Frank had become a grandfather. His son, Travis, had welcomed his first child, Hope, with his fiancée Tatiana.

Madison was glad to toast baby Hope, but figured that

news might make it a little more difficult to relay her own news to her mother. Madison was buddies with her cousin Travis. She was happy for him...and maybe even a little jealous. Maybe someday Travis would hear that Madison had had a baby, too. At least Madison could hope so.

She couldn't help a quick glance at Oren. Unlikely that they'd ever get into a relationship like that, but the idea somehow felt good to Madison, especially now that Alec was no longer part of her life. Interesting, though, that Travis's fiancée, Tatiana Davison, was his co-CEO at the company he'd started, Colton Plastics. And maybe even more interesting was that she was the daughter of serial killer Len Davison.

Their dinner went well, fortunately. Madison, sipping on her red wine, figured she would wait till they were nearly done to address the issues she needed to with her mother. That way, they could enjoy themselves for the longest time possible.

Her soup was, of course, as delicious as the last bowl she'd had here—and she did partake in some challah on the side, as well as her tasty coleslaw. Her siblings and mother appeared to enjoy their food, too, as well as the company.

Although the camaraderie didn't include Oren much. Oh, sure, he mostly sat with them and occasionally even caught Madison's eyes as he then scanned the room with his own, making it clear to her that just because he sat with them didn't mean he wasn't watching out for her safety. And for her family's.

Her mother glanced at Oren a lot, as if wondering who this man who'd joined them for dinner was and why he kept looking around. Plus, he occasionally rose, excused himself and walked away, potentially giving the impression he was off to the restroom, but Madison knew better.

And even when he just sat there and ate, he appeared alert and uneasy, which didn't help Madison's state of mind. Maybe this wasn't the best place to have the conversation that would inevitably start soon.

But it did make sense for her to be with her two siblings when she had the discussion with their mother.

They understood. They'd back her up.

And hopefully her mom, who wouldn't be thrilled, would understand.

As they ate, most of the conversation centered around their mother's day at school.

Once they'd all finished their meals, they still had drinks on the table, and Madison sipped more of her tart red wine as she looked at her mom, who was across the table from her. She, too, held her wineglass, and she looked away from Jillian to Madison, who sat beside her sister. And yes, Oren was once more on her other side—for her protection, of course, though she wasn't about to tell her mother that right now, though she'd have to eventually.

She didn't have to explain to her law-enforcement siblings, who knew the facts.

"This has been a fun evening, but I think it would be more fun if Alec was with us so we could discuss even more of the wedding plans than we can without him. But I haven't heard anything from you lately about where things stand, even whether you found a dress on your out-of-town shopping expeditions." She paused. "Did you?" Her glance darted quickly to Oren at Madison's other side, then back.

Madison resisted the urge to put her wine down and

hold Jillian's hand for reassurance. Or, even more entic-
ingly, Oren's. But neither would be appropriate.

Instead, she waited a moment before responding, allowing her ears to take in the sounds of some of the conversations around them, all sounding upbeat, at least
from a distance.

She, likewise, attempted to sound happy. "Alec and I
decided to call off the wedding, Mom." She made herself smile a bit.

But Mom's blue eyes grew huge. "What?" she exclaimed, so loudly that Madison cringed and glanced
around at the nearest tables. Sure enough, some patrons
there were staring at them.

Madison shrugged as nonchalantly as she could. "We
talked about it, Mom. Both Alec and I agreed that we
really weren't cut out for each other. Yes, we like each
other a lot—he's a nice guy—but more as friends than
a man and woman in love or planning a future together.
In fact, we agreed that we really don't love each other, so
it would be better for us to end our engagement. Maybe
that way we could each even find someone else more
suited to us." Madison felt an urge to glance at Oren but
stopped herself. That might give him, or the others at the
table, the impression that she considered him possibly
more suitable for her.

Well, why did she have that urge to look at him?
Surely *that* idea wasn't really in her mind…

Although… Well, this wasn't the time to consider
it, but in the brief period she'd known Oren, she found
him a lot more suitable for a potential long-term—forever—relationship. She knew she could count on him.
That he would take care of her, to the extent she needed
taking care of.

But, heck, that was his job. That was all.

Although…well, Madison had to admit to herself that she was a lot more sexually attracted to this man who happened to be in her life than she'd ever been to Alec. And she liked the idea that Oren was so close to Olivia.

Bryce and Jillian seemed fine that Madison had broken things off with Alec. Would her siblings be okay if she ever entered into a relationship with Oren?

Didn't matter. That wasn't going to happen.

"I… I don't understand, honey," her mother said, her expression appearing…well, anguished. "I know you care for one another, or you wouldn't have gotten engaged in the first place. And there's nothing standing between you, preventing you from getting married. Did you have an argument? You need to contact Alec again, fix the situation, get your plans back together."

There were tears in her mom's eyes and that made Madison mist up as well, but not for the same reason. She believed she understood what was really on her mother's mind. "I'm so sorry, Mom, but that's not going to happen. We're through. But this situation—my situation—isn't at all like what you went through with Dad. He had reasons to leave…" At least at first. And soon Madison was going to have to fill her mother in on that part of the current situation as well.

First, though, she needed to convince her mother that her breakup with Alec was for the best.

"Yes. Yes, he did," Mom said, now looking down at the table in front of her. "But Alec isn't in the military. And that's why, if there's nothing in the way, you should just move forward as you planned. Get married. Continue with the rest of your life…"

Madison glanced at Jillian, then at Bryce. Both appeared utterly sympathetic, but neither jumped in to help her.

She was the first of all of them to even get engaged. Of course, she was the oldest. But the situation just wasn't right.

And her mother couldn't expect her to move forward with the wrong man, no matter what had happened in her own life.

Madison suspected that her mom wanted her children each to find someone and marry quickly so they'd never have to go through what she did with their dad—having the man she loved die before they'd ever gotten married. Or at least that was what she'd believed.

At least things at the table had quieted down, so no one else appeared to look their way. And Olivia had joined them. Oren handed his sister a credit card, which Madison really appreciated. Of course she would pay him back, but at least they would all be able to leave as soon as it seemed appropriate.

And Madison added generosity to the list of things she liked about Oren.

Now? Well, she really wanted to talk more with her mother, find a way to prevent her from stewing over what had happened.

"I can understand why you're upset, Mom, but I really am continuing with the rest of my life just the way I should."

"It's *not* the way you should." Her mom's voice was raised again, once more drawing attention to the table. She stood all of a sudden and pushed back, almost knocking over her chair, making Madison cringe. "Excuse me. I need to— Where's the restroom?"

She didn't wait for an answer. She turned her back on them and hurried away.

"I'll go with her," Madison told the others, but just then her phone pinged, which made her hesitate.

"I'll go take care of her," Jillian said, rising and hurrying after their mother.

Madison checked her phone, although she planned on following them as fast as she could.

Until she saw the message from an unknown sender.

How nice that you have the whole family here together. Time for me to make sure all of you are gone so the man who killed my father will suffer even more. See you around, in the deli—maybe the bathroom. Who knows? But you will all see me soon.

OREN HAD BEEN watching Madison with sympathy while she engaged in that anticipated disagreement with her mother. But not watching too closely. Out in the open like this, he wanted to keep an eye on their surroundings.

But when Verity dashed away, Oren rose, figuring Madison would follow her mother. Jillian joined her, but Madison had stopped. Looked at her phone.

A text, Oren figured. And judging by the horror on Madison's face, it was bad. Real bad.

She'd only gotten as far as the end of the table, and he joined her quickly as the other two women continued walking away. "What is it?" he demanded.

He didn't wait for her to reply. Instead, he carefully grabbed the back of her hand. Her phone was cradled in its palm, and he pulled it toward him. And looked.

And swore.

He let her go gently and pivoted to stare at the rest of the room. Again.

Where was that damn Darius? In the ladies' room? Somewhere else, laughing at them, while he prepared to kill them all?

He needed to know, to protect Madison's family—but Madison came first.

He needed, therefore, to enlist Bryce. No need to yell anything at him, at least. Madison's brother had joined her, too, and stood in front of her.

"What is it?" he asked, his eyes on Oren.

"You need to go get your mother and Jillian. And then…" An idea came to him immediately. "We all need to meet at the Grave Gulch PD right away. I'll call Brett and let him know." At least he now had the interim chief as a contact. And now he might need to become even more.

"A threat?" Bryce questioned but didn't wait for an answer. Instead, he dashed toward the ladies' room.

"What are we going to do?" Madison asked. Her voice was shaky, and so was she.

He knew because he kept one arm around her. His left arm, in case he had to grab his gun from his pocket.

"You heard me. You and I are heading straight for the police department, and your relatives will meet us there. I trust your FBI brother to make it quick. Do you?"

The look in her green eyes revealed terror. "Yes, but—"

"No *buts*," Oren interrupted. "Let's go."

He felt furious. But Oren was most concerned about Madison. Rightly or wrongly, he really liked her. He would protect her—and her family—from Darius, no matter what.

Chapter Fourteen

With Oren in control, they started down the center aisle of the restaurant.

Olivia stood near the front speaking to some customers in a booth. She looked at Oren, then beyond him, where the others followed. "What's going on, bro?"

"Tell you later, but we've got to leave now." Fortunately, the waitress had returned with his credit card and receipt, and he'd added a healthy tip. He'd work things out for partial repayment by the others whenever he was able.

He realized how concerned his sister was, judging by her wide-eyed expression as she looked from Oren to Madison and back. "Is everything okay?" she asked but obviously knew the answer.

"I don't know, but hopefully we'll be taking any trouble with us." He certainly didn't want anything to happen to Olivia, her customers or her restaurant, another good reason to leave fast. He leaned toward her, though. "Keep an eye on things," he said softly, "and if anything looks even a little wrong, call 9-1-1. I'll explain later."

"But—"

Oren had taken Madison's hand again and started hurrying toward the exit once more, not wanting to take time to explain now—or to stay and potentially make things more dangerous at the deli. He stopped just inside the door, keeping Madison right behind him, and again looked around. Of course he might not be able to see one person in the slight crowd outside or in a car driving by, but for now all appeared okay. He looked back into the deli beyond Madison and was glad to see Bryce and the other women not far behind.

And though he hadn't told Bryce much, the FBI agent was doing as Oren did and looking around constantly, hand on his pocket, as he led his relatives out of there.

But as they got outside and those in law enforcement looked around, Verity said, "What the hell is going on here? You're all freaking me out. Is this some kind of game to make me stop pushing Madison? Or—"

"Enough, Mom," Madison said sharply, getting close to her. "There's a lot you don't know about but should. We're—we're all going to the police station right now, and we'll tell you about it. *I'll* tell you about it. It's incredible, and you won't believe it, but it's also really dangerous right now. So just follow Bryce and Jillian, and listen to what they have to say. When we get there, I'll fill you in."

"You'd better." Verity scowled at her older daughter, but at least she listened and started walking again between her two younger children.

"Wow," Madison said to Oren. "She is actually paying attention now."

If he'd thought he had time, Oren would have called a car right away—but they had to leave immediately. He didn't want to drive Madison's, in case Darius had rigged it to explode. But time was important.

Oren did see a police car driving by, with two uniformed cops in the front seat. He stepped onto the street and flagged it down. "Hey, we're on our way to the station because of an urgent matter. Can you drive us there? You can contact Interim Chief Shea to check on us." He gave his name and Madison's. "And if you've another car in the area, please drive those three, also." He gestured to the group behind them. "One of them's with your department."

"I recognize CSI Colton," said the cop in the passenger's seat, staring where Oren pointed. "Yeah, come in, and we'll get another patrol car here in a minute."

"Great." Oren opened the back door and helped Madison in. "I want to ride with you to the station, too," he said to the cop, "but there's something I need to check first. I'm walking around the back of the deli to check Madison's car. Please pull around and pick me up."

"No!" Madison's voice was loud and adamant. "Get in this car, Oren. It's unsafe to even be out there, let alone checking on my car. You know Darius knows what it looks like."

"Exactly," Oren said, and he nodded at the uniformed officer closest to him. "I've had some bomb disposal training as part of my job," he assured Madison, assuming that was at least part of her concern.

"We'll stay in visual contact with him," the same cop said after turning slightly toward Madison, and Oren silently cheered the guy. He probably knew nothing about the situation, but possibly thanks to the mentioned GGPD connections, he trusted them and was willing to protect them.

"Thanks," Oren told the tall, thin, serious guy, whose name tag on his uniform said he was Werther.

The easiest way for Oren to get to the parking lot to

check out Madison's car would be to head between the
buildings the way he usually did. But that might leave
him vulnerable to an attack started from the Italian restaurant next door. Plus, he wouldn't be able to stay in visual contact with the cop car, as Werther had proposed.

Oren was pleased to see another cruiser pull up to the
curb, and the others started getting in. He then walked
to the far side of the Italian restaurant along the minimally crowded sidewalk, intending to sprint down the
driveway beside it to the parking lot in the rear of both
eating establishments.

He was glad to see the police car driving slowly beside him, then also turn into the parking lot.

Except—as Oren started to dash down the driveway,
with the cop car right behind him, a black SUV tore
down it in the other direction. A familiar-looking vehicle, and Oren stared toward the driver.

And found the guy also staring briefly and angrily
at him. It was Darius Amaltin, Oren was sure: a young-
looking, thin guy with long brown hair and an intense
gaze. The guy didn't attack him, most likely because of
his police escort. Had he been waiting for Madison to
go get her car? Was the text he'd sent intended to get her
to leave the deli quickly—and drive away?

Oren was furious at Amaltin. And frightened for
Madison. At least she was under police protection now.

And Darius was the one driving away. At the end of
the driveway he screeched off to the right.

No way would Oren be able to follow him, and even
the cop car was unlikely to catch up with the suspect,
since it would have to turn around first.

Oren had already stopped on the driveway, and now
he looked at the two cops in the front seat of the police

car. He hurried to Werther's window, and the officer rolled it down. "The driver of the SUV that just left is the source of the danger to us," he blurted. "If you could get someone after him, that would be damn helpful."

"We'll give it a try." Werther frowned as he pulled out his phone.

"Want to get in and let me try to catch up with him?" asked the driver.

"No!" Madison called from the back seat. "Please, no. He may be waiting for Oren to come after him so he can hurt him."

Oren was glad she'd been the one to veto the proposition; no way was he allowing the people guarding Madison to chase down a criminal. It might be possible to catch him, Oren thought, but it was unlikely. He was more concerned that, if the guy was waiting somewhere around here, it would be for Madison.

"We need to get to the station as soon as possible. It would be best if you could get someone else after that car. But—"

"But?" the driver echoed.

"But let me take a quick look at Madison's car." Just in case, Oren thought, and he hurried down the drive into the parking lot.

He quickly reached Madison's vehicle. When he looked back toward her, she was aiming her key fob toward her car.

"No!" Oren shouted, afraid Darius had somehow rigged it... He got down on his knees and looked toward the undercarriage.

Sure enough, he saw a box there with wires that seemed attached to the car.

Damn! If this went off, it might blow up the entire

area, including Madison, the cops, Oren himself and even Bubbe's Deli and his sister and everyone there. He was suddenly terrified for all of them.

He rose quickly and returned to the cop car. "Don't even try opening the doors!" he yelled to Madison. "Give one of these officers your key." Then he turned back to Werther. "Better call in a well-equipped investigation team for this one, with people primed to deal with explosives. Have a unit from your station get here to evacuate the area, businesses and all, plus get someone on patrol here right away to make sure no one else gets near the car—or they're liable to get blown to pieces."

As the cops started driving away, Oren called Olivia. "There's a bomb out here," he said.

"Oh, no!" Olivia exclaimed. "I'll get the place and neighboring stores evacuated right away."

Good. Oren knew his sister would do it and do it right. He next called Deputy Kathy Smith, one of the marshals now guarding Wes/Richard in Kendall, to warn them, too, in case Darius had rigged something there to kill his prey—or gotten an ally prepared to do it.

"Thanks," she said. "We'll check things out."

Oren believed her—but he still couldn't relax. Not under these circumstances.

He could only hope that they'd catch Darius now, or at least prevent him from harming anyone.

MADISON TURNED OVER her car keys to one of the officers in the front—realizing her hand was trembling. All of her was trembling. Hard. She was terrified.

If it wasn't for Oren—

She was glad he had gotten into this cop car, too, after discovering the problem under her car, which she couldn't see but assumed was a bomb since Oren had mentioned getting blown up.

At least he hadn't attempted to remove it—and kill himself by setting it off.

Terrified? No, she was panic-stricken, and trying hard to hide it. Thank heavens she had Oren with her. His presence was highly welcome, and maybe did calm her just a little.

Now they were presumably heading for the police station, where her mother and siblings should already be.

She'd have to explain it all to her mom. Jillian and Bryce already knew. But how would she be able to ensure they all remained safe?

Could the cops do that? Protection wasn't in Jillian's job description at the GGPD. Maybe it was in Bryce's at the FBI, but Madison doubted that. It apparently was in Oren's, at the Marshals Service. He'd helped Madison's father with his current identity. He'd helped Madison with her survival. But—well, he was now probably on Darius's list along with her, and her mother and siblings, according to that text.

And her father.

Madison at least needed to tell her mom about her father soon.

Finally—it seemed like forever, although it was probably only five minutes—they reached the police station.

Were her mother and siblings there yet? Surely they were. She and Oren had been delayed a bit as he'd checked her car and they'd watched Darius drive off and also waited for the next cop car to arrive so no one else could get close to her vehicle.

"Madison. You're here." That was the highly welcome voice of Jillian, who definitely knew her way around the police station. She hurried from behind the gated front desk to where Madison, Oren and their police companions had just entered.

"Yes," Madison said when Jillian reached them. "It was…a bit of an experience. A damn scary one. I'll tell you about it. Are Mom and Bryce here, too?"

"Yes. They're in a conference room. I'll take you there now. We're waiting for Brett to join us so we can discuss what to do next."

"Any idea how long he'll be?" Oren asked.

"He's in the middle of something, but he promised to join us as soon as possible," Jillian said.

"Hey, I think you're okay now," said the cop who had driven them here: Officer Scott, according to his metal ID badge. "We'll be heading off, maybe to see what's going on with that rigged car of yours."

Madison shuddered. She liked her car—but she might never want to drive it again, even if it survived. "Thanks so much. I really appreciate all your help."

"Ditto here," said Oren from beside her, and he reached out to shake the officers' hands.

Madison entered first and saw that her mom and Bryce sat at the long wooden table that took up the center of the room, similar to the last conference room Madison had visited. Her mother immediately stood.

And Jillian was with Madison, who was so relieved her family members were all okay that she felt tears fill her eyes.

Her mom spoke. "I want an explanation, Madison. Both Bryce and Jillian keep telling me that you need to be the one to tell me what's going on. Does this have something to do with your foolish decision not to marry Alec?"

"No, Mom," Madison said. "Well, maybe indirectly since I first saw…" She didn't finish. That was almost humorous, but she didn't think she had any real laughs within her after a near-death experience. "But I think you'd better sit down."

Her mother frowned and shook her head, but she did as Madison said.

Madison also sat, with Jillian and Oren beside her. Their supportive presence made her feel almost cool and human and ready to deal with the emotions her mother was likely to evince once she revealed the story that started all this.

Almost.

Everyone was looking at her. She understood that, but she also wished she had another glass of wine in front of her to relieve some stress.

She began talking anyway. "Mom, I know you're aware that I first went to Kendall to look for a wedding dress a bit over a week ago."

"Yes," her mother responded.

"While I was there, I saw…someone who looked familiar." She shot a gaze toward Bryce, who smiled encouragingly. She saw Oren's hand move on the table, as if he wanted to help boost her mood by holding hers, which of course was utterly inappropriate. Even if he had just saved her life.

"Someone you know?" her mom encouraged.

"Well, yes. As it turned out, you know him, too." Madison paused, then forced herself to continue. "I went back there this week to look for him again, maybe talk to him to see if my imagination was totally out of control… but it wasn't. Mom, it was our father, Richard Foster."

"What!" her mother screamed and stood up. "You're

joking. I've told you… I've told all of you that your dear, sweet father… He died years ago in the war."

Jillian rose beside her and placed her hand on their mother's shoulder. "Please, sit down, Mom," she said. "And listen to what Madison has to say. You need to hear it. Our lives—yours included—depend on it." She shot a look at her elder sister.

"But—"

"Please, Mom," Bryce also said. He, too, encouraged their mother to sit down. And, finally, she did. But her expression, the stiffness of her posture, suggested she wouldn't believe a word of what Madison said.

Madison wished she didn't have to believe it—well, all of it—either. She was delighted that their dad was still alive but couldn't completely accept why he'd remained out of their lives, even if it was because of supposed danger after he'd helped put a killer behind bars. And even if his reappearance in their lives had almost just killed Madison herself.

Even though what he'd grimly prophesied was now somewhat coming true.

Her voice hoarse, Madison said, "Dad is in witness protection. He stayed out of our lives, Mom, to keep us safe and to get justice for a murdered man. And as much as I didn't want to believe that when he first told me, what's going on now shows it was the truth."

She started from the beginning, her first trip to Kendall when Grace had come with her. She explained that she'd seen a man who looked a lot like a much-older Bryce. She glanced at her brother, who nodded in encouragement, which she appreciated. She said that her not understanding, not wanting to believe it, made her return the next week to find the fellow again and maybe even talk with him.

She described how she'd seen him, how she'd followed him and how she'd been grabbed and arrested while jaywalking right behind him. This time, she looked at Oren, who raised his black eyebrows and smiled at her.

She couldn't help smiling back again for just a moment, even remembering her first, angry feelings about Oren as he arrested her. She felt a lot different about him now, with his always being there for her. Protecting her.

"Really?" her mother asked.

"Really." Madison explained then who Oren was, how Richard Foster was now under the protection of the Marshals Service, with Oren as his main contact. How he had been under that protection for years, after witnessing a murder and testifying. How Amaltin had died in prison twenty years ago after threatening Richard's life, but Amaltin's son Darius was still threatening him and his family. Shea joined them in the conference room then and took a seat. The chief said nothing, just listened as Madison continued.

Madison described briefly how Oren and she had been forced off the road on their drive here to Grave Gulch—by that son. She then told what had happened when Oren and she left the deli a short while ago—and how Oren had checked out her car and found the explosives. "But it's not just me," she said. "He threatened all of us. He sent me a text message that included my family in his threats. Every one of us needs to be really careful now."

"And go live in a safe house," Brett said, standing, leaning over the table and looking at each of them in turn. "All of you."

Now, that was something new, Madison thought. She glanced at Oren, who appeared slightly puzzled, too, but he nodded at Brett nonetheless.

"What do you mean?" their mom asked, and Madison was glad. She wanted to know more of what Brett intended, too. She was scared, sure. More for her mom and siblings—and father—than herself. But she'd no intention of making any major changes except being a lot more alert and careful.

And try hard to keep her terror under control. She didn't want to die, but she had to do what she could to help her family.

Brett explained he'd been in touch with Oren's marshal colleagues now in Kendall keeping watch over Wesley Windham. Wesley had also received some texted threats not only against him but against Verity and their children, presumably from Darius.

Plus, the investigators who'd looked at Madison's car found some pretty lethal explosives there, and the officers who'd attempted to find Darius when he'd driven off had had no success.

"It's dangerous out there," Brett finished. "We've done well with safe houses when there've been other people in trouble here in Grave Gulch, and I've got some members of our police force who know what they're doing to help out. Until we get this Darius, we need to keep you safe, and that's the best way. So—got it? All of you Coltons who are here are going to be kind of like Wesley Windham in Kendall. You'll be in a special place under our direct protection, starting immediately."

Good idea, Madison thought…but only for their mother. Maybe Jillian and Bryce, but they were both in law enforcement so a safe house was most likely unnecessary for them.

And her? No way was she going to hide that way.

It would be much better if she stayed at least somewhat visible—and brought Darius into the open to be captured.

She looked straight into Oren's eyes. He was staring at her, too, as if attempting to read her thoughts.

Well, she'd tell him and the rest of them.

And hope they all got it.

Chapter Fifteen

That expression on Madison's face… Not that he could read her mind, but if he had to guess, she was against the idea of a safe house, at least with respect to her.

She confirmed it. "Thanks so much," she said to Brett, looking steadily into the police chief's eyes. "I think it's a wonderful idea—to protect my mother and siblings, if they're willing to stay there for a while. But… Well, I want to do whatever is necessary to capture the man who intends to kill us all. He seems to be mostly after me now, so I don't just want to hide out. Although I do intend to be careful, I need to be around to see if the guy will try to get me so he can be caught. Not that I'm in law enforcement, but if Oren can still help…"

She looked at him with a pleading expression.

Hell, he should say no. Despite his willingness to use all efforts to protect her, he was terrified that wouldn't be enough. He should convince her somehow to head to that safe house and stay far away from any possibility of that jerk Darius finding her.

But if that happened, he'd have no excuse to stay here and protect her. The local PD would have that obligation, which they might meet well. Or not.

As much as he hated to admit it, she was right. If they

really wanted to catch the guy, it would be better to have a target who was visible to him. A *well-protected* target.

Before he responded, Bryce spoke. "I understand what you're saying, Madison, but you can't do that. And—"

"I don't like it either, but…" Oren broke in, again staring at her, as if his look would make her change her mind. If it did, he'd just have to live with it.

"Please, Oren," she said. "Or are you going back to take care of our father? You said other marshals are doing that now."

"They are. But the idea of you purposely placing yourself in the crosshairs of that intended killer—"

"With you here to protect me," she said, which he certainly intended if she stayed around.

And as much as he hated admitting it to himself, her trusting him that way made him feel rather proud.

"Look, this is what I think," Bryce said. "If I had a choice, I'd send you to the safe house, Madison. I don't like your making yourself a target by remaining in your usual life, especially when you're right—the guy's apparently after you first. But here's my suggestion. I'll avoid the safe house, too, at least for now. That way, I can help protect you, as Oren does, as well as doing all I can to help find the suspect. And if Jillian goes there, not only will she be safe, but she can help to ensure our mother's safety." He looked at Madison. "Does that work for you?"

She nodded at her brother. "Sounds good."

Oren kept himself from cheering. That certainly worked for him, as long as Madison wasn't going to listen to reason and head to the safe house herself. He'd take care of her, and now he'd also have her brother's help.

Plus, he'd do what he could to make sure her students weren't jeopardized, either.

And she was actually right, he admitted to himself. They were much more likely to find her potentially lethal stalker sooner if Madison stayed in his sights, in her regular life, as much as possible.

"Okay," Brett said, nodding enough for his red hair to shift at his collar. "I'll call a couple of my colleagues here who've put together safe houses before. They've already got at least one location available they've used in the past, and you two, Verity and Jillian, can pick up your essential belongings with those cops with you for protection, then head there tonight. Okay?"

Oren wondered if Jillian would be okay with it. Sure, she was a member of the GGPD, but she did crime-scene investigations, not protection. It was their mother, though, she'd be protecting.

Fortunately, Jillian was fine with it. "I'd really like both of you to join us, Madison and Bryce—especially Madison, since you don't have any kind of law-enforcement background and the guy does seem to be after you now." She looked at her sister but didn't wait for Madison's response. "But I'm willing to go to a safe house for my own protection under these circumstances, and much more so if I can also help take care of our mom." Her gaze moved to land on their mother, who didn't even look at her. But her expression was grim.

Oren figured some of what Jillian said was to placate their mom and make sure she was willing to do as she'd been told: stay in that house for a while. Having one daughter there with her had to make the situation at least a little more palatable.

Even though her other kids would be out in the world, potentially in a lot of danger.

All the more reason for Oren to help protect Madison—and to find the dangerous man threatening them all.

Mostly Madison, which stoked his motivation even more. And continuing to protect Madison on his own? Oh, yeah. Sure, it was his job. But he was beginning to recognize that it was turning into a whole lot more. Yes, he cared for her. And as he considered what he would be up to in the future—well, he was starting to wonder if Madison could remain part of it.

"All right," Verity finally said, standing and shaking her head. "Richard's really alive? And that's the reason for all this?" She looked again at Madison, who nodded, a sympathetic look on her face. "Okay, then. I want to know more. A lot more." She crossed her arms and sat back down. "I know you kids are always concerned about me, and this is a difficult situation. So for now, I'll go to that safe house with you, Jillian—as long as Madison and Bryce promise to be careful. I guess they won't be able to visit us, then leave and come back, since that might give the location away. But please, please, consider changing your minds and joining us. Okay?"

"Oh, Mom, I'm so glad," Madison said, hurrying over to hug her mother. "And I'll keep in touch the best way I can, through the police department. Okay?" She looked up toward Brett, who nodded.

"Sounds good," he said. "You, too, Mr. FBI." His gaze moved to Bryce.

"Yep." Bryce also nodded. "And I'll want to discuss contacts with you—whether Oren and I, and Madison, should keep in touch with you directly or who in your department we should rely on."

"Good idea," agreed Brett. "Once I get all the safe-house details and personnel worked out, we'll talk. In fact, we'll talk more about it tonight."

Though Oren wanted to get Madison somewhere else immediately, there wasn't any place safer than the police station. And it wouldn't hurt to learn more about the safe house.

Brett left the room and soon returned with his K-9, Ember, and a couple of cops, after apparently getting a team together to establish and prepare for running the safe house with Verity and Jillian living there.

The group described the location that would be used, a remote house a distance from downtown Grave Gulch, one with thick walls and lots of other homes around, though not too close, and no woods or anything else to obscure it from the team protecting its inhabitants. Oren gathered that it was owned by the police department, although the deed designated some former cop who'd retired—and still cooperated—as the owner. Oren looked forward to seeing the place, but that might take a while unless Madison changed her mind and decided to stay there with her mother and sister.

The two safe-house specialists Brett introduced them to were armed uniformed officer Daniel Coleman, a K-9 at his side, and Detective Troy Colton. They both regarded everyone in the room with curiosity. They might not be the only ones to provide the planned protection, but at least initially they would be in charge of the location where Verity and Jillian would stay, ensuring they remained out of sight and safe.

Brett then let his safe-house staff know who the others in the room were, not just the two women they'd be taking care of. "For safety's sake, you shouldn't all be in communication with each other much," Brett said after completing the introductions. "We'll get a few burner phones, though, so you can talk now and then on a limited basis."

Finally, it was time to leave. Almost. Oren would need to call the marshals' office in Grand Rapids soon and speak to some of his superior officers. He'd still be protecting Madison, which remained his assignment, but he needed to inform his superiors about the recent events—and learn if they had any additional orders to convey.

Meanwhile, the trainees he'd worked with had driven here to Grave Gulch from Kendall in two cars, one of them Oren's since he'd left it to accompany Madison here in hers. They had both departed in the other car, and Oren's SUV was parked down the street in an indoor parking lot. They'd dropped the keys off at the station after a brief phone discussion with Oren.

Brett now stood with his safe-house folks and Verity and Jillian, as they got better acquainted. Madison and Bryce stood off to the side. Jillian seemed at ease, but their mother appeared anxious. Not surprising. Hopefully, as things progressed, she would relax a bit as people including the two they'd just met attempted to keep her safe.

And Madison? Keeping her safe was definitely Oren's job, his responsibility, his chosen goal—although now he would also have the assistance of Bryce, which was a good thing—now that he was starting to care for her so much. Probably too much. But so what? As he'd been pondering, he wasn't sure what the future would hold, but for once he was wondering if this could turn into some kind of relationship. A real one.

Oren got his car keys from the front desk.

Before they left, Madison said to both Oren and Brett,

"I intend to keep my life as much on course as possible—without endangering other people. I want you to know that. I'll go to my school tomorrow but hopefully won't be in my classroom, since I'll want to protect my students. I've given special programs in one of the empty classrooms before, and I'll tell our principal I'll hang out there tomorrow to plan one of those programs. And I'll try to continue to do that till Darius is in custody."

Good idea in some ways, Oren thought. He looked at Brett, though, and said, "I'd imagine our suspect will figure out the potential trap and maybe stay away."

"Which isn't a bad idea, of course." Brett nodded as he considered it. "But tomorrow, at least, I'd like you to do everything you normally do. It's more likely to draw our suspect out. But I'll also have a lot of protection there, including undercover cops who'll look like teachers, others patrolling the streets, in case the guy decides to show up. We will keep everyone there safe, not just Madison. And we'll see then if it makes more sense afterward for you to stay out of your classroom. I'll also run this by the school's administration and security staff."

He didn't allow for any argument. Oren wasn't entirely happy, but of course he would also be there, protecting everyone he could.

And Madison? "As long as you're sure you can take care of everyone," she said.

Oren knew Brett couldn't be certain, but he did say, "We'll certainly do our best."

"We've got to go now, Madison," Oren said. Of course, it wasn't quite that easy, though she did say a hasty goodbye to her family members and promised her mother and sister she'd stay in touch as much as was reasonable.

As an added protection, Brett had an officer drive them to the parking lot where Oren's car was now located so Madison and he wouldn't have to walk along the street in plain view. Fortunately, there weren't many people walking around the area, and still no more demonstrations outside the police station, a good thing.

The cop dropped them off around the corner, and a few minutes later they were on their way to Madison's condo.

"I assume you're still intending to do your regular day of teaching now that Brett told you to."

"Yes." Her tone suggested she expected him to argue about it. They'd stopped at a traffic light, and he looked over at her.

"I can't completely disagree with Brett about it, even though I don't like it. But I'll definitely stay in close touch with Bryce, and even more so with Brett to ensure he actually does have protection around your school and its students, especially yours."

The expression on her lovely face looked anything but convinced. "So we, and the kids, will be safe?"

Oren made the final turn onto Madison's street. "Sure," he said, hoping he wasn't lying. He certainly would do his part, but he knew there were no guarantees that Madison wouldn't be hurt. Which worried him. A lot. "Why else would I hang out with you?"

Madison laughed. "Why else, indeed?"

Soon Oren had parked in the condo's lot, although his navy SUV now occupied a guest space and not one associated with Madison's unit. He wasn't sure what had happened with her car but figured the cops would take care of it till she could start driving again, assuming the explosives had been removed and the car was otherwise okay.

"Wait for me," he ordered as Madison started to open her door.

She stopped and waited and scowled. "I guess this is my life for now," she said.

"Yep, unless you want me to handcuff you and take you to the safe house." Not that he'd really do such a thing, but he figured he was making a point, at least somewhat humorously, with this woman he found really attractive. So attractive he wanted to do a whole lot more than share kisses with her. Like, not only checking the safety of her room, but spending time in it, with her, in bed— No. Forget that. It wasn't humorous…and it also was a bad idea…

"Of course I do." She turned and held her hands, wrists together, out toward him.

He laughed, and she laughed back. But in a moment she grew somber. "I really do appreciate what you're doing, Oren. And I recognize I may need some continued tutoring on what I can and can't do to stay safe. Thank you."

He nodded and exited the car, then removed his changes of clothes from the trunk. Tutoring? Well, she was a teacher, and in some ways he would be educating her on things he felt would keep her safest under these difficult circumstances.

At this moment, at least, he felt she actually would listen to him.

He kept looking around them as he guided Madison out of the car and into her building, then insisted on entering her unit first and looking around.

On the other hand, he thought, as Madison poured

them both beer and they sat down in her living room, maybe Darius really had just wanted to scare the family members—while he headed back to Kendall and his real target.

Well, Oren trusted his colleagues who were there and again had Wes in protective custody.

But the only way to be truly certain they were safe was to catch this guy...and he wanted to be the one to do it. To know that Madison would be safe.

How to do it? Well, even considering Brett's help and Bryce's, too, Oren was certain he was in a better position than anyone else, thanks to the woman he was now protecting. Unfortunately. Darius had already threatened her and would undoubtedly come after her again, unless he was no longer in town—and maybe even then, in a while.

They chatted as they drank their beer, mostly about nothing but also including Madison's concerns about a safe house. She rightly assumed that Oren knew quite a bit about them thanks to his work, but she still seemed worried for her family, and no wonder. He was even worried for Olivia, after that bomb threat so close to her restaurant. Still, he tried to comfort Madison with some anecdotes about how people he'd known who'd stayed in safe houses not only survived but were often allowed back to their real lives after those threatening them had been caught.

And despite not wanting to leave her company, he again encouraged her to head for the safe house and stay with her relatives.

Big surprise. She said no. He was secretly glad, though, that they'd be alone.

She also soon reminded him that she needed to get up early tomorrow to go to school.

"And yes," she said, "I understand the risks of staying in my usual life. My biggest concern is that Darius will show up there and hurt someone other than me."

Oren couldn't promise otherwise, but he reminded her that Bryce would be there, too. "What I don't understand is that man's thinking. Yes, he wants revenge on my dad, but what good would it do him to kill anyone now, either him or a family member? Or all of us?"

Oren had no good answer, although he'd worked in law enforcement long enough to know that some suspects just had a desire to do bad things. He stood. "Apparently it's something he's thought about for a long time."

Oren had an urge to end their evening together on a lighter, more humorous note. "Anyway," he said. "it's bedtime. I'll follow you into your bedroom."

She looked at him with a smile that did appear a bit amused, but there was a look in her eyes that suggested more. A lot more. She looked him up and down, stopping for an extra second at the area of him that started to harden immediately when she said, "Oh, I like that idea." Her voice was low and hoarse, which only got him more aroused. And now her eyes connected with his.

Her beautiful, sexy green eyes.

Was she serious?

"And," she continued, "I gather we may be living together for a while, so we might as well not waste any more nights when we're both in my condo."

She sure sounded serious. And he had an urge to grab her hand and lead her into her bedroom. A very strong urge.

But his professionalism fortunately dashed through him suddenly. He had to patrol the area inside and out before he went to bed. And having sex first would be one humongous distraction—one during which Darius Amaltin might well show up at the condo.

Besides, she couldn't really be serious. She'd just ended her engagement, even if she'd never really loved Alec... Oren directed that thought to the part of his body that was telling him otherwise.

Still...

Okay. Enough. Joke or not, he would treat it as such. For his own sake, as well as hers.

"I enjoy the promise of things to come," he said with a sly grin. "Sometime. I'll see you to your bedroom, sure, and look around it to make certain all looks safe. But anything else? Nope. We'll save that for another night."

He winked, then grew somber. "Distractions, even fun ones, are not a good idea in my line of work. So think about what we could be doing as you fall asleep tonight. I will. But I won't allow it to distract me from my protection of you."

Chapter Sixteen

Okay, she'd asked for that dismissal of her invitation. Oren was a marshal, doing his job—not her live-in lover. But as Madison lay alone in her bed that night, she felt her body continue to react to the sexual innuendos she had tossed at Oren earlier. She'd realized she wanted him in a way she'd never wanted Alec. Or any other man, for that matter.

Oren was now lying on her sofa as he had before, probably sleeping. Or not. But he wouldn't be awake for the same reason she was. At least not entirely.

He might be thinking about having sex with her someday—or not. But he was most likely listening for any concerning noises in her condo or the area. Or maybe he was even up and about, checking to make sure everything was in order and Darius wasn't around.

And the idea of going to her bedroom with her other than just to ensure it was safe? That apparently wasn't on his mind, or he must have shoved it far from his consciousness.

Unfortunately. And frustratingly for Madison.

Had she been serious about wanting sex with him? Oh, yes. Too serious. She was much too attracted to the man, for too many reasons, such as his thoughtfulness, his protectiveness, his funniness—and his drop-dead good looks.

But she recognized, despite her discomfort and embarrassment at having even broached the subject, that Oren had done the exact right thing.

Rejected her. Even if she wanted nothing more than to spend the night with him right here, in her bed.

SHE WAS GLAD to awaken the next morning to the sound of her clock radio. She'd actually slept. And she felt herself grow slightly red from the embarrassment that hadn't left her overnight.

Fortunately, Oren didn't mention her inappropriate hints when they met in her kitchen for their quick cereal-and-coffee breakfast. He carried his sports jacket but wore his slacks and a new black T-shirt, which somewhat showed his muscular physique. His dark hair was tousled... Wow. It was a good thing Madison knew she had to head to work.

While they drove to school, a pang shot through Madison as she realized her mother must have taken a leave of absence from her job. She wouldn't be teaching this day, or for a while, most likely.

If only there was something more Madison could do to help her...

Beyond making herself an obvious target to draw Darius out? Surely that was enough.

She didn't mention that to Oren, though. But she did want his confirmation that her going to school that day was a good idea. They'd talked about it before and now did so again. No matter that she was willing to put herself in danger, and she'd made that clear. She couldn't help being scared, though, and she would do anything to protect the people she loved and otherwise cared about, like her own students—even risk her own life. And Oren would do she same, she felt sure.

Sure, the place would be under surveillance by authorities anyway, but there would likely be more of it with her presence. And the police chief, and maybe Oren, too, believed it was preferable for her to be there with lots of protection around, both uniformed cops and undercover, to keep an eye out for the guy—although Oren would of course be with her no matter where she headed that day or for the foreseeable future.

On their way, Madison noted when Oren slowed the car or turned corners to go around blocks but figured he was checking to see if they were being followed. Apparently not, fortunately, since he kept going and didn't contact Brett or anyone else in the police department.

But the GGPD definitely had a presence nearby. Madison usually didn't pay attention to patrol cars, but she'd have noticed this many in the area before. At least half a dozen drove by in their direction or the opposite way.

If Darius was around here, he'd know he was being sought, which in some ways was a good thing, both for her safety and for that of others at her elementary school.

But that might also keep him away—for now. Or brave and foolish enough to challenge all those out to get him. Madison certainly hoped that wasn't the case, but the little she'd seen and heard of him made her assume it could be.

Once they reached the school, Oren checked the parking area, then accompanied Madison inside. "Good morning," she said to fellow staff members as she passed them in the hallway. She didn't see Alec, but she might later—and here she was again with Oren, whom her ex had seen her with before. Well, Oren wasn't a new romantic interest—which was a shame—and doing his official duty had to come first.

As before, she headed first to her classroom, with her gorgeous, caring, professional bodyguard whom she'd really wanted to have sex with last night...

Okay, she couldn't keep thinking about that. Oren was right to keep things more casual. He even acted completely friendly as she greeted people in the hall, even as he clearly studied them, but of course none was Darius.

They soon reached her classroom, where she was jolted by the appearance of someone she'd never seen in the school previously. Her brother sat in the chair she usually occupied in the front of the room when she faced her students for classes.

"Hi, sis." He looked up from the phone he'd been studying and approached them. "And hi, Oren." He seemed to study Oren's face, and Madison figured her brother was attempting to read the degree of concern there and whether Oren had seen any potential danger on his way in.

"Good to see you," Oren told him. "I assume all appears well here, since you were just sitting there. Anything exciting show up on your phone?"

Bryce laughed. "Nope. Anything exciting last night or on your way here?" Bryce's gaze first on Oren, then her, appeared to attempt to read their minds. *Anything exciting?* Maybe he was searching for more info they had about Darius, but Madison wasn't sure. Was it so obvious that there was at least some degree of attraction between Oren and her? She felt herself turn hot with embarrassment.

"All seems pretty calm since we last saw you," Oren replied, seemingly unbothered.

"Have you talked to Jillian or Mom or anyone at the safe house?" Madison asked. "Is everything okay there?"

"Yes, yes and yes," Bryce said. "I've talked to them all and everything seems fine."

Good, Madison thought. She'd have to speak to them later, too. "Since you were allowed to come in," Madison said, "does anyone know why you're here?"

"I was directed to one of the security guards since I came here so early." At Madison's quizzical look, he added, "I've been in your classroom for over an hour now. Anyway, apparently the guards have been primed to know there's some potential for danger around here. The one I talked to—his name was Bob—seemed fascinated by my FBI ID, but he figured I was related to you since we share a last name. Anyway, he promised to patrol the halls, and he was aware there'd be cops from the PD around, too, mostly in casual dress."

"That all sounds okay," Madison said. "And if you don't mind hanging around here a little longer, I want to go visit our principal and find out what she knows— and possibly fill her in on more."

After she locked her purse in her desk near where Bryce sat down again, she turned to Oren. "Do you want to go talk to Principal Nelson with me? I assume she already knows what's going on, or at least some of it. But I want to make sure she's dealing with it okay."

"Sure," he responded. "I'm fairly sure Chief Shea contacted her himself, but it won't hurt for her to have another contact if she needs it."

"Like you?" Madison asked.

"Like me."

After confirming once more that Bryce would hang out there, Madison led Oren to the end of the hall. Once more, since it was early, Principal Nelson's assistant wasn't in the outer office, so Madison knocked on the inner door.

And as before, the principal opened it nearly immediately. "I was hoping to talk to you this morning," she said to Madison, then shot a quizzical glance again toward Oren. "I've talked to the current chief of police, no less, and he told me some of what's going on, but not everything."

Today, she wore a charcoal dress adorned with a large green pendant. Her hair was pulled back into a clip at the nape of her neck. She waved for Madison and Oren to sit again on the chairs across from her desk. "Okay," she said. "I gather whatever's going on has something to do with you and your family. I considered telling you to go back home today, but Chief Shea indicated it would be better for you to be here, under guard." This time, she stared at Oren. "With you, of course," she continued, "as well as the cops both in uniform and undercover who're around today. It's okay for today, but we'll have to see how things go to decide about what happens next. I can't have law enforcement in my school every day."

"I understand," Madison said. "And my idea is, if the person who's being sought isn't captured today, I'll teach remotely. That way, my students will be safer."

And if anyone's hurt—or worse—it will only be me.

"Well, that's a possibility." Her boss didn't appear happy about it. "But if things appear too potentially dangerous, I'll have to put you on leave for a while."

Madison wanted to object, but that made sense. She knew she was juggling a bit here, wanting to do her job

and protect her family—and herself. She would definitely listen to what her school's principal told her. "Of
course," she agreed, though her gaze lowered to her fingers clasped in her lap.

"I agree that we should see how things go today,"
Oren said, "and maybe for the next few days. For the
safety of everyone, we need to get this guy into custody."

Madison glanced at Oren, who wore a determined
expression on his face.

"I certainly want to help anyway I can to bring this
situation to a conclusion that's safe for your family,
Madison—and especially for this school," the principal said."So let's touch base often, and please keep me
informed—" again her dark-eyed, intense gaze landed
on Oren "—about how things are progressing. Okay?"

"Okay," Oren agreed.

This conversation over, Madison thanked her boss
and led Oren from the principal's office. She took him to
the cafeteria, where she got them each a bottle of water.
Her throat felt dry, as if she'd been teaching all day—
maybe because she was so close to Oren. Or maybe it
was simpler than that: her hydration decreased as her
nervousness grew.

They headed back to the first floor. Madison chatted about inconsequential things with Oren, partly to
calm her uneasiness. There were many people in the
halls she didn't recognize. A few were in police uniforms, and those who weren't she assumed included undercover cops.

Fortunately, none looked like Darius. Not that she was
certain to recognize him. But she trusted Oren, and he
didn't seem to see Darius there, either.

They returned to her classroom. Her students had

begun to arrive, and Bryce was talking to them, demonstrating some simple origami by making designs out of construction paper he must have found in her desk. The kids seemed enthralled. And happy. Which made Madison happy, too.

She greeted her students as always and had fun watching Bryce teach some of his skills with folding paper. Then, at her class's normal starting time, she was glad to see that both her bodyguard and her brother moved from the front of the room to the back, where they watched the kids sit down at their table seats after removing their backpacks.

Soon, Madison began her regular classes of reading, printing, spelling and beginning arithmetic. It felt so much like a regular day.

Except that she had two adult men sitting at the back of the room keeping watch over her, looking out the windows along the side of the room a lot, leaving the classroom presumably not only to find the little boys' room but also to patrol the halls and watch for danger. Watch for Darius.

Eventually it was time for recess, which worried Madison. But things went well then, too. It didn't hurt that there were a few people she didn't recognize, both men and women, who most likely were also undercover cops hanging around on the playground. There were even a couple of uniformed cops. Soon, they all returned indoors, and Madison continued her lessons.

And finally, kindergarten was over for the day.

Unlike usual days, though, Madison didn't return to her classroom after they'd gone, to make her typical plans for the next day. Instead, she headed down the hall, with her entourage still protecting her. But while they were near the end of the hallway, Principal Nelson started toward them. "I was just about to come visit you in your classroom," she said. "All of you. Do you two think we're all safe here?"

Oren was the one to answer. "No indication otherwise." And before she could say anything else he added, "My suggestion is that we continue this daily, at least for now—unless we see anything that suggests otherwise. It seems best for all of us."

Did Madison agree? Well, she'd seen no sign that Darius was around that day. No suggestion that anyone in or around the school had been in danger. The idea of going about her daily life felt very welcome, even if she had to keep up the facade that everything was all right.

"All right, then," Principal Nelson said. "We'll continue this tomorrow. But you do promise you'll let me know if anything at all suggests the situation is changing in any bad way, don't you?"

"Of course," Madison said, trading glances with her brother and Oren. Neither said anything to disagree.

They returned to her classroom, where Bryce said goodbye. "It's early enough that I should be able to get on the road and start hunting our quarry, even if he isn't hunting us. My mission right now, while I'm not keeping an eye on you, Madison, is to go after that gunrunner's son and bring Darius down before he can even threaten anyone else. And you—" he faced Oren "—you'll take damn good care of my sister. Got it?"

"Got it," Oren said with a grin.

And what else could Madison do but hug her brother and agree? But of course she said, "That would be wonderful, bro. But please, please stay safe."

"You, too, sis."

Bryce headed out the door.

"So tonight," Oren said. "And us." He looked her straight in the eye in a manner that made her body quiver suddenly with desire. Even though she knew full well that wasn't what he had in mind.

Or even if he did, nothing would come of it.

"Same old, same old." Madison smiled in a way she hoped didn't reveal her inner thoughts.

Chapter Seventeen

First thing as they drove away, though, Oren called Brett, putting his phone on Bluetooth. He wanted to confirm that the police chief also thought things had gone well enough that day at the school.

Which he did. "I talked to Principal Nelson. She called to say you'd left and that you'd spoken with her about having things go the same way tomorrow as today, with the patrols inside and out. I assured her we'd keep an eye on things similarly tomorrow, and she sounded glad. Plus she indicated, Madison, that you were welcome to conduct your classes the same way. At least for now."

"Great!" She sounded as if she truly was pleased. Then she asked Brett if she could call her mother and sister at the safe house. He agreed and gave her the number for the phone they were currently using—a burner phone.

Oren was glad to see Madison so happy. Which kind of surprised him. Or not. He was beginning to like her too much, and he hoped he could contribute to her happiness.

She conducted that conversation with her mother and sister in the car, too, with her phone on Speaker so Oren could hear. Her family members seemed fine, but her mom asked, "Please, even with all this going on, is there some way I can see...your father, Madison?"

Good thing they were at a stop sign, since Madison turned and stared at Oren. Of course. He was the one with the knowledge and connections, even in Kendall. "Assuming he's okay with it, we'll work it out," he said, loud enough for Verity and Jillian to hear.

And in fact, after Madison ended her call to her family, promising to get in touch again soon, Oren parked at the curb and called his boss, explained the situation and got his approval to contact one of the two marshals assigned to protect Wesley Windham.

"It should be fine to take him to their safe house to say hello," his supervisor said, "as long as everyone there remains alert."

"And as long as I don't show up there with our wonderful gunrunner's son's other main target, Madison Colton," Oren added, sending an apologetic glance in her direction.

They talked a little more about logistics. When Oren got off the phone and started driving again, he said to Madison, "It sounds all set. You may want to let your family know that Richard Foster will most likely be visiting them tomorrow, assuming everyone follows through right away—and also assuming he's okay with it."

Which Madison did. And when that call ended, they were finally at her condo. Once inside, Oren called his sister and arranged for her to send a sandwich for him and matzo ball soup for Madison. The meal arrived in just over half an hour, and Oren went to get it from the delivery person, silently thanking his sister for working so fast.

During dinner, Oren dived into topics of conversation with Madison about kids and origami and why he got into law enforcement: he'd wanted to help after growing tired of seeing on the news that so many bad guys got away.

Madison seemed interested in all he said and got into some topics of her own, including that she'd decided to become a teacher because, growing up, she'd had some really good ones and some really bad ones, and she had wanted to use the good stuff she'd experienced to educate other kids.

Oren liked that, despite how different their careers and backgrounds were, they both aspired to the same goal: helping people.

Soon it was time to start getting ready for bed—with Oren sleeping on the sofa as usual.

Only... That night he felt relieved that all had gone well at Madison's school again that day. Glad to be in her company for the foreseeable future. Glad...well, hell. When she said good-night and started down the hall toward her room, he had to accompany her to check it out.

At her door, she looked at him. Her gorgeous face appeared to assess him again, looking him up and down suggestively with her amazing green eyes. "So," she said, "are you going to come in and check there's no one waiting for me in my room?"

"Of course." He pushed the door open and slid beside her into it, his chest just grazing her arm, but he was definitely aware of the contact.

There, he walked around as he had before, arcing around the queen-size bed that had pillows and a coverlet in pretty pastel colors of lavender and pink similar to the look of her sofa and other furniture. He could see around the tall bureau and bedside table and into the lush bathroom adorned with fluffy coral-colored towels. He checked under the bed, not that he expected to find

Darius there or anywhere else in this place—for now. "Okay," he finally said. "Everything's fine."

But as he looked back at her face, she looked troubled. "Everything's not fine," she said.

His hackles immediately rose. "What's wrong?"

"I'm going to be lonely in here by myself tonight, especially after the stressful day we had."

Was she really going where he thought she was with this? He felt his body react in a manner that was completely inappropriate—and yet completely appropriate. He grew warm and felt an erection begin to grow. Really grow. "So you want me to stay with you?"

"Yes." Her tone was soft and almost pleading. How could he say no?

But notwithstanding where his thoughts had drifted before, could he say yes and risk her life and maybe his own, too?

"I understand what you're thinking," she said, and even looked down at his increasing arousal. "You don't need any distraction when you're trying to protect me. But what if we both really concentrate not just on what we're doing, but also on what we're hearing around us, and—"

He couldn't help it. She'd taken a step toward him, and now he bent down and took her into his arms. "Bad idea," he whispered. "But—"

But when she grabbed his butt and ground her body tightly against his, how could he resist?

MADISON KNEW SHE was being foolish. But she was so sexually aroused by this man that she simply had to do something.

Something wonderful. Or so she anticipated.

The hot encounter she envisioned and craved shouldn't take very long anyway. Not the way she wanted him to kiss her, touch her, sink into her, then move them both to completion. And she suspected that this hunk of a man wouldn't prolong their intimacy. He'd want it hard, fast and entirely, rapidly enjoyable, as she did. So they wouldn't spend too much time on their distraction…

She felt more desire than she ever had before. Her skin tingled. Her whole body hungered for more…now.

She'd backed away from Oren just a bit—just long enough to begin unbuttoning his shirt. He'd left his sports jacket over the chair in her kitchen as they ate, which of course she had noticed. Not that he'd revealed a lot of his body that way, but the shedding of any piece of clothing over dinner had been enough to tempt her, at least a bit.

"Oh, here," he muttered, finishing the job she'd started and dropping the shirt, and the slacks he removed, onto the floor. He stood there, his muscular chest and arms uncovered, in his gray briefs with the front extended, and Madison had an urge to drop to her knees, pull his shorts off and begin kissing him there.

But she didn't have the chance. Instead of just standing there, Oren moved toward her again, and soon her dress joined his clothes on the floor. And then her bra and panties. And then—

Then they lay on her bed. Oren's hands were all over her. Not to be outdone, she finally pulled his shorts down and grasped him.

He growled and grew closer yet, kissing her breasts, tickling them a bit with his facial hair, holding her most intimate area and using his fingers to stimulate her even more. She, too, began kissing him, there, also stroking him, wanting—

Fortunately, though she hadn't had a lot of reason to keep condoms here despite her engagement, she had a supply. She extracted one from the drawer at the top of the stand beside her bed and helped to put it on Oren.

She got what she wanted when he soon lowered her gently to the bed, pulled himself on top of her and entered her. And began moving in and out, slowly at first, then faster. As she moved in harmony below him, holding him close yet shifting her body to help provide the deepest and most delightful sexuality, she listened to his groans and her own. "Oh, Oren," she breathed— and felt herself reaching her climax at the same time he apparently reached his, since he inhaled deeply and stopped moving.

And she? She felt amazed—gratified and fulfilled and full of joy at this unique and wonderful experience.

Madison allowed herself to return to a bit of reality afterward. "That was… I can't even tell you how wonderful it was." She heard the hoarseness in her voice and felt her breathing begin to slow down.

"Now, just lie here for a while with me," he said, holding her closely against his hard, hot body. "We'll listen together for anything that shouldn't be around here."

Which made more reality crash down on Madison, but he was right.

And he had done exactly what she'd wanted—made incredible love with her. Probably for the only time that night. The only time forever, or at least until Darius Amaltin was caught?

Not if she could help it.

For now… Well, she soon realized she was falling

asleep. Oren's breathing seemed deeper, too, but when she moved slightly so did he. "You okay?" he asked.

"More than okay." And then she wanted to know. "Will you stay in here with me tonight? I mean, we don't *necessarily* need to partake in any more enjoyment, but I'd love to have you near me, and we can both listen for…whatever."

"As long as I don't disturb you when I wake up and patrol the condo to keep an eye out for…whatever." His tone was light, despite the seriousness of what he was saying, and he pulled her closer against him once more, their bodies still bare and hot, and Madison felt stimulated yet again.

But she would restrain herself now.

"You definitely won't disturb me, whatever you do." Madison added a bit of suggestiveness to her tone just in case Oren wanted to have another go. But if he didn't, she'd certainly understand—and hope for more another night.

"That's fine, then." Oren tightened his arms around her. "I'll stay."

OKAY, HE'D WANTED this to happen. Boy, had he. And what he'd gained was a reward far, far greater than he'd imagined. And he'd imagined a lot.

Had anything happened to endanger Madison when he was lost in the delight of making love with this amazing woman? He didn't think so. He'd managed sometimes to let his mind escape the wonders his body was engaged in and think. And listen.

And then return to the ecstasy…

What now, though? He would continue to make certain she was safe.

Might they repeat this sometime? He could only hope so. Because, damn it all, right or wrong—he was falling in love with her.

Now, he let himself lie there holding Madison for a short while, then pulled gently away, albeit reluctantly.

"Are you patrolling?" she asked in a voice that suggested he'd awakened her.

"Yes," he said. "But I'll be back soon." He hoped. He also hoped he'd find no indication that Darius was anywhere around or that he even knew where Madison lived—although that was highly unlikely.

Still, Oren got up, dressed and conducted his inspection. All seemed fine, so he returned to bed and actually fell asleep with Madison's still-naked body against his. Fortunately, he'd put his shorts back on before lying down, and the warmth of her, her delectable curves, her sweet female aroma… Well, he managed to get some sleep without stirring up any more arousal. This time.

But closer to dawn, when he awakened for the fourth time, he decided he needn't resist any longer.

And their sex this time… Phenomenal.

Before he got out of bed, he found himself wondering what would happen once he'd found Amaltin and no longer had to be with Madison. He didn't want to think about that.

The next morning was pretty much the same as they'd experienced before: cereal and coffee for breakfast, then heading to school.

But not really the same. The way they spoke to one another was even warmer, with a bit of suggestive humor thrown in. And they shared kisses before getting out of the car.

Oren accompanied Madison to her classroom, and

that was a bit different since Bryce wasn't there that day. But Madison's brother called her at the same time they'd first seen him yesterday. At Bryce's apparent request, Madison put him on Speaker on her phone. "Just so you both know," he said, "I'm working today on a couple of cases. Oren, you were made aware of them. I've been given a lead on finding Len Davison, so I've got to follow up on it."

On looking more into what was going on in Grave Gulch, including the former demonstrations at the police station, Oren had heard of that situation beyond what they'd discussed with Interim Chief Shea. In fact— "Isn't that one of the killers who got away thanks to Randall Bowe playing with the evidence?"

"Yeah, the guy Brett talked to us about," Bryce replied. "That's one of his many misdeeds. But one good thing about Len Davison is that he's Tatiana's dad."

"Well, I hope you succeed with that lead and bring a killer down."

"Thanks from me and the rest of the FBI, buddy," Bryce said. "And I will be in touch. If there's anything urgent you need from me to keep Madison safe—"

"I'll definitely let you know," Oren concluded. He hoped he hadn't sounded any different to Bryce, now that he'd slept with the man's sister.

"Be careful, bro," Madison said. "Let's stay in touch."

After she hung up, Madison looked at Oren. "Guess I'd better get ready for the day," she said.

"Good idea. I'll go on my first patrol of the morning."

Which Oren did. He soon returned to Madison's classroom and sat in the back, as he had yesterday. And later went on further patrols.

Nothing that day appeared different from the prior

days—except that several students approached Oren one at a time and said hi or otherwise tried to interact with him, which he found cute. These little ones certainly had charm. And definitely needed to stay safe.

When he could, Oren watched Madison interact more with the kids.

How would she be with children of her own? Their own?

Don't even think about that, Oren warned himself.

And when they started back to Madison's that night, Oren wondered if that night would seem the same as the prior one. He hoped so.

One possible similarity was that they could order another meal later from Bubbe's Deli.

And beyond? He ordered his mind to stay focused... even as he hoped there would be more distractions that night as well.

Chapter Eighteen

Oren had been quiet on the drive back to her condo, so Madison let her thoughts loose as they cruised through the familiar Grave Gulch streets.

She didn't let herself get too excited about the possibility of spending another night with Oren. Due to practicality and professionalism, it most likely wouldn't happen again. The fact that all had gone well—amazingly well—this morning, no awkwardness, nothing, didn't mean they should take any further chances.

When she'd been with Alec—well, mornings had felt uncomfortable too many times, and Madison was always happy when they left for school. What if Oren and she enjoyed themselves that way one more time? Okay, she admitted to herself, she was beginning to care for Oren. A lot. In fact…well, she believed she might be falling for him. Hard.

Which probably wasn't a good idea. Oren's job was in another town—and he'd undoubtedly be putting himself in danger frequently, even after things got resolved with Darius here.

A real relationship? He might disappear on her, die for real, the way her father had pretended. Which would be horrible.

Although… Oren did remain friendly that day, but she sensed some distance between them. What if he hadn't enjoyed himself as much as she had?

What if he didn't really like her as much as she was beginning to like him?

After all, he was there to guard her as part of his job, hanging out with her a lot, even at her school. And he did his job diligently.

But maybe a kindergarten teacher just wasn't his speed.

If so, then she would have to tamp her emotions down. *Way* down. She loved her job.

The right guy could be Oren. But only if the feeling was mutual. Or what if he wanted just something physical, not forever?

Enough. To turn her mind in other directions, she asked Oren about what they were going to eat that night.

She offered to cook but Oren said, "I think things went well enough last night. Are you okay with another dinner from the deli? We can order different food, of course, and I'll have it delivered again."

"Sounds great to me." And it actually did. She didn't need to pretend. She enjoyed cooking but she appreciated that she didn't have to now—plus, she enjoyed food from the deli. Besides, Madison appreciated seeing how close Oren was to his sister. And his love for his family only made Madison care for him more.

Oren said he'd call his sister once they reached Madison's place.

Then Madison thought about the phone call she wanted to make. She asked Oren if he thought it was okay for her to contact her mother and sister to learn if they'd been able to get together with her father, and if so, how it had gone. Oren insisted on their calling Brett again first, while they were still in the car, to get his okay. Good thing they did, since apparently the burner phone being used at the safe house had been changed. Brett gave Madison the new number.

They had just pulled into the parking lot of her condo. Oren chose a spot near the end of an aisle of the area for visitors, different from before. As always, he checked around first before helping Madison out of the car and walking cautiously to her unit.

Once they were inside, they discussed what they wanted for dinner, and both chose matzo ball soup and challah, plus a salad. Oren smiled and called Olivia. As he did so, Madison, sitting on her living-room couch near him, took the number Brett had given her for the latest burner and entered it into her phone.

Jillian answered. "Hi, Madison." Her tone was odd, Madison thought—soft and sad and somehow angry at the same time, though Madison wasn't sure how she could interpret that from two words.

A lot of questions crossed her mind, but she just asked, "Anything new?" Like, *did our dad actually get transported there today in protective custody to visit you?* Madison stared at the cream-and-gold pattern on the area rug on her wooden floor as if she could read answers there.

"Oh, yeah!" That sounded loud and upset. Madison prepared to ask what was going on, but Jillian continued. "Wesley Windham—yes, the former Richard Foster, our father—was brought here to visit today. And…well, it was so weird. He was friendly to me but remote with Mom. What he said sounded like a combo of apologetic, defensive and also cold, as if it wasn't all his fault. And before you say anything, I know it didn't start off being his fault, but…" she paused, then continued in a sorrowful tone "…how can someone go from not being your father for twenty-five years to suddenly being alive? Now I'm almost twenty-eight, and suddenly my dad is alive?"

"I understand." Madison wished she could hug her sister. "And I relate to all you're saying. I don't know how things will be among all of us when Darius Amaltin is caught." And with Oren and Bryce and even Jillian and others on the GGPD working on that, she felt he would be…eventually. Hopefully soon, before he could hurt anyone he'd been threatening. She raised her gaze and regarded Oren, who was also looking at her with an expression that seemed both curious and caring. She nodded slightly and looked toward the floor again. "But we'll stay in close touch and we'll…we'll learn more."

"Maybe." Jillian now sounded curt. "But the whole visit… Well, it was highly emotional, as I'm sure you can guess. Mom seemed somewhat glad to see him but angry and hurt, and she demanded answers he wasn't prepared to give."

"How about you?" Madison asked softly. "How did you feel, seeing him?"

"Mostly confused."

"How did you leave it?" Madison felt her body tense up. With all that emotion, would their father decide just to disappear from their lives again? Or…?

"He was only here for a couple hours, and then the people watching him, apparently from the US Marshals Service like your bodyguard Oren, swept him away, heading back to whatever safe house they have set up for him in Kendall. We all kept things open as they left, hinting we'd do this again, if possible, but nothing absolute was discussed with the marshals—or with our dad. I just hope—" Her voice softened, then stopped.

"Hope what?" Madison urged. That they would get together again? That hopefully she could join them?

Or that their father would just leave their lives again and never return?

"I'm not sure," Jillian said softly. "I'm just so confused, and I mostly want the best for Mom."

"I know," Madison said. "I don't know what's best. I'm sure it's going to take some time to sort out."

Madison asked to speak to their mom, and Jillian agreed. But their conversation was short. "It…it didn't go the way I'd hoped, Madison," Mom said. "But I sensed that he still cared, that he was still being protective, and he indicated before he left that we'd see each other again."

That sounded somewhat different from what Jillian had implied, but Madison certainly wasn't going to make things any worse for their mother now. "Sounds promising." She tried to sound enthusiastic.

"Yes," her mother said. "But I have to say goodbye now. One of the nice people staying with us wants me off the phone. Let's talk again soon."

And Madison hoped they'd be able to. She hung up after also saying goodbye. Then she looked at Oren and gave a brief rundown of what her sister had said.

"Wow," she sighed as she finished. "I wish I could have been there, too. That wouldn't have made him act kinder to our mom, though. I feel awful for her, and for Jillian. But if I'd tried… W-well, we don't know where Darius is, but there might have been more of a chance of his finding the rest of my family if he's actually doing a good job of following me without being obvious."

"True," Oren agreed, "but of course I hope not. Maybe, with so many people involved in protecting you, he's just backed down and not following through with any of his threats." But Oren's heated expression suggested that wasn't really what he was thinking. Maybe he was upset for her mother's sake, too. What a sweet, caring person he was.

"I can't help thinking more about my father and how he was with my mom," Madison found herself interjecting. "I'm really sad about it."

"Yeah, me too. After all he's done and all the time that's passed—Well, it's not really my business." But Oren looked deeply into Madison's eyes, and she saw even more anger there.

Which only made her care even more for Oren. She wanted to hug him. Tightly. And kiss him. Rub herself against his body. Oh, heavens. She was really falling for this man. Hard. Time to change the subject. "Will our dinner be here soon?" she asked. She didn't want to talk about the sorrow now percolating inside her.

"Yep," Oren said. In fact, his phone rang just then, and it was the delivery person. "I'll go out and get it."

And in a short while they ate the delicious dinner. Or at least Madison tried to eat. And she attempted to keep their dinner conversation light, and not focused on her family.

Soon, it was time for bed. Madison didn't want to become any more disappointed than she already was, so she just invited Oren to check her room while she finished cleaning up in the kitchen.

But when she headed toward bed, she found him still there. "I'd like some company again tonight," he told her hoarsely. "But this will only work if you understand—"

"I understand this is just a way for both of us to make a difficult situation easier to deal with. We'll both keep our senses aware of what's going on around us and stop if there's any indication of trouble. Right?"

"Right," Oren said, and Madison stepped into his arms.

OH, YES, OREN thought the next morning as he showered and prepared for the day. Another day of protecting the woman he was slowly falling for. He'd reminded himself often it was a bad idea to get involved with someone on the job, as wonderful as sex with the beautiful, sensual Madison had continued to be.

He also reminded himself about his various relationships that had gone bad and told him he shouldn't really attempt to get close with a woman any way but physically.

But those reminders also prompted him to keep his mind and ears alert for Madison's protection, even as the rest of his body continued to enjoy what he touched and felt and experienced.

When he'd finished showering, shaving and trimming, and dressing, he joined Madison in her kitchen. He could only tell her, "Look, Madison, last night was great. Again. I'm not going to demand that we stop such wonderful experiences, but of course I'm concerned I'll miss—"

She put her index finger on his lips to stop him—and he couldn't help kissing its warm, sexy length. "As long as we spend nights together, we might as well enjoy them," Madison said, stroking his lips slightly with that finger. "But of course we both need to stay careful." The expression in her eyes as she looked him up and down made him want to drag her back to bed yet again, but he knew she was teasing him—but also still enjoying the reality of what they'd done.

"Sounds good to me," he said. "Especially the careful part."

"And the enjoyment part," she reminded him, and he couldn't resist taking her back in his arms. Too bad there wasn't time to follow through. She was on her regular schedule this school day.

Their breakfasts were now a routine, and soon they were on their way to her school. This day should be like the last couple, Oren figured.

Once again, though, Bryce wasn't in Madison's classroom. On Speaker, Madison filled Bryce in on her conversation with Jillian and their mother from the safe house, and Oren could hear his clearly frustrated reactions. He told his sister he wished he was there with her this morning. But he couldn't be. Once again, he was off on his real assignment, but the lead he'd been told to follow to find that serial killer Len Davison had gotten him nowhere so far. He was utterly frustrated that nothing had panned out yet. But he was determined to get the guy.

Oren was glad when Cora came into the room and Madison joined her at the front to go over what would go on that day, or so Oren believed. But he kept Madison's phone since they hadn't hung up. "Look," Oren said quietly, turning from Madison and continuing the call with Bryce. "Right now things are fine, but I want to be sure you'll be available to help if something happens and I need you to help protect your sister."

"Of course I will, but—"

"But you also have to do your job. I understand. Now,

I've been considering what you're doing and that lead you're following. I've just got a few minutes before I need to start patrolling here, but let's discuss your strategy. We can continue talking about it later, if that makes sense."

"It sure does," Bryce said enthusiastically.

Then Madison continued her conversation with Cora, who now sat beside her at the teacher's desk. Though Oren doubted Cora would be much help if the wrong person entered the classroom before the kids did, she'd at least provide a distraction. Not that Oren wanted Cora, or the kids, of course, to do anything to protect Madison, or even potentially need to protect themselves. But at least he felt he could now leave and start his own brief patrol, including checking where the school's security guys currently hung out.

One way or another, Oren was going to make sure Madison was safe. That was more than his job now. He really cared.

Waving to Madison to make sure she knew he was leaving, Oren exited into the hallway, and was glad, but not surprised, to see Bob, one of the guys in the school's security detail, walking slowly by.

Since they'd introduced themselves before, Oren just said hi. "Everything look okay around here?" he asked.

"Yep." The guy must be approaching his senior years, considering all the lines etched into his face. But his body appeared solid, and Oren had no reason to believe he'd be anything but good at his job. "All okay with you?"

"Yes," Oren replied. "I'm about to get my first exercise of the day walking around here." He tossed Bob a smile that told him the reason for the walk wasn't just exercise.

"Well, you know where the security office is," Bob said.

"I do," Oren acknowledged. "And if you need anything from me, feel free to call." They'd previously talked and waved when they saw each other in the halls, but now Oren handed Bob a card, and Bob did the same to him.

"Great," Bob said. "See you around."

"Sure will." Oren saluted good-naturedly.

For the next half hour, he walked up and down the halls, mostly staying on the first floor, where the kindergarten room was. As he reached the back of the building he saw Principal Nelson exit her office. They traded morning greetings, and Oren continued on his way.

When he returned, the kids had started to arrive. Madison stood in front of her desk, bending to hold a conversation with the little girl she'd called Marti yesterday so her lovely red hair surrounded her face. They were talking about a children's book Marti held open, and Madison pointed at one of the pictures with the finger Oren had kissed earlier. A couple of other students stood nearby listening, including a boy named Buster, who held sheets of paper that appeared to have letters to copy on them.

Oren joined Madison briefly in the cafeteria at lunchtime but didn't eat his sandwich at the table near her since she had several students with her. He enjoyed watching the way she interacted with them informally here, unlike her more structured way in the classroom.

His prior wonderment of how Madison would be with kids of her own—*their own?*—flew through his mind and he again quashed it.

But his eyes mostly scanned where she sat and beyond to ensure there weren't people there who shouldn't be—one in particular.

They headed back to the classroom soon so Madison could finish her classes. Afterward, she hung out there longer to work on her lesson plans for the next day, Oren figured, since that was what she'd done before.

Later, he drove her back to her condo, again using roundabout routes to avoid potentially being followed. While they were on their way, Bryce called and asked to join them for dinner, and Oren was happy to agree.

The routine they'd been establishing was slightly different that evening, thanks to her brother. But this way, Madison had two protectors with her, which pleased Oren. A lot. The more, the merrier—and the safer. Even if he sometimes wished they were alone, just the two of them, for more intimate time.

Over dinner, Madison and Bryce had another discussion about their father and his visit with their mother and sister. "Yeah, I want to see him, too," Bryce muttered at Madison's question. "But sometime when he's with all of us and owning up to who he is—and why he left us for so long. He thinks he has an excuse, since his gun-runner's son is now after us, but there wasn't any kind of problem like that for all these years."

"Not to stick up for him," Madison said, "but he was warned by Louis Amaltin before he got killed in prison that there were a lot of colleagues of his ready to kill our father thanks to his testifying against him. They could have come after us, too, even when Amaltin was dead, so maybe there was some protection in mind when our dad stayed away."

"Yeah. Maybe." Bryce took a large bite of his sandwich and a swig of the beer they'd also ordered from the deli. Then he looked at Oren, across the kitchen table. "Well, I'm glad I'm working with you to protect my family, although I apologize for not having as much time as I thought I would. But I certainly appreciate what you're doing, Oren. And I'll do all I can to bring that Darius down. Still, seeing our father isn't exactly at the top of my priority list."

Not Oren's, either, despite his assignment. But Oren now despised how Wes/Richard had treated his kids—especially Madison.

"Please, Bryce," Madison said. She was sitting next to her brother. "You need to for Mom's sake, if she wants you to."

"I guess so, sis," he said after a moment, and the smile he sent to Madison appeared at least a little apologetic.

Oren was glad he wasn't involved with that decision, only the protection of Madison and her family—and, yes, her father, too.

Bryce left a short time after dinner.

And there they were, alone again.

Madison looked stressed, probably thanks to that discussion with her brother. Even so, Oren figured this was the best time to do his next patrol of her condo property that night. All seemed fine. No sign of Darius.

When Oren started back toward the condo, his phone rang. The ID indicated it was Brett.

"Hi, Chief," Oren said.

"Hey, you'll want to hear this," Brett said. "We got a call a few minutes ago from your buddy Darius Amaltin." That definitely got Oren's attention. "He said he knew our police department was now involved in attempting to protect the people he was after. He referred to them as Coltons and part of the family, acknowledged or not, of Richard Foster, who had helped to get his father killed. He told us to bug off, since he'd not only succeed in getting rid of them but also disappear after that, so we might as well stay out of his way, since he'd succeed no matter what we did."

"You're kidding," Oren heard himself say, realizing that no one would be kidding about anything to do with Darius.

"Nope," Brett said. "And though he called on a burner phone, there were background noises that gave us a good sense of where he was. Around a train stop not far from the safe house, apparently, though I don't know how he learned its location. I've got a team on the way to bring him in, but I figured you'd want to know."

"Thanks," Oren said. "Give me more detail about where he is. I may want to watch him being taken down."

"Sure. In fact, I'd really like to have you with us since you know what Amaltin looks like and you've seen him in person, although we do have copies of his ID photos."

"I'll see what I can do," Oren said.

Brett gave him the cross streets, then they hung up.

Good idea to leave Madison here alone? Well, if Amaltin was otherwise occupied, like in fighting off the police a distance from here, why not?

And Oren rethought what he would do next. He'd definitely like to see Darius taken down by the cops, too.

But that seemed too easy.

He could get the scoop about it later, if all went well. And if it didn't... Well, it would be much better if he hung around here with Madison.

And kept her safe.

Chapter Nineteen

Madison knew something was on Oren's mind when he got back from his patrol of the area and shut the condo door carefully behind him. Something important, considering how his black brows that so matched his wavy hair were narrowed over his eyes.

"Everything okay out there?" She kept her voice light. Standing in her living room not far from him, she wanted to run right up and give him a big, soothing hug, no matter what he was thinking.

But if there really was anything wrong, a distraction wouldn't faze him, nor would it make him happy. Especially if he had seen danger.

"Didn't see any problems," he said, and Madison started to take a deep breath in relief but stopped herself. Something was definitely on his mind. "I'm ready for another beer, though."

"Sounds good." Madison turned to head to the kitchen. "But is there a reason?"

Hearing nothing over her shoulder, she turned to face him again. He appeared as if his mind was somewhere far away.

She nevertheless got a couple bottles of beer from her

refrigerator, opened them and handed one to Oren. "So tell me what you're thinking about," she said, persisting.

Interesting. She'd never had a desire to learn what was on Alec's mind that way, to comfort him. But Oren? She'd do anything to help him feel better.

He sat down at the table and so did she. The swig of beer he took seemed shallow, but it appeared to soothe him somehow. "Okay," he said. "Here's the thing. Under other circumstances, I'd be off with Chief Shea and his troops in the GGPD somewhere else in town, maybe somewhere near the safe house. He invited me, in fact, since the police apparently received a call from Darius, who claimed to know where the house is and threatened to come after the people there. It came in on the station's main system and was recorded, so they've been able to go over it."

"Oh, wow." Madison, who'd been raising her beer bottle toward her mouth, suddenly grew stiff. "I gather they believed him."

"They didn't want to take any chances. Brett said a large group are on their way to track him down and take him into custody assuming he wasn't lying, although apparently the phone he used is another burner giving no ability to use GPS to track him."

"I hope they find him." Madison took a large swig of her beer. "Especially if he has any idea of where the safe house is. I certainly don't want him to find my mom and sister and start his threats—or worse—against them. But…you seem worried."

He shrugged, smiled at her and took another sip of beer. "I'd just love to be there when they take him down. But… Well, surprise, surprise, but I don't trust the guy. He told the cops something he wanted them to know.

That doesn't make it true...and he's also putting himself right in their crosshairs."

"Of course not," Madison said. "But even so..." She got the impression that Oren somehow believed it. Or he wanted to find out the truth himself. Or what if he wanted to stay there with her? Could he be seeking to prolong their time together? She could only wish...

Maybe by going with the cops he'd help find Darius searching for the safe house. The safe house. Madison had hoped that Amaltin wouldn't find out about it at all, or if he did, that he had no idea where it was.

That might not be the case. And if so...

"I guess we'll learn tonight or tomorrow whether the cops find our buddy Darius." Oren took some more beer. "I certainly hope so, although I can't help being skeptical."

"Me, too." Madison had a thought. "And— Well, I have the impression you don't want to wait to learn the truth. That maybe you want to go along with the cops to check out the safe house area for any sign of Darius. Right?"

"Not really." But Oren's tone didn't exactly sound truthful, and his words weren't exactly a strong denial. "Although Bryce intends to be there, and Brett indicated he'd like me to be with them, since I'm more likely to recognize Darius than the rest of them."

"Then, go with them," Madison insisted. Not just because he wanted to, but also because it might help her mother and sister. "Please. Leave now. I assume Brett will bring you up to date about where he and the other cops are at the moment, since he contacted you in the first place. I can stay here, make sure all doors and windows are locked, including the building's front door, have my phone in my hand in case I need to call Bryce or you. Too bad I don't have a gun—but even if I did, I wouldn't know how to use it the best way possible. But I do have nice sharp knives in the kitchen. Darius can't be two places at once, so hopefully you and the authorities will find him, and they'll take him in, and I'll stay here nice and safe."

"I appreciate your offer." Oren stood. "And it sounds good. Too good. But if I agree, I'll get in touch with Brett and make sure he ups the number of patrols in this area. A lot."

"Fine." That made her feel a little safer, at least. "Go now, Oren." Madison spoke the words one at a time, making sure they sounded like an order. "I hate to have you hanging out with me when you clearly would rather be somewhere else. And the police chief wants your help. Plus, it'll benefit my family. And it's not like I'll be dashing about the schoolyard or somewhere that Darius could see me and come after me."

"But he probably knows where you live. And—"

"And I'll be locked in, and you'll be closer to him than I will."

Since Oren was already on his feet, Madison joined him, took his beer bottle from his hand and placed it back on the table. Now, if she only wasn't so worried about him.

"If you're sure…" he said.

"I'm sure. I'll even put your beer back in the fridge, and we can drink some more before we go to bed tonight while you tell me how Darius was caught. Now go."

She was suddenly in Oren's arms. Their kiss was hot and hard—and Madison had a horrible thought that it could be the last one they'd share. Well, she'd be okay, carefully locked in here. But what about Oren?

"Go," she repeated, pulling back. "But please be careful." She looked up into his blue eyes as they regarded her with…well, it seemed like more than mere affection. Attraction? Heck, yes. And could that be gratitude? He had nothing to be grateful about. He'd been here for her since they'd met, and he was due for some time away from her, anyway.

And the time he'd be spending helping to bring down Darius could only be helpful to her, too. Even if he was endangering his life…and her heart in the process.

"Okay, but I'll stay in close touch. Keep your phone with you at all times. Do you have it now?"

"I will in a second." She hurried into the living room, where she'd deposited her purse on the coffee table. She pulled her phone out and waved it at Oren, who'd followed her in there. "See? And here." She pulled her condo keys out and gave them to him. "Now you can come in and out of this place whenever you want. So get on your way, Marshal."

"Yeah. In a minute." Madison felt a rush of further gratitude—and, yes, love—when Oren called Brett and asked him to beef up the patrols in her neighborhood, both patrol cars and cops on foot, even visiting her property. "He's on it," Oren said to her as he hung up.

He shoved her keys in his pocket and grabbed her yet again for a deep, quick kiss.

Then he left. She heard him rattle the door as he apparently tried the knob before he went away. She wondered if any neighbors would see him dash down the stairs and into the parking lot and question what that was about. Hopefully, they were all relaxing in their units.

Madison suddenly felt her body deflate. Damn, but she would miss Oren. And worry about him. And…well, she'd worry about herself a bit, too. Yes, she should be good and safe here, although she tried opening the door and also confirmed it was locked. This time of year, she never opened windows so she knew they were secured. She couldn't look out to see the patrolling police, but she'd no doubt they would be there. Oren had arranged for those patrols. He would protect her, even if he wasn't here.

She returned to the kitchen, sat down at the table and finished her beer. And kept her mind—and heart—on the man getting farther and farther away with each step.

 OREN HURRIED DOWN the hall to the stairway, ignoring his urge to go back and try Madison's door again. To make sure the woman he was coming to adore was safe, that no one could get to her. Or maybe open it with the key she gave him and go back inside.

But she was right. He hoped. He'd been asked by Brett to help bring the dangerous son of the gunrunner in, and he might have the unique ability around here to recognize Darius, although the guy probably looked like his ID photos that the cops would have access to.

But he was a law-enforcement officer, too. Bringing down bad guys was part of his job.

So was protecting the innocent…but wasn't Madison his responsibility, too?

Of course. And he'd arranged for more official protection in her neighborhood.

He hurried down the stairs, seeing no other building residents, which was normal. He opened the outside door, shut it and tested it.

He did a quick walk around the building and parking area. Of course he didn't see Darius. Maybe the guy had already been caught.

Getting into his car, Oren called Brett before starting out. "I'm on my way there," he told the interim chief. "But did you get him?"

"Not yet, but we've got patrols around the train station, near the safe house and more, including several in Madison's area. They'll be patrolling her street often, and at least a couple will walk around her development a lot." Which was exactly as Oren had hoped.

"Glad you're coming." Brett gave Oren directions where to meet up with him and his subordinates who also sought the suspect.

"Okay," Oren said. "I'm leaving now." He started his car and drove quickly through the parking lot and onto the street.

Where he pulled over by the curb—just for a minute, he told himself, till he convinced himself once more that he was doing the right thing.

Only that conviction didn't come. His heart—and his mind—were back at Madison's condo with her.

The officers apparently saw no sign of Darius or anyone they might think was him, or Brett would have let Oren know.

Sure, Darius had warned them he was heading toward the safe house.

Sure, the cops had recorded that call and heard a train in the background that helped them figure out where Darius probably was.

But the main word there was *probably*.

The idea of leaving Madison alone, even in a locked building, a locked unit, with lots of patrol cars going by as well as police on foot—but that Darius out there possibly playing games with the cops… Nope.

Maybe he'd feel bad later about not helping Brett.

Maybe Madison was completely correct, that she was safe there in her locked condo, especially since they didn't know for certain if Darius knew where she lived.

But Oren nevertheless turned the car around and headed back into the parking lot, taking the first undesignated space.

And headed back inside the building to personally protect Madison.

Not wanting to scare her, he called first rather than just unlocking the door to her unit and coming in.

She met him at the door. "I don't understand. Didn't they find Darius?" she said.

"I don't entirely, either," he admitted. "But—"

A loud noise echoed in Madison's bedroom. What the hell? It sounded like the window breaking…

Oh, yeah, he'd been right to come back. He wouldn't let anything happen to her.

WHAT WAS GOING ON? At first, Madison was irritated that Oren had returned. Surely she could take care of herself for a while, in her locked-down home.

But that noise—

She ran behind him to her bedroom, in time to see a man who could be that guy who'd run them off the road a few days earlier shout something unintelligible, grab the chair she kept at her computer table and bash Oren in the head with it.

Oren crumpled to the ground.

"What are you doing?" Madison screamed, not bothering to demand how Darius, who was supposed to be a distance from here near the safe house, had entered her condo. "Oren!" She ran over and knelt on the carpet beside where Oren lay, not moving.

"What the hell is he doing here?" was Darius's shouted reply. "I fixed it so he'd be leaving when I got here, and I even saw him drive away in his car."

"Well, he came back," Madison spat at him, wishing Oren responded. Hoping he was okay—or would be. She needed him to be. What should she do without him, her lover and protector?

He was definitely unconscious now. Or could he be pretending so he could leap up and subdue this guy? She didn't think so. She only hoped he was still alive. She stroked his head and its wavy black hair. He didn't move, and she had to prevent herself from crying. But at least when she touched his throat she felt a pulse.

"Get out of here," she demanded, glaring toward Darius. "The police are on their way." She wasn't lying about that, of course. Or she didn't think so. Brett had promised Oren to send some patrols.

"Yeah, sure they are," Darius scoffed. "I set things up with a call that would make them figure I was near the train station closest to where I think your family's safe house is—assuming my idea about it is right. But soon as I did that, I headed here, since it wasn't hard to learn where you live, my dear Madison. So here I am."

Madison had seen Darius Amaltin before, of course. Only for a few seconds and not close up. But she recognized him.

Mostly she'd noticed his eyes staring at them from his car as he tried to run them off the road on their way from Kendall to here and shoot them. Now, she saw those wild, dark eyes darting from her to Oren and back again. He looked midtwenties. He was skinny, had long medium-brown hair and wore a green-camouflage shirt over black jeans.

And why was she studying him like this? She'd want to be able to identify him later, after he was arrested, so she could testify against him.

Assuming she remained alive...but why was he targeting her instead of her dad or her other family? Was it just because he knew where she was? Not that she wanted any harm to fall on any of her family, not even her father.

Darius suddenly knelt on the floor on Oren's other side and grabbed his throat. "Your buddy's alive," he hissed. "Well, not for long. Gee, he could have lived, if he'd just gone to join the cops." He looked back at Madison. "But I want to take care of you first, and though he's breathing, he hasn't reacted to my touch so I figure he'll be out cold for a while. A good thing. You and I are going into the other room now." He rose quickly and yanked Madison's arm painfully, dragging her to her feet. "I'll make some calls, then you and I are leaving. Maybe we can have a little fun before I kill you."

"What? No! Leave me alone!" she shrieked, panicked. But Darius's grip on Madison was tight and she couldn't pull away. Why did he want to kill her? So her father would suffer the way Darius had when Louis was killed?

If only they were in her kitchen and she could grab one of those knives she'd mentioned to Oren.

If only she could help Oren...

Maybe she could dash off to the kitchen from the living room, which appeared to be where Darius was taking her. Why?

"Come on, dear Madison." Darius's tone seemed

mockingly warm. "I want you to be the first. We'll take care of it here."

They were in the living room now, and he shoved her toward the couch. She stumbled but managed to turn enough to wind up sitting on her sofa rather than falling to the floor.

Madison liked that couch, before. Especially since she and Oren had sat there several times talking.

When would they be able to talk again?

Would they ever be able to talk again?

"What do you mean?" she finally responded to Darius. "What will we take care of?"

"Oh, we're going to talk a little about why I have it in for your family, although I think you know about some of it, at least, thanks to your buddy Oren—and your wonderful killer of a father, Richard Foster, or whatever his name is now."

Darius had moved her coffee table away and put one of her armchairs in front of the sofa to block her from getting up and running.

"Okay," he said. "First, I need you to tell me exactly where that safe house is. Like I said, I have a general idea, but that's not enough. I'll have to find your father again, too, up in Kendall, but that will come later. I'll want him to doubly suffer by learning that all of you are dead first, before I kill him, too." His tone had been almost friendly before, but now he leaned down so his head nearly touched Madison's, and he grabbed her throat. "So where is that safe house?"

Madison began gagging. He released her slightly, maybe because he realized she couldn't talk that way. But even when she was back to near normal, she wasn't going to answer his question—not that she actually knew where the safe house was—so she pretended she still wasn't able to talk.

"Where. Is. That. Safe house?" Darius clearly wasn't giving up.

"I don't know," she managed to say, telling the truth.

"Yeah, right." He tightened his grip again, and Madison gasped. Was he going to choke her to death?

Did she have an idea where the safe house was? Not really. But she could guess…

He apparently planned to kill her, anyway. Why even give a hint of where she believed it was and make it easier for him to target her mom and Jillian, too?

She tried to stop focusing on him. How could she save herself?

How could she save *Oren*?

What was she going to do?

Oren was conscious. Just barely. But he'd been aware of Darius kneeling by him. Grabbing his throat. Choking him—in addition to the injuries he'd incurred when Amaltin slammed him with a chair.

He still lay on the floor, concentrating on his efforts to breathe. But Madison was with Darius. He had to go save her.

Assuming he could move.

At least he heard them somewhere down the hall. They hadn't left…yet. But Oren was certain Darius wasn't just going to hang around here indefinitely with Madison.

Why was Darius after her this way? Oren might have his suspicions, but he just hoped he would have an opportunity to ask Amaltin as he took him into custody.

Was she still okay? He heard her voice in the short

distance, although he couldn't understand what she said. She *had* to be safe. He wouldn't know what to do if that man had gotten his hands on her...

He moved slowly, hoping to rise so he could go help, ignoring his dizziness. Ignoring his pain. But he definitely wasn't strong enough to break into the room and confront Darius, even though Oren was still covertly carrying his weapon. Although...still lying there, he carefully rubbed his hand down his side toward the pouch where he kept his sidearm. And didn't feel it. Had it fallen out? Had Darius seized it? It didn't matter.

Damn! He felt naked, even more exposed. Terrified for Madison.

He needed help. And he knew just who he needed.

He pulled his phone from his pocket, and that wasn't an easy feat. He managed to look at it and made sure the sound was off. He kept looking at the door to the hallway to make sure Darius didn't appear from the room at the end, where Oren believed he was holding Madison. Quickly, Oren began typing a text message. To Bryce.

In Madisons condo. Darius here and has her. We need help.

In a few seconds he felt the phone vibrate and received the reply he'd hoped for: On my way.

Great. But of course Oren couldn't wait. He had to act.

As he attempted again to stand he grew dizzier—and the room disappeared.

Chapter Twenty

As calmly as she could, Madison had explained that the cops never told civilians where a safe house was, that she wished she knew. But she was actually glad, at that moment, that she didn't.

How long had they been there, she wondered now. Two minutes? Twenty?

She managed somehow to convince Darius to join her in the kitchen, and she pulled a beer for him from the refrigerator. Acted like his buddy. Like she understood what he'd gone through. Quivering inside, desperate to determine the best way to handle this—especially to help Oren—she'd encouraged Darius to give her his side of the story, why he hated her father so much, why he was determined to avenge himself against Richard Foster and all his family.

But where was Oren? Still in one of the rooms down the hall, most likely.

But was he okay? If he'd been fine, he would be here helping her…

And the thought that he wasn't made her frantic with worry.

At least while Darius was in here, he wasn't hurting Oren any more than he already had. But he clearly wasn't concerned about the marshal bursting in and arresting him.

That meant Oren must be badly injured. And although Madison had tried once to go in and see him, help him, Darius had made it clear she was to stay right there. Away from Oren.

With Darius.

If she wanted to remain healthy.

But what was she going to do? Oren needed help. He might even be *dying*.

Yet if she didn't remain alive, there'd be no way she could help him at all.

At least, as long as she stayed in the same room as Darius, the guy was almost cordial. He answered her questions about his father, who he claimed had been innocent, convicted because of Richard Foster's so-called lies, and his determination to kill that man's family as retribution.

And all the while, he was acting friendly, even as he urged her to tell the truth and let him know where the safe house was.

Which of course she wouldn't, even if she knew. She kept changing the subject back to his father. And so far, despite what she'd seen in him before, Darius kept his cool, didn't attempt again to choke the information he wanted out of her.

Yet.

But she couldn't be sure what would happen next. How long he would let this go on before he did something physical again. Shook her, hurt her, or worse.

And she stewed inside, contemplating how she could physically retaliate against him. Like jump up, run to the drawers near the sink and pull out a knife to defend herself with.

But he was bigger. Probably stronger. And if she pulled out a knife, would she be able to keep control of it if he grabbed it?

It didn't help that she sat quite a ways from the sink. There were cabinets nearer where she was, where she mostly kept things for school: notebooks and even some reference texts she could look at for additional ideas.

Well, this couldn't go on forever—their discussion, his cordiality. And so she dwelled on how best to distract him...while still considering how she might arm herself.

So far, she hadn't figured it out.

"So now you know what it was like for me to have a dad in prison for just trying to make a living," Darius finally said, leaning over the kitchen table toward Madison.

Making a living as a gunrunner wasn't exactly admirable, but apparently Darius was okay with it as he described his childhood, twenty-odd years ago, with his father in prison...and then dead. The way he told his story was designed to make Madison feel sorry for him, she figured. And in a way she did.

She'd feel a lot sorrier for him if he hadn't tried to run them off the road and shoot them. If he hadn't burst in here and hurt Oren. If he wasn't targeting her entire family.

If he wasn't now keeping her prisoner. And if he didn't, apparently, intend to kill her.

"That had to have been so hard," Madison replied nevertheless, still trying to keep things calm.

"It was. I was so young. And I've suffered ever since,

you know? So you have to understand why I want Richard Foster to pay for what he did."

"I sympathize," Madison said. "But will causing others to hurt really make you feel better?" she wheedled.

Darius stood up, shoving the kitchen chair behind him, and grabbed Madison by her throat, forcing her to stand, too. "Yes," he hissed. "It will. Now tell me where that damn safe house is."

OREN SNAPPED AWAKE AGAIN. Damn, but he hurt all over. Especially his head. It had been the target of Darius's chair-swing. But his shoulders and neck hurt, too.

Even so, he couldn't lie there any longer. He'd been here far too long already. He needed to rescue Madison.

Oren knew Darius still had Madison in the condo, outside this bedroom. He could hear their voices. He had no idea of Madison's condition, though. Physical or otherwise.

If only he didn't keep losing consciousness…

The hell with it. He couldn't stay here, not without knowing how Madison was.

His job was to protect her.

His life was to protect her. He had no doubt now that he'd fallen in love with the brave, determined teacher, appropriate or not.

This time when he moved, he forced himself to stand, grabbing the mattress for support. He took a couple of steps toward the closed door, unsteady at first.

But he had to get out there. Take charge. Bring Darius into custody. And he wouldn't necessarily need to do it on his own, although he had to be prepared to do so. He believed it had been a while since he'd texted Bryce. He had no idea where the FBI agent was now, but at least he was on his way. How long would it be till he got here? Who knew?

Oren didn't want to call 9-1-1 or anyone else now, since Darius would hear his voice. And he'd already held an important text conversation with Bryce.

The idea of having help on the way finally gave Oren the impetus he needed now that he was remaining conscious.

Time for him to get out there and do all he could for Madison. Bryce could show up any minute now to help. But once Oren got started, maybe he wouldn't even need Bryce's help.

Not that he could count on that, especially considering his current state. No, any help Bryce could provide would be critical.

But now was the time.

He'd act carefully, though, and not just because of his pain and unsteadiness. He wasn't sure exactly where Darius and Madison were.

Damn, but he was worried about her. Hearing her voice at least assured him she was alive, but in what condition? And for how long? This time, he managed to take a few more steps despite some residual dizziness. First thing, he opened the bedroom door a slit and waited. Darius didn't shove it open or come after him. He opened it farther and looked down the hall.

And heard voices again. They were in the kitchen.

It was time. He was moving. He felt stronger. Not his usual self, but at least a bit better.

He slid into the hallway, back against the wall, flexing his hands, and maneuvered slowly, carefully, silently, toward them both.

Yes, Darius was there with Madison. She stood

facing the criminal, her back toward the door where Oren entered.

Darius, facing Madison, therefore saw Oren first. "You! I thought you'd be out a lot longer than this." Darius shoved Madison aside, his eyes even wilder than Oren had seen him before. He dashed toward Oren.

Who couldn't take time to wait. Not for Bryce or even his own thoughts to take control.

He'd been hit by one of the chairs and definitely injured. Those pieces of furniture therefore could come in handy.

Madison turned and called out, "Oren!" She moved as if to run over to protect him. But he grabbed the nearest chair and faced Darius.

Once their attacker almost reached him, Oren swung the chair at Darius's head.

And made the kind of hard, injurious contact he'd hoped for.

This time, Darius crumpled.

Oren wasn't about to take any chances, though. Bracing himself against the pain, he knelt on the hard tile and checked Darius's pulse. He was alive but didn't move.

Oren had had a pair of handcuffs in his pants pocket along with his firearm but didn't know where they were now. Darius might have swiped them along with the gun. He patted Darius down. Nothing. Worse—or better?— no gun. But Oren had to make certain Darius couldn't flee if he regained consciousness—or, more important, that he couldn't attack either of them again.

He looked up at Madison. "Does a schoolteacher happen to have any rope around? Or even a scarf that can be turned into a bond I can tie onto this guy?"

"I have scarves," Madison said, "but I'm not sure

any of them can be twisted into a good rope. They're in my bedroom, but I don't think I ought to leave here right now."

"Oh, he's not conscious," Oren said. But he recognized that his own speech was somewhat fuzzy thanks to his injuries. He saw the concern on Madison's face.

"Good." She sounded skeptical—and frightened. How could she remain so beautiful, so determined-looking despite what was going on? "How about a cord from one of my appliances?" she asked. "My electric frying pan has one that comes off. Or even my phone charger."

"Sure," Oren said. He should have thought of that, or something like it. Obviously, his mind wasn't back to normal, even if he didn't fear losing consciousness again. "Let's give it a try."

"No way!" Darius suddenly came wide-awake, pushing himself up from the floor, shaking but definitely conscious. And apparently full of more strength than Oren.

He immediately faced Oren, teeth gritted, hands out, grabbing toward Oren's throat—just as the marshal heard the unit's door burst open and slam against the wall.

"Hey, Madison, I'm here," called Bryce as running footsteps sounded in the hallway. "Oren, you okay?"

"What the hell—" Darius shouted, turning slightly to look at Bryce as he appeared at the kitchen doorway.

Great timing, since the distraction allowed Oren to look around the kitchen for one of the cords Madison had mentioned.

"Get down on the floor," Bryce hollered toward Darius, his gun now aimed at the man who had started moving toward Madison.

She yanked open a drawer in a cabinet near the wall

and pulled something out. A book, large and heavy-look-ing. A dictionary?

"Here, you horrible jerk!" she shouted, then smashed Darius's head with it, and the man who wanted to kill her and her family members tumbled back down to the floor.

Clearly unconscious again. Not that Oren was taking any further chances. "Electrical cord?" he demanded of Madison, and she grabbed the one used for her electric skillet. Oren bound Darius's hands behind his back with it, even though the guy didn't move.

"Glad to see you, bro," Madison said as Oren watched Bryce stick his gun back in the holster at his waist. He replaced the electrical cord with a set of handcuffs.

Madison went to give her brother a big hug as he said, "Ditto, sister. And you, too, Marshal Margulies. Hey, I expected you to have things better under control, guy."

All Oren could do was shrug. "Hey, what can I say? I was waiting for help from the FBI."

"And you got it." Madison had moved away from her brother, stepping over Darius's legs, and approached Oren.

This time, the hug was for him, and he reveled in it.

It was over.

At least the threat to the Colton family from the Amal-tins was over.

But did that also mean that everything was over—in-cluding his bond with Madison? Because he hoped not. He could see so much more with her—a future, even. But would Madison feel the same way?

Chapter Twenty-One

I did it!

Oh, she'd had help, but Madison was thrilled that she was the one who had finally brought down the prospective killer of her family, Darius Amaltin.

With a weapon of her own choosing, too. Well, she hadn't been able to get to the knives she'd had in mind. But of course a teacher would use a nice, big, handy book. And it had worked well. Not that she'd tell any of this to her students.

Nearly an hour had passed, and now her condo was filled with members of law enforcement. Oren, of course, her wonderful brother, Bryce, and others were talking in her kitchen. They'd also called in Chief Shea, and Madison had learned that Brett and Bryce had been in touch—and her brother had let the cops know that they could leave the safe house, since Darius had set them up to go there when he came here to kill her.

Oren had taken a hit for her. He had been protecting her, as usual. And now he talked to the cops, letting them know his side, and therefore her side, of what had happened that night. He seemed okay now, thank heavens. Maybe not his usual strong self, but a whole lot better than he'd been.

A couple of officers had taken Darius into custody. He'd been well enough by then to go with them to the police station and not the hospital, although they'd said they would call a paramedic in to check him out. Her dictionary hadn't killed him, and she was glad of that.

At the moment, Madison sat on her sofa, waiting for whatever happened next. One of Brett's investigators had already interviewed her, so there was nothing for her to do but be patient. And worry. And grow sleepy, since her energy had been sapped by all that had gone on.

Then, it was truly over, at least for the night. Brett joined her, and he was smiling. His rugged face, beneath his red hair, looked relaxed. "Thanks for all your help, Madison," he said. "I'll head back to the safe house now and tell your mom and sister what's happened—and that they can go home. We'll eventually need you to testify when Mr. Amaltin is put on trial, and we may need more input from you before that, but I don't anticipate further danger in this matter. Let me know, though, if you think otherwise."

"Thank you, Brett. It'll be so good to have this all behind us."

Oren walked Shea to the door, while Bryce stayed with Madison. "We'll need to throw a party in celebration," he said.

"Maybe so." Madison hugged her brother, then he left.

Only Oren remained in Madison's unit with her then, standing a distance from her in the living room. "Hard to believe it's finally over." His voice was cool, his expression relieved.

And Madison felt almost as if he'd shoved her to the floor. It was over. All of it?

She should never have let her emotions loose around him...

"I assume you'll let the marshals guarding my father know what happened."

"Of course," he responded.

"Will you be staying here for the night?" she asked, unhappy about her voice's raspy quality. She couldn't help it. She allowed her feelings to show in her longing look. *Please stay,* her mind pleaded. *I want you; I need you. Darn it all, I love you!*

His gaze seemed to mirror what she was thinking. "Of course," he said, "as long as I'm invited."

"Definitely," Madison replied, and he immediately came close and drew her into his arms. Their kisses helped her feel better. But when they stopped, she pulled away. "Do you feel okay now?"

"Still a little pain here and there," he said. "But I'm a whole lot better now that Darius is in custody at last— and can't hurt you."

"Or you," she responded with a smile, which he returned. Then she told Oren, "I've got to make a call."

She tried using the burner-phone number she had for her mother and sister, but it no longer worked. She wanted to talk to them, though, after they'd been informed by Brett, and by Bryce, too, about all that had gone on that night.

Fortunately, they called her a short while later. Bryce was with them. Her relatives all expressed how glad they were that she was okay and also thanked her for all she'd done to protect them.

They decided to get together for dinner the next night to celebrate. And, yes, they wanted to go to Oren's sister's deli again. Of course Madison had suggested it. She had come to care for Oren so much and wanted to get to know his wonderful sister more, too.

So that was finally settled, and Madison was delighted. She wanted to talk to their father, too, but Oren said she'd need to wait till at least the next day, and he would set it up.

Oren. They spent the night together, and she was thrilled. So maybe it wasn't all over. At least not yet.

Still, their night together was short. Too short. But sexy. For yes, they engaged in several highly heated encounters despite Oren's injuries, which he mostly ignored, except for an occasional grimace. Madison hoped she wasn't acting frantic, as if she wanted to get as much into this night as possible…in case it actually was their final night together since Oren's official duties, and therefore his official reasons to remain in this area, had ended. Of course that meant their relationship, such as it was, would have to end, too.

But the next day was Friday, a working day for Madison, so they rose as they had been doing since Oren began staying with her. Madison showered and threw on one of her usual school-day dresses, a teal one with a wide matching belt.

Oren didn't have to accompany her to school that day, so he didn't. Madison understood. But she also wondered if that was the first step of their distancing themselves from one another.

Still, she felt so relieved about the capture of Darius before he'd hurt any of them badly that she had a wonderful day of teaching, making sure all her students enjoyed their lessons as much as possible. She of course had reported to Principal Nelson first to let her know all was well.

Oren showed up at lunchtime just as Madison headed toward the cafeteria. She was thrilled. "So good to see you," she said.

"I just wanted to put you in touch with your father," Oren told her. Which also made her happy.

Though he looked around the empty room, then engaged in an erotic kiss with her, he didn't seem inclined to stick around after giving her the current burner-phone number Wes/Richard was using. Was the kiss a clue that he would spend a little more time with her before he left? She wanted him to stay in her life, but so far he hadn't given any indication he wanted the same thing.

She thought about Alec. At least he was local—but she had no desire to get back together with him.

After she'd grabbed lunch with some other teachers, Madison's conversation with her dad was brief, but he seemed really happy. "Good thing I didn't know what you were up to," he said. "I'd have worried a lot about my little girl. I was already worried about what that SOB Darius was up to regarding me and the rest of the family, but I never imagined you'd help to capture him."

She wondered what her dad had been told. And why he suddenly was calling her *my little girl*.

"I didn't set out to," she said.

"Well, I'll want to hear all about it. I hope to head to Grave Gulch soon, now that I don't have to stay in protective custody. I may still have some commitments around here first, at the bookstore. But I'll be there as soon as I can."

"Great!" And Madison meant it. Maybe she was too optimistic, but she hoped, now that the pressure was off regarding their lives being at risk, that her mother and father would now get a good opportunity to get to know one another—again. And see what came of it.

Back to her classroom. Rather than teaching her full class, she'd worked out a session with only half a dozen students that afternoon, while Cora worked with the rest on basic addition. And Madison? She had her students, including Marti and Buster, each choose a picture book, and she read to them close-up so they could see.

Sweet kids. They reminded her of wanting children of her own someday. With Oren? She could hope so, but didn't feel optimistic that would happen.

Afternoon lessons were soon over, and the kids went home or to their day care for the rest of the day.

It dawned on Madison then that she didn't have a ride home. With all that had gone on, she hadn't yet gotten her car back.

"Of course," Oren said when she called him while alone in her classroom, sitting behind her desk. "I'll pick you up. And I've already checked with Brett. They still have your car at the repair shop near the station, but it's nice and safe and ready for you to pick up despite the dent still being there. We'll get it this afternoon and leave it at your condo. I'll drive us to the deli."

So she'd not only see Oren later that day, she'd get to ride with him. To talk to him.

He'd even eventually wind up with her at her condo, since he'd have to at least take her home after dinner.

And then?

Well, maybe Madison could seduce him. Invite him to stay in her life, which was what she really wanted.

But what did *he* want? She hoped she'd find out, and that she'd be happy with it.

She soon put everything away and went to the entrance of the school building. Sure enough, Oren was there, sitting in his car, waiting for her.

She slid into the passenger seat, stifling an urge to bend over the console to kiss him. He gave her a friendly-enough greeting but immediately got the car started.

"How are you feeling now?" she asked. "Last night was fun, and I know you've been driving today, but are you well enough?"

His brow furrowed beneath the black hair over his forehead. Was he in pain?

"I'm okay," he said. "Not perfect, but I've continued to improve all day, and I have been careful. I'm fine with what we've got planned for the rest of today."

She hoped so. She wanted to hug him, kiss the spots where he'd been injured, as she'd done before. Maybe more. But he was already cool toward her. Now that his job protecting her was over, was he determined to end their intimacy, too?

He soon got her to the large lot where her car was being held, not far from the police station. Brett wasn't there, but the guy in charge had all the paperwork as well as the keys, and Madison soon had her car back. They said they could take care of the dent when she was ready, too, and she said she'd be in touch. She'd contact her insurance company again first.

"I'll follow you to your condo," Oren said, which he did. Madison kept checking her rearview and side mirrors. He must be feeling okay, she figured.

Soon, she pulled into the driveway and parked in her designated space—no need to hide any longer—with Oren right behind her. He got out of his car and opened his passenger door for her since he would be driving to the deli. He looked straight into her eyes before she slid in, and her urge to throw her arms around him and kiss him seemed all-consuming.

But she saw no similar emotion in his friendly smile as he held out his hand to help her in.

She turned and blinked away the tears that rose to her eyes. She didn't want him to know how devastated she felt.

And yes, she did feel devastated and feared it would only get worse the more they were together...for now.

Well, the evening was just beginning. And it turned out delightful—but not because of any interaction between Oren and her.

Bubbe's Deli was busy, as usual. Her mom reached Madison first and threw her arms around her. "I'm so proud of you, honey! Bryce told us all about what happened yesterday. I'm so glad you're all right, and I heard you were the one who essentially captured the man who was threatening us."

"Well, it wasn't like—"

"Close enough." Oren's smile toward Madison made her feel all warm and gushy—and more hopeful than she'd been over the past few hours. Perhaps he wasn't so averse to being around her after all...

"I'll leave you all alone now," Olivia said. She was also smiling, and Madison also wanted to hug Oren's sister for owning this great restaurant.

"Thanks so much," Madison said. "I'm looking forward to my matzo ball soup."

Which made Olivia laugh. Nice lady, Madison thought, not for the first time.

And she had one wonderful brother, in many ways...

Okay, for this evening Madison wouldn't obsess over

Oren. He had helped to save her life, as he'd promised, and she'd even maybe helped to save his.

But that didn't guarantee a long relationship, no matter how much Madison had come to like the guy. *Like?* Heck, she'd already admitted to herself that she'd fallen in love, felt more for him than she'd ever felt for Alec. *This* was the type of forever she wanted.

But what did Oren think of her? She knew he was attracted to her, but did his feelings go any deeper than that?

He seemed to fit right in with her family here. They were chatting, and Madison was pleased that Oren sat at her side as had become their habit. She was eating her matzo ball soup, as was also her habit. Bryce was across from her, eating a corned beef sandwich, and that was what Oren and Jillian had ordered, too. Their mother, like Madison, was eating soup.

They all talked about what had happened the previous day—mostly to Madison and Oren, though those protected in the safe house had heard that the man who threatened to kill them was on the loose. Eventually, they learned that Madison had been involved in bringing that man down. Now, they cheered her, as well as Oren and the cops who'd been taking care of them.

"So I heard you went back to school to teach your students today as if nothing happened." Mom shook her head as she smiled at Madison.

"Of course," Madison said. "Life goes on. I've returned to my usual routine, and I assume Jillian and you will, too."

"Yep," said Jillian. "My normal routine."

"Boy, I don't envy any of you in law enforcement," Madison said, looking from Jillian to Bryce and then to

Oren. "All that potential danger from people who want to hurt others…and you."

"That's part of the fun of it." Oren winked at her.

Okay, she didn't like that idea of him being in danger. But at least he was lighthearted about it.

And his wink at her made her insides start fluttering again.

What would things be like that night? Would he stay with her after taking her back to her condo?

She'd wondered about that before and kept wondering about it as they finished their meals.

They all chipped in to pay the bill, although Jillian mentioned they needed to do an accounting sometime regarding previous meals mostly paid for by Oren. Tonight, Oren attempted to treat Madison—another good sign? Or was he just being a protective gentleman and a remote professional?

"I'm assuming you're staying the night with me again," Madison said as Oren drove them to her place. He didn't have a home here, after all—although she figured he could stay with his sister if he wanted to.

"Sure," he said, as he turned into the condo's parking lot. "If it's okay with you. I can sleep on the couch."

"Why not sleep in bed with me?" Madison said, forcing herself not to feel hurt at his rejection. That evening she'd occasionally seen him flinch in pain as he walked or sat down or rose. "I gather, from the way you've been wincing now and then, that your injuries from yesterday are still giving you some pain. Sleeping on the uneven sofa might make you feel even worse."

"Maybe so," he said. "Thanks. But just because we're in the same bed doesn't mean we have to…well, enjoy each other."

"Or," she countered, "even if we don't have to, we can still probably have some fun, though we'll need to find a way that won't hurt you."

There was something about his not particularly happy smile after he parked and turned off the car's engine that made her be the one to wince—inside. What was he thinking?

He told her a little later, after they'd gone inside, watched a little television news and drunk some water, since they'd had wine with dinner.

"Time for bed," he finally said. "And, well, we've already discussed having some more fun there. But before you decide, I want to let you know I'm heading back to Kendall tomorrow to make sure all's under control there, and after that I'm returning to my job at the marshals office in Grand Rapids. So even though we've had a great time together, I don't want to lead you on."

Of course. That was who he was, a marshal. He'd been engaged in his job of protecting her while he was here, but now that was over. She'd allowed herself to hope he'd find a way to stick around, but apparently that wasn't what he wanted.

A wave of despair swept through her. But there was nothing she could do to change his mind.

So she made herself pretend to be blasé about it. "So I figured," she said. "But that doesn't mean we can't enjoy ourselves on our last night together."

"If you're okay with it," he said, "I am."

"But let me know if you feel any pain."

They were soon in each other's arms, and then they made their way to her room and her bed...

And Madison allowed herself to engage in the most

wonderful sex possible that night with the man who had stolen her heart and was now about to break it.

She might as well enjoy one last time, she told herself. And she did.

But how was she going to go on without Oren in her life from now on? She didn't want to face that. But she would have to.

Chapter Twenty-Two

Oren couldn't stop thinking about Madison as he drove toward Kendall. He'd had breakfast with her this morning, and of course she didn't have to go to school that day since it was Saturday. He'd done his best to keep her at an emotional distance, but there was no denying she'd crept into his heart.

He wondered what she'd do over the weekend. Probably go back to whatever she used to do on weekends before she'd first seen the man who turned out to be her father—and all the chaos that had erupted as a result. At least, whatever she'd done outside her then-fiancé's presence.

She didn't need Oren any longer. Sure, they'd seemed to be developing a relationship. But thanks to his prior experiences, Oren didn't believe in relationships. They nearly always seemed doomed to failure, so why take a chance?

He recognized that Madison cared at least a bit for him, as he did for her—well, maybe he cared a lot, but so what? They lived in different towns. Led very different lives. Had no chance at a real future together.

Which hurt. So much. But he would deal with it.

He'd already become too close to the subject of his

protective assignment. Enjoyed it? Hell, yes. But that had to be the end.

Despite the tears he'd seen in her eyes as she said goodbye to him that morning.

At least she still had relatives in Grave Gulch, and none of them were hidden in a safe house any longer. If Madison hadn't any other plans, at least she could get together with one or all of them.

He'd passed the area where Darius had run them off the road a while ago and he'd let out an internal cheer. Darius would pay for that and for nearly murdering Nita the clerk—and all his crimes.

Now, Oren approached the final turnoff to Kendall. He intended to visit Wesley Windham one last time. Darius had been questioned, and no former associates of his father were known to be after Richard. He'd been the only one. Therefore, Wes no longer needed protective custody, Oren's or anyone else's. Still, Oren always liked to check on those who'd been under his protection one final time to make sure all was well with them. And he hadn't had to go far out of his way on his route to Grand Rapids.

It was late morning now, and Oren headed to the bookstore where Wes worked. He'd already called the guy, let him know he was on his way to say goodbye.

Wes. Madison's dad…

Okay, he had to stop thinking about Madison. He could stay in touch with her, sure, just on a friendly basis.

And when he visited his sister in Grave Gulch? Would he visit with Madison then, too?

The idea sounded much too good—and much too complicated.

He soon entered the town and drove through Kendall till he reached the street where the bookstore was located.

And that boutique next door that sold wedding gowns. So much here reminded him of Madison...

Enough.

He parked and got out of his car, then went inside the store. Wes was behind the counter talking to a younger man. "Hi, Oren," he said immediately after glancing in his direction. "Come over here."

He introduced Oren to the other guy, Reggie Blandi, who owned the store, a young fellow with lots of brown facial hair. He seemed delighted to meet Oren. "He couldn't talk about it before, apparently, but Wes has been telling me all about his background now—and how much he owes to you, Marshal Margulies."

"Just Oren," he told Reggie. Then he looked at Wes. "Do you have time to grab a cup of coffee?" And talk, of course, but that didn't need to be mentioned.

"Of course." Wes glanced at Reggie. "I assume that's okay, right?"

"Sure. No need for you to hang around much today or otherwise. I know you've got things to do."

The young man grinned and waved, and Wes nodded in the direction of the store's door. "So let's go," he told Oren.

There was a chain coffee shop across the street, and Oren wasn't surprised it was the place Wes chose because it was so convenient. In just a few minutes they both had their orders, Oren's a large, regular black coffee and Wes a medium latte. They chose one of the half dozen unoccupied inside tables and sat down on two wooden chairs facing one another.

Wes started their conversation, leaning over his edge of the round table toward Oren. Having spent some time with Bryce, Oren now saw what Madison did—their resemblance.

"I've heard all about what happened in Grave Gulch," Wes said, "thanks to my most recent herd of protective deputies like you." He held up his drink as though offering a toast. "Here's to all of you. I appreciate it."

"You're very welcome. I'm just glad Darius didn't accomplish any of his highly nasty goals—like killing your family members first and then killing you."

Wes paused to take a sip from his cup. "And his father put himself in the position that wound up getting him killed. Anyway, I'm glad to see you here...but where's Madison?"

"Home in Grave Gulch." Oren felt his throat constrict as he thought yet again of possibly never seeing her again.

"But I thought... Nearly every time Madison and I spoke after you accompanied her there, I knew you were with her. And the way she talked about you, so fondly and more, well, I thought you were becoming a couple."

Oren inhaled deeply. "I... I do care a lot about your daughter. But what we had wasn't a relationship... I was protecting her. You certainly must understand that."

He was surprised when Wes half rose from his chair and glared at him. "Don't be me, you fool. If you care for her, go after her. Stay with her. I can't begin to tell you how much I've regretted not breaking out and going back to Verity before."

"You're not with her now," Oren pointed out, not wanting to think about any similarity between how he felt about Madison and what Wes had done with his life.

"No, but I hope to be. You know, when I visited them at the safe house...the moment I saw Verity again after twenty-five years, all my love for her came pouring back, but… Well, I'm determined to at least try to win her trust back, even though it might be impossible. Same with my children. But the risk is worth it. You know why I don't have to spend much time in the bookstore today? I've resigned! I couldn't leave while that idiot Darius was out there, but I'm heading to Grave Gulch later today to stay there and see what I can do to make myself part of my family again. But you…you don't have to do anything like that. You care for my Madison? Then go get her, Marshal."

Oren's heart sang at the very idea. But he couldn't even trust his own heart. And what did she really think of him? She let him go that morning, acting very nice and polite and accepting. Surely she wanted to move on with her own life…

Or did she? He had seen tears in her eyes. Or had he imagined it?

"You heading back to Grave Gulch with me, Marshal?" Wes pressed, swigging down the rest of his latte.

"Well, I can follow you back and make sure you arrive safely." That was the best Oren could do.

And on the way, he'd call Madison and let her know he was accompanying Wes to Grave Gulch. But would he get to see her?

He simply wasn't certain.

REALLY? SITTING ON her living-room sofa while the contractors hired by the condo association fixed her broken window, Madison was on the phone with Oren.

His call had been very unexpected.

He let her know he'd followed her father on his drive to Grave Gulch, and they were just arriving in town. Yes,

Richard—or Wes—was on his way here and hoped to talk to her mother. And maybe her and her siblings, too.

Wow! Her family was finally coming back together after so long apart.

But Madison couldn't focus on that now. Oren had decided to come, too, to make sure her father arrived here safely. Even though there were no threats anyone knew of against him now. No more Darius.

So why was he really coming? To see her? He'd made it clear he wasn't interested in pursuing anything further with her, so he had to be accompanying her dad back to town, to make sure there were no more threats to his life or his family. That must be it. Oren was, once again, just doing his job.

She had to ask. Shaking her head, drinking some water from a bottle she'd gotten out of her refrigerator, she said, "Am I going to see you while you're here?"

"Would you like to?" he responded.

If he'd been there, she might have kicked him. Or not. He was probably still sore from his injuries, but he surely knew how she felt.

"Yes," she said forcefully. "I'd like to see you." And then she decided to go for it. After all, she hadn't been sure she'd ever talk to him again, let alone possibly see him. "Oren, in case you haven't figured it out, I really care for you. And not just because I enjoy you in bed, or I'm grateful for all you did to protect me. And those feelings have nothing to do with my former fiancé no longer being in my life, in case you're wondering. But I... I need to know how you feel about me."

She could picture him with his scowl of concentration as he drove, although he did shoot her frequent smiles when she was sitting beside him.

Did she really want to know how he felt about her?

Well, she'd already asked.

"This is better said in person," Oren began, and Madison clutched the phone. Was he going to admit he wanted nothing more to do with her? She braced herself, preparing to tell him that was how she really felt, too. Assuming she could lie that well. "But... Well, I do want to see you when I'm in Grave Gulch, although I don't know where this will go. I don't think I'm ready to get involved with someone who's fresh out of a relationship, despite what you said, someone I was just working to protect..." He hesitated, and Madison shut her eyes.

Was this going where she thought? And did he even want a family?

Well, she loved him. And she'd be willing to see how things went if they actually got together.

Wouldn't she?

He hadn't resumed what he was saying, so she had to prompt him. "So how do you really feel? What do you want?"

"I love you, Madison. But—"

She felt her mouth open, her body tense. She didn't know where the *but* was going, and Oren didn't continue. "I love you, too, Oren," she responded breathlessly, hopefully, despairingly. "But—"

"But I'm not sure we can go anywhere," Oren finished.

"I get it," Madison lied. That's when her phone started to ring with a second call. She glanced at it. Jillian was calling. Good. An excuse to end this painful conversation right now. And to take it up again later? Maybe in person? All she said was "Hey, Oren, sorry. I have to get off this call. I've got another one coming in that I have to take. Can I call you back later?"

"Of course," he said and immediately hung up, leaving Madison feeling heartsick even as she answered the call from Jillian.

"Hey, Madison, did you hear?"

Madison suspected she knew what her sister was talking about but asked anyway. "Hear what?"

"Our father just arrived in town. He's at Mom's now. He'd apparently called to say he was coming, and she got in touch with me to let me know since we've stayed in even closer contact since that safe-house thing. Anyway, she said she'd confirm it after she'd had a chance to talk with Dad. I'm calling him that in the hopes that he really will be acting like one of the family now. Which I gather he is. Mom wants Bryce, you and me to come to her place for dinner tonight. Dad'll be there. Are you available?"

"Oh, yes. I wouldn't miss that for the world," she said, relieved to be discussing something other than Oren. "I can't assume all will go well, but I'll at least want to be there for Mom."

"Great! Unless we hear otherwise, we're supposed to be there at six. Okay?"

"See you then." Madison felt highly excited as she hung up. Were things going to improve now for Mom? For the rest of them?

What would they all really think of Wes Windham— uh, Richard Foster? Hopefully, he'd at least let them know what name he intended to go by from now on. He'd come back from the dead, and his feelings must still persevere for him to want to see them and their mother now. That appeared to be true love—but was that really what she had with Oren?

She continued to sit there and think. She'd said she would call Oren back. Though he hadn't sounded particularly excited about the idea, she decided to do so.

To stay in touch with him as long as she could.

After all, he'd admitted he loved her. But was that just some kind of soft excuse to supposedly make her feel better as he exited her life? He'd told her he couldn't be involved with her.

Before calling Oren again, though, she had to go talk to the guy who'd finished fixing her window. She looked the area over and thought it looked fine but hoped the condo association would have someone check it out, too. "Thanks," she said to the guy and handed him a tip.

And sat down again after seeing him out.

Her life might never return to what it had been like before she'd seen her father in Kendall, but at least it was taking small steps in that direction.

Taking a deep breath, she called Oren.

She heard noise in the background. "Where are you?" she asked.

"At the police station in Grave Gulch. I'm going to be meeting with Brett soon to get his update and to thank him for his help."

"Thank him for me, too," Madison said and then grasped for what she should say next.

She didn't have to. Oren was the one to speak. "Look, Madison, I think we need to talk. In person. Could you meet me for dinner tonight?"

Her heart sank, even as a tiny shred of hope swam through her. "Sorry," she said. "I've got a family dinner planned—with our father, at our mother's house. I'm really excited, and curious about how it will go."

"Well, I'll probably still be around tomorrow, although till I'm done talking here I won't have much idea about my schedule. I'll call you if I'm available, and you can let me know if whatever I can do works for you."

That sounded as if he was inching his way away from her. Not making getting together with her a priority, despite how he allegedly felt about her. And she wasn't going to settle for a lukewarm relationship again.

Trying to hold back the sorrow she felt, she attempted to sound normal.

Happy.

"Okay," she said. "I'll wait to hear from you tomorrow."

And when she hung up, she was glad the worker was no longer there to see her cry.

HE'D HAD A sudden urge to see Madison that night. Heck, he had a constant urge to see her all the time.

But she'd brushed him off despite admitting she cared a lot about him, too—even loved him. Sure, her reason for not seeing him made sense. She'd be getting together with her family.

Without him, of course. But in a way he also wished he could be there to see what happened once Wes joined the group and would most likely try his best to start mending fences.

But for now…

Yes, he'd followed Wes the entire way to Grave Gulch, and right now Oren was parked in a lot near the police department, since Wes had decided to ask Jillian to accompany him to her mother's place. Probably to act as some kind of buffer if Verity wasn't as pleased to see him as he hoped. Wes had gone inside already, and Oren wasn't certain when they would head to Verity's. Maybe they'd already left.

Oren considered going inside and talking to Brett but decided he'd better make his plans for the evening first. He obviously wasn't going to be staying with Madison that night.

Hopefully his sister would let him stay at her place.

Rather than calling first, he headed to Bubbe's. It was midafternoon, and Olivia was likely to be there. In fact, she was there nearly all hours, even on weekend days like this, although she did choose times to take off each week and leave the place in the hands of trusted staff.

She wasn't behind the counter but walking down the aisle toward it. Toward him. Customers filled the booths and tables that she walked by, even at this hour of the day, and Oren was glad his sister's business remained so successful.

She raised her hand to wave at him. "Why, hi, bro," she said as she reached him. "I thought you'd left town for a while."

"Well, my intention was that it would be for a long while—like, I was heading back to Grand Rapids."

Her face scrunched into a frown. "What do you mean?"

He cocked his head. "I mean to go home, where my job is."

"But… Hey, come into my office, Oren. I've got some questions for you."

That didn't sound good. Oren figured his nosy sister intended to ask him about Madison. Well, he'd at least be able to ask Olivia if he could spend the night at her home. And discuss Madison? He hoped not.

He followed her up the stairs behind the counter and through the door into her office.

"Okay, Oren. What's the story between Madison and you? I know you haven't known her long, but when I've seen you together, I've seen something really good starting there. Am I wrong?" Her eyes glared at him.

"Well, I'm attracted to her, sure. What sane guy wouldn't be? But she was my assignment, and that assignment is over."

"But the attraction is still there, right? How strong is it?"

Hell, Olivia was his sister. He could be honest with her. "Pretty damn strong," he acknowledged, looking down at his hands on his lap. "We've both even admitted that we care a lot for one another." No need to mention love yet.

"Then, have you at least invited her to come with you?"

"She's a schoolteacher here, Olivia. You know that. She wouldn't come with me. Assuming I wanted her to. And she just ended another serious relationship."

"But you want to be together. I can see that and hear it in what you're doing. So...find a new job here. Grave Gulch has a good police department. Or maybe your office could use a presence here. You at least need to check. Even if this is new, don't give up on it just yet. Explore what you feel for Madison."

"But—" He brought his gaze up and glared at his sister. "You're telling me to get into a full-fledged relationship with Madison, right?"

"Right. Assuming you care about her as much as you appear to."

"Okay, I do. But that could lead to marriage, and—"

"And marriage can be a good thing, at least for some people. Look, stop living in the past and looking at how you hadn't found the right woman before. Look toward the future. Potentially with Madison. If she's the right woman for you, don't let her go. Got it?"

"I hear you," he said. And damn if he didn't find what she said to make sense. A lot of sense. It allowed him to start being truthful to himself. And the truth was— "Is it that obvious?"

"That you really care about Madison after knowing her even for so short a time? Hell, yes. Go for it, bro."

"I'll think about it," he said. And of course he already was.

"You do that. And more."

"Meanwhile… Well, can I stay at your place tonight? One way or another, I'm not heading back to Grand Rapids tonight now."

"Fine with me," Olivia said. "But think about the place you've been staying all the other nights since you arrived here."

He did think about it. A lot, as he gave Olivia a hug, kissed her cheek and thanked her.

He left Bubbe's Deli then, his mind swirling.

And trying to focus on what he wanted to do next.

Chapter Twenty-Three

It was wonderful, Madison thought.

She was in her mother's kitchen as Verity, with assistance, prepared dinner for all five of them: Jillian, Bryce and Madison, and now their father, too.

A roast was cooking in the sizable oven in the especially lovely kitchen. Everyone chipped in. Madison was helping Jillian put a salad together. And Bryce and their father were peeling potatoes that they would boil and mash in a while. All of them were working on the shining granite counter that ran down the center of the kitchen.

Unsurprisingly, Mom kept popping over to check on the potatoes' progress—and to talk to Dad. The two of them seemed to be getting along phenomenally. Now that they were together again, did they feel the love they'd once had?

Would they stay together now? Marry?

That seemed a bit much after all this time, but Madison hoped things went the way Mom really wanted them to, whatever it was.

The smell in the kitchen was delightful. And Madison was really enjoying being with her family members.

Even so…

"Are you okay?" Jillian scooted over closer to Madison. "You seem…well, quiet." She paused. "Where's Oren tonight?"

Madison grabbed another head of lettuce and began pulling it apart, pretending to concentrate on it rather than what Jillian had brought to mind. "Actually, I'm not sure," she finally said, as coolly as she was able.

"Is he in town now? Or—"

"Yes, as far as I know he's in Grave Gulch tonight. He followed Dad here from Kendall to make sure he arrived safely." Madison kept her voice low so their father hopefully wouldn't hear her—and possibly participate in this part of the conversation.

"Then—"

Madison looked at her sister. "I don't want to talk about him, Jillian," she said softly, hoping no one else was listening. "Not now. We can talk later. I… There's a lot going on in my head about him. I'd like your sympathy, but not now."

"Sympathy? Then…okay, we'll talk later." At least Jillian's voice was soft, too. And having a caring sister to talk to might help Madison get through this night, and the following ones, with at least a bit less emotion. She'd only known Oren a few days—she couldn't really love him, surely. This would pass…but she would most likely need compassionate company. Madison was certain she'd lost Oren. Not that she ever really had him, other than as her protector.

And lover. Her wonderful lover…

Okay. She had to pay more attention to the salad, or she might fall apart here as much as the lettuce that was being torn apart.

"Good job," her mother said a few minutes later as

Madison and Jillian combined the salad ingredients in the large wooden bowl in front of them. "Let's all go into the dining room and start with the salad while the roast, potatoes and veggies continue cooking." Mom had also started steaming some broccoli in a pan.

Madison followed Jillian into the dining room and sat between her sister and brother, across the table from their parents.

Their parents. Together...

This was definitely an emotional night, in many ways, Madison thought. She didn't have much of an appetite, but she managed to start eating her salad, even enjoying it.

And she attempted to eavesdrop on what her dad was saying. "I don't think I need my undercover name much longer, if at all, so I'll probably go back to my real name, if the authorities say it's okay. And if that's okay with you." He looked at their mother's face, and the smile on it seemed so warm and loving that Madison felt her insides grow warm.

Well, maybe two people at this table were looking at a happy ending, even if she wasn't.

She sighed and took another bite.

But they also discussed where their dad would live while he was in Grave Gulch. It sounded as if he'd stay in Kendall at first and visit often to spend time with their mother—and also look for a place to live.

Maybe eventually—soon—at their mother's.

And as they were discussing Grave Gulch and what it was like these days, Madison's phone rang.

It was Oren, so of course she answered. She stood up from the table and walked into the hallway to talk so she wouldn't disturb anyone.

"Hi, Oren," she said, knowing puzzlement sounded in her voice. "Is everything okay?"

"I hope so," he said. "Could you come outside for a minute? I'm in front of your mother's house. There's something I want to discuss with you before I leave."

Her heart sank. Well, at least he was saying goodbye.

She waved at her family. "I've got to check on something outside," she called and then went to the front door.

She walked onto the front porch before seeing Oren standing at the side of the lawn under a dim pole light. She headed there.

Her heart started racing as she saw him. He was so handsome. And like it or not, he had hold of her heart.

Though this might be the last time she saw him.

As she neared him, she said, "What's wrong, Oren? Is there anything I can do to help?"

His smile was wide—but there was something about it that suggested worry. "Nothing's wrong, Madison. Not yet, at least. But yes, there's definitely something you can do to help."

She stopped right in front of him. "What—" And then she gasped as Oren dropped to one knee on the grass in front of her. He held a small box in one hand that he held out to her.

"Madison Colton, I love you. I want to be with you forever, here in Grave Gulch or wherever. Will you marry me?"

No need to think. Never mind that she had just exited an engagement. That had been with a man she'd liked but hadn't really loved.

But Oren? "Oh, yes, Oren. Yes!" She held out her hand, not for the ring but to touch him, touch his arm, be in contact with him.

But he opened the box and pulled out a lovely ring with a large diamond surrounded by smaller ones in it. He reached out, and Madison put her hand in his.

The ring fit as perfectly as if he'd measured her finger beforehand. Maybe that was another thing marshals did as well as they somehow kept track of the people they were protecting...

And as Madison threw herself into his arms, against his wonderful, hard, sexy body, she heard some noise from behind them.

Her family was cheering, yelling "Congratulations!"

But Madison didn't want to talk to them. Not yet. She drew even closer to Oren, threw back her head and said as closely into his ear as she could, "And I love you, Oren Margulies."

DAMN. AFTER HIS discussion with his sister that had focused him on how he really felt about Madison, he had become certain that he wanted to marry her. To spend his whole life with her. To have kids with her.

He'd wanted their commitment to begin immediately. That was why he had bought that ring.

And hoped her answer would be the positive one it had been.

As a result, Oren certainly had planned to spend the entire night of their engagement with the wonderful woman who had become his fiancée hours ago, and he had accompanied her home. But it was late now, and he'd just pulled his car into the dark parking lot behind Bubbe's Deli, parked in his usual employee spot that wasn't far from one of the dim lights mounted on the building. He grabbed his weapon as he exited the vehicle.

And was glad to see others in the parking lot, too: several cops in uniform, one with a K-9. They came over to him, and he immediately showed his ID. They advised him that their interim chief knew he was here.

Olivia had called him. She had stayed long after closing the place to go over some things in the books, she'd told him, her voice shaking. "I've been robbed," she cried. "Can you—"

"I'll be there in a few minutes," he'd told her. "But have you called 9-1-1?"

"Yes, and a couple of officers are already here."

"Good. You do as they tell you, and I'll see you soon."

Of course the call had interrupted an absolutely wonderful session between Madison and him in bed. His gorgeous, naked fiancée was sitting up, her red hair mussed, holding a sheet around her. "What's wrong?"

He told her as he got dressed in his suit. He needed to appear official, even though his main reason for being there would be to take care of his sister.

"Can I come, too, to help Olivia? She'll be my sister-in-law soon, after all. And what happened sounds so horrible."

"You'll stay right here," Oren commanded. "I don't want to have to worry about you, too." He left soon, after giving Madison, now wearing a robe, a deep, loving kiss and promising he would return as quickly as possible.

"Stay safe," she'd told him and kissed him again.

And now he was here. He hurried to the front door and entered the deli, which was full of more cops. Some of them were collecting fingerprints around the checkout counter.

Olivia was sitting at one of the tables near the front

with several cops surrounding her, including Brett, with Ember sitting beside him. Oren hurried over there.

"Olivia, what happened?"

Though there were tears in her eyes, she managed to smile grimly at him. "Hi, bro." Her voice was trembling. "I may be able to show you a little of what happened if these wonderful police who showed up so fast can get footage from some of my neighbors' security cameras."

Good. If that worked, they should be able to identify whoever it was.

And in fact, Brett stood up and joined Oren, Ember at his side.

"I'd like you to contact Bryce. I have his number, but it would be better if you called. And he might be very interested in what happened here."

Curious but wanting to cooperate fast, Oren immediately walked away and called Bryce. The guy sounded groggy at first, till Oren finished his quick explanation of what had happened. "I don't know why the chief thought the FBI would be interested, but—"

"I'll be right there," Bryce said.

After they hung up, Oren returned to his sister's table and asked her to elaborate on what had taken place. He held out his hand, and Olivia put hers in it. Brett remained at the table, but the other cops had risen to patrol the inside of the restaurant, even though it sounded as though the perpetrator had left a while ago.

Olivia talked first about closing time, the customers who'd been there and dawdled a bit. "It was late, and I was alone, of course, going over the books. This man suddenly burst in. He had a gun, and I was terrified." Her voice hitched with emotion, and Oren, looking into her blue eyes, waited till she could talk again. And strangely, she wound up smiling, though sardonically. "Would you believe he demanded a corned beef sandwich?"

"Hey, that sounds good to me, too." Oren lifted his brows, kidding, of course, but hoping to lighten things up even more for his sister.

"Then, come back when we're open."

"Got it."

Olivia continued. The guy had left after eating the sandwich she'd of course put together for him, but that wasn't all. "He made me grab all the cash I had in the register, plus from my purse. He left with hundreds—but I can't complain too much. He didn't hurt me. Only... Well, he said he really liked the corned beef sandwich, so he'd be back to try the pastrami. Or kill me, I don't know."

Damn. Oren asked her a few questions, then talked to Brett a bit. Yes, the cops here now on patrol, including K-9 officers, were looking for the guy.

And the detectives on call that night at the station had already gone over the security footage. "You were very lucky, Ms. Margulies," Brett told Olivia. "It turns out your visitor is known to us—too well. He's a serial killer, in fact. Name of Len Davison." He looked at Oren. "That's why I thought your FBI connection would be great to bring in here."

Olivia nodded. "I thought he looked like the images that have been circulated everywhere, but I didn't know for sure. I was too scared to think straight."

Bryce entered the deli then. "Hey, tell me about that robbery here." He turned to look at Olivia. "Are you okay?"

She stood up. "I... I think so. But—" She said to

Brett, "He's a serial killer? And he said he'd be back?" She sank back down on the chair. "Maybe I'm not so okay, after all."

She clearly needed some cheering. This seemed a good time for Oren to relay his news to her. "Well, you were certainly okay before, when I was here yesterday. Smart, of course. Inspirational."

Olivia looked up at her brother. "What are you talking about?"

"I proposed to Madison tonight…and she accepted."

Olivia screamed happily and rose again and threw her arms around him. "That's fantastic! Congratulations, Oren." She stepped back and scowled at him. "But you didn't tell me."

"I was going to bring Madison here tomorrow—uh, today—to surprise you. I still might, though it won't be a surprise. And will you be opening later?"

"I—I don't know." Olivia looked from him to Brett to Bryce. "Would it be okay? Although, I'm sure this is a crime scene." She choked a bit. "He said he'd be back for more." She was clearly shaking.

"Let's hope he does come back," Bryce growled. "So we can catch him at last." But he took a couple of steps toward Olivia, hugging herself in obvious fear, Oren thought. He was about to chastise Bryce when the FBI agent said, "I'm going to hang out with you, Olivia, till he's been captured, whether he's caught here or somewhere else. Well, consider yourself in my protective custody till we get this resolved, okay?"

"O-okay," she stammered, then looked at Oren as if wanting his okay as well.

He gave it. He had full faith in his future brother-in-law.

"And yes," Bryce said, "after we do our crime scene investigation, like checking any security footage, dusting for prints and whatever else makes sense as we go along, you should open the deli today, both for your own peace of mind and because it might attract Davison back sooner."

A while later, after further discussions with the cops patrolling the area, who'd not found Davison, Brett said he was going to leave. "We'll have patrols around here all night and into the day, too. And we'll count on the FBI's services here as well."

"Good," Bryce said.

"And I'll be back here during the day," Oren told Olivia. "With my new fiancée."

Olivia's squeal wasn't frightened; now, it was just excited, Oren was glad to note. "I can't wait! But don't make it too early. I may even get some rest tonight, and I'll have to help clean the place when the police say it's okay." She glanced at Bryce. "And I guess I may have company then, too."

"Right," Bryce said, nodding. "Unless we're lucky and catch the guy tonight."

"I hope so." Oren shook hands with Bryce, then walked out the door with Brett and his dog. Something had been on his mind to talk to Brett about. "By the way, since I've gotten engaged to a local girl, I'll probably want to stay around Grave Gulch."

He felt sure his parents would understand if he moved here to be with his future wife. They'd probably even visit here more to see Olivia, too. Still, that remained uncertain. But he had introduced them to Madison via a video call, and they seemed delighted.

Madison and he had also promised to visit them soon.

"Sounds good," Brett said.

"Not sure if the Marshals Service will have a job for me here, though—but how about the Grave Gulch PD? Do you think I could come work for you?" Oren continued.

Brett turned under the dim light in the parking lot. "Let's talk about it when we're both wider awake, okay? Maybe we can find something here…"

"Excellent!" Oren exclaimed. They shook hands, and Oren headed for his car.

He drove to Madison's as quickly as he could, then used the key she'd given him to get in.

Unsurprisingly, she was in bed, but not sleeping—not deeply, at least. She sat up immediately when he entered her bedroom and turned on a lamp beside the bed. "You're back," she said. "I'm so glad. Is your sister okay?"

"A bit scared, of course, but she'll be fine," Oren said. Especially with Bryce watching over her to make sure her assailant didn't return and hurt her. "But how about me? Aren't you going to ask if I'm okay?" He'd sat down on the edge of the bed and was now staring down at her with a pretend frown.

"Aren't you? You look fine to me. In fact, you look delicious."

They were suddenly in each other's arms, and their kiss was definitely delicious and more. He could hardly wait to show his fiancée off to his sister. But right now, he was glad he was home safe, in the arms of the woman he loved, the woman who would become his wife. This was where he needed to be—now and forever.

He held Madison tightly against him. "I love you, Madison."

"And I love you, Oren. How about we prove it to each other again?"

"Oh, yeah," Oren said and stood again to pull off his clothes.

* * * * *

MILLS & BOON

THE HEART OF ROMANCE

A ROMANCE FOR EVERY READER

MODERN

Prepare to be swept off your feet by sophisticated, sexy and seductive heroes, in some of the world's most glamourous and romantic locations, where power and passion collide.

HISTORICAL

Escape with historical heroes from time gone by. Whether your passion is for wicked Regency Rakes, muscled Vikings or rugged Highlanders, awake the romance of the past.

MEDICAL

Set your pulse racing with dedicated, delectable doctors in the high-pressure world of medicine, where emotions run high and passion, comfort and love are the best medicine.

True Love

Celebrate true love with tender stories of heartfelt romance, from the rush of falling in love to the joy a new baby can bring, and a focus on the emotional heart of a relationship.

Desire

Indulge in secrets and scandal, intense drama and plenty of sizzling hot action with powerful and passionate heroes who have it all: wealth, status, good looks…everything but the right woman.

HEROES

Experience all the excitement of a gripping thriller, with an intense romance at its heart. Resourceful, true-to-life women and strong, fearless men face danger and desire - a killer combination!

To see which titles are coming soon, please visit

millsandboon.co.uk/nextmonth

WANT EVEN MORE
ROMANCE?
SUBSCRIBE AND SAVE TODAY!

'Mills & Boon books, the perfect way to escape for an hour or so.'

MISS W. DYER

'Excellent service, promptly delivered and very good subscription choices.'

MISS A. PEARSON

'You get fantastic special offers and the chance to get books before they hit the shops.'

MRS V. HALL

Visit millsandboon.co.uk/Subscribe
and save on brand new books.

MILLS & BOON
Desire

Indulge in secrets and scandal, intense drama and plenty of sizzling hot action with powerful and passionate heroes who have it all: wealth, status, good looks…everything but the right woman.

MILLS & BOON
MEDICAL
Pulse-Racing Passion

Set your pulse racing with dedicated, delectable doctors in the high-pressure world of medicine, where emotions run high and passion, comfort and love are the best medicine.

MILLS & BOON
True Love
Romance from the Heart

Celebrate true love with tender stories of heartfelt romance, from the rush of falling in love to the joy a new baby can bring, and a focus on the emotional heart of a relationship.

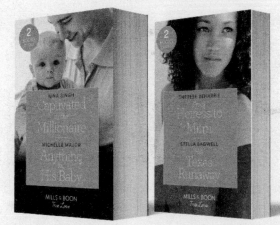